Stars of Delphinus

Chapter 1

August 31, 1999. The sun had dipped below the horizon hours ago, casting the city into a realm of twilight mystique. The 32nd San Diego Comic-Con had just drawn to a close. But just beyond the glittering façade of the Convention Center, where caped crusaders and masked heroes had paraded their otherworldly talents, our story narrative takes an unexpected, dark, and somber twist.
High above the streets, in the pulsing heart of downtown, a gripping drama was unfolding.
There, on the twenty-second-floor balcony of the towering Marriott Hotel, we find Sam, his silhouette a stark contrast against the fading twilight. His heart raced, his fingers trembling, clinging to the railing, teetering on the precipice of a decision.
"You win," he shouted at the night sky, his words a desperate cry. Half-drunk and teetering on the ledge, he inched closer to nothingness. With one last glance at the lights atop Soledad Mountain, he closed his eyes. Sam had lost everything he held dear, leaving him with a profound sense of emptiness. It felt as though he had nothing left to live for. With hesitation, he inched closer to the edge, his mind filled with the tumultuous events of the past few months, as he contemplated taking that fateful step into the abyss...

****

If there were a Wheel of Time, Sam would undoubtedly discover it. He'd turn it back, but not for years or decades, not to learn lottery numbers or peek into the future of the stock market. Instead, he'd go back just a month, just far enough to undo a handful of regrettable decisions. The speed at which the wheel turned wouldn't matter, as long as he could relive the month of his thirty-nine-year life.

He'd release his grip on the wheel when time had wound back to the last Friday of July in 1999, a time when he felt like the king of the world. It was a moment when he hadn't yet realized how fragile and delicate the threads connecting us to our loved ones could be. Before comprehending that life is the sum of our decisions, whether right or wrong, and that these decisions define not only our lives but also who we are.

Chapter 2

"End of the world!" The blaring magazine cover caught Sam's eye. He picked up the magazine and walked toward his office window, thinking, "*Old News*". With 1999 drawing to a close and the new millennium looming, the Y2K bug had everyone on edge. The fear was that when the clock struck midnight on New Year's Eve, all computer programs would come to a screeching halt. However, Sam's mind was preoccupied with a different countdown – the minutes left until his wedding anniversary party that night.

From his office perched atop a hill in Sorrento Valley, Sam idly flipped through the pages of the magazine, his gaze drifting out the window to the sprawling University of California, San Diego campus. The lush green expanse lay just beyond the Interstate 5 freeway, which snaked through the landscape like a colossal anaconda weaving through a forest of trees. As his daydreams threatened to transport him back to the nostalgia of the '80s, the tranquility of the moment was abruptly shattered by the sudden swing of his office door.

Intruding into Sam's office, a tall, red-haired man disrupted the stillness. "Are you decent?" he blurted, his presence filling the room with an unexpected energy.

"Hey Damien, what's up?" Sam greeted, his frame casually leaning against the wall adorned with eight retired racquetball racquets. It was a display of his favorite sport, one that kept him both physically and mentally sharp. Each racquet, as it aged, found a place on the wall, a silent testament to the games and victories it had witnessed.

Hope, Sam's efficient yet irked office secretary, swiftly emerged. "He just barged in, as usual," she huffed, her irritation palpable.

Sam, ever the peacemaker, reassured her, "Don't worry, Hope, I'll knock some sense into him." His words hung in the air, attempting to restore the disrupted equilibrium.

"Just let me know when it's time to throw him out," Hope demanded with a triumphant grin, stuck her tongue out at Damien, who arched an amused eyebrow. "You know I can hear you, right?" he pointed out, injecting a note of camaraderie into the room.

Hope, victorious, left the space, her exit a blend of confidence and satisfaction. Damien, contemplating the dynamics, mused, "I should have gotten her some flowers for Secretary's Day," shaking his head in mock regret.

"Respect can't be bought, my good friend," Sam remarked, a wry smile playing on his lips.

"Blah, blah, blah," Damien babbled, reaching for a framed picture on Sam's desk. A smile graced his face as he gazed at the group photo. The image featured friends, including Sam, Damien, Luke, Brenda, and Nicole, all taken on Watermelon Day at UCSD. It was an annual tradition where a Watermelon Queen was selected to drop a watermelon from the top of the Urey Hall building, allowing physics students to measure its splat. This quirky custom had its roots in 1965, with the record set in 1974 at a whopping 167 feet 4 inches."

Damien, an old college buddy of Sam's, was one of his closest friends. A loaner at 42, he remained a bachelor, and his personality was marked by shyness and a reserved nature. Armed with a degree in finance, he had previously worked as an internal auditor for The Price Club until 1994. Unfortunately, he became one of the early casualties of the digital technology boom, finding himself replaced by a Compaq 66MHz PC.

Recognizing that his friend was struggling to secure new employment, Sam extended a helping hand by offering him a role in the company's accounting department. Damien quickly demonstrated his worth and became a valuable asset to the organization. His dedication and skill eventually led him to rise through the ranks, culminating in his appointment as the Chief Financial Officer upon the retirement of the current CFO."

"How you been?" Sam inquired, his grin carrying genuine warmth as he reached into the mini-fridge, retrieving a couple of water bottles. His gaze briefly pierced through the reflective Meade telescope at UCSD before tossing a bottle to Damien.

"Just fine, and I'm sure you're doing great as usual," Damien replied, his eyes briefly glancing at the 5000 piece framed puzzle on the wall. Memories flooded back of the months spent assembling the colossal puzzle of the old world map, a project that had overtaken the dining table at Sam's apartment.

Sam, twisting the cap off his water bottle, casually leaned against his desk, creating an easygoing atmosphere. "How do the numbers look for June, Mister Almost CFO?" His inquiry held a subtle playfulness, a blend of professional curiosity and the shared history between the two.

Damien, pride evident in his eyes, nodded. "We just finished reviewing them. They look solid. That deal you negotiated with those sheiks in Dubai was a game-changer. You never told me how you managed to win them over. We all thought the Dutch had that contract locked in. Congratulations on the big fat bonus you scored on top of your commission."

Sam's raised eyebrows hinted at a mix of surprise and perhaps a touch of discomfort at the public acknowledgment. "I thought that was confidential information," he pointed out, navigating the fine line between professional decorum and friendly banter.

Damien, chuckling, dismissed any formality. "Don't be puzzled, Sam. I see all the numbers, even yours. I couldn't resist giving credit where it's due." His words, though candid, carried a hint of solidarity.

Leaning forward, Sam's smirk suggested he enjoyed the recognition. "Do you think I deserved it?" His tone, though light, invited Damien to share in the banter.

Damien, realizing he might have pushed the envelope, let out a grumble. "Well, forget I said anything. Just letting off some end-of-the-month steam." The acknowledgment of boundaries came with a touch of self-amusement.

Sam, however, brushed it off with a smile. "It's Friday, Damien. Let's put work aside until Monday." The words hung in the air, an unspoken agreement to enjoy the upcoming weekend and set aside the intricacies of office life.

Damien paused at the threshold of the office, a sudden spark of curiosity igniting in his eyes. He turned, his casual demeanor giving way to something more intense. "By the way," he began, his voice tinged with intrigue, "what's up with this special board meeting on Monday?"

Sam, momentarily taken aback, his face a canvas of surprise and confusion, replied, "Special board meeting? That's news to me."

Damien leaned in closer, his voice dropping to a hushed tone that seemed to carry the weight of confidential information. " Rumors are swirling that the board has called an urgent meeting, summoning all the key players."

Sam reclined in his chair, his arms crossing in a gesture that seemed both dismissive and contemplative. "Well, since I stepped down from the board, their affairs don't concern me anymore."

But Damien wasn't deterred. With a sly grin, he teased, "Maybe you're not on the board, Sam, but your shadow still looms large over their decisions. They can't seem to let go of your legacy."

A light chuckle escaped Sam, his eyes narrowing with a hint of mystery. "Let's just say my calendar for Monday is already filled with... different pursuits." His words lingered in the air, shrouded in ambiguity, inviting speculation about what clandestine plans might be unfolding beyond the boardroom's reach.

As the Director of Sales at Genesys, a genetic engineering company he co-founded a few years back, Sam had gradually eased off his workload to prioritize time with his family. The fact that he hadn't been informed about the impending special meeting raised his suspicions. If he possessed the gift of foresight, he might not overlook it, but at the moment, only one thing was on his mind - returning home to Nicole and their children.

Each year, they marked their wedding anniversary on the last Friday of July, following the same tradition of a dinner cruise on San Diego Harbor. The cuisine might not have been exquisite, but the mesmerizing view and the cherished memories they created brought them back, year after year. This year, however, they'd opted for a grander celebration, planning a soirée at the B Street Café, surrounded by their closest friends and family.

Before departing from work, Sam retrieved a gift box from his desk drawer and opened it, admiring its content. Like many times before, he contemplated how Nicole would react. With the gift in hand, he left the building and approached his sleek black Aston Martin DB9. Sam paused for a moment, just to savor the rumble of the engine before shifting the car into gear.

Driving past the UCSD campus toward his home atop Soledad Mountain, he marveled at the remarkable growth it had undergone in recent years. Where tall trees once stood, vast blacktop parking lots now stretched out. As often happened on this route, a wave of nostalgia washed over him, transporting him back to the vibrant memories of the 1980s.

Chapter 3

Let's journey back to the first day of the 1983 fall quarter at UCSD, where Sam, Damien, and Luke eagerly reunited after the summer break. Standing in line to pay their tuition, they reveled in the joy of old friends reuniting, just like kids back in grade school. The air was filled with stories of their summer adventures, with Damien sharing tales of his visit to Florida, unable to contain his enthusiasm. However, the ever-playful Luke had his own mischievous agenda.

"Dude, who gives a darn about your family tales," Luke chimed in with a naughty grin, "we're just dying to find out if you got laid in the Sunshine State."

The usually well-mannered Damien was momentarily taken aback, speechless. Luke was his complete opposite, rarely serious, and always living for fun.

"Enough, man," Damien retorted, his patience waning. "Just go there for the spring break, you won't come back disappointed."

Luke promptly suggested, "We should all plan a trip there together." He was known for his good looks and a charming personality. Raised near Moonlight Beach in Encinitas, where his mother trained lifeguards, he had been a beach aficionado since the age of four. He got his lifeguard certificate the day he turned eighteen. His naturally blond hair had nearly turned white from endless hours in the sun. Luke lived life day by day, using his earnings to chase the world's best waves. A student of marketing and design, he aspired to one day design and manufacture his own line of surfboards.

"My love life in California is complicated enough," Sam chimed in. He had recently ended a relationship in which his girlfriend, expressing a desire to explore the world while she was still young, suggested a 'break.' Sam, perceptive to the nuances, recognized it as a graceful way of being dumped. Going to Florida seemed unnecessary, as he navigated the complications of his romantic entanglements at home.

Luke countered, "See, that's your problem dude. Where there's no love, there's no complication. What happened to pure lust in this world? And since you and Yassmin are no longer together, what's there to complicate?"

Sam exchanged glances with Damien before facing Luke. "I suppose good news travels fast," he said, alluding to a phone conversation with Damien in which he'd asked him to keep it quiet. Sam knew that Luke, with his matchmaker tendencies, would jump at the opportunity to set him up.

Damien offered a casual shrug, accompanied by an apology, recognizing that his words had slipped out hastily. Sam responded in jest that Luke would now attempt to arrange him in a date with his usual type.

"You mean, hot and sexy?" Luke teased.

"No," Damien interjected with a grin, "he means dumb and easy."

"Exactly, the best type," Luke replied, a playful grin on his face.

Sam's focus wavered from the monotonous line, stolen by the magnetic presence of a girl at one of the cashier's booths. A sudden stillness overcame him, a spell cast by the allure of an unexpected moment. Luke, sensing Sam's detachment, attempted to pull him back into the rhythm of the ordinary.

But Sam resisted, turning slightly, his eyes remaining entranced by the enigmatic figure at the counter. His voice, usually assured, trembled with a mix of curiosity and an unnamed emotion as he uttered, "Who is that?" The question hung in the air, a whisper of wonder that betrayed a depth of intrigue beneath Sam's calm exterior. And then, as if overwhelmed by a surge of unspoken feelings, he fell silent again.

As the girl concluded her transaction, she gracefully glided past Sam on her way out. His eyes, drawn irresistibly, traced every step she took, and an unspoken gravity anchored his intense gaze upon her. Sensing the weight of his scrutiny, she turned around, and in that fleeting moment, their eyes collided.

A spark ignited between them, a silent acknowledgment of an invisible thread connecting their worlds. The twinkle in her eyes radiated a subtle luminosity, casting an enchantment that momentarily illuminated Sam's surroundings. Her elegant eyebrows, delicately arched, framed eyes reminiscent of a captivating constellation, the hue of blue holding the secrets of an uncharted galaxy.

Locks of chestnut-brown hair, a cascade of artistic strokes, gently embraced her face, revealing features sculpted with a divine touch. They flowed over her shoulders, embracing her like a curtain of silk. The radiance of her skin, akin to a canvas kissed by the sun, absorbed the admiration of Sam's watchful eyes.

Straight, white teeth peeked through the gateway of her bee-stung crimson lips, a dazzling smile that echoed the warmth within. The contours of her shapely figure, adorned in a fitted top and Jordache jeans, created a silhouette that left Sam awestruck in the wake of her passing.

With a graceful gesture, she brushed a few loose strands of hair from her face. Turning toward the exit, she bestowed upon Sam a smile so inviting that it felt like a warm embrace. The door began to close, severing their connection like the closing curtain of an ephemeral scene, leaving Sam suspended in a moment touched by the fleeting magic of an unspoken connection.

Meanwhile, Luke, with his keen eye, spotted a piece of paper left behind on the counter by the captivating girl. In one fluid motion, he snatched it up. "Almost forgot this," he quipped to the cashier before she could react and swiftly disappeared into the bustling surroundings.

"Will I ever see her again on this huge campus?" Sam pondered, still gazing outside, but the girl had vanished from sight like a fleeting dream.

"Just go after her, you goof," Damien advised.

"I wouldn't even know what to say. I'd probably make a fool out of myself," Sam confessed, his voice tinged with a blend of wistfulness and self-doubt.

Luke burst back in, his arrival marked by a flourish of excitement. In his hand, he brandished a piece of paper, which he theatrically waved in front of Sam's eyes like a magician revealing his final trick. "No worries, my friends, no worries," he proclaimed, his voice bubbling with a blend of triumph and mischief. A wide, naughty grin stretched across his face as he added, "For starters, her name is Nicole."

Sam's eyes lit up with a mix of eagerness and surprise. He quickly reached out, his fingers deftly snatching the paper from Luke's grasp. As he scanned the document, he realized it was Nicole's class roster. One particular entry leaped out at him, as if highlighted by fate itself: "Genetics, Biology 130," neatly scheduled on Tuesday and Thursday afternoons. A quick mental check confirmed there were no conflicts with his own schedule.

A spark of resolve ignited in Sam's eyes. "Hey, guys, I need that class to graduate anyway," he declared with a newfound determination, mentally adding the class to his schedule.

Damien, leaning against a nearby table, couldn't help but comment, his tone a mix of admiration and disbelief. "That's crazy and romantic at the same time," he observed, his eyebrows raised in amused skepticism.

Luke, ever the eternal optimist and instigator, chuckled heartily. "It's crazy, just crazy," he agreed, but then added a dose of reality, "What if she's already taken? Not that it ever stopped me, but we're talking about you here." His eyes twinkled with a blend of challenge and camaraderie. "How about we go out this Saturday night to one of the fraternity parties? I guarantee you'll forget all about her," he suggested, slapping Sam on the back with a friendly gusto.

Just then, the cashier called for the next person in line, breaking their huddle of conspiracy. Sam, stepping forward, cast a thoughtful glance over his shoulder. "But I don't want to forget about her," he mused softly, his voice barely audible over the din of the bustling office.

As Sam walked away, Luke, undeterred, flashed him an enthusiastic thumbs-up. "Awesome," he exclaimed, his voice laced with both encouragement and a hint of playful challenge.

****

Sam's passion for math had been an unwavering constant, a flame ignited in the days of preschool innocence. In his childhood reveries, he painted a future adorned with the robes of a mathematician or an engineer, his mind dancing with the elegance of equations and the allure of algorithms. Yet, in this symphony of aspirations, a discordant note emerged — his father harbored different dreams. The paternal wish was for Sam to tread the path of medicine, to follow the ancestral trail of healing rather than the abstract realm of numbers.

"Besides helping people, you'd have a brighter future as a doctor," his father would gently advise. Swallowing the dissonance between paternal expectation and personal yearning, Sam reluctantly acquiesced to his old man's desires. As fate would have it, he found himself in the final throes of the premed program, standing at the crossroads where dreams met reality, and the road to medical school beckoned.

Amidst the sea of prescribed courses, Sam added the genetics class, a beacon leading him closer to the intersection of his passions and the mysterious allure of a certain girl named Nicole. The anticipation was palpable as he counted the days until the first class, each moment stretching like an eternity.

Finally, the much-awaited day arrived, and Sam, buoyed by a blend of excitement and nervousness, made his way to the Peterson lecture hall well before the class was slated to commence. It wasn't just genetics he was about to unravel; it was the tapestry of possibilities and perhaps a connection that transcended the boundaries of academia.

The lecture hall echoed with the departing cadence of students, a bustling river flowing out as the previous class reached its conclusion. Finally, the doorway stood clear, revealing the vast expanse of the 350-seat auditorium. Sam, a lone figure among the ebbing tide of students, peered into the cavernous hall, his eyes scanning for the elusive presence of Nicole.

With a heartbeat of anticipation, he claimed his cherished spot in the second row, dead center. Anxiously, he stole a glance towards the doorway, yearning to catch the first glimpse of her. In the brief interlude of extracting his notebook, pencil, and eraser from his bag, the room had transformed. Seats were swiftly claimed by others, leaving Sam scanning the growing sea of faces in a quest for Nicole. The room, now a whirlwind of activity and jostling bodies, obstructed his view.

As the minutes ticked away, frustration curled within him like an impatient storm. "Where are you?" he silently fumed, the weight of expectation hanging heavy in the air, each passing moment intensifying the longing to find her amidst the labyrinth of the lecture hall.

"Alright, settle down, everyone. Let's kick off the class," a voice resonated through the speakers. Sam swiveled in his seat, attention now fixed on the casually dressed man commanding the podium. Dr. Mills, as he introduced himself, emanated an air of nonchalant confidence, his tattered shoes sparking Sam's curiosity.

In his introductory address, Dr. Mills navigated through the terrain of his teaching philosophy, the grading landscape, and a set of rules etched in stone. Sam, perched on the edge of his seat, absorbed each word, his intrigue deepening with every passing moment.

"I hope you all have a soft spot for math, especially statistics, because this genetics course is one part biology and a whopping three parts statistics," Dr. Mills declared, his words cascading like a harmonious melody into Sam's eager ears. However, a collective 'aah' of dismay reverberated through the lecture hall as those less fond of the numerical dance expressed their disappointment.

With a flourish, Dr. Mills etched a problem on the blackboard, a moment that would act as the seismic shift, forever altering the trajectory of Sam's life.

Chapter 4

In the heart of a crisp morning on Charles Street, the scent of freshly brewed coffee lingered in the air, revitalizing Dr. Bijan Larabi's spirit as the clock inched towards 5:30 AM. His steps slowed, drawn by the inviting aroma of a cup of coffee and a Boston cream donut, but he resisted the temptation. He vividly remembered the last time he'd indulged at the end of a grueling forty-eight-hour on-call shift at Massachusetts General Hospital—it had stolen sleep from him for hours.

Inside his modest apartment, a trail of discarded clothing traced his path from the door to his bed, marking his descent into a deep slumber. As the day aged, sunlight spilled through the window, casting a warm, golden glow upon his form, stirring him from his rest around half-past three. With a longing gaze outside, he decided that it was time to explore the vibrant city of Boston for the very first time on that fateful Saturday, October thirteenth, in the year nineteen fifty-six.

After a leisurely stroll from his apartment, he found himself in the tranquil embrace of Boston Common Park. His appetite called for a quick bite, leading him to an enchanting ice cream vendor nearby. As he continued his unhurried walk, he stumbled upon a group of spirited young people ardently distributing campaign flyers. Among them, one girl shone like a radiant star, her charm accentuated by her long skirt and a vibrant blouse. Her moonlit hair, elegantly arranged, complemented her enchanting misty-green eyes, and her rosy cheeks blended seamlessly with her luminous, porcelain-like skin. With a warm smile, she extended a flyer towards him.

"Have you registered to vote yet?" inquired the slender, blonde girl, her smile as inviting as a sunbeam. Bijan was spellbound by her presence, a desire to engage in conversation brewing within him. Puzzled momentarily over the question, the intricacies of the American election process foreign to him, he began to read the flyer, all the while savoring his ice cream.

The flyer advocated for President Eisenhower's re-election. "Isn't he already the President?" Coming from a background of monarchy, he was entirely unfamiliar with the U.S. election system. The girl chuckled, thinking he was jesting. "You're quite amusing. So, who are you leaning towards?"

'Leaning towards,' he pondered, suspecting there were other options but unsure. "What are my choices?" he inquired. "Wow, you're really serious," she said with a playful gleam in her eyes.

This conversation marked his first genuine interaction outside of work since arriving in the U.S., an opportunity to make friends. Having been granted a full scholarship for pediatric surgery by The Imperial Government of Iran after graduating from Medical School, he had immersed himself in his specialty upon moving to America, leaving no room for anything else. Unaware of the upcoming election news, he asked the girl to explain it to him as he finished his ice cream.

She shared her reasons for supporting President Eisenhower, and he found himself captivated by her, more so than by her politics. His stomach growled audibly, drawing a light blush from her as she smiled. "Apologies, my stomach is reminding me how hungry I am," he interjected, his stomach grumbling once more. "What you're saying is fascinating, and maybe we can continue over a meal."

"Thank you, I'm not hungry," she replied, her eyebrows knitting together momentarily, just handed him a pamphlet, and hastily returned to her group. He realized he'd inadvertently asked her out on a date and recognized how impolite he might have sounded. "Miss, miss," he called after her. She hesitantly turned back, her expression shouting - What do you want? He apologized for any perceived disrespect, clarifying that it was his hungry stomach talking, and that ice cream was all he had that day.

"Then get something to eat, goodbye," were her parting words. As she began to walk away, leaving Sam standing there, he couldn't let her go so easily. He squeaked, asking if she could direct him to a nearby good restaurant, admitting his unfamiliarity with the area. A subtle relaxation of her facial muscles accompanied her turn toward him, and her gentle, soft voice reassured him. The genuine smile gracing her face spoke of her belief in him.

She directed him to a nearby restaurant, Gino's Diner, and enthusiastically mentioned their best Philly cheesesteak. Though unfamiliar with the dish, he maintained composure, determined not to reveal his ignorance. Repeating the name in his mind, he strolled along Boylston Street, checking every store display window. Suddenly, he felt a tap on his shoulder. To his disbelief, the same girl from the park stood before him.

"Hello again," he greeted her, captivated by her dreamy green eyes. She smiled and casually stated, "I think I'll take you up on your offer." She had felt a twinge of sympathy for the new stranger in the land and decided to catch up with him.

Excitement and eagerness to see her again surged within him. Straightening his jacket, he attempted to be very proper. "Of course, of course, thank you," he responded cautiously, choosing his words carefully. She extended her hand for a handshake. "I'm Jacqueline."

"It's very nice to meet you, Jacqueline. My name is Bijan," he replied, gently shaking her hand. Their laughter intermingled, punctuated by the unmistakable growl of his stomach.

"Let's get some food in your stomach," she suggested, leading the way. The subtle dance of emotions between them hinted at the beginning of an unexpected connection, fueled by the promise of a shared meal at Gino's Diner.

The bond between these two strangers ignited like a brilliant star in the night sky, and within a year, they pledged their love and devotion in a heartfelt wedding ceremony. In the vibrant dawn of 1960, their family welcomed a bouncing baby boy, a bundle of joy whose name would soon fill their lives with laughter and dreams.

By 1961, a new chapter beckoned as they embarked on a journey to Iran, their hearts filled with anticipation. Bijan's completion of his specialized training was the gateway to a life-changing adventure. Settling in the enchanting city of Shiraz, they took root, with Dr. Bijan Larabi weaving his expertise into the fabric of Namazi Hospital. The pivotal year of 1964 witnessed the grand inauguration of the pediatric surgical department, a testament to their dedication and the brighter future they were building together.

In 1966, the Larabi family experienced another joyous chapter with the arrival of a radiant daughter named Ariana. Two more years on this remarkable journey, and Jacqueline's ambition soared to new heights as she established a unique private elementary school, uniting American and Persian educational traditions into a harmonious blend.

Their days were bathed in tranquility and contentment. Jacqueline thrived in her new home, embracing the rich culture, and savoring every moment spent at her place of work. The backdrop of their lives was a serene canvas painted with love, ambition, and shared dreams. But in 1979, the winds of change swept in, forcing Jacqueline to bid a sorrowful farewell to the cherished home she had come to adore.

Chapter 5

As Nicole walked into PH 108 on that fateful first day of the Genetics course, her friend Brenda's enthusiastic wave beckoned her to a saved seat right next to hers. Fate had randomly paired Brenda as Nicole's roommate at the Muir college dormitories, and their bond quickly deepened. Brenda, a stunning Southern belle from Dallas, possessed a wild beauty and an infectious personality that seemed to enchant everyone who crossed her path. Her golden-blond hair, often permed in the style of the '80s, flowed like liquid sunlight. She took great care to maintain her smooth skin with the perfect sun-kissed glow and made sure her fashion-forward wardrobe showcased her heart-stopping figure, all funded by her affluent oil tycoon father.

Nicole greeted Brenda and settled into her seat, her heart dancing to the rhythm of their friendship.

"Hello, gorgeous," Brenda said, her tone playfully flirtatious as she switched off her Walkman. Brenda leaned in, her voice a seductive whisper after Dr. Mills' voice had echoed throughout the large classroom.

"Alright, settle down, everyone. Let's kick off the class," Dr. Mills announced, taking command of the room and starting to write on the blackboard. His engaging voice filled the space. "If there are sixteen people in a conference room and at the end, all shook hands before leaving, how many handshakes took place?"

Suddenly, a bold student's voice pierced the silence. "One hundred and twenty," his response echoing through the hall. Dr. Mills turned his way, but the student seemed to be scanning the back of the class, as if looking for someone.

Dr. Mills continued, presenting a more challenging question. "In a class of twenty students, there are twelve girls and eight boys; seven of the students are A students. If a student is chosen at random, what is the probability of choosing a girl or an A student?" The room fell into a thoughtful hush as everyone grappled with the problem.

"Not enough data," the same student's voice emerged again. This time, all eyes turned toward him. Slowly, he shifted his gaze to the front of the class, meeting Dr. Mills' direct gaze.

Nicole's voice trembled as she recognized the boy from the registrar's office. "Oh my God, that's him," she whispered to Brenda, lightly squeezing her hand. She had told Brenda about her intriguing encounter earlier.

Dr. Mills, impressed by the student's response, introduced some additional data to the problem. "What if three of the seven A students are girls."

Nicole and Brenda were five rows behind him. Brenda leaned in, scrutinizing him closely. He appeared to be writing on the desk as if the solution were emerging from his fingertips.

"Eighty percent," he answered calmly, projecting confidence as he looked directly at Dr. Mills.

"Sixteen out of twenty, or eighty percent. By the way, it's so nice of you to finally join us. I was beginning to think the answers were written on the back wall," Dr. Mills quipped, eliciting a soft laugh from the class.

"That's the 'stare freak'?" Brenda asked, recalling the details Nicole had shared.

Nicole shook her head, a faint smile playing on her lips. "Oh, you've got it all wrong," she murmured, her voice a blend of amusement and secrecy. "The way he gazed at me... it was the kind of look every girl dreams of: unfiltered, heartfelt, brimming with sincerity. And from what I've gathered, he's not just a pair of dreamy eyes; he's got the brains too."

"Maybe you should ask him, what's the probability of both of you ending up in the same class," Brenda suggested, her tone laced with doubt that it was not merely a coincidence.

As Dr. Mills continued the lecture, delving into the intricacies of probability and its role in explaining diversities in nature, Sam, the unsuspecting protagonist, remained blissfully unaware of Nicole's gaze. Every word from the professor fueled his interest, creating a harmony of fascination within him. With the assignment of homework marking the end of the first day of class, Sam prepared to leave, eager to embark on a quest to find Nicole. However, his plans took an unexpected turn when Dr. Mills called out his name.

Disappointed yet curious, Sam picked up his backpack and approached the front of the classroom. Dr. Mills, initiating a conversation, remarked, "You're very quick in problem-solving. What's your major?" Flustered but flattered, Sam explained his major in premed and minor in math. Yet, his attention was divided, stealing glances at a girl in the back who repeatedly turned to look at him.

Catching on to Sam's distraction, Dr. Mills playfully teased, "Not only are you smart, but you have good taste, too." Sam, rendered speechless and bashful, turned toward Nicole once more.

"Run, young man. What are you waiting for?" Dr. Mills urged, his hand landing reassuringly on Sam's shoulder. Sam nodded, feeling his heart pounding like a drum in his chest, and darted off in his quest for Nicole. As he approached the exit, he was met with a scene reminiscent of two mighty rivers colliding: students flowed in and out of the entrance in a relentless, swirling current. Like water crashing against rocks, they rushed in and out of the class, their movements fluid yet chaotic. Sam wove through this human torrent with determination, but Nicole had already vanished into the tumultuous stream of bodies. She had become like a whispered legend in the river's flow, leaving Sam to navigate the rapids of fate in his search for the girl who had unwittingly ensnared his thoughts.

****

As the hours of two seemingly eternal days trickled away like grains of sand in an hourglass, destiny finally orchestrated their paths intertwine once more. On the dawn of the second day of the course, Nicole's eyes remained fixated on Brenda, who was immersed in the melodies of her Walkman, seemingly cocooned in a world of her own. The music played so loudly that the lyrics, unfamiliar yet catchy - words like 'Holiday' and 'Celebrate' - spilled into the surrounding air through the tiny headphones, invading Nicole's space and fraying the edges of her patience.

Her annoyance simmering just beneath the surface, Nicole's voice was tinged with exasperation. "For heaven's sake, Brenda, can you take off your headphones when I'm trying to talk to you?" The words tumbled out, frustration carving deep lines on her face.

In response, Brenda, oblivious to Nicole's irritation, simply beamed and offered her headphones like a peace offering. "Listen to this. You'll love her music," she said, her voice imbued with an infectious enthusiasm that seemed to dance to the rhythm of the very tunes she cherished.

Nicole rolled her eyes and shook her head dismissively. Brenda switched off her Walkman and casually set it aside. "You're looking hot today. Your boyfriend would be over the moon," Brenda teased, winking mischievously at Nicole.

Those were precisely the words Nicole had secretly yearned to hear, but she craved reassurance and sought it, albeit playfully. "Oh, stop it. But seriously, how do I look?"

"Stunning," Brenda declared with a flirtatious blow of a kiss. "Speaking of the devil, there he is, and it seems like he's searching for someone. Hmm, I wonder who?" Brenda playfully winked at her friend.

Sam, previously unnoticed by Nicole, was now just a few rows away. Brenda, the spirited and fearless one, playfully raised her hand to catch his attention, halted only by Nicole's more reserved demeanor.

"Are you out of your mind?" Nicole hushed Brenda, feeling a tinge of envy at her boldness.

Contrary to his customary spot in the middle of the second row, Sam chose a seat across the aisle from Nicole after he noticed her. Dr. Mills initiated his lecture on genes and alleles, followed by a problem-solving session. Sam, typically vocal, remained silent, refraining from participating in answering any of the questions. The problems escalated in complexity, delving deeper into the intricacies of genetics.

The fourth problem presented a formidable challenge, leaving the class momentarily stumped. "Who knows the answer?" Dr. Mills inquired, his patience wearing thin. Various responses were offered, all of them incorrect. "Stop guessing. Does anyone have the correct answer?"

Nicole's gaze kept drifting toward Sam, who seemed intent on keeping a low profile in his seat. However, unable to resist the urge any longer, he finally provided the correct answer.

"Finally," Dr. Mills exclaimed, shifting his gaze toward the source of the correct response. "I was wondering where you've been hiding, Sam."

In the classroom, a sudden shift occurred as all eyes turned towards Sam. There was a palpable sense of curiosity and surprise among the students, their gazes converging on the unassuming figure who had just inadvertently stepped into the spotlight. Sam, feeling the weight of their stares, sank a little lower in his seat. He kept his head down, his eyes fixed on his desk, hoping to evade further scrutiny. Yet, unbeknownst to him, it wouldn't be the last time Dr. Mills would single him out, casting him into the spotlight in the days to come.

Meanwhile, across the aisle, a subtle but significant exchange took place between Brenda and Nicole. Brenda leaned closer to Nicole, her voice a low whisper tinged with intrigue. "And now we know his name," she said, giving Nicole's hand a gentle squeeze. Her words were laced with a mix of revelation and curiosity.

At the end of the class, Dr. Mills' voice sliced through the chatter, reminding everyone to submit their assignments before leaving. The room, abuzz with the frenetic energy of students eager for freedom, seemed to pulse with life.

In the midst of this controlled chaos, Sam stretched onto his tiptoes, his gaze darting through the sea of heads in search of Nicole. As he navigated the crowded aisle, fate orchestrated a serendipitous encounter. Their eyes met, locking in a moment suspended in time. The world around them blurred into obscurity, leaving only the magnetic pull of their shared gaze.

In Nicole's eyes, Sam found himself adrift in an azure sea, her lashes like delicate oars rhythmically propelling him deeper into her soul. Each blink was a symphony, a siren's call beckoning him closer. Yet, as the spell of the moment wove its magic, reality's tug reminded him of the path he needed to forge.

With a courteous nod, he stepped aside, his voice barely above a whisper, "Please, go ahead."

Nicole's smile, warm as the lingering sunlight, bathed him in a glow of recognition. "Thank you, Sam."

His heart skipped, "You're welcome, Nicole." His words were a bridge he hoped to cross, to linger in her presence a moment longer.

But before he could build on this newfound connection, Brenda, a whirlwind of energy, interjected herself into their orbit. "Would you know my name too, Sam?" Her question, playful yet pointed, derailed Sam's thoughts.

Confusion clouded his expression, a silent struggle played across his face.

Nicole's brow furrowed in curiosity, "What's happening here?"

Brenda's eyes sparkled with mischief as she faced Sam, "You're practically a legend here, thanks to Dr. Mills everyone knows your name. But how do you know Nicole's name?"

Cornered by Brenda's inquisitiveness, Sam grappled with the awkwardness. Nicole's gaze, now tinged with genuine intrigue, intensified the pressure. As they neared the exit, the table to leave their assignments loomed, mirroring Sam's rising panic.

Internally, he chastised himself, "Focus, Sam, focus!"

Grasping at straws, he mumbled to buy some time, "Seems you're the guardian angel of her." Then, inspiration struck. With a confident tilt of his head, he asked, "Isn't that right, Brenda?"

Brenda paused, taken aback. Sam's subtle gesture towards her homework, her name emblazoned across the top, defused the tension.

Nicole chuckled, "A guardian angel, huh?" Her eyes shone with a mix of amusement and intrigue.

Luke and Damien, positioned near the exit, had been entrusted with a vital mission: to make sure that Sam didn't miss another chance to connect with Nicole. In case Sam was held for any reason, they were prepared to delicately stall Nicole, ensuring Sam had the opportunity to join.

"I see you've made new friends. Wonderful," Luke said with a wink as he put his arm around Sam. "I'm Luke, and this is Damien."

"I see the whole cashier's office crew is here," Nicole remarked, introducing herself and Brenda.

Luke wasted no time and strolled over to Brenda. "The weekend is nearly here. Where are we heading?"

Brenda playfully teased Luke, "You must be the nerd's 'fun' friend. What's your idea of fun? A marathon study session at the S&E library until closing time?"

"My idea of fun might be considered illegal in some states," Luke quipped, a mischievous glint in his eye. "But if you're up for it, I might just show you one day or one night, your choice. Although I have to admit, it might get too loud for S&E. It's probably safer if you told me what's your idea of fun, Ms. Sheena Easton," referring to how she was dressed like a pop sensation. Her hair, teased to the heavens and styled with a bold scrunchie, a black mesh crop top, black fingerless lace gloves, a black skirt over leggings, and stars and crucifixes necklaces and multiple bracelets, dramatic eyeliner, and a confident red lip. These elements captured the rebellious and fearless spirit that defined the iconic fashion era of the 80s. Adding the finishing touch, a Boy Toy belt adorned her waist.

Brenda corrected him with a playful grin, "FYI, Madonna, not Sheena Easton. Get with the program." She had been captivated by Madonna's music ever since the release of her first single and she had boldly adopted her fashion.

Luke unruffled, whispered into her ear, "I may not know who Madonna is, but you certainly look delicious."

"Perhaps a bit too fiery for you," Brenda whispered back with a teasing smile.

"Hot and Spicy is my favorite, but I've got a sweet tooth too. Let's go to Pannikan? It's Damien's treat," Luke suggested, steering the conversation towards a popular downtown La Jolla coffee shop known for being a UCSD students hangout, serving a variety of coffee and tea long before the days of Starbucks.

Damien, staying silent, seemed to have little choice but to agree.

Seeing an opportunity to be alone with Nicole, Sam quipped, "Looks like taming these two wild beasts might be a bit of a challenge. I think they'd prefer some privacy."

Nicole nodded with a grin, "You guys have fun. We'll take a rain check."

Luke and Brenda exchanged awkward glances as Damien also made a hasty exit, using the excuse of having other commitments.

An electrifying anticipation hung in the air, palpable and exhilarating. For Sam, it manifested as a thrilling pulse of energy, a current of excitement that made his heart race. He was in disbelief at his fortune. Only minutes after their first exchange, he found himself in the intimate company of Nicole.

As they wandered through the lush campus paths, their conversation initially orbited around their shared class. However, Sam, driven by a spur-of-the-moment impulse, suggested they chase the day's sunset to the summit of Mount Soledad. This unexpected twist transformed their evening into an adventure.

In his Nissan 280 ZX, a mix cassette tape hummed New Wave music through the speakers, showcasing the car's impressive sound system. They ascended the serpentine Via Capri, a road that mirrored the rugged beauty of its namesake island in Italy. On one side, the vast ocean stretched to the horizon, and on the other, the imposing silhouette of Soledad Mountain loomed.

In this enchanting setting, Nicole initiated a deeper conversation, inquiring about Sam's origins. Her curiosity piqued as he narrated his intricate journey: born in Boston, a chapter of his life unfolding in Iran, and finally anchoring him in San Diego since 1979. When Nicole asked, "Then, are you Persian?" a moment of introspection washed over Sam. He delved into the complexities of his mixed heritage, revealing layers of his identity.

This exchange marked a turning point in their interaction. The connection between them deepened, echoing the intertwining paths of the road they ascended. Their stories, each unique yet relatable, began to weave together, creating a tapestry of shared understanding and mutual fascination. Under the waning light, their evening was transforming into a journey of discovery, not just of the scenic beauty around them, but of each other's intricate worlds.

As Sam's car crested the final incline to Mount Soledad Park, the sun teetered on the brink of the horizon. Its descent painted the sky in breathtaking shades of crimson and gold, the ocean below reflecting this fiery spectacle. Sam, with a gallant flourish, swung around the car to open Nicole's door. She played along, gracefully extending her hand as if she needed assistance rising from the low-slung seat of the Nissan 280 ZX.

Together, they strolled to the park's edge, where the sun appeared to dip its fiery edge into the ocean, as if testing the water's temperature before plunging into its nightly retreat. The date, October 6, 1983, seemed to pause in this moment of natural grandeur.

As the last embers of daylight flickered out, the sky transformed into a canvas of deep blues and purples, reminiscent of a peacock's tail just before it vanishes from sight.

Nicole, captivated by the scene, whispered in awe, "This is beautiful." Sam, his eyes not leaving the horizon, responded with a knowing tone, "It always is."

Nicole and Sam meandered through the park, an electric current of unspoken desires and subtle tension pulsing between them. Each was keenly aware of the other's presence, yet hesitant to breach the physical distance that separated them.

Suddenly, Nicole's gaze was drawn skyward to a celestial spectacle: a slender crescent moon, suspended over the darkened ocean. It hung there like a cosmic chaperone, its slender arc casting a mystical glow over the waters. This celestial body, in its understated elegance, seemed to oversee the night, turning the ocean beneath into a canvas of shimmering silver.

The sight was nothing short of magical. The moon appeared as a delicate sailboat, its waning sail drifting toward the horizon, leaving in its wake a sky now dotted with stars and distant planets. It was as if they were witnessing a celestial dance, a meeting of cosmic forces at the end of the day as the celestial sailboat soon disappeared below the horizon. The world around them seemed to stand still, wrapped in the enchantment of the universe's grandeur, providing a backdrop for their own unfolding story.

Seated on a bench beneath the bewitching night sky, Nicole nestled closer to him, a soft sigh escaping her lips. "If only I could read the secrets of the stars about my future."

Sam's response was gentle, tinged with a hint of mystery. "The stars, they're silent storytellers, not fortune tellers." He shifted, drawing her into a shared gaze toward the heavens. "Yet, we can weave tales from their patterns." He shared a childhood memory of rooftop stargazing, "When we were children, we claimed a star as ours? Look there," he gestured, "those three stars with the brightest in the center."

Her eyes traced the celestial line. "Is that your star?"

"No, that's a childhood friend's dream. But follow me," he guided, his voice a whisper of adventure, "from that star, draw an unseen line leftward. What do you see?"

With a playful flourish, she mimicked drawing in the sky to be led to that hidden treasure.

Closer still, their cheeks brushed in a moment of tender complicity. Sam's arm encircled her, his fingers gently guiding hers through the starlit ballet. There it was, a quartet of stars, dancing in a diamond formation.

Her gaze locked onto the constellation, a soft gasp of realization parting her lips. "I see it now." As they wrapped in a celestial embrace.

"Those four, they're my cherished stars," Sam's voice was a velvet ribbon, binding them in the moment.

Nicole's eyes fluttered closed, a smile playing on her lips. "A lone star wasn't enough for you? You had to get a quartet to call your own, what do you call them?"

"I simply called them 'My Stars' until a friend called them the 'Kite Stars' for their unique formation." His hand drifted, leading hers to a fifth star. "In the grand tapestry of the sky, they're part of Delphinus, the Dolphin, a constellation that leaps across the night. The legend has it that Poseidon, the Greek God of the Sea, put the image of Delphinus among the stars out of gratitude for persuading Amphitrite to accept Poseidon's marriage proposal."

Under the canopy of the night sky, a silent exchange of glances unfolded between Sam and Nicole, each look heavy with unspoken promises. The air around them was thick with anticipation, the stars above witnesses to the burgeoning connection between two hearts.

Nicole's playful challenge, an inquiry about buying one of Sam's cherished stars, hung in the air, her eyes twinkling with a mix of mischief and curiosity. Sam, finding himself unexpectedly contemplating the idea, felt a surge of excitement at the thought of sharing something he valued so personal.

In a world where the value of a star could only be measured in the currency of the heart, Sam playfully suggested a price—a kiss. To him, it seemed a fitting tribute to the celestial wonders that had captivated mankind for eons. Nicole's response, a blend of humor and allure, was a turn of her face towards him, an unspoken acceptance of his whimsical proposition.

As they moved closer, the moment stretched, time seeming to slow. Sam wrapped his arms around her, and as their lips met, a cascade of sensations overwhelmed him. He was acutely aware of every point where their bodies touched, the warmth of her skin, the softness of her lips, a kiss that was both tender and full of longing. In that instant, Sam realized this was a moment etched in memory, a kiss that spoke volumes more than any words could.

Nicole, playful yet poignant, reminded him of the significance of their shared star. Her fingers danced over his shirt button, a gentle reminder of the bond they were forging.

In response, Sam pulled her closer, his actions speaking louder than any words. Their second kiss was deeper, more urgent, as if trying to communicate everything unspoken between them. He whispered near her ear, his breath warm, a promise of never forgetting this moment.

Their exchange continued, each kiss a seal on their shared ownership of the celestial wonders above. With each embrace, the connection between them deepened, a dance of passion and tenderness. Nicole playfully asserted her claim to more stars, each kiss a step closer to an unspoken agreement, their bodies pressed close in the cool night air.

Sam's senses were fully engaged, each kiss intensifying the connection, his hands exploring the contours of her back, fingers entwining in her hair. The more they kissed, the more he craved her presence, her taste, her scent. It was an intoxicating cycle, each moment feeding the next, an endless spiral of desire and connection.

Finally, as they parted, breathless and exhilarated, Sam proclaimed her the co-owner of the Stars of Delphinus. Nicole, ever playful, teased that her contributions warranted more than just a shared ownership. Sam, his heart alight with joy and affection, playfully rebuffed, insisting that some things were too precious to give up entirely.

In the intimacy of that night, under the silent gaze of the stars, they wove a tapestry of memories, each kiss a stitch in the fabric of their shared story. The universe itself seemed to conspire in their favor, the Stars of Delphinus shining a little brighter, as if to acknowledge the birth of a new constellation in the hearts of two lovers.

Regrettably, their time beneath the stars had to end. Nicole's lips, sore from their sweet encounter, told a tale of their memorable night. As they parted ways, Nicole stood by the entrance to her dormitory and remarked on the fun day they had shared. Sam, with a twinkle in his eye, offered her a secret remedy for sore lips. He kissed her again, playfully stating, "Be careful, this remedy may be habit forming."

Nicole rubbed her lips thoughtfully and quipped, "It did make them feel better. I wonder how long its effect will last." Sam responded with one more kiss, their connection deepening as they confessed their dreams for the night ahead, sealing the promise of more to come.

Under the dark sky, their joy lingered like stardust, and the echoes of their shared stories reverberated in the quiet night. As they walked away in opposite directions, the invisible thread of their celestial encounter remained intact, connecting their hearts across the vast expanse of the universe, whispering secrets to the night, carrying the essence of a love that had just begun to bloom.

Chapter 6

The pulsating music slammed into Sam like a tidal wave as he steered his car into the parking lot of the apartment complex. The thumping bass and infectious beats, synonymous with Luke's nocturnal revelries, reverberated through the air. Sam hastened his steps toward the apartment he shared with his bold and spirited roommate.

Upon crashing through the door, the relentless music still echoing in his ears, Sam froze in his tracks at the unexpected sight that met him. Luke, the unapologetic showman, held court in the center of their living room, transformed into a one-man dance extravaganza. His clenched fist doubled as an impromptu microphone, and the gleaming buckle of his belt proudly proclaimed "BOY TOY," a testament to the unbridled audacity that defined Luke's character.

Sam couldn't stifle his laughter at the sheer absurdity of the scene. "Luke, are you okay?" he managed to ask between bursts of amusement, making his way to the turntable and swiftly silencing the music. Luke had been grooving to the iconic Madonna tune "Holiday" on a single 45 RPM record.

"What in the world are you listening to, and where did you find that ridiculous belt?" Sam inquired, shaking his head in disbelief.

Undeterred by the interruption, Luke responded with a playful grin. "That, my friend, is the timeless music of Madonna. Get with the program." He winked mischievously at someone lurking just around the corner.

Intrigued, Sam took a few steps toward the corner and discovered Brenda sitting at the dining table. Her laughter echoed through the room as she reveled in the entertaining spectacle before her.

Brenda's laughter cascaded through the room, a melodic symphony of mirth that seemed to dance in the air. "Your friend is absolutely bonkers," she exclaimed, her eyes twinkling with uncontained amusement.

Sam, leaning against the wall with a half-smile playing on his lips, nodded in playful agreement. "You don't have to tell me," he replied, his chuckle mingling with the remnants of Brenda's laughter. There was a warmth in his voice, a hint of affection for the friend they were discussing.

Brenda leaned in, her curiosity a tangible force. "Where's Nicole?" she asked, her voice lowering to a conspiratorial whisper.

Sam's demeanor subtly shifted, a sigh escaping him as if he were releasing a weight he'd been carrying. "She went back to her dorm," he said, his voice laced with an undercurrent of something unspoken, a depth of emotion not yet revealed.

In that moment, Luke burst into the conversation, his eyes alight with an excitement that was almost palpable. "Hey, bro, how'd it go? We need all the juicy details!" he exclaimed, his enthusiasm infectious.

Sam, however, seemed uninterested in delving into those details. His gaze drifted away, a silent refusal to engage in the topic. "I'm hitting the hay," he declared with a finality that closed the chapter on that conversation. As he moved towards his room, he added, almost as an afterthought, "By the way, Brenda, Luke's car has a habit of stalling when you decide to leave...if you catch my drift."

Luke retorted quickly, a playful edge to his voice, "Just shut up and go to bed, Sam."

Brenda, clearly enjoying the playful banter, chimed in with a wink. "And make sure your door is shut tight if you want any sleep tonight. I might need to give Luke's engine a jump start."

The atmosphere in the apartment shifted as Luke exclaimed, "Awesome!" His grin was infectious, spreading like wildfire as he started up the music. Brenda joined him on the makeshift dance floor, their movements a celebration of the moment.

Chapter 7

Midway through the semester, Sam finally mustered the courage to approach Dr. Mills for a recommendation letter, the last crucial piece to complete his medical school applications. The anticipation was palpable as he voiced his request, hoping for a swift and affirmative response.

However, Dr. Mills' reply was far from what Sam had anticipated. "Are you absolutely certain about this decision?" he inquired, casting a shadow of doubt over the moment. Sam had expected a simple "my pleasure" or, at the very least, a nonchalant "no problem."

Dr. Mills probed further, "Do you genuinely believe that medical school is the right path for you?"

Sam hesitated, his gaze drifting to a world of contemplation. "In an ideal world," he admitted, "I'd dive into the wonders of mathematics. But in reality, it's the doctors who drive fancy cars and own grand homes, not the math teachers."

Dr. Mills, undeterred, gestured for Sam to take a seat, as if inviting him to explore an uncharted territory. "How about we consider another path?" he suggested. "Have you ever entertained the notion of pursuing both an MD and a PhD simultaneously?"

Perplexed, Sam inquired, "What would be the point of that?"

A spark of enthusiasm lit up Dr. Mills' eyes as he outlined a proposition. "If you apply to the graduate program in genetics," he explained, "I can personally ensure your acceptance into the MD-PhD program. In seven years, you could hold a doctoral degree in genetics while completing your medical education."

Dr. Mills elucidated the program's intricacies and urged Sam to take some time to mull it over. "Give me a few days to prepare your recommendation letter. Meanwhile, consider my suggestion."

In the days that followed, Sam delved deeper into Dr. Mills' proposition, immersing himself in research and the realm of genetics. As he peeled back the layers of this new opportunity, he realized the vast potential it held. The evolving science of genetics fascinated him, and he saw countless uncharted avenues of exploration that could be his to discover.

Eager to embrace this unorthodox but enticing path, Sam submitted his application to the genetics program. The following year, he embarked on a journey that would intertwine his passion for new discoveries and genetics, unveiling a world of possibilities that he had never before envisioned.

Nicole was set on her path from a young age and worked hard to achieve it. In 1986, Nicole proudly graduated from UCSD with a degree in Biology, a moment that marked the first step on her journey towards becoming a cardiologist. The same year, she embarked on the arduous path to medical school. It was a challenging endeavor, but her unwavering determination and commitment propelled her forward.

The years in medical school were demanding, pushing Nicole to her limits. She sacrificed countless hours of sleep to grasp the complexities of the human body, particularly the intricacies of the heart. Her fascination with cardiology deepened as she learned about the organ's vital role and the various ailments that could afflict it.

After years of rigorous study and grueling clinical rotations, Nicole earned her medical degree. She was now Dr. Nicole Larabi, and the road to becoming a cardiologist stretched before her. Residency followed, and Nicole immersed herself in the world of cardiology, studying under experienced mentors and gaining hands-on experience.

Throughout her career, Nicole's love for cardiology only grew stronger. She felt privileged to be part of a field that could mend and heal the human heart, both literally and figuratively. The most profound moments in her career were those when she witnessed patients recover their health, their hearts mended by her skillful hands and deep compassion.

As the years passed, Nicole's reputation as a cardiologist grew. Patients admired her not only for her medical expertise but also for her empathetic approach. She took the time to listen to their concerns, to understand their fears and hopes, and to guide them toward healthier lives.

Chapter 8

Let's travel forward and rejoin Sam on his journey back home, a man navigating the labyrinth of his own thoughts. The memories of his time at UCSD cradling him in a cocoon of nostalgia and reverie. The hum of the tires against the asphalt was a lullaby to his contemplative mind, taking him deeper into the caverns of his thoughts. Yet, this tranquility was suddenly shattered by the urgent ring of his phone.

Sam's eyes darted to the screen, revealing his office number. A web of questions spun within his mind, like a spider weaving a complex tapestry. He silenced the music that had been serenading his solitude and answered with a curious, "What's up, Hope?"

Hope's voice, when it finally reached him, was tinged with concern, a note of disquiet. She had a matter on her mind, one that had caught her attention like a distant storm gathering strength on the horizon. Sam listened intently, wondering why her voice quivered in the conversation. The impending storm was the special board meeting slated for Monday, a meeting announced with disconcerting spontaneity.

A whisper of dread swept through Sam as he realized the gravity of the situation. "You mean they just planned it today?" He asked, lowering his music even further, his tone more solemn. Hope confirmed it, and a sense of foreboding loomed like a shadow in Sam's thoughts.

Hope's last words lingered like a haunting melody, "I hope it doesn't involve our department." Her words echoed in his mind, setting a curious fire of intrigue within him. "I don't need this now," Sam mumbled to himself, his fingers dialing a number, a decision that would ripple into uncharted waters.

Meanwhile, in the opulent confines of the Genesys Director's office, a congregation of five individuals was engaged in a crucial discussion. Their deliberations were disrupted by a persistent ring, the office phone clamoring for attention. The man behind the imposing desk reached for the phone, but before he could answer, he pointed to the caller ID, and they watched it ring with unease. Four more rings sounded before it surrendered to the voicemail.

Their conversation veered toward the roots of the company's success, a silent acknowledgment of the missing piece in their meeting. The President, seated behind a grand mahogany desk adorned with the name "Allen Phillips," began to emphasize this point when his personal cell phone intruded on the atmosphere. Without a second thought, he declined the call, his gaze unwavering.

Moments later, another cell phone chimed in, only to be similarly ignored, as the participants exchanged troubled glances, leaving their unspoken thoughts to simmer in the room's luxurious air.

Back in the streets, where life flowed at its own pace, Sam continued his journey. He crossed the street into Via Capri, placing his cell phone on the seat beside him, an act of willful detachment from the world of corporate intrigue that he had momentarily touched.

His gaze found solace in the cross atop Mount Soledad, a sentinel that oversaw his first date with Nicole. Sam turned right, a homeward-bound course set in motion, blissfully unaware of the tempest slowly brewing in the corporate realm he had left behind.

Sam's arrival home was marked by the jubilant cries of his son, Cameron, who greeted him with unbridled enthusiasm. "Daddy's home, daddy's home," Cameron exclaimed, adorned in a Bob the Builder tool-belt, launching himself into Sam's waiting arms. Father and son, their bond strong and unbreakable.

"Let's play, let's play," Cameron implored, a burst of youthful exuberance. Sam couldn't refuse, but first, he needed to reconnect with the rest of his family. "Sure, just give me a minute to say hi to everyone. Where are the girls?"

"In Mom's room, doing girly stuff," Cameron said with a mischievous grin.

Sam, carrying Cameron on his shoulder, embarked on a journey through their home. In Nicole's dressing room, he found Tara trying on her mother's bracelets, in the mirror of the woman she admired. As soon as Tara spotted her father and brother, she abandoned her treasures and rushed into Sam's embrace, declaring, "It's my turn." Sam, feeling the warmth of family enveloping him, traded places with Cameron, hoisting Tara onto his shoulder. Together, they ventured toward Nicole's closet, a sanctuary of her style and grace. There, she stood, radiant in a black, strapless dress that accentuated her curves, a goddess of beauty.

"Hi, honey," Nicole purred, her eyes gleaming with love and desire. Sam couldn't help but jest, "I missed you too, but control yourself in front of the kids."

Cameron, always ready to join in the fun, chimed in, "Yeah, Mom, control yourself," as he chuckled.

With their children's giggles echoing through the room, Sam directed them to their quarters, promising to help them get ready. Tara and Cameron scampered off to their rooms, leaving Sam and Nicole to bask in a moment of intimacy.

"How do I look?" Nicole inquired, strutting out of the closet in her alluring dress, her confidence emanating like a fragrant bloom.

Sam, caught in her gravitational pull, approached her, a glint of mischief in his eyes. "Let me take a closer look," he murmured, reaching for the zipper of her dress, teasing her with his sensuality.

"Be serious," Nicole chided, pushing him away playfully. She gazed at herself in the mirror, unsure if her allure was complete.

However, Sam had one more enchantment tucked away, waiting to be unveiled. Gently, he guided her to the chair before the mirror, their eyes meeting through the glass. "You're absolutely breathtaking," he breathed, draping her bare neck with a necklace resplendent in diamonds from the velvet-lined box. "Happy anniversary."

Nicole's eyes sparkled like the gems on her neck, her hand reaching for the necklace, her gratitude reflected in her loving smile. She leaned in, planting a kiss on Sam's lips before turning back to the mirror, her desire intensified by the elegant gift she now wore.

"I hope this is acceptable as the down payment for what I'm getting tonight," Sam hinted, his voice laced with passion.

Nicole, her eyes still locked on her radiant reflection, replied with a sultry smile, "This should be enough for the next twelve months."

Chapter 9

The B Street Café, nestled within the city's heart, was transformed under the spell of a live band. Melodies emanated from the stage, breathing life into the atmosphere, while the song "Closing Time" by Semisonic reverberated through the room. It was an evening that brimmed with the promise of stories yet to be told.

Into this scene, Sam and his family made their entrance. The café's warm ambience enveloped them, wrapping them in the embrace of old friends and cherished memories.

At the bar, Luke and Damien found solace in a world of their own. Laughter and the clinking of glasses flowed from their corner, creating a symphony of camaraderie.

Damien, his eyes filled with the twinkle of familiarity, extended a hearty embrace to Sam. "Twelve years, huh?"

Luke, the guardian of countless shared moments, drew Nicole into an affectionate hug, his smile reflecting the weight of their history. "I feel your pain," he quipped.

Tara, the inquisitive one, couldn't resist a query. "Uncle Luke, when are you going to get married?"

Luke, forever the jester, placed a dramatic hand over his heart, humor twinkling in his eyes. "Don't scare me like that. You almost gave me a heart attack."

Cameron, youthful and candid, joined the conversation. "My mom says you'll never get married."

In the midst of the playful banter, Nicole, wise and affectionate, interjected, "He'll get married once he finds the right woman."

Sam, adding a touch of levity, remarked, "We just have to wait for the day he grows up."

Tara, undeterred, ventured, "You should marry Aunt Brenda," nonchalantly reaching for a snack.

Brenda, an enchantress in her own right, graced the gathering with her presence. Luke, the eternal gentleman, rose to offer her a seat, displaying the courtly manners of a bygone era. "It's always a delight to see you. Tara thinks that we should get married. Let's start the arrangements I say."

Brenda, moved by Tara's pure-heartedness, expressed her affection. "You're so sweet," she said. Her hand reaching for Nicole's, creating a silent bond. "You look as gorgeous as ever, honey."

Brenda, a touch of longing in her gaze, softly smacked Luke on the back of the head. "How come I can't find the right guy?"

Luke, playful and teasing, couldn't help but respond. "I sang and danced for you the first day we met. Nicole had to wait three years."

Sam, with a hint of humor, chimed in, "Don't forget about the 'Boy Toy' belt either."

Hope and her husband arrived, followed by Sam's sister, Ariana, and Nicole's parents. The room buzzed with the energy of old friendships and close-knit family bonds, weaving a tapestry of life's experiences.

Amidst the gathering, Damien seized the moment to raise his wine glass for a toast. The clinking of glasses and the symphony of celebration filled the air.

"To Sam and his beautiful life,
To his kids, his heart, his wonderful wife,
To friendship, to love, to days of our youth,
To Nicole, the eternal flame of his truth.
Cheers."

Sam, swept up in the atmosphere and the depth of his emotions, rose from his seat. His gaze sought out Nicole, the one who had been his constant companion through the winding journey of life.

"The first time I saw you," Sam began, his voice laced with vulnerability, "it made me wonder if I was seeing an angel. Obviously, only an angel could tolerate me all these years and still laugh at my lame jokes."

As Sam's words resonated through the room, Nicole mouthed her response, "I love you," a single tear escaping the corner of her eye.

Sam continued, "Nicole, you complete me."

Nicole, pulling Sam closer, whispered, "Shut up. You had me at hello," sealing their words with a tender kiss.

Amidst the soft murmurs of the gathered audience, Sam, ever the entertainer couldn't help but steal a nervous glance toward Nicole's father. "I don't know what came over me, sir. I never do this sort of thing to your daughter."

The retired Marine officer, a man of few words but boundless wisdom, offered a simple piece of advice. "Just wipe the lipstick off your face."

After dinner, the band shifted to lively salsa music. Hope and her husband demonstrated intricate dance moves to Sam and Nicole, infusing the room with a whirlwind of motion, laughter, and spontaneous joy.

Sam, caught in the spectacle, couldn't resist asking Hope, "Is this the famous Dirty Dancing?"

Hope chuckled, shaking her head. "No, that is," she replied, nodding towards Luke and Brenda, who seemed to float across the dance floor.

Nicole quipped, "That ought to be the forbidden dance."

Moments later, Nicole's mom, seizing a moment alone with the couple, expressed her concern. "Are you ready for your trip?"

Nicole replied with determination, "As ready as we can be."

Worry etched her mother's face. "Are you sure it's safe to go to Iran?"

Sam reassured her, "We'll be fine."

Nicole's mom persisted. "Shouldn't they come here instead? I'm sure we have better medical care here."

Sam, unwavering in his decision, explained, "That's why I'm taking the best heart doctor with me," with a fond pat on Nicole's back. "Please excuse me; I have to get the doctor a drink."

Hope, standing at the bar and ordering a drink, was approached by Sam. He ordered a cosmopolitan and Bourbon and inquired, "Having fun?"

Hope's expression shifted, and she spoke with a note of seriousness, "I did some digging about that board meeting. I think you should postpone your trip. I casually asked Miranda, Mr. Phillips' secretary, if she knew anything. She just said, 'Don't worry, it's nothing.'"

Sam considered her advice thoughtfully and mused, "Maybe you should just listen to her."

Hope's demeanor grew nervous as she confided, "Of course, that's not good. It's the way she said it, with the pauses she made, while looking at me above her glasses, wobbling her pen in her hand, and that fake smile. I know she's hiding something."

Sam lightened the mood with a warm smile, saying, "You know my dad is ill, and I am leaving Sunday no matter what." He picked up the drinks and tipped the bartender. "

Nicole's father, a man of experience and wisdom, took a moment to reflect on his own history. "I've told you before that I was stationed at the American Embassy in Tehran when I was a young Marine. What a beautiful city it was."

The memory of the vibrant city stirred emotions in the room. The sense of anticipation for Sam and Nicole's upcoming journey to Iran added a layer of complexity to the evening.

Guests mingled amongst themselves, conversations ebbed and flowed, and the band transitioned into a new song. As the music pulsed through the room, Nicole turned her gaze toward the stage. The opening chords of "Take Me With U" by Prince filled the air.

Sam had taken the stage, a single spotlight casting a warm glow around him. He raised the microphone, his eyes locking onto Nicole's. The room held its breath, the atmosphere electric.

"I love you," he mouthed, and a tender kiss blown in her direction.

Her radiant face, bathed in the dim setting of the cafe, transported Sam back to a day in the mid-80s. The memory of that moment, how vividly he still remembered every detail, played out like a cherished scene in the story of their life.

****

Amidst the fading chords and breakups of his beloved bands like Duran Duran, The Police, Wham, and Van Halen, Sam found an enduring joy in the summer of 1986. It was this radiant season that witnessed his timeless promise to Nicole, a vow etched in the fabric of eternity, unyielding to time's relentless tide.

As the sun ascended in the sky, its gentle rays casting a warm, golden glow over the commencement ceremony, the multitude of black robes and caps enveloped Nicole, melding her form into a sea of eager anticipation. Among the crowd, her friends and family nestled, waiting with bated breath for the announcement of her name. However, the tranquility shattered when Jacqueline, a mother known for her unfiltered honesty, cornered Sam.

Jacqueline's voice sliced through the moment, her candor catching Sam off guard. "When are you going to pop the question?"

Sam blinked, his surprise momentarily stealing his words. "I haven't given it much thought," he replied, his gaze briefly drifting to Nicole, who seemed lost in the ceremony. "I don't believe Nicole's in any rush either."

Ariana chimed in, her lips curved in a sardonic smile. "Are you genuinely clueless or simply playing the part?"

Jacqueline leaned closer, her intense gaze locked on Sam. "Every girl dreams of donning that pristine white dress, of being swept off her feet by a loving groom. You should be acutely aware of that dream, Sam."

Amid the playful banter, Bijan couldn't resist sharing his own romantic tale. "I can still vividly recall the day I swept your mom off her feet," he quipped, a mischievous twinkle in his eye.

Sam signaled discreetly, mindful of Nicole's parents sitting nearby. "Keep it down."

Bijan leaned in, his voice soft but filled with conviction. "Believe me, they're even more eager for it than we are."

Sam furrowed his brow, contemplative. "But how can one be sure of the right moment?"

Bijan, his eyes locked with Jacqueline's, held her hand tenderly. "The very first time we kissed." As Sam's mother smiled, her eyes glistened with nostalgia. "And in that instant, I knew I wanted to spend my life with her," Bijan concluded, sealing his words with a tender kiss on Jacqueline's hand.

Nicole's mother interrupted the banter as her daughter's name approached on the program. "Her turn is coming."

Nicole stood on the stage, a vision of elegance in her academic regalia, awaiting her long-awaited diploma. As the crowd erupted in jubilant cheers, her name echoed triumphantly through the speakers. Sam couldn't help but be captivated by every nuance of her being—the radiant smile that illuminated her face, the way her hair gracefully swayed in the gentle breeze. In that moment, he realized that the right time had been by his side all along. The moment to ask her the question that had lingered within him, yet had remained elusive due to his own innocence. Swiftly, Sam approached the stage, his heart brimming with affection, and embraced her as she descended the platform. "You do know how much I love you, don't you?" he whispered, his voice tinged with a touch of vulnerability.

Nicole, somewhat bewildered by his sudden ardor, replied, "I surely hope so. Is everything all right?"

Sam held her close, a mixture of happiness and remorse tugging at his heart. "I want you to know that I will cherish you for the rest of your life. Never doubt that," he assured her, his eyes reflecting the guilt of waiting too long to express his feelings.

As their jubilant group gathered around to celebrate with Nicole, she blew a tender kiss to Sam while sharing an embrace with Bijan. Little did she know, the night held more delightful surprises as Sam whisked her away on a romantic dinner cruise along the picturesque San Diego harbor.

As the rhythmic country beats filled the air, most passengers twirled and swayed to the music. Yet, Sam and Nicole found themselves on the deck, captivated by the enchanting nocturnal panorama of the city. Nicole leaned gently against the railing, her gaze fixed on the sparkling downtown lights.

Sam encircled her in his embrace, the soft graze of his lips against her neck sending shivers down her spine. "You see how perfectly you fit in my arms," he whispered, his words an intimate caress, "just like the active site of an enzyme, snugly nestled within the receptor site of a cell."

A playful smile graced Nicole's lips. "I've been sensing your 'active site' for a while now," she teased, nuzzling closer to him.

Sam tightened his hold, the world around them vanishing in the tender magic of the moment.

Walking back inside, Sam grappled with a profound realization that life is an ever-evolving journey, and for their relationship to thrive, it must adapt and grow. In his heart, he had already committed to a lifetime with Nicole; all that remained was the formality of a piece of paper.

"I'll be back shortly by the time you decide on some desserts," Sam mentioned as dinner concluded.

The band embarked on a heartfelt rendition of "Take Me with U" by Prince, the notes gliding through the air like whispers of destiny. Nicole, in sync with the song's rhythm, swayed to the melody, her legs moving effortlessly. "Take Me with U", a melodic gem from the movie 'Purple Rain,' and the chart-topping soundtrack of 1984 with the same title was more than a song; it was the anthem of their love, a cherished memory woven into the fabric of their relationship. Each time the song graced their ears, Sam couldn't help but sing along with the familiar chorus, "Take Me With U."

Then, unexpectedly, she heard Sam's voice slicing through the melody. "This song is dedicated to the love of my life."

Turning toward the stage, Nicole found Sam, microphone in hand, gazing intensely at her. His concealed hand, beneath his jacket, seemed to echo the rhythm of a heartbeat, his unwavering gaze locked on her. With unwavering focus, he sang, as if the song's lyrics were etched into his soul, each word carrying a promise:

"I can't disguise the pounding of my heart"
"It beats so strong"
"It's in your eyes what can I say"
"They turn me on"

"I don't care where we go"
"I don't care what we do"
"I don't care pretty baby"
"Just take me with you"

Sam then descended from the stage and began to slowly make his way toward Nicole. His voice continued to weave the enchantment:

"I don't care if we spend the night at your mansion"
"I don't care if we spend the night on the town"
"All I want is 2 spend the night together"
"All I want is 2 spend the night in your arms"

As he finally reached Nicole, his eyes held a question that needed no words:

"To be around u is so-oh right"
"You're sheer perfection"
"Drive me crazy, drive me all night"
"Just don't break up the connection"

Kneeling before her, Sam's love flowed through the words:

"I don't care where we go"
"I don't care what we do"
"I don't care pretty baby"
"Just take me with you"

"Honey," Sam's voice, soft and intimate, carried the weight of a promise "under this starlit sky, with the gentle caress of the ocean's whispers as our witness," As Sam's words hung in the air, Nicole's heart danced to their rhythm, every word etching itself into her memory. Her eyes, glistening with emotion, met his, and she knew that this moment was bound to be the turning point of their forever.

In that suspended instant, with the world fading into the background, Sam's trembling hand extended a token of their love—a ring that sparkled like a promise. "If you say yes," he continued, his voice filled with a blend of vulnerability and unwavering commitment, "I promise to make you feel like the only girl in the world for as long as I live."

Overwhelmed by emotion, Nicole knelt beside him, tears of joy shimmering in her eyes, mirroring the brilliance of the ring. Her voice, laced with delight and the depth of her affection, quivered as she whispered her answer, "Of course, I will."

As the ring found its place on her finger, the room erupted in a symphony of applause, a chorus of love and well-wishes, celebrating the union of two souls destined to be together.

The bandleader, sensing the magic of the moment, raised a toast to Nicole and Sam, inviting them to lead the next dance. The timeless melody of "I've Been Waiting for a Girl Like You" by Foreigner swirled around them, the perfect soundtrack to their enduring love story.

As Nicole admired her ring, a soft breeze ruffled her hair, and the moonlight cast a gentle glow on their faces, enhancing the magic of the moment.

"Sam, this is beautiful," Nicole whispered, her eyes shimmering with affection. "I'll cherish this night forever. What you promised means the world to me."

With a tender smile, Sam enveloped her, his embrace a sanctuary where their love flourished. "I meant every word with all my soul," he assured her, his voice a gentle serenade. "And I hope you understand that I'm not letting you go back home tonight. This night, my love, you belong to me."

Nicole's laughter, like a melody, filled the air. "As for tonight, you won't get rid of me even if you tried." She assured him. With that, she sealed her words with a loving kiss, the taste of their future on her lips.

On their journey back, Nicole's curiosity was piqued when Sam turned into the valet parking area of the Marriott Hotel at 333 West Harbor Drive. "What do you have in mind?" she inquired, a playful smile on her lips.

With a mischievous gleam in his eyes, Sam answered, "Tonight, everything has to be perfect. We're not going back to my apartment with Luke and who knows who else in the next room."

Nicole chuckled, her heart pounding with anticipation. "I didn't even bring a change of clothes," she admitted as they made their way to the hotel's front desk.

Sam leaned closer, a hint of excitement in his voice. "Where we're going, you won't need clothing."

Nicole's laughter was a sweet symphony as she tried to keep up with Sam's brisk pace. At the front desk, Sam made a special request, his eyes never leaving Nicole. "We'd like the honeymoon suite," he told the clerk.

The clerk quickly checked the availability, her eyes twinkling with understanding as she calculated the rate. Sam didn't seem fazed; he was determined to make this night memorable.

"You don't have to do this," Nicole whispered when she heard the cost, her love for Sam shining in her eyes.

Sam simply shook his head, his commitment unwavering. "This one's a gift from Mr. Larabi Senior," he revealed, handing the clerk his credit card.

As the elevator whisked them to the twenty-second floor, Sam placed the "Do Not Disturb" sign on the door before closing it. The world outside melted away, leaving only the two of them, the promise of their future, and the magic of their love.

****

Back at the Café in 1999, Sam's voice soared, filling the room with the cherished notes of their song. With every word, he aimed to make her feel like the only girl in the world:

"I can't disguise the pounding of my heart"
"It beats so strong"
"It's in your eyes what can I say"
"They turn me on"

He presented the microphone to her, determination in his eyes. "You know I'm not giving up," he reiterated, his voice unwavering. She accepted the microphone; her silent words to him filled with affection and a touch of playfulness, and sang;

"I don't care where we go"
"I don't care what we do"
"I don't care pretty baby"
"Just take me with you"

She encircled her arms around him. Together, they serenaded each other with the lyrics. Their voices grew softer, but their lips drew nearer. Their performance culminated in a tender kiss.

As the night wound down, Sam and Nicole expressed their gratitude to their guests, creating memories that would linger in their hearts. The guests once again offered their congratulations as they departed, leaving behind a night filled with love and melodies.

****

Luke approached Brenda after Sam and Nicole had left, his eyes filled with a lingering excitement. "The night is still young, and the music is keeping the energy alive. Want to stay a bit longer?" Luke suggested with a charming smile.

Brenda glanced at the clock, her curiosity piqued. "It's not even midnight yet, and it's a Friday night," she remarked as she playfully pulled him onto the dance floor.

With a mischievous glint in his eye, Luke leaned in closer. "Damien is my ride home. Would you be my knight in shining armor if he leaves?"

Brenda couldn't help but wink at him. "You know I've got your back. Send him on his way."

Soon, they were back on the dance floor, the last souls lingering as the place began closing down. Their conversation flowed like a gentle river, the night's enchantment never quite dissipating.

Brenda stifled a yawn. "I can't remember the last time I stayed out this late."

"Maybe age is finally catching up with you," Luke teased, a playful grin tugging at his lips.

She nudged him gently. "Shut up. You're older than me, anyway."

Luke chuckled. "I was kidding. Thank you for staying, Brenda. We should do this more often."

Brenda met his gaze, her eyes locking onto his. "Are we doing this again?" she asked, her voice tinged with curiosity. "I've lost count of how many times we've started and stopped, every time without a reason."

A wistful smile tugged at Luke's lips. "You know what, Brenda? We've shared sixteen incredible years together. That's a lifetime, isn't it?"

"You're a great friend, Luke. Sometimes, I even miss you," Brenda admitted, her tone tinged with affection.

Luke reached out, gently rubbing her arm. "Well, what are you wearing during those times?"

Brenda rolled her eyes, her tone teasing. "Be serious for once, will you?"

A hint of vulnerability surfaced in Luke's eyes as he sat upright. "I have a confession to make. I still dream about our first night together."

"That's all you think about, isn't it?" Brenda shook her head in disappointment. "How about all the other stuff we did together?"

Luke reminisced, a glint of mischief in his eyes. "Remember that time in Vegas when I dared you to use the men's room? Too bad you lost the bet."

Brenda's face lit up with a defiant spark. With a hearty laugh, she playfully slapped his shoulder. "I didn't lose, you jerk. I waltzed right into that restroom filled with guys. But, come on, I draw the line at sitting on a grimy urinal. Instead, I left the stall door open. On the other hand, you, my dear friend, were the one too scared to play the part of a blind man and accidentally grab the girl's boobs in the red skimpy top."

A sly grin tugged at Luke's lips as he made his confession. "Well, I didn't want to end up in jail."

Brenda's laughter bubbled forth. "Exactly—chicken, chicken, chicken."

"We sure did have our share of fun, didn't we?" Luke mused, his voice laced with nostalgia. "I can't figure out why we kept drifting apart. Maybe we're just too much alike. Sam's got a point; perhaps it's time to grow up."

"Growing up, huh?" Brenda said thoughtfully. "Maybe he's right."

As they arrived at Luke's place, Brenda parked the car in front of his house. She held his hand, a soft smile playing on her lips. "Perhaps it's time for both of us to catch up with our age. Just promise me you won't lose your sense of humor. Don't let me miss your jokes, even when age catches up with you."

Luke grinned and leaned in, planting a gentle kiss on her cheek as he prepared to exit the car. "I might be older, but I'll still ask you to come in."

Brenda rolled down the window and chuckled. "Perhaps this time, we should do things the right way."

Luke continued to smile. "What do you suggest we do?"

Brenda's eyes sparkled with amusement. "Let's pretend this was our very first date. Call me tomorrow, like a true gentleman, thank me for the fantastic time you had, and ask me out again."

"Perhaps that's part of growing up," Luke mused.

Brenda flashed a warm smile. "Perhaps."

As Luke gently kissed her cheek, Brenda gazed at him. "Wasn't that a perfect first date?"

His grin was infectious. "Absolutely. Now I have to rehearse what to say for an important phone call I have to make tomorrow."

"Don't be too nervous," Brenda advised. "I have a feeling she's going to say yes."

With that, she drove away, leaving the night behind, filled with endless possibilities.

Chapter 10

On the bustling morning of Saturday, July 31, the day following their enchanting anniversary celebration, Sam and Nicole found themselves in a whirlwind of activity. With their departure for Iran looming on the horizon, the impending qualms of work and the uncertainties of the situation weighed on Sam's mind. Despite these concerns, they managed to put those thoughts aside and focus on packing their essentials for the journey.

"All set with the packing," Nicole sighed, her fatigue evident, stretching her arms in the dimly lit room.

"Go brush your teeth and prepare for bed. I'll come in to tuck you in shortly," Sam told Tara and Cameron, exhaustion evident in his eyes. He arranged the suitcases by the door, making sure everything was ready before attending to his children.

As he settled Tara under her covers, Sam couldn't help but ask, "Are you excited about the trip?"

Tara's eyes shone with anticipation as she replied, "I can't wait to see Grandma and Grandpa. You know how they always bring me toys and gifts when they visit us. I wonder if they'll still give me presents when we go there."

A chuckle escaped Sam's lips as he lovingly tucked her in. "So, do you miss them or their gifts?"

Tara giggled and planted a sweet kiss on her father's cheek. "I love you, Daddy."

"I love you too. Don't worry; you'll be thoroughly spoiled over there," Sam assured her, the tenderness of the moment warming his heart.

With Tara settled, Sam moved to Cameron's room, his heart still aglow from his daughter's sentiments.

"Will there be other kids to play with over there?" Cameron inquired as Sam lovingly drew the blanket over him.

Sam grinned as he replied, "I'll take you to the alley of the Grandpa's house. I had a blast growing up on that long, narrow road. I'm sure you'll have a great time too."

Cameron's eyes sparkled with curiosity. "That sounds like fun," he said with a yawn.

"In the afternoons, we'll walk to the local pastry shop that makes the best cream puffs in the whole wide world, and at night, we'll sleep on the roof so we can watch for shooting stars," Sam shared with his son, who was barely keeping his eyes open.

With a loving kiss goodnight, Sam left Cameron to his dreams and headed back to his bedroom.

Sam entered his room, the soothing sound of the shower running a gentle welcome. Curiosity piqued, he approached the steamy glass, the fogged surface hinting at the outline of Nicole's form within. With a playful yet tender intent, he silently shed his clothing and quietly slid open the shower door.

Nicole, caught off guard by his sudden appearance, let out a soft gasp, quickly turning it into a laugh. "You and your surprises," she said, her voice a blend of mock reproof and warmth.

"Do you need any help in there?" Sam asked, his tone light yet laced with unspoken promise. "I'm quite skilled in the art of back scrubbing, or perhaps any other service you might require."

Nicole's eyes sparkled with amusement and affection. "Always the joker, aren't you? But I won't say no to a little help."

As Sam stepped into the warm embrace of the shower, the water enveloped them both, creating a world that was theirs alone. He reached for the soap, his movements gentle yet intentional, as he began to trace patterns on her back.

The closeness in the confined space of the shower, the steam around them, and the touch of Sam's hands were all Nicole needed to feel the depth of their connection. She turned to face him, her smile an invitation.

"Maybe we can think of other ways to enjoy this shower together?" she suggested, her voice a soft murmur.

Sam met her gaze, his eyes reflecting the same playful yet deep affection. "I'm sure we can come up with something," he replied, his words hinting at the shared intimacy of their past and the promise of the moments to come.

In the steam and warmth of the shower, they found a quiet, passionate world away from the rest of their lives. It was a dance of water and warmth, a moment where time seemed to pause, allowing them to savor the connection that had always been the foundation of their relationship.

Sam later lay on the bed, waiting for Nicole to come to bed. As minutes passed, he started to drift into a light doze.

"Sam, are you awake?" Nicole's soft voice roused him from his slumber.

He mumbled in response, "I am now."

Nicole's tone shifted, her voice tinged with concern. "How do you feel about this trip? Is everything going to be okay? When I tell people I'm going to Iran, they give me these strange looks, as if I've lost my mind. They question if it's safe for Americans to visit. Are you worried too?"

Sam, now fully alert, pulled her closer and embraced her, his reassurance providing comfort. "I'm sure it will be just fine. My mother, who is American, lives there without any issues, and my father wouldn't have us go if he thought there could be a problem."

"You're right. I was just thinking out loud," Nicole replied.

"You should get some rest; we have a twenty-six-hour flight ahead of us," Sam gently advised, sealing his words with a tender kiss. He watched over her as her eyes closed, offering a silent promise of protection and love.

With Nicole sleeping in his arms, Sam's thoughts turned inward. The past few weeks had been a whirlwind of preparing passports, documents, and legal paperwork, leaving him little time to contemplate what Nicole had just said. Suddenly, it dawned on him that they were returning to a place he had to leave in a hurry, almost like an escape rather than a voluntary departure. A wave of uncertainty washed over him. He began to worry about potential complications leaving Iran, the children's health, Nicole's experience among new faces, and his father's health. But he pushed those anxieties aside, choosing to focus on the warmth of reconnecting with old friends, revisiting his high school, and strolling through familiar neighborhoods filled with cherished memories.

However, one nagging thought surfaced, making him feel guilt and shame – the thought of seeing her again. Roxana's image seemed to intrude into his consciousness, and he couldn't help but wonder about her appearance now. As he lay there, tormented by these thoughts, he turned away from them, trying to banish any lingering memories and guilt, seeking solace in the comforting embrace of sleep.

Chapter 11

"A sudden jolt rocked the airplane, causing Sam to stir from his slumber. He checked the KLM monitor in front of him, displaying the aircraft's current location. It had been a grueling journey, involving two connections and twenty-two hours, but now the plane had just crossed into Iran's airspace, with the border of Azerbaijan fading away behind them. An announcement over the intercom reminded passengers that alcoholic beverages were prohibited and that women should adhere to the country's strict Islamic dress code. These messages served as stark reminders that the Iran Sam was returning to was vastly different from the one he left in 1979.

    Ariana leaned over to Nicole and suggested, "It's time to put on our gowns and scarves." Women began forming a line near the lavatories, which seemed almost magical. They entered the restroom in Western clothing, complete with makeup, and emerged wearing loose-fitting dark gowns, their heads gracefully covered with scarves. The plane initiated its descent and landed gently at Tehran's Mehrabad Airport. Buses awaited passengers to transport them from the runway to the arrival terminal.

    Their moment came at the immigration booth, and Sam approached a stern-looking Islamic Republic official. The atmosphere was tense, and even the calmest traveler might feel a hint of trepidation. The official took their passports without making eye contact, tapping away at his computer keyboard. Finally, he looked up and spoke in Farsi, "Khanoom bacheha baare avaleshone miyan Iran?"

    "Baleh," Sam replied.

    The inspector continued to input data into the computer. Curious, Nicole whispered to Sam, "What did he say?"

    Before Sam could answer, Tara chimed in confidently, "He asked if it's our first time in Iran, and Dad said yes."

    The inspector, his demeanor now transformed, became friendly and welcoming as he stamped their passports. "Your Persian is very good," he complimented Tara, addressing her by name. "Welcome home." He handed Tara and Cameron hard candies, saying, "This is your reward for speaking Farsi."

    The kids smiled and expressed their gratitude with a heartfelt "Merci."

    It was about 4:30 in the early hours of Tuesday morning as they exited the airport. A crowd of eagerly awaiting family members stood behind the glass windows, their faces etched with anticipation. While Sam's immediate family resided in Shiraz, their destination the following day, they didn't expect anyone to welcome them at this stop. However, as they walked through the exit, Sam's name echoed through the arrivals hall. Perplexed, he turned to see a man holding a bouquet of flowers, calling his name.

    Ariana leaned toward Sam, whispering, "Who's that?" They began their slow approach, navigating through the bustling crowd.

The man, overwhelmed with excitement, enveloped Sam in a warm hug and planted kisses on both sides of his cheeks. "Saam, I can't believe it's you! Your mother told me you were coming back, and I couldn't wait to see you." He hardly allowed Sam to respond before continuing, "And where's Ariana?"

Ariana mumbled a timid "Salam."

Turning to Ariana, the man couldn't contain his laughter. "Oh my God, Ariana, you've grown so much! The last time I saw you, you were just a kid in middle school."

Finally, Sam recognized him through the rapid hand gestures that constantly touched his head. Suddenly, the realization struck him, and he embraced the man warmly, "Farhad, how are you? It's so good to see you."

Farhad pulled away with a perplexed expression. "Did you just recognize me right now?"

Sam chuckled, patting Farhad's round belly, "I'm sorry, but the last time I saw you, it was twenty years and twenty kilos ago."

Turning to Nicole, Farhad offered an apologetic greeting in English, "Forgive me; I was too eager to see Sam." He extended his hand to Nicole, shaking it vigorously. "You must be Nicole; I've heard so much about you from Sam's parents." Farhad then turned to the kids, greeting each of them in turn.

Once the introductions were complete, Farhad retrieved flowers and handed them to Nicole, offering a warm welcome. Then, noticing Ariana, he swiftly took back the bouquet and plucked a couple of roses before giving them back to Nicole. He handed the Roses to Ariana and said, "Welcome home; I got these for you."

Ariana accepted the flowers with a hint of sarcasm, thanking him for his gesture. Farhad retrieved two gift-wrapped boxes from an oversized bag and handed one to Tara and the other to Cameron, urging them to open the presents. Their excitement was palpable as they uncovered their gifts.

Nicole suggested heading to the hotel, concerned about the kids' exhaustion. However, Farhad had other plans. He grinned, informing them that their reservation had been upgraded. Confused, Nicole turned to Sam for an explanation.

Sam explained, "Don't you know Iranians by now? You know that he's not going to let us go to a hotel. He's taking us to his home."

As they drove toward Farhad's house, the early morning sky gradually brightened with the rising sun. Observing the family, Farhad saw that they had all fallen asleep. In a hushed tone, he encouraged Sam to rest as well. Sam was about to respond, but the sight of a familiar monument in a square caught his eye.

"There's Shahyad Square," Sam pointed out.

Farhad corrected him, "It's called Freedom Square now."

In that moment, Sam realized that the change in the appearance of an old friend was not the only transformation. The gritty streets, jammed with old cars, and the way people were dressed struck him as hallmarks of profound change. In a very short span, Sam understood that the country he left twenty years ago was no longer the same place.

Farhad sensed Sam's contemplative mood and inquired, "What's on your mind?"

Sam replied, "Just how much everything has changed."

"Of course it has," Farhad acknowledged. "Twenty years have gone by. Hasn't your hometown in America changed in the past two decades? And don't forget about the revolution and the change of the establishment. We went through eight years of bloody war with Iraq, and the population has doubled since."

Sam nodded, choosing to remain silent. He knew that nothing stays the same, but he was also aware that some changes are for the better while others are not. Farhad was correct; San Diego had changed over the past two decades, but it wasn't a transformation as dramatic as Tehran's. Sam had seen how some less appealing areas in San Diego had evolved into charming neighborhoods in recent years, but he couldn't say the same for Tehran, and that left him with a sense of melancholy.

En route to Farhad's house, Sam couldn't help but notice how the city had significantly expanded in size. Unfortunately, the results of poor urban planning had eroded the city's once-distinctive character. Many of the charming single-family homes that used to resemble Los Angeles' Bel Air area had been replaced by towering apartment buildings. What struck him most were the narrow alleyways that had remained unchanged, leading to frustrating traffic snarls. Sam couldn't help but acknowledge that both places had changed over the years, but it was clear that one had thrived while the other had deteriorated into a less favorable transformation.

Sam and Farhad had a history that went back to their shared high school days in Shiraz. Although they weren't particularly close friends at the time, fate had other plans. Both managed to secure coveted spots in the same medical program in Tehran and, as luck would have it, they became roommates.

Fast forward to the present, and Farhad's life had taken an unexpected and prosperous turn. Following the establishment of his private medical practice, a fortuitous opportunity led him to delve into the import business, starting with latex medical gloves from Malaysia.

This venture grew exponentially, evolving to encompass a wide array of medical supplies sourced from various corners of the globe. With the extraordinary profits this new business brought, Farhad set his sights on yet another endeavor—construction.

He turned his attention to constructing high-rise apartment buildings, gradually shifting his focus away from practicing medicine. His sprawling penthouse, occupying the entire thirty-fifth floor of one of his residential creations, showcased his transition from healer to a business mogul.

Their arrival at Farhad's penthouse was nothing short of grand. Jafar, his dedicated butler, had been summoned in advance and waited in the parking area to ensure a smooth transition.

"Welcome," Jafar greeted them. "Please make your way upstairs, and I'll tend to your luggage."

As they stepped into the elevator and Farhad swiped his access card, the ascent began. Upon arrival, the elevator doors opened to reveal a grand foyer, complete with awe-inspiring, floor-to-ceiling glass windows that framed an enchanting view of the sprawling city.

"Wow, this place is nothing short of astonishing," Sam marveled, moving closer to the panoramic windows to take in the breathtaking vistas. "I can only imagine how your patient count has soared with a residence like this!" Sam playfully complimented Farhad.

"Very gorgeous and charming indeed, is there a Mrs. Farhad?" Nicole inquired, subtly prodding for information.

Farhad, the ever-jovial host, didn't miss a beat. "Not yet," he replied with a wink. "I haven't found the right one yet. Besides, I must lose some weight first."

Sam couldn't resist a teasing comment. "Or maybe you're just too smart to get trapped."

Ariana, with her quick wit and a dash of mischief, decided it was high time to spice up the conversation, with her eyes gazing out the window, chimed in with a touch of dry humor, "You are almost above the smog level."

Farhad, always ready with a witty response, shrugged and quipped, "Another byproduct of civilization, I'm afraid."

Jafar came to the rescue, arriving with their suitcases and politely offering, "Allow me to show you to your rooms."

The kids, not to be outdone, rushed in with their discovery. "Mom, Dad, you have to see this!" Tara and Cameron cried, pulling their parents toward the vanishing doors that opened to the terrace. "Look, he's got a pool on top of the roof!" Tara exclaimed with infectious excitement. "Can we go for a swim? Can we, can we, please, please?"

Nicole, being the voice of reason, knew the importance of rest. "You guys must be very tired. Take a nap first," she suggested.

Cameron, however, was determined, using his newfound pool as leverage. "Now that I've seen the pool, you know I can't go to sleep," he pleaded.

Sam, understanding the allure of the pool, glanced at Nicole and grinned. "You know we can't make them go to sleep now."

Nicole agreed but with one condition, "Fine, but you must ask Uncle Farhad first."

Farhad, always up for some fun, was more than willing. "Of course, it's okay. I'll jump in too."

Ariana decided to join the festivities. "Heck, I'll go too. There'll be plenty of time to sleep later," she added, heading to her room to change.

Sam, perhaps thinking about the elusive promise of sleep, opted out. "Not me. I need my beauty sleep."

Farhad took charge. "What are you guys waiting for? Go get ready."

As Ariana reached the poolside, she tested the waters, both literally and figuratively. "It's cold," she commented, dangling her feet over the edge. "It always takes me a while to get in."

Farhad, the pool expert, approached with a mischievous twinkle in his eye. "That's because you don't know the trick," he declared mysteriously.

Ariana couldn't resist. "And what is this secret trick?"

Farhad flashed a sly grin and without further warning, he playfully pushed her into the pool.

Ariana surfaced, sputtering and wide-eyed. "Very immature. Just remember, I'll get even." With a mischievous glint in her eye, she retaliated by splashing him.

Farhad's laughter filled the air. "I had to show you the trick!"

Ariana shot back, "Ha, ha, very funny," before swimming away. When she reached the opposite side of the pool, she noticed Farhad perched atop the diving board. In a playful jest, she couldn't resist teasing him. "You better jump in quick before that board breaks off under you."

Farhad took the bait with a chuckle. "I can't believe you're still mad at me." With that, he launched himself off the board, creating a tremendous splash that sent ripples of laughter throughout the rooftop pool area.

Amid their boisterous laughter, Nicole lay in her room and couldn't help but overhear their merry antics. Her own curiosity was piqued. She noticed that Sam was also awake, his eyes lingering on her.

With a sense of adventure, she sat up on the edge of the bed and decided to join the poolside fun. "They're having a good time. I'm gonna join them," she announced.

Sam, his gaze still fixed on her, replied, "You go ahead. I'll be there shortly too."

Nicole began changing into her bikini, and the subtle thrill of anticipation hung in the air. Sam, watching her with a glint in his eye, couldn't resist playfully suggesting, "You know, I can show you some good times right here." He tapped the bed, an invitation filled with a hint of mischief.

Nicole, intrigued by the offer, paused in the midst of putting on her top. She leaned over the bed, her hand disappearing beneath the blanket. "Really... you'd actually do that for me?" she inquired with a sly smile. However, before Sam could respond, she decided to leave him with his thoughts and continued dressing. She donned a robe over her bikini and left the room.

"You tease," Sam groaned playfully to himself.

As she made her way to the pool, Nicole noticed that Jafar had thoughtfully prepared the breakfast table. When Jafar offered her tea, she responded with a query of her own. "Kaveh daary?"

Jafar acknowledged her coffee request, signaling a brief wait. While Nicole picked up a slice of fresh, warm bread, paired with carrot jam and cream, Jafar promptly returned with a steaming cup of coffee.

"Merci," she expressed her gratitude before leaving the table, coffee in hand, to join Ariana, Tara, and Cameron by the pool. They had all teamed up against Farhad, playfully splashing him. Farhad humorously feigned drowning, only to rise up with a monstrous roar and a triumphant display of victory. His attention then shifted to Nicole, who couldn't contain her laughter. "They started it," he said in playful defense.

Tara, ever the enthusiast, splashed a little water at Nicole and eagerly invited her to join in the aquatic revelry. Nicole, now torn between the poolside fun and the tempting breakfast table prepared by Jafar, made her decision. "You guys should see the breakfast table Jafar has prepared," she suggested.

"I wanna stay in the pool," Cameron protested.

Without missing a beat, Farhad, the master of fun and games, called for Jafar. He requested that breakfast be brought to the poolside, ensuring that no one would have to choose between fun and food. He then turned his attention to Nicole. "Where is your lazy husband? Have him come out for breakfast."

With a grin, Nicole promised, "I'll get him," and embarked on her mission to entice Sam from his room.

Upon Nicole and Sam's return, they discovered Ariana wielding the water hose like a pro, directing a high-pressure stream of water squarely at Farhad, who was now thoroughly soaked. She couldn't resist rubbing in her triumph, repeating, "I told you I'd get even. I told you."

"Okay, okay, I surrender," Farhad pleaded, lifting his hands in surrender as they all shared a hearty laugh.

Dripping wet and in high spirits, they eventually gathered around the breakfast table, which was thoughtfully arranged under the welcoming shade of the canopy. Farhad regaled them with amusing stories from his shared history with Sam, adding to the joyful atmosphere with each recounted memory.

That evening, Farhad treated everyone to a captivating sightseeing trip to the picturesque heights of Farazaad and Darakeh. Street vendors adorned the bustling pathways, tempting passersby with an assortment of fresh fruits and delectable snacks. Pausing by one particular vendor, Sam recommended the black Persian mulberries, known for their exquisite flavor. He ordered six bowls for everyone to savor.

The young vendor, barely in his teens, handed over the six bowls brimming with succulent mulberries. "That'll be 2400 tomans."

"Twenty-four hundred tomans?" Sam seemed momentarily startled. "Is he joking?"

Unfazed, Farhad effortlessly procured a stack of bills and paid the vendor. "You know that's only $2.50, right?"

Sam felt a twinge of embarrassment, realizing he'd caused a scene over just $2.50. He hadn't yet adapted to the new, inflated prices. In his memory, 2400 tomans was equivalent to $350, with the exchange rate of seven tomans to a dollar. But given the relentless devaluation of the toman following the 1979 revolution, it was now worth a mere $2.50.

"These mulberries are a true delight. Let's have another round," Sam suggested to the vendor.

The boy happily handed over six more bowls. "Sir, we accept dollars too," he noted, hinting at a preference for the greenbacks over tomans.

Sam handed him a $5 bill. "Keep the change."

The evening continued with laughter and merriment, and the group returned to Farhad's place, falling asleep almost instantly. The next morning, they readied their suitcases and left them by the elevator. Sam spotted two additional suitcases and asked Jafar, "Whose suitcases are these?"

"Those belong to Mr. Farhad. He's joining you on the trip to Shiraz."

"Wait, you're coming with us to Shiraz?" Sam inquired, clearly taken aback.

"I could use a break and spend some quality time with you, all while visiting my family," Farhad explained with a grin.

Chapter 12

A covert meeting was taking place at Genesys, but nothing escaped the watchful eyes of Hope. From her discreet vantage point, she meticulously observed every detail, tracking every individual entering and exiting the conference room. A man of diminutive stature, seated near the room, piqued her curiosity. She pondered what role he might be playing in this secretive affair.

Hope seized a random folder and walked past the man, casually making her presence known. "Hi," she offered a warm smile. The man simply nodded. Deliberately, she collided her hand with the chair next to him, sending the folder and its contents scattering across the floor. "Damn it. What a way to start the week."

The man, though hesitant, began assisting her.

"Don't worry, I'll take care of it," Hope sighed, feigning frustration. "Thanks a lot. I'm Hope."

The man remained tight-lipped.

"I've never seen you before," Hope remarked, angling to extract some information.

"I'm just waiting to be called in," he gestured toward the board room with his briefcase.

"I'm familiar with these meetings. You'll be here forever. Let me get you a cup of coffee. Please come with me." She sauntered away toward her office without allowing him any room to object.

"I thought you were in a hurry heading the other way," he noted.

Hope continued walking. "Oh yes, about that... it's time for my break. What's your name?"

"Rashid," he replied.

Once inside her office, Hope poured two cups of coffee. "There you go." She intentionally knocked his briefcase, causing coffee to spill onto his shirt.

The hot liquid elicited a string of Arabic curses from Rashid, "sharmuta."

"I'm so sorry. I don't know what's wrong with me today," Hope apologized, feigning ignorance of his Arabic expletives. She quickly fetched some napkins, attempting to clean his sleeve.

"Where is the bathroom?" Rashid grumbled.

Hope guided Rashid toward the door, directing him to the restroom farthest from her office. As soon as he left, Hope opened the briefcase and began sifting through the papers. Unsure of what she was seeking, she methodically reviewed the contents. She scurried around her desk, extracting her recently purchased digital camera from her purse. She photographed the pages one after another, her actions guided by a growing sense of unease. Suddenly, she heard the doorknob twisting open.

Quickly, she locked Rashid's briefcase and pretended to be cleaning it. "I managed to get some coffee on your briefcase too," Hope stammered nervously.

"The sign on the door says this is Mr. Larabi's office," he grumbled.

"Oh my, is there a problem with that?" Hope innocently inquired.

"I can't be here," Rashid retorted, hastening back to the conference room.

Hope pondered the mysterious connection between Rashid and Sam. She wasted no time in emailing all the documents to Sam, eager to unravel the enigma that was unfolding at Genesys.

Chapter 13

We strive to protect our children from harm's way from the moment they enter this world, doing all we can to ensure their safety. That's why when Sam's father couldn't secure seats on the only Airbus airplane available for the Tehran-Shiraz route on the day of his son and family's arrival, he opted to delay their reunion by an extra day. The alternative, a journey on a Russian-made Tupolev airplane, was a risk he was unwilling to take.

The quality of Iran's airline fleet had significantly dwindled due to the U.S. sanctions imposed on the nation after the takeover of the US embassy in Tehran. With each flight, the sanctions cast a gloomier shadow on the country's aging fleet. In the pre-revolution era, Iran Air had boasted a state-of-the-art fleet, equipped with the latest aircraft. It had been a pioneer, second only to Pan Am in introducing the Boeing 747 jumbo jets, and was considered the most advanced airline in the region. Iran Air had even preordered the prestigious

Concorde supersonic airplanes, which had graced Iran's skies before the company's tragic downfall.

Fast-forward to 1999, over two decades since the Shah's time, and the Iranian airline was still operating the same aging, outdated fleet. The stark contrast between its former glory and the diminished state of the country was an undeniable reminder of the consequences of the disastrous revolution.

Flight #23 completed its six-hundred-mile journey from Tehran to Shiraz, gently touching down at 11:35 am on Wednesday, August 3rd. The overhead speakers blared the flight's arrival, a familiar announcement that drew friends and families to the airport to welcome their loved ones returning from lengthy journeys. The terminal buzzed with anticipation as the crowd eagerly awaited Sam's return. Upon hearing the announcement of the plane's landing, Dr. Larabi and the group rushed excitedly toward the expansive glass windows overlooking the runway. The Airbus came to a slow stop, strategically positioned near the main terminal building, and a mobile staircase was deftly maneuvered into place for the passengers to disembark. Though everyone was anxious to spot the arrivals emerging from the plane, the distance made it difficult to distinguish individuals, especially with the women draped in Islamic attire.

"Look, Bijan, there they are," Jacqueline exclaimed, her keen eyes picking out Sam and his family as they descended from the plane. As they entered the terminal, the welcoming party greeted them with a joyous, hearty cheer. Nicole had never before experienced such a warm and jubilant reception, with more than fifty well-wishers holding vibrant bouquets of flowers to offer their greetings. "You never told me you were this popular here," Nicole teased Sam.

As Sam surveyed the exuberant crowd, he spotted the familiar faces of his parents, and Tara and Cameron dashed toward their grandparents for warm embraces. With each step, Sam recognized more and more vaguely familiar faces, and upon reaching the heart of the crowd, they were enveloped in an outpouring of tight hugs and affectionate kisses.

The moment was a bittersweet blend of joy and sorrow as Sam was reminded of those who had passed away during his absence. As he held his aunt close, memories of his cousin Ali, who had lost his life in the Iran-Iraq war, came flooding back. Among all his cousins, Sam had shared a unique bond with him. Ali had become involved with a religious faction that had motivated him to volunteer for the war, a mission laden with peril. Tragically, he did not return from one of his deployments. As he embraced his aunt, Sam felt the absence of Ali and his younger brother, who had also perished in the conflict at the tender age of 14, driven by the same ideology, promising an eternal life in heaven in exchange for their sacrifices.

Over the course of their reunion, Sam found himself grappling with the challenge of recognizing once-familiar faces that had changed over the span of two decades. Some of his relatives had not even been born when he left in 1979. The children he had known as little ones had grown into adults, with some having embarked on their own journeys into parenthood.

Chapter 14

The nail-biting wait had finally come to an end as Hope saw the conference room door swing open. Her sharp eyes immediately caught Rashid, who wasted no time heading for the exit. The rest of the participants began emerging one by one, wearing their customary smiles and offering handshakes, but Hope's attention was fixed on Damien. It struck her as peculiar to see him leaving the meeting, given that he wasn't a board member. As she watched him approach her office, expertly buttoning his double-breasted suit, Hope couldn't help but nervously bite on her pen. Her thoughts raced, wondering what piece of news he might be carrying. The sight of Damien's presence in the meeting did offer some reassurance, as she knew that if the proceedings had any connection to Sam or his department, Damien would stop at nothing to safeguard Sam's interests.

Hope had experienced a challenging life and couldn't bear the thought of losing the job she cherished. Luck hadn't always been on her side. She was born in the Azores, a picturesque archipelago of Portuguese Islands in the vast Atlantic Ocean. Her parents immigrated to the United States after their home village was devastated in a volcanic eruption at Ponta dos Capelinhos in 1957. She learned to support herself financially from the tender age of thirteen, stepping into the role of a dental assistant at just sixteen. Most of the doctors overworked her and underpaid her for her efforts. But her fortune finally took a turn when she landed a job with Dr. Lew, a dentist who appreciated her work. It wasn't long before she became the office manager, enjoying a comfortable living and the respect of her new boss. For the first time, she had a boss she genuinely admired. However, her world turned upside down when Dr. Lew announced his retirement, with Dr. Petal set to take over the practice.

Hope was well aware of the terrible way Dr. Petal treated his staff. Her already high-pitched voice squeaked even higher as she exclaimed, "Good luck, but I won't work with Dr. Petal."

While the East Coast was being battered by the "storm of the century" in February 1993, an unseasonably warm day graced San Diego. On this beautiful day, as the rest of the staff headed out for lunch, Hope wasn't in the mood for food. She remained in her office, engrossed in tackling overdue accounts. Sorting through charts and records, she heard the door chime. Glancing at the round clock adorned with the cheerful image of Sea World's Shamu, she noticed it was only 1:40, and there were no appointments scheduled until 2:00. Turning her attention to the man in the waiting room engrossed in magazine covers, she inquired, "How may I assist you?" When he turned and she recognized him, Hope greeted him with a warm smile. "Good afternoon, Mr. Larabi. How are you today?"

"I'm doing well, Destiny," he replied.

"It's Hope, sir," she corrected with a chuckle. "But you're getting closer; last time you called me Faith. Your appointment is at 2:00. You can stay here or enjoy the beautiful day and return at your appointment time." She secretly hoped he'd choose the latter.

"I'll stay," he decided. "I don't get much time to read magazines at work. And I promise to get your name right next time."

"It's all good Mr. Larabi," Hope assured him with a hint of sadness. "I won't be here for your next appointment anyway."

Sam looked taken aback. He was aware of Hope's dedication to her job and asked, "Why's that?"

"Never mind," she sighed.

Sam had built a close rapport with Dr. Lew during his visits. Their conversations often ran long, causing Dr. Lew's schedule to fall behind. While Sam was reading the list of Oscar nominees for that year in an Entertainment Weekly magazine, he couldn't help but wonder about Hope.

"I heard Hope might be looking for a new job. Would you recommend her?" Sam inquired from Dr. Lew.

Dr. Lew spoke highly of Hope, saying, "She's a gem—loyal and honest. Dr. Petal would have a tough time finding someone like her. It surprises me that she discussed it with you. She usually keeps office matters separate from patients."

"Do you think she could handle the corporate world?" Sam inquired.

"With the right training, absolutely," Dr. Lew assured.

"Would you mind if I spoke to her about a potential job opportunity with us?" Sam asked.

"As long as she stays with me until my last day on March thirty-first," Dr. Lew replied.

Before leaving, Sam handed Hope his business card and requested her to call him, emphasizing that Dr. Lew was fine with the idea.

Chapter 15

Nestled amidst the majestic Zagros Mountains, the ancient city of Shiraz occupies the heart of Iran's south-central region. While the city's oldest standing structure, the Jaameh Mosque, dates back a remarkable 1100 years, historical records trace Shiraz's roots to a staggering 4000-year history. It serves as the capital of Fars Province and holds the legacy of the formidable Persian Empire, a grandeur initially established by the visionary Cyrus the Great in 559 B.C., a transformative empire that once commanded unprecedented strength and vastness across the known world.

Before the turbulent Muslim Arab invasion of Persia in 651 A.D., a time that saw the enforced conversion of Zoroastrianism to Islam, this province was named Pars, thus bestowing the title Persia upon the land. The transformation, however, was not confined to faith; it extended to language, marking a profound shift. The Arabic alphabet, distinct in its absence of the letter "P" and the corresponding phonetic pronunciation, led to the substitution of "P" with "F" in some Persian words. As a result, "Pars" metamorphosed into "Fars," initiating a significant change, resonating through the annals of history. The same linguistic influence manifested in the transformation of Parsi into Farsi, a remnant of Arab rule.

Arab dominance over the Persian realm was marked by brutality, with fervent attempts to eradicate the Persian heritage and identity, compelling Persians to embrace Arabic. Yet, the indomitable Persian spirit refused to surrender completely to the occupiers. It took centuries, replete with battles and wars, for Persians to gradually reclaim their land, expelling the Arab rulers. However, the legacy of the conquerors was deeply imprinted within the people and their consciousness. Although the Persian language was resurrected, the indelible marks of Arabic influence persisted. Today's Persian language is an intricate tapestry, woven with countless Arabic words that have either supplanted their Persian counterparts or rendered them obsolete, epitomized by the ubiquity of "Farsi" instead of "Parsi, and Fars instead of Pars."

Cars filled with friends and family celebrated Sam and Ariana's return by harmoniously honking their horns as they approached the Larabi family's timeless abode. Sam had woven countless tales about his childhood home, nestled at the far end of an alley that seemed to stretch forever, branching off from Bagh-Eram Street.

After twenty long years, Sam found himself at the entrance of the alley where his childhood home was nestled. Stepping onto the familiar asphalt, a cascade of memories engulfed him, each a vivid echo from his distant yet intimately close past.

The alley, marked by the passage of time, was still abuzz with vibrant life. The sound of children's laughter filled the air, a timeless melody that transcended the decades. They played spirited games, their joyful shouts intertwining with the alley's rich tapestry of life, just as they had during Sam's youth.

Above, crows circled and soared, their stark black figures etching silhouettes against the sky. Their caws, a familiar soundtrack of the alley, added to the symphony of sounds that had resonated throughout Sam's childhood. These birds, with their watchful eyes and commanding presence, had been silent observers to the ebb and flow of life here.

Stray cats, reminiscent of those from Sam's childhood memories, roamed with an air of quiet ownership, their paths intersecting with the playing children. One ginger cat, in particular, wound its way gracefully among the youngsters, its movements a dance of coexistence.

Closing his eyes, Sam inhaled deeply, letting the unique aromas of the alley fill his senses. The scent of freshly baked bread from the nearby bakery mingled with the subtle fragrance of jasmine that grew in Mrs. Shahim's garden, a garden that seemed to defy the passage of time. The aroma was a comforting embrace, a sensory reminder that some essences of home remained unchanged.

Neighborhood chatter filled the air, a warm, familiar sound. Neighbors, who knew each other's stories by heart, exchanged greetings and news. Their conversations, a blend of concern and camaraderie, were a testament to the deep bonds formed in this close-knit community. These were the people who had seen each other through life's highs and lows, their lives intricately woven together.

Sam's steps on the asphalt were in sync with a sense of belonging. He realized that this alley, with its amalgam of sounds, sights, and familiar faces, was an integral part of him. Despite his years abroad, the essence of this place, where friendships lasting a lifetime were forged, had always lingered within him.

As he delved deeper into the alley, past the watchful crows and amid the laughter of children and the warm exchanges of neighbors, Sam felt an overwhelming sense of homecoming. This place, with its asphalt paths and enduring friendships, was more than a mere location. It was where Sam's story began and where his heart had always remained.

Standing there, enveloped in the spirit of his old alley, Sam experienced a profound sense of peace. He was home, not just in place but in essence. The alley, with its changes and constants, mirrored Sam himself – transformed by time yet fundamentally unaltered. His years in the USA had shaped him, but the core of his being, forged in this small corner of Iran, was untouched by distance or time.

Ariana found herself back in her cherished childhood room, while Sam and Nicole made themselves comfortable in his old quarters. Tara and Cameron eagerly claimed the room next door.

Jacqueline extended a warm invitation to Farhad. "Would you like to stay with us while Sam is in town?"

"Absolutely," Farhad replied, his enthusiasm undeniable.

Stepping into his room Sam felt like stepping back in time; it seemed almost frozen in the past. Sam gazed out of the window, anticipating the kids' imminent plunge into the inviting pool. His heart swelled with excitement when he spotted his cherished motorcycle gleaming in the backyard. It was a moment of sheer disbelief that his parents had preserved it all these years. He raced down to the bike, as if reuniting with an old friend, and to his amazement, it was in impeccable condition.

"We had it meticulously serviced for you," Bijan mentioned, passing him the key. "We knew you might want to ride it again."

Sam mounted the bike, turned the key in the ignition, and confidently kick-started it. The engine roared to life, unleashing a symphony of memories and an exhilarating thrill.

"The mechanic assured us it's as good as new," Bijan reassured him.

Sam closed his eyes and revved the engine, savoring the familiar and powerful sound that brought his memories rushing back.

****

In the quiet aftermath of his siesta, Farhad meandered into the family room, his steps slow and deliberate. There, he found Ariana, a figure of concentration, her attention fully absorbed by the old photo albums spread before her. A curious smile played on his lips as he approached, a playful spark in his eyes. "What have you unearthed there?" he asked, leaning over her shoulder.

Ariana looked up, her eyes dancing with nostalgia. "Memories from another lifetime," she said, turning the photo album towards him. "This was taken the day we left Iran. Can you believe I was only thirteen?"

Farhad's gaze lingered on the photograph, a chuckle escaping him. "Ah, I remember that day vividly. You were in your... how do you call it... the ugly duckling phase?" His teasing was light, but it struck a playful nerve.

Ariana feigned a scowl and snapped the album shut, her mock indignation evident. "Hey, that's enough from you!"

"I'm sorry, I'm sorry," Farhad quickly interjected, his voice softening. "I was only jesting. You know, you've transformed, Ariana. From that young girl to... well, a swan of sorts."

Her eyes narrowed in playful reprimand. "Farhad, you really must work on your compliments. With charm like that, it's no wonder you're still single."

Farhad's laughter filled the room. "Well, if I'm single for lack of charm, what's your excuse?" he retorted, a mischievous glint in his eye.

Ariana's response was swift and laced with mock severity. "Men like you, obviously."

Sensing the shift in the air, Farhad extended a peace-offering hand. "I apologize if I crossed a line," he said, his touch conveying a sincerity that words alone could not.

Ariana's mood softened as she reopened the album, pointing to a photograph of Farhad and Sam in their Tehran apartment. "And look at you here," she teased, "proof that you were once as thin as a straw."

Farhad leaned in, examining the photo with a self-deprecating smile. "It appears the rumors are true then. I did have a skinny phase."

As they continued their journey through the past, the pages of the album flipping gently between them, Farhad's eyes brightened with an idea. "Why don't we take a walk to Bagh-Eram? It's one of the few places that remain untouched by time."

Ariana, pleased by his suggestion, couldn't help but throw in a final jibe. "Finally, a stroke of genius from you today."

Their laughter mingled, a symphony of old friendship and shared history, as they closed the album and prepared for their nostalgic stroll to the Bagh-Eram, a place suspended in the past, much like the memories they cherished.

Unbeknownst to Ariana, Farhad's subtle hints of admiration were beginning to reveal themselves, even though she still saw him as an old friend. Their relationship was slowly evolving, laying the foundation for a future beyond friendship.

Shiraz, the enchanting 'City of Flowers and Nightingales,' conjures images of exquisite gardens and poetic romance. Among its verdant treasures, the Bagh-Eram botanical garden stands as the crown jewel, celebrated for its towering cypress trees, the grandest of them all;

Sarve-Naz. This majestic site draws admirers from near and far, a testament to its allure. Once the private domain of Khosrow Khan, a formidable leader of the Ghashghaei tribe, it fell into the hands of the Shah's government after forcing him into exile. A twist of fate brought him home after the 1979 revolution, leading him to selflessly bestow this priceless haven and its resplendent three-story palace upon the people of Shiraz. Tragically, the grip of the newly established Islamic Regime proved ruthless. The very hands that offered this gift were unjustly silenced, a haunting reminder of the regime's unrelenting pursuit of power and its ruthless suppression of any perceived threats.

Bagh-Eram's serene charm belies the turbulent history of its surroundings, nestled on a street that bears its name, just a few blocks from the former U.S. consulate in the Shah's era. This picturesque avenue, flanked by the cool shade of trees, witnesses young lovers strolling hand in hand along its romantic pathways. It was here that Farhad sought the ideal backdrop for the burgeoning romance he envisioned.

****

As Sam descended the stairs, the muted undertones of a conversation seeped out from the kitchen, wrapping the house in a cloak of uncharacteristic solemnity. The distant cadence of his parents' voices, intermingling with the soft clinking of utensils against ceramic plates, created an atmosphere thick with unspoken words.

Sam treaded softly towards the kitchen, his senses heightened. He caught the tail end of his father's somber statement, "We have to tell him sooner or later."

His mother, Jacqueline, her voice a delicate blend of worry and resolve, replied, "Yes, but later. His vacation shouldn't be clouded by this. Can you hold onto a secret just a little longer?"

Bijan, standing by the window, exhaled a deep, weary sigh. The secret he had harbored for two decades, shared only with a trusted few, seemed to weigh heavier with each passing moment.

The clink of a spoon against a cup ceased as Sam stepped into the room, his presence slicing through the hush. "What's going on?" he asked, his brow furrowed with concern. "What do you need to tell me?"

Bijan and Jacqueline exchanged a glance laden with unspoken words. Bijan moved towards Sam, placing his hands on his son's shoulders with a tenderness that belied his inner turmoil. "There's something important, Sam, but let's wait until after tonight's party," he said, his voice steady but eyes avoiding Sam's gaze.

Sam's mind raced, his thoughts clouded with apprehension. "This will weigh on me all day. It's about your health, isn't it?" he ventured, his voice barely above a whisper.

Jacqueline stepped in, her maternal instinct to protect surfacing. "Yes, it is."

Bijan turned towards the garden, his gaze distant. "My heart, it's been stronger than anyone expected. But it's growing weaker," he confessed, the pain in his voice spilling into the room. "My time may be limited, but I'm blessed to have my family close in these days."

Sam's heart clenched at the revelation, a tumult of emotions swirling within him – fear for his father's health, the ache of the secrets yet to be revealed, and the shadow of change looming over them.

He reached for his father, their embrace a silent exchange of strength and vulnerability. "We can't just give up. What about a transplant or other treatments? There's got to be something," Sam pleaded, his voice laced with desperation.

Bijan gently disentangled himself, his eyes meeting Sam's tear-filled ones. "I've never given up, Sam. But we must face our reality," he said, his voice a calm anchor in the storm of emotions.

Their moment was interrupted by Nicole's arrival. She entered quietly, her smile trying to dispel the heaviness in the air. "I hope I'm not intruding," she said, settling into a chair.

Jacqueline, ever the gracious host, welcomed her. "Not at all, dear. Let me get you some coffee."

Nicole, sensing the tension, reached out to Sam, her fingers tenderly brushing his hair. "Is everything okay?" she asked, concern etching her features.

Sam mustered a semblance of composure. "I'm fine," he lied, his voice barely a whisper.

Ariana and Farhad's laughter echoed through the house as they returned, their cheerful mirth punctuated by Farhad's quick wit and humor. Sam, greeted by their arrival, couldn't help but jest about their extended slumber.

"Where have you guys been? I thought you were still sleeping," Sam inquired.

Farhad, his infectious laughter lingering, replied, "We ventured to Bagh-Eram. Your sister has agreed to help me shed some weight. We swung by here to fetch our running shoes for a jog."

Sam's playful response was swift, a good-humored tease. "I thought you stayed here for me, but it seems you've opted for the prettier sibling."

Ariana's laughter bubbled forth. "Don't tease him, that's my department."

While the duo awaited Ariana by the house's entrance, Sam's nostalgia found its voice. "I have so many memories of this alley," he reflected watching the alley "We used to play soccer here late into the night without fear. But now, we won't even let our children step outside alone, not for a second."

Farhad's tone was tinged with melancholy. "Life was much simpler back then. We didn't have Nintendo or PlayStations, but a cheap plastic soccer ball kept us entertained all day."

Sam nodded in agreement, peering down the alleyway, where they had once played, replaying old memories. Yet, his gaze caught sight of an ominous transformation. The houses that once stood open and welcoming had now metamorphosed into fortresses. Tall, sharp metal fences adorned the tops of walls that had been sufficient barriers in the past.

"What's happened here?" Sam queried, his voice heavy with concern. "Why do these houses now look like fortresses?"

Farhad sighed, a grim acknowledgment of the city's transformation. "It's for peace of mind. There have been so many break-ins in recent years that people had to add these sharp fences atop their already towering walls. With unemployment skyrocketing and an inflation rate of twenty-five percent, people are pushed to unimaginable lengths just to put food on the table."

Sam's voice held a note of sorrow as he observed the changes. "It's hard to believe that this is the same country, the same people."

It was a poignant moment, a testament to the stark transformation wrought by the Islamic revolution. What had once been a lively and welcoming community was now besieged by the burden of economic hardship and insecurity. The creeping consequences of the revolution were slowly pushing the nation to the brink of destruction, and the burden of suffering was disproportionately placed upon those not connected to the regime—those who refused to barter their souls, dignity, and pride for survival in a world where such values held diminishing weight.

Chapter 16

As Damien stepped into Hope's office, her composure stood unshaken, like a lighthouse amidst a brewing storm. His entrance was like the first drops of rain – foreboding and filled with unspoken dread.

"It was brutal in there. Sam should've been here," Damien said, his voice a low rumble of concern. The gravity of his words seemed to echo off the walls.

Hope, her senses heightened, rose from her chair, her eyes searching his for hidden truths. "What happened, Damien? Why are you so worried about Sam?"

Damien hesitated, his gaze falling to the floor before meeting hers again. "It's bad, Hope. Emirates Genomic is accusing our company of bribery in securing the last contract." His words hung heavily in the air.

Disbelief flashed across Hope's face. "Bribery? That's ludicrous. But what's Sam got to do with this?"

Damien's reply was weighed down with implications. "They're pointing fingers at him as the paymaster."

Hope's shock was palpable. "But such practices are common in business, aren't they? As long as no one can trace it back..."

"That's just it," Damien interjected, his tone somber. "Where did Sam slip up?"

Hope's defiance flared. "Don't twist my words, Damien. That's not what I meant."

Damien's next words cut through her defense. "Sam's on forced leave. The board had no other choice."

Hope felt a chill run down her spine. "But he's not even in the country. What are we supposed to do?"

Damien's explanation revealed the harsh reality. "The Emiratis are calling the shots. Our revenue is too tied up with them. Phillips will bend over backward to keep them happy."

Hope paced the room, her frustration bubbling over. "This isn't right. Sam doesn't deserve this. Phillips knows it, you know it, we all do."

Damien's loyalty was clear. "I agree. That's why I stepped up to fill his shoes temporarily. It's better me than someone with less regard for Sam."

Hope's skepticism was evident. "Volunteered? It's a top position, Damien. Don't play the martyr."

Damien's expression hardened. "Would you rather have someone else in charge? Someone who doesn't care about Sam?"

Hope's anger dissipated, replaced by regret. "I'm sorry, Damien. You're right."

Their tense exchange was interrupted by a knock. Mr. Phillips walked in, his presence commanding yet fraught with the day's burdens.

Damien excused himself, leaving Hope to face Phillips alone. The CEO gazed out the window, his thoughts seemingly far away. "I never understood Sam's choice of view," he mused.

Hope cut to the chase. "What's happening, sir? I heard about Sam."

Phillips sat down, his demeanor serious. "Sam was integral in building this company. But we had to sideline him. There's pressure from Emirates Genomic. He might even have to sell his shares."

Hope, struggling to grasp the financial implications, voiced her disbelief. "But this must be some mistake. Sam wouldn't jeopardize the company."

Phillips's expression softened slightly. "I've always wondered how Sam secured those contracts. He has a knack for it, but sometimes the methods are... unclear."

"Why wasn't Sam warned earlier? You must have known," Hope pressed.

Phillips sighed. "It wasn't that simple. The Emiratis insisted on board-level disclosure first. We couldn't risk the fallout."

"But why target Sam?" Hope asked, her confusion evident.

Phillips stood, ready to leave. "I think it's more about them saving face. I'll talk to Sam myself. For now, work with Damien as if Sam were here. We're hoping for a swift resolution."

As Phillips left, Hope sat back, her mind racing. The walls of the office seemed to close in, echoing with the weight of unsaid words and unasked questions. The future was uncertain, and the only thing clear was that a storm was brewing, one that would test them all.

Chapter 17

In the warm, bustling kitchen, Farhad found Ariana at the heart of family life, seated casually at the table, a cup of tea in her hand. Her laughter mingled with the lively chatter around her, creating a scene of comfort and belonging.

Farhad leaned against the doorway, his gaze landing on Ariana with playful intent. "I see you've abandoned our morning run for the seductive allure of cream puffs and tea," he remarked, his voice laced with mock disappointment.

Ariana glanced up, her eyes sparkling with humor. "Today's calorie-burning adventure can wait until tomorrow," she retorted with a smirk. "We've got a party to gear up for tonight, after all."

Farhad's laughter filled the room, resonating with a lightness that seemed to lift the spirits of everyone present. "In that case," he declared, reaching for a cream puff, "I see no harm in joining this delightful indulgence."

Jacqueline, observing the exchange, couldn't help but join in with a knowing smile. "Some things never change with you, Farhad."

Ariana shot back, her tone playfully teasing, "Well, except maybe for that extra little bit you're carrying around the waist." Her words danced in the air, leaving a trail of laughter as she gracefully exited the room to prepare for the evening.

Farhad stood there for a moment, a wide grin plastered on his face, the flirtatious undertone of their banter lingering like a sweet perfume.

In Iran, the essence of summer parties came alive under the cloak of night, typically starting way after dark and stretched their joyful echoes into the dawn. Sam and Ariana's welcome gathering took place in their uncle's garden nestled in the western part of the town. These gardens, blessed with fertile soil, nurtured a diverse range of produce, from the crimson jewels of pomegranates to the zesty allure of limes and plums. But the true crown jewel of the region was the grapes. These grapes were renowned worldwide, celebrated not only for their succulence but also for their historical role in winemaking. Prior to the seismic shift brought about by the 1979 revolution, these grapes were expertly transformed into wine. However, in the wake of the new Islamic Government's stringent regulations prohibiting alcohol production and consumption, people had turned to crafting their own wines in the privacy of their homes.

Shiraz natives, seasoned vintners with a tradition spanning millennia, had seen their beloved nectar banned by multiple ruling parties throughout history. And much like their predecessors, the current regime was encountering a degree of resistance. It was a cycle that had repeated itself time and time again. Interestingly, the oldest remnants of wine production in the world, dating back nearly 7,000 years, had been unearthed just beyond the city's boundaries. These ancient clay jars spoke of a history where the art of winemaking thrived in the region.

Today, Shiraz grapes had found new homes in vineyards across the globe. Countries like Australia, South Africa, and the vineyards of Napa Valley in California eagerly embraced these grapes, creating a diverse array of wines. The Shiraz grape had risen to prominence as a key player in the world of winemaking, solidifying its place among the most renowned labels worldwide.

Sam had prepared himself for an evening restrained by the country's strict social laws, expecting a muted affair devoid of the usual party staples. However, the reality that unfolded before him was a startling defiance of his expectations.

As guests flowed into the garden, they were initially draped in the customary black robes, a uniform of modesty that blended into the night. But as the party's heartbeat grew stronger, these layers were shed in a bold metamorphosis, revealing a colorful array of contemporary fashion. The transformation was symbolic, a shedding of societal norms in favor of personal expression.

Sam, still acclimating to this unexpected vibrancy, leaned towards Farhad with a hint of concern. "Aren't we risking trouble with the Revolutionary Guards?" he whispered, his eyes scanning the merry scene.

Amir, overhearing the conversation, flashed a knowing smile. "Worry not, my friend," he replied with a mischievous glint in his eye. "Certain... arrangements have been made. In Iran, the right connections can make many problems disappear."

Sam's mind, ever analytical, processed this new information with a mix of amusement and cynicism. "So, it seems the enforcers of law have become somewhat akin to a mafia," he mused.

Amir laughed heartily, the sound mingling with the music and chatter around them. "You're too caught up in thought, Sam. Here, we learn to navigate the tides. If Darwin were to visit us, he might indeed reconsider his theory, suggesting perhaps it's the survival of the wealthiest."

The party blossomed around them, a clandestine garden of forbidden delights. Music, laughter, and dance wove together, creating a tapestry of rebellion and joy. For Sam, the evening was not just a revelation of Iran's hidden facets but a lesson in the resilience and adaptability of its people. Amidst the revelry, he found himself swept up in the rhythm of a world that thrived in the shadows, pulsing with life and defiance under the starlit sky.

The live band came to a halt around midnight, heralding the serving of dinner. While Tara and Cameron were eager to continue playing with their newfound friends, they were obliged to finish their meal before they could dash off.

In the soft glow of the garden lights, Nicole observed Ariana and Farhad's figures meandering down the illuminated path, their silhouettes merging with the gentle sway of the trees. Turning to Jacqueline, she asked in a hushed tone, "Have you noticed anything different about Ariana lately?"

Jacqueline's smile held a depth of understanding. "I saw it the moment we were at the airport. The way Farhad's eyes lingered on her... it's part of the reason I suggested he stay with us."

Nicole's gaze followed the pair as they strolled, lost in their own world. "Do you think Farhad could be the right match for her?" she inquired, a note of curiosity in her voice.

Jacqueline considered this, her eyes reflecting the soft lights. "Only time can truly tell. Farhad is kind-hearted, well-educated, and comes from a respectable family. Those are good signs."

Nicole added with a playful tone, "And let's not forget, he's quite wealthy."

Jacqueline's laughter was a gentle sound in the night air. "Yes, there's that too."

The conversation paused momentarily before Jacqueline reached out, taking Nicole's hand with a touch as light as a feather. "Do you know what every parent's deepest wish is?" she asked softly.

Nicole responded with a tender gesture, her hand gently caressing Jacqueline's cheek. "You have the wisdom of experience, Jacqueline. Enlighten me."

Jacqueline dabbed at her eyes, a mix of nostalgia and melancholy in her gaze. "As parents, we naturally want success and prosperity for our children. But as years pass, what we truly long for is their happiness, their fulfillment. You're never completely at peace until you know your children are content. There's an old Persian saying, 'the truth is bitter.' I must face that Bijan's time with us may be limited. At this stage of our lives, all I yearn for is to see Ariana settled, to know she's found her path while Bijan and I are still here."

Nicole's response was a comforting whisper. "Ariana will find her way, married or not. She's a strong, independent woman."

Jacqueline's smile was tinged with a mother's wisdom. "You're still too young to fully understand, but one day, you will. The deepest desires of a parent's heart are often simple, yet profound."

In the tranquility of the evening, the conversation between Nicole and Jacqueline wove a tapestry of understanding, bridging generations with the timeless language of a parent's love and hopes.

As the night unfolded, Sam found himself swept into a lively debate with old friends, a discussion that was a familiar refrain among many Iranians. The topic? The ever-present desire to leave Iran for the United States, a place they perceived as a land of opportunity and freedom. The air was thick with their frustration with the current state of their homeland, igniting a collective yearning for a better life elsewhere.

Sam, however, felt a need to ground the conversation in reality. "Life in Iran has its own joys that you might not find in America," he cautioned. "It's not all about leisure and freedom there. Often, it's a relentless cycle of work."

One friend, eager to counter, stressed the ideals that drew them to America. "We're talking about fundamental values, Sam. Law, freedom - these are the cornerstones of any society."

The talk took a lighter turn when another friend curiously asked, "So, Sam, how often do you hit those famous American discos?"

Laughing, Sam admitted, "Honestly, not as much as you'd think."

Their playful retort branded him "boring," as they fantasized about a life filled with nightly escapades in vibrant nightclubs, inspired by images from "Saturday Night Fever."

The conversation then took a sharp, unexpected turn. An acquaintance, his eyes glinting with mischief, probed, "But really, Sam, tell us about the dating scene there. Is it easy to find a girlfriend?"

Sam's discomfort was evident. "Why ask such a thing? You're married."

What Sam hadn't fully grasped was the profound shift happening in Iran. The economic strain and soaring inflation were pushing young girls into prostitution as a means of survival. Many were fleeing oppressive family situations, seeking anonymity and refuge in the big cities.

In this environment, the Islamic restrictions were, paradoxically, fueling a rise in covert activities. Many married men openly engaged in "sighehs" or temporary marriages, an aspect of Shiite doctrine that allowed a man to have multiple, short-term marital arrangements. These arrangements, criticized by many as thinly veiled prostitution, were justified by clerics as a means to avoid paternity disputes.

The practices surrounding these temporary marriages varied widely. Some men maintained separate residences for their sighehs, most kept them hidden from their wives, and a few were quite open about the arrangements. These marriages were formalized with agreements on duration and a negotiated dowry, but their resemblance to prostitution sparked fierce debate and condemnation.

As the night wore on, unraveling layers of complex societal changes and contradictions, Sam found himself immersed in a narrative far removed from their experiences in the United States. By the time they returned home and settled into bed, the clock had already ushered in the early hours of the morning, around four, marking the end of a night filled with revelations and reflections.

Chapter 18

The morning sun spilled its gentle warmth through the curtains, bathing the family room in a soft, inviting glow. Sam, still feeling the remnants of the previous night's late hours, strolled in, his movements slow and heavy. There, he found Farhad deeply engrossed in his morning stretches, a look of resolute determination on his face.

"Good morning. What's all this?" Sam asked, his voice tinged with both amusement and curiosity.

With a grin that bordered on naughty, Farhad replied, "Embarking on a fitness journey, my friend. I plan to be back in shape before you head back."

Just then, Ariana breezed into the room, her timing impeccable. "At the rate he's going, you might need to extend your stay for another six years," she teased, her eyes twinkling with humor.

Farhad feigned a sigh of disappointment. "You're not exactly a cheerleader, are you?" he joked, his eyes still alight with playfulness.

Ariana turned to Sam, her tone shifting to one of concern. "How are you holding up with the news from back home?" Her eyes conveyed a deep empathy.

Sam, his brow furrowing in confusion, responded, "What news are you talking about?"

Ariana, pausing at the doorway with Farhad in tow, said, "The situation at your work. We should get going." With a swift exit, they left Sam standing in a cloud of uncertainty.

It was then Nicole entered, her keen eyes immediately picking up on Sam's troubled expression. "Are you alright? You look like you've just seen a ghost."

Sam, his unease growing, shared his concern. "Apparently, there's some trouble at work, and it seems I'm the last to know."

Nicole gently guided him to sit down, her hands offering a comforting caress through his hair. "Hope called yesterday. The board has placed you on a leave of absence," she explained softly.

Sam's shock was palpable. "And you all thought it wasn't necessary to tell me?"

Nicole met his gaze squarely, her voice steady yet caring. "Would knowing have made last night as good? Your mom wanted you to enjoy the party without this hanging over you. And I agree with her."

Sam's frustration was evident as he reached for the phone, his voice tinged with determination. "I need to know what's going on."

After the call, Sam's demeanor softened. "I'm sorry for overreacting," he apologized, pulling Nicole close. "Forgive me?"

Nicole, her voice soothing, responded, "Just take a moment before reacting next time. Did Hope explain anything?"

"She said Phillips would discuss it with me when I return. I'll talk to Damien too," Sam replied, the uncertainty in his voice now mixed with resolve.

Nicole cupped his face in her hands, looking into his eyes. "Have you done anything that could cause this situation?"

Sam responded with conviction, "I own a significant share of the company. Why would I do anything to harm it?"

Nicole smiled reassuringly. "Then let's not worry now. Enjoy our vacation, and we'll face whatever it is when we return. Deal?"

"Deal," Sam agreed, a sense of relief in his smile. "I wonder where my parents are. They usually don't sleep this late."

Sam's knocks on his parents' bedroom door echoed, each one a silent plea for a response that never came. Slowly, he pushed the door ajar, the creaking hinges adding an eerie note to the silence that greeted him. "Hello, Mom, Dad," he called, the words hanging in the air, met only by the quiet vacancy of the room. The disheveled bed, left unmade, bore witness to a hasty departure.

As Sam entered, his eyes fell on an abandoned room, revealing the abruptness of their exit. It was clear that something had occurred, something that had called his parents away in haste. With urgency and uncertainty gnawing at his chest, he reached for the phone perched on the bedside table. His fingers danced across the familiar buttons as he dialed his mom's cell phone number.

"Hi Mom," Sam's voice trembled, laden with concern. "Where are you guys?" His ear pressed against the phone's receiver, Sam strained to catch every word, his heart pounding.

Amid his mother's hushed and hurried explanation, Sam's brows furrowed. He drew a shaky breath before responding, "I'll be right there." The phone call ended abruptly, and he placed the receiver back in its cradle with a sense of urgency.

Without a second thought, Sam darted out of the room, his footsteps quick and determined. He could feel the seconds slipping away as his mind raced, fraught with worries and questions. His voice, tinged with apprehension, cut through the air. "I'm going to the hospital."

Nicole, her eyes wide with concern and curiosity, couldn't hide the fear that welled up inside her. "Hospital? Why?" Her voice, though filled with inquiry, held a note of understanding, sensing the gravity of the situation.

Sam's response was swift and single-minded, his hand reaching for the car keys, the cold metal offering a semblance of stability. "Dad was taken to the hospital. I don't know the details. I gotta go."

A surge of worry enveloped Nicole, her concern pushing her into action. "Wait, I'll go with you." Her determination was palpable, echoing the unspoken bond that tied them together.

Driving through the chaotic streets of Iran, Sam felt a sense of nostalgia mixed with anxiety. It had been two decades since he had last navigated this tangled web of traffic, and as he pulled the car out of the house, the memories came rushing back. He realized that here, the concept of courteous driving was nothing but a distant dream.

With a deep breath, Sam swiftly made a right turn into the bustling street, his instincts taking over. Nicole, sitting beside him, couldn't contain her fear as the other cars seemed to come perilously close. Her voice, tinged with panic, cut through the air. "What are you doing? That car almost hit us."

Sam's knuckles whitened on the steering wheel, his grip unwavering as he ventured deeper into the chaotic traffic. "You must drive like a maniac here if you want to get anywhere," he explained, his voice resolute. "Lines, lanes, traffic lights, even pedestrians don't mean anything here."

Nicole, her nerves on edge, clung to the dashboard, her knuckles turning pale under the pressure. She had to constantly stop herself from screaming about the recklessness surrounding them. The streets were filled with drivers who zigzagged through the chaotic traffic, a symphony of car horns that seemed to play incessantly. People darted across the road, their actions mirroring a chaotic game of survival.

Pedestrians navigating the bustling streets resembled the iconic video game of Frogger, a constant dance with danger. Drivers showed no mercy for those on foot, refusing to yield an inch. Instead, they accelerated, hoping to deter pedestrians from venturing too close and forcing them to slow down.

In this whirlwind of traffic, Sam and Nicole found themselves navigating a world where chaos reigned supreme, where traffic laws were mere suggestions, and where survival often depended on who could be the most daring amidst the vehicular frenzy.

Their driving adventure brought them to Namazi Hospital, a place of personal significance to Bijan. He had once walked these halls, a part of the hospital staff before his health had forced him into early retirement. The hospital bore the name of its founder, Mr. Namazi, whose legacy had left an indelible mark on Shiraz. Decades prior, Mr. Namazi had amassed a fortune in the United States in the late '40s and early '50s. Upon returning to his homeland, he had established the Namazi Foundation, a beacon of hope and progress for the city. The streets, schools, squares, and countless other places bore his name as a testament to his benevolence.

In 1955, the philanthropist had breathed life into the hospital that now stood before Sam and Nicole, a structure set within a sprawling garden at the far end of Zand Street. The significance of the moment had been so profound that the federal government had issued a series of commemorative stamps in honor of this grand endeavor.

As Sam and Nicole stepped inside the hospital, a heavy sense of disquiet washed over Sam. The hospital they remembered had been a paragon of sanitation and modernity, its corridors bustling with a helpful and friendly staff. But the present was a stark departure from the past. The hospital seemed overwhelmed, its corridors clogged with patients lying on beds in hallways, a striking testament to the strains of time and mismanagement of the government at every level.

Their destination lay to the west, in the direction of the CCU (Cardiac Care Unit). Sam marched forward, his pace unwavering, except for a fleeting moment when he slowed, catching Nicole's eye. His gaze focused on a sign: "Larabi Pediatric Surgery Section." The emotions welled up, but the gravity of the situation kept him moving, one step at a time.

Jacqueline stood at the doorway, a sentinel of hope, her gaze flickering back and forth between the room where Bijan lay and the bustling hospital corridor. The sight of Sam and Nicole approaching in the distance pulled her away from the threshold, beckoning her to step out to meet them.

Sam's arms wrapped around his mother, an embrace of both comfort and concern. "How is he doing?" he inquired, his voice infused with a mixture of emotions.

Jacqueline's response held a glimmer of relief. "He is better," she shared, the words carrying the weight of an arduous few hours.

Inquisitiveness sparked within Nicole as she sought to understand the situation. "What happened exactly?" she probed gently, her voice laced with care.

With a deep-rooted worry etched across her features, Jacqueline began to recount the day's ordeal, a sense of urgency still resonating in her words.

Nicole's empathy extended further. "How long have you guys been here?" she inquired, concerned about the strain that had already marked the day.

Jacqueline glanced at the time, her weariness evident in the lines that had formed on her face. "Since six o'clock," she replied, the hours of vigilance etched into her countenance of the past five hours.

Sam's words carried both admiration and a touch of reproach. "Wow, you guys did not get any rest," he remarked, his voice brimming with a desire to support his parents. "You should have called us. Nicole would have helped."

A resilient smile touched Jacqueline's lips as she brushed aside the notion of needing assistance. "I'm not new to this," she asserted, her eyes reflecting years of experience and unwavering dedication. "You should go in. He'll be happy to see you guys." The warmth in her gaze held a silent reassurance, inviting them to reunite with Bijan in his time of need.

Bijan was sipping on a glass of orange juice and perusing the morning paper. His eyes rose as Sam and Nicole entered the room.

"Hi, Dad," Sam greeted with a hug, an undertone of worry in his voice.

"Hi," Bijan replied warmly, extending his arms toward Nicole. "Come here, give me a hug."

Nicole's concern was palpable as she embraced him. "How are you feeling? You should have called me to check on you."

Bijan, ever resilient, reassured her, jestly continued. "Don't worry, I'm OK. I enjoy coming here for its breakfast."

Nicole moved to the monitors, her medical instincts guiding her. She analyzed the displayed numbers. "Everything seems to be stable."

Sam leaned in, his question revealing a desire to see his father return home soon. "Does that mean he will get released soon?"

Their conversation was momentarily interrupted by the arrival of a doctor, who offered a friendly greeting. "I see you have visitors. How are you feeling, Mr. Doctor?"

Bijan responded with a light-hearted tone. "Excellent, Mr. Doctor. I'm just waiting for you to discharge me."

The doctor began to examine him, the routine checkup interspersed with small talk. "What's the hurry? Don't you like our services?"

Bijan pointed to Sam. "Do you know who this young man is?"

The doctor, while listening to Bijan's heartbeat, glanced at Sam. Recognition sparked in his eyes. "Oh my god. Is this Saam?"

Sam, delighted by the recognition, extended a warm greeting. "Doctor Mir, I'm so happy to see you again."

The doctor, now fully aware of the connection, "I didn't know you were back in town. And who is this pretty lady?"

Sam introduced his wife with a smile. "This is my wife, Nicole."

Nicole extended her hand for a friendly shake. "Nice to meet you."

Dr. Mir, with a nostalgic tone, shared his connection with Sam. "I have known your husband since he was only about this big," he said, placing his hand about three feet above the floor.

Nicole, gracious in her response, acknowledged their shared profession. "Nice to meet you too. I see you are taking excellent care of Dr. Larabi."

Bijan, with a hint of paternal pride, added, "She's a doctor too, Doctor. A well-known cardiologist in San Diego."

Dr. Mir, now aware of Nicole's background, was quick to prioritize Bijan's health. "Then I should know that you're not here on vacation to see more hospitals. I'll be quick to make sure Mr. Doctor can be discharged."

As Dr. Mir continued his examination, a lighthearted moment unfolded. "Dr. Larabi," he said.

Both Bijan and Nicole, almost in unison, responded. The simultaneous answer brought about laughter, with Nicole playfully redirecting the spotlight.

"I think he meant you," Nicole said with a smile, sharing a knowing look with Bijan.

Dr. Mir, in good spirits, patted Bijan's back before delivering a final word of advice. "I will let you go, but remember to take it easy. You need your rest. No more late-night parties, OK?"

As Dr. Mir prepared to leave, Nicole seized the opportunity for a medical briefing. "Do you mind briefing me on his case if you have a minute?"

As Dr. Mir shared his insights with Nicole, Jacqueline and Sam gently helped Bijan prepare for his departure. In the midst of the room's controlled chaos, there was a precious, unspoken connection among them, a quiet affirmation of family bonds during a challenging time. Amid the murmur of voices and the shuffle of feet, Bijan couldn't help but share the headline from the morning paper with Sam, knowing it would bring a smile to his son's face. It was a small yet significant moment that spoke of their shared history and affection.

The headline of the paper blared, "The Last Solar Eclipse of the Century." Sam eagerly seized the paper, his eyes scanning the article's enticing details. "There's going to be a full solar eclipse on August eleventh, and Isfahan is one of the prime spots to witness it."

Bijan, brimming with enthusiasm, chimed in, "That's next week. I know how much you appreciate these celestial phenomena. I'll arrange the trip."

Concern etched on Jacqueline's face as she cautioned, "But dear, please remember that you need to take it easy."

Bijan's excitement remained undeterred. "This is a once-in-a-lifetime opportunity to witness a full solar eclipse, and I've been wanting you all to experience the beauty of Isfahan. It's like hitting two birds with one stone."

While contemplating the rare event, Sam voiced his reservations. "I've seen a few solar eclipses and there is nothing like it. However, your health should be our priority."

Jacqueline suggested a quicker mode of travel. "We could fly there. It's just a forty-five-minute plane ride."

Bijan, though appreciative of the suggestion, waved it away. "Nonsense. It's only a four- to five-hour drive. Sometimes, we've been stuck in traffic longer than that. Besides, it'd be a new experience for Nicole and the kids to witness the small villages and towns along the way."

Jacqueline asserted her final word with a commanding tone. "We'll leave it to Dr. Mir's discretion. We'll only go if he says it's safe. End of discussion."

"Yes, ma'am," Bijan playfully saluted.

After concluding his discussion with Nicole, Dr. Mir joined the conversation. "In fact, a little getaway could be good, as long as you turn it into a mini-vacation. Don't make it a day trip. Stay there for a few days, enjoy the many sights in Isfahan, and make sure you don't exhaust yourselves."

Bijan, eager to get going, extended his hand to Dr. Mir, expressing his gratitude. "Thank you for everything."

Sam conveyed his appreciation as well. "It was great to see you again."

Dr. Mir, while shaking everyone's hands, offered a final wish. "I hope to see you all under different circumstances next time. Have a safe and enjoyable trip to Isfahan."

Chapter 19

The late afternoon sun cast a warm glow over the lively streets. Cameron's eager voice broke the gentle hum, "When are we going for the creampuffs you promised me?"

Checking his watch, Sam noted the time; it was around five o'clock. "Let's gather Tara and head there right now."

In the midst of their daily merriment, neighborhood kids played "haftsang," a game of agility and strategy as a pair of stray cats witnessed the action. Two teams, each eyeing a stack of seven flat stones stacked on top of each other, took turns attempting to topple the stack with a well-aimed tennis ball. Team members scattered in all directions as the other team chased the loose ball. The objective was for the first team to rebuild the stack and shout "haftsang" without falling prey to the opposing team's ball. Players struck by the ball were eliminated from the round. Teammates needed to work swiftly, taking advantage of the chaos caused by the ball's unpredictable path. The game concluded either with a triumphant call of "haftsang" or when all members of the first team were struck.

"Can we join in the game with the kids?" Cameron asked.

"Of course," Sam replied with a smile. "But first, let's pay a visit to the pastry shop."

The trio strolled to a local bakery, one that had held a special place in Sam's childhood. The store had undergone a significant transformation, transitioning from its previous incarnation as "Reza Shah Pastry" to its present identity as "Imam Reza Pastry." The shift in nomenclature bore witness to the convulsions of a nation in flux. Originally, the store's moniker had paid homage to the founder of the Pahlavi Dynasty, Reza Shah, harking back to a time before the tide of revolution swept over the nation.

In the wake of the seismic sociopolitical changes, a mandate was issued to sever ties with any remnants of the former regime, casting a shadow of uncertainty over business owners and citizens alike. As part of this sweeping transformation, enterprises found themselves compelled to shed any vestiges of association with the Shah's rule, thus resulting in the renaming of streets, schools, hospitals, and all traces of the previous regime. The alteration of this humble pastry shop's name from Reza Shah to Imam Reza, the eighth Imam of the Shiite faith, was emblematic of this larger societal upheaval.

As they waited their turn, Sam encouraged Tara and Cameron to pick their favorite pastries from the display case. Sam noticed a framed picture of the former owner hanging on the wall, a customary gesture to honor the previous generation's legacy. He greeted the new owner, a man who had known him since childhood.

"Welcome back, Mr. Larabi," the owner said as he extended his hand across the counter. He mentioned that Sam's mother had informed him of his return during a recent visit to the shop for his welcome party. He peered at Tara and Cameron and remarked, " are they yours?"

Sam introduced the children with a warm smile. "Yes, this is Tara, and this is Cameron. I've told them all about your father's famous creampuffs. By the way, my condolences. May his spirit rest in peace."

"Thank you," replied the owner. "May God grants your father a long and healthy life."

Sam inquired about the owner's son's involvement in the business. "Does your son help you like the way you helped out?"

"My father, may God bless his soul, wasn't wise enough to provide me with a formal education," the owner responded. "He gave me all he had and shared all he knew. But I've made sure my son goes abroad to study in Sweden. He's working towards becoming an engineer."

The shop owner couldn't help but lament the state of their country, where raising children had become increasingly challenging. The school system required children to conform, to stifle their thoughts and abide by rigid religious standards. Even if they weren't religious themselves, they had to attend mandatory prayers and praise the leader and clergy. This was a facade, as most people secretly despised these authorities. But these were the sacrifices required to advance in this society. Sam listened intently as the owner continued, expressing his desire to keep his son away from this oppressive culture. His son had been sent abroad at the tender age of thirteen, free from the stranglehold of a society that demanded multiple personalities to navigate its complexities.

Their conversation drifted as the pastries were carefully boxed. The owner tied the box with a ribbon and handed it to Sam. "Enjoy."

"Thank you," Sam said, pulling out his wallet. "How much do I owe you?"

The owner, with a gracious smile, replied, "Don't mention it. This one's on the house."

Returning to Iran after years away, Sam had almost forgotten the nuanced dance of "taarof" that governed social interactions, a ritual that wove through the very fabric of Iranian society. Taarof was a deep-rooted tradition, dictating the intricacies of human connections and politeness, and was an essential part of being a gracious host. It embodied a verbal duet between the giver and receiver, a subtle, unspoken contest in which both parties fought to be the most generous. At its core, it was an intricate cultural phenomenon where one persistently refused what they actually desired, while the giver insincerely offered something of value for free.

The act of taarof blurred the lines between genuine gestures and mere formalities, creating a social dance at times both enchanting and frustrating, an enigma cloaked in pleasant words and gestures. It often led to ambiguity, for one could never be certain of the other party's true intentions. It was a uniquely Iranian practice, built upon centuries of foreign invasions and oppressive regimes that had necessitated such intricacies for survival.

After a while, those immersed in the culture learned to distinguish between sincere and artificial taarof. For instance, in a shop, when a customer inquired about the price, the first response from the salesperson was typically "ghabel nadareh," meaning "it's not worthy of you." Yet, both parties knew this was a false taarof, a mere formality. The customer, sensing this, would switch to "khahesh mikonam," signifying "I beg you," a polite way of saying, "please tell me the price." After this brief exchange, the seller would openly reveal the total cost. The irony manifested when a customer dared to ask for even the slightest discount. The seller would embark on a detailed explanation of how they hardly made any profit, barely met their expenses, and how, if a discount were feasible, they would have surely offered it. The same seller who initially acted as though they would give the items for free now adamantly refused to budge on the price. They had the knack for making customers feel guilty for seeking discounts.

However, authentic taarof existed too. For instance, when dining at your aunt's house, if you claimed to be full after finishing your meal, she would insist you eat more. "Please don't taarof, I know you're still hungry," she'd say, and proceed to replenish your plate, disregarding your protests. In this scenario, she may think you're merely performing the ritual of taarof, unaware that you genuinely have no room for more food.

The shopkeeper's words resonated with sincerity, "Don't even mention it. It's impossible for me to take your money this time. You're our guest, and it would be a disgrace to have you pay." Sam recognized the authenticity in his offer, knowing that this time he wasn't just taarofing. With a resigned smile, he conceded, signaling to Tara and Cameron to do the same.

As they left the pastry shop, the owner bid them farewell, a warm smile on his face. "Have a wonderful day, and please give my regards to Mr. and Mrs. Doctor," he said, a term affectionately reserved for Bijan and Jacqueline.

In Iran, the honor of earning a doctorate came with a distinct nomenclature. Once the title of "Doctor" was acquired, it wasn't merely a designation; it became their primary identity. To family, friends, and acquaintances alike, the appellation "Doctor" supplanted their official names, becoming the lens through which they were viewed and addressed.

This singular title's influence even extended to the immediate family. Jacqueline found herself known as "Mrs. Mr. Doctor," while

Sam and Ariana were forever branded as the "son and daughter of Mr. Doctor." The significance of these titles was not lost on anyone in Iranian society, where the honorific "Doctor" was held in the highest regard.

    Stepping out of the quaint pastry shop, Sam couldn't help but notice the presence of a new neighbor next door: the Serpico Internet Café, as proclaimed by the bold lettering on the window. It was a testament to the ever-changing landscape of the city. With Tara and Cameron in tow, Sam made his way back to the alley, eager to share the freshly acquired pastries with the children engaged in a spirited game of haftsang. Each child offered a polite "Merci" as they graciously accepted the treats from the pastry box.

    Turning to the young players, Sam inquired, "Would you mind if Tara and Cameron joined in the fun with you?"

    The children, ever welcoming, replied in unison, "Of course."

    Leaving the delightful pastry box in the children's care, Sam retraced his steps to the Serpico Internet Café. The interior was charmingly adorned with small, round tables, each hosting its own computer station. A poster of the classic 1973 movie "Serpico" graced the wall, featuring the iconic Al Pacino. Sam ordered a cup of tea, which arrived in a delicate, clear crystal glass, and settled in at one of the stations. He logged into his email account, the mundane surroundings contrasting with the gravity of the situation.

    As he read through the email sent by Hope, he opened the attached documents. Disbelief washed over him as he scanned the contents; they were copies of his own emails, meticulously compiled and meticulously forwarded to him.

    A thought gnawed at his mind: How had someone gained access to his private emails? In a move to secure his digital realm, he immediately changed his password, yet the nagging question remained: Who stood to benefit the most from his potential downfall?

    Frustration welled up within him, and he swiftly closed the attachments, signing out of his account. With a deep breath, he sat back in the chair, silently sipping his tea, his gaze drifting to the café's other patrons. Apart from a solitary elderly man, the tables were occupied by young couples. The atmosphere seemed to be in defiance of certain societal norms, from teenage boys and girls mingling at the same tables to girls displaying more hair than was typically allowed, all accompanied by the rebellious strains of Western music.

    Then, without warning, the café's mood took an abrupt turn. The music ceased, and the boys scrambled to separate themselves from the girls. Sam was left perplexed, trying to decipher the sudden shift.

The pieces fell into place when the café's door swung open, revealing an uninvited guest.

Chapter 20

Nicole's unease intensified as she scanned the alley and questioned the whereabouts of her husband. The pastry shop, she knew, was just around the corner, yet his prolonged absence cast a shadow of concern. With a swift and practiced motion, she adorned herself in a headscarf and a flowing coat before venturing outside.

Stepping into the lively alley, she was greeted by the sight of her children, Tara and Cameron, running around, their youthful exuberance on full display. "Where's your father?" she inquired with a soft yet assertive tone.

Cameron, a bundle of youthful energy, eagerly pointed to the end of the alley, his eyes brimming with curiosity. "He went that way," he gestured.

Nicole embarked on a stroll through the alley, past the inviting display of an ice-cream shop and a chic women's boutique. As she walked, the nightgown featured in the boutique's window display caught her eye. Yet what truly arrested her attention were the mannequins within. These female figures were conspicuous for their lack of heads, some cleanly amputated beneath the lip line, their anatomical features showing any bulge conspicuously absent.

Her fascination was abruptly interrupted by the grating shriek of a car coming to a sudden halt. A middle-aged man with a bushy beard, his armpits bearing the telltale marks of perspiration, sprung from the vehicle with fervor. He commenced a methodical inspection of the shops, scrutinizing each one before moving to the next.

His tirade began inside the ice-cream shop and swiftly progressed to the women's boutique. As he assessed the items on display, Nicole struggled to comprehend the nature of their conversation, her eyes remaining fixed on the boutique's offerings.

The man, an arbiter of societal compliance, loudly criticized the mannequins' attire. "This mannequin reveals too much of her bare arms," he declared. "Only hands could be shown. Cover her arms and neck with a long coat."

The owner, pleading for clemency and respect, repeated the words "chashm haj-agha." These words, steeped in Iranian culture, conveyed obedience and reverence without resorting to self-degradation. He was acutely aware that the inspector wielded the formidable power to abruptly shutter his beloved store, the lifeblood of his livelihood, with no need for a court order, or worse, to have him apprehended without a warning.

The man's inspection extended to the mannequins' feet. "Put a pair of socks on that model. Her feet are bare," he ordered.

Nicole watched the owner, well aware of the consequences that could befall him if he contested the man's authority. In a society where the prosecutor held the role of both judge and jury, compliance outweighed defiance.

His critique continued, addressing the length of a child mannequin's hair. "Child figures may reveal their faces and hair, but her long hair suggests she's past puberty," he pronounced.

With more instructions given, the man moved on to the next shop. After peeking through the window he entered the coffee shop.

Nicole, intrigued by the unfolding events, took the opportunity to enter the pastry shop and inquire about her husband's whereabouts. "Welcome," the owner greeted her. "How may I help you?"

Nicole, torn between languages, cautiously attempted to bridge the communication gap. "I'm looking for my husband, Saam," she uttered in her nascent Farsi.

Recognition quickly dawned on the owner as he endeavored to converse in English. "Saam, yes, yes, I see go coffee," he replied, attempting to accommodate her in the unfamiliar language. "OK? OK?"

Nicole, graciously accepting the assistance, replied with a word that resonated across languages. "OK, merci," she said, exiting the pastry shop in search of Sam.

Chapter 21

The coffee shop door swung open, and an imposing man, his pants sagging below his ample belly, strutted in, clutching a CB radio. He wasted no time reprimanding two girls at a nearby table. "Fix your headscarves," he ordered, as he made his way towards the cashier. The girls obediently tucked in their hair without acknowledging him.

He approached a group of boys with a stern look, carefully inspecting their attire. "Button up. Your chest is showing," he warned.

"Your place is becoming a hangout for boys and girls," he chastised the owner, who was already accustomed to these confrontations. "This immoral behavior belonged to the last regime."

The shop owner responded with a placating nod, muttering, "Chashm haj-agha," a gesture of utmost deference. "As you see they are not sitting together."

The morality police agent wasn't satisfied. "Do I look like a fool to you? I saw them from the street sitting at the same table. There are also reports that you play corrupting western music."

"I promise it won't happen again, haj-agha," the owner said as he prepared two cups of tea. "I'm just trying to provide for my family. Please, have a tea and take one to your friend in the car."

The agent accepted a tea cup and a handful of sugar cubes, creating a tense silence in the shop as he scrutinized the surroundings. "You should replace these pictures on the walls with Koranic verses."

Meanwhile, Sam observed the scene intently, wondering about the rigid enforcement. "What are you looking at?" the agent barked at Sam, his irritation mounting.

"Just observing," Sam replied calmly, taken aback by the agent's rudeness.

The agent threatened, "You should be more careful and know who you're talking to. Continue, and you might find trouble."

"I didn't mean any disrespect," Sam said, surprised by the agent's harsh tone.

The agent decided to probe further, clearly identifying Sam as an outsider. "You've come from overseas, haven't you?"

"It's my second day here," Sam replied. "May I ask why you enforce such strict separations? It seems unnatural."

The man studied Sam, clearly unsettled by his open curiosity. He turned his gaze towards the crowd and angrily responded, "So you're one of those cowards who fled the country. Do you even know what we've been through? Where were you and your kind when Iraqis dropped bombs on our homes? Now you're back from your plush life and want to teach me how to do my job with your corrupt mind."

The tension escalated as the agent moved menacingly closer to Sam. "It's all Khatami's fault that let guys like you come back."

Just when it appeared the situation might spiral out of control, the cashier intervened, patting the agent on the shoulder. "Please forgive him. He's new here. He never learned the proper manners. Don't get yourself worked up over nothing."

A profound hush had settled over the cafe until the door's chime jingled and broke the stillness. The patrons scarcely reacted until a woman's voice pierced the air, "Sam." It was Nicole, her voice tinged with fear upon seeing the agent confronting her husband.

In the sudden silence, every pair of eyes in the establishment swiveled in Nicole's direction as she advanced towards Sam. Her gaze flitted warily to the agent out of the corner of her eye. She leaned in, her voice a cautious whisper, "What's going on?"

The cashier implored, "Please forgive him. His wife is here."

Sam wondered, 'Forgive him, for what? What have I done?' But he decided to remain silent.

The agent turned his attention to Nicole. "Is she your wife?"

Sam nodded.

"She's a foreigner, right?"

Again, Sam just nodded.

The agent declared, "After all, they are guests in our country. This time I'll overlook it. I hope he realizes the consequences he could face and remind him that he's not in America." Without looking at Sam, he picked up his teas and left the store.

Immediately, the shop returned to its normal state. Boys and girls sat together, and the cashier resumed playing music.

"What happened here? What did you do?" Nicole's concern was evident in her voice as she whispered to Sam.

"Let's leave before he comes back," she suggested, her unease palpable.

But then, a kind, elderly man seated alone interjected, addressing them in perfect English. He folded his newspaper and gestured for them to join him. Immaculately dressed in a suit and bowtie, he exuded a sense of authority that was comforting.

Nicole hesitated, her fear of trouble lingering. "We ought to leave. We don't want any trouble."

The man assured her, "I fully understand," before inviting them to sit. "Please, sit, relax, and have a tea with me. I guarantee he won't come back," he reassured them, signaling to the cashier for two cups of tea. "I am Dr. Mehr. Thank you for staying."

With newfound hope, Nicole and Sam introduced themselves to their newfound friend.

"As long as they can demonstrate their dominance over the people, they are content," Dr. Mehr explained, his voice laced with resignation. "That's precisely what he was doing. He knows you're not here to incite a revolution. If he intended to apprehend everyone who expressed dissent, there would be no one left on these streets. But the moment they sense even the faintest whiff of a threat to their power, that person is as good as dead."

"I don't understand what I said wrong," Sam protested.

"Perhaps it would be prudent to keep your opinions to yourself next time," Nicole suggested.

"I hate to admit it, but she's right," Mr. Mehr added. "You challenged the system by voicing your true feelings. That is simply not tolerated here."

"I'm surprised no one came to my defense," Sam remarked.

Dr. Mehr took a contemplative sip of his tea. "You're new here, and you're yet to grasp the intricacies of how things operate in this country. You'd be on your way to prison if anyone had openly supported you. Unity among the people is forbidden. By remaining silent, we were, in our own way, assisting you." He paused briefly to take another sip of his tea.

I got my PhD in history from Northwestern University in Chicago. Probably before you guys were even born. For twenty years, I taught history at Pahlavi University until, after the revolution, they made an attempt to coerce me into instructing their distorted rendition of history, rather than adhering to the truth. When I refused, I was swiftly fired, labeled as a western-minded corrupt. Despite the students' protests, they shuttered the universities for two years, dismissing professors who defied the new mandates and expelling students who exhibited the slightest divergence from the regime. It may sound amusing, but they informed me I was no longer allowed to wear this," he said, clutching his bowtie. "There were many like me who refused to compromise the truth. We all lost our jobs."

Nicole was empathetic, telling Dr. Mehr, "What you did is truly admirable. You didn't sell out."

Dr. Mehr shared his doubts, "I've heard all these speeches before, but none of those words put any food on the table for my family. Sometimes I ask myself, was it all worth it?"

Nicole offered encouragement, "I hope the conditions get better soon."

"Maybe not in my lifetime, but someday it will," he replied. As if transported back in time, he continued, "Throughout its 7000-year history, Iran has endured far graver trials. Some of these endured for centuries, but no force or power has ever succeeded in altering our identity. Even the invaders found themselves adopting our way of life. Consider the tumultuous invasion by the Arab Muslims in the name of a single God. Persians had practiced a similar ideology for millennia, but the invaders used their facade to justify their actions and deceive the common people. First, they burned our books, and then they banned the use of Parsi language or our tongues would be gouged out."

He spoke as if he were a witness to that distant era. "Their efforts were relentless, as they aimed to obliterate our identity and strip away the essence of our national pride. Yet, it was we, the Persians, who introduced culture to the nomadic Arab invaders. Soon, Persians were governing their vast territories. While Arabs were skilled in looting lands for wealth, they had little knowledge of managing their newfound domains. Persians, with their advanced administrative skills, assumed control over much of the conquered lands and sought to reconnect with their roots. The revival of the Persian language after three centuries was a pivotal moment. Iran remains the sole country that retained its culture, customs, language, and heritage after the Arab invasion. This demonstrates our unwavering pride in our ancestors."

He continued, "In contrast, all those nations beyond the Arabian Peninsula, such as Egypt, Iraq, Syria, and numerous others, have lost their heritage and languages, adopting Arabic due to the Arab invasion. The Islamic revolution is dubbed as the second Arab invasion, but just as the Persians preserved their identity then, we will retain it now. The mullahs may attempt to erase our Persian heritage and replace it with Islamic traditions, but they will not succeed. The Iranian identity exists in a duality, part Persian, part Islamic. Time has proven that these two aspects can never fully blend. It's like oil and vinegar, no matter how vigorously you shake them into each other they will never completely dissolve into one. The Shah erred by imposing Western culture, while the mullahs enforce Islamic rules upon our society. We already know how the story of the Shah ended, and the same fate awaits this regime."

As Dr. Mehr prepared to leave, he paused, turning back to Sam and Nicole with a look that held both warmth and sincerity. "Please, when you return to America, extend my regards to its people," he said, his voice imbued with a genuine respect. "Let them know that here, we hold respect for all humankind. The animosity that seems to loom so large is only between those in power, those who hunger for more than they have."

He offered a small, heartfelt smile, adding, "And if your travels ever take you to Chicago, remember me. Find a cozy spot in one of the coffee shops on Randolph Street, and have a cup of coffee in my memory."

With these parting words, Dr. Mehr departed, leaving behind an air of contemplation. Sam and Nicole stood there for a moment, absorbing the weight and warmth of his message. It was a reminder of the common humanity that binds people together, beyond the political strife and power struggles that too often dominate the headlines.

"Never a dull moment," Nicole said. "First your dad, and now this."

Sam added with a touch of humor, "With all these daily excitements, who needs Disneyland?"

Sam felt a growing unease as he pondered the mysterious hacking of his emails. It was imperative to uncover the identity of the individual or group behind this intrusion, and Shervin, his trusted contact in Dubai, seemed like the perfect ally for this mission.

With a sense of urgency, he reached for his phone and dialed Shervin's number. As the call connected, he explained the situation and the breach of his sensitive emails, emphasizing the potential repercussions on his business.

Shervin listened attentively, understanding the gravity of the situation. He promised to initiate a discreet investigation to unearth the culprits responsible for this breach, a shadowy quest that could reveal a web of hidden motives and adversaries. Sam knew that the answers they sought lay in the digital shadows, waiting to be uncovered, and he couldn't afford to be complacent in the face of this clandestine threat. He emailed all he had to Shervin.

Chapter 22

In the tranquil evening, as the sun dipped below the horizon, Javad, the gracious butler, prepared two sets of beds on the rooftop – one for the kids and the other for Sam and Nicole. With a gentle breeze in the air, he skillfully hung the pashe-bands, a delicate mosquito screen forming a protective canopy over the beds. As the twilight deepened into night, the rooftop mattresses took on a refreshing chill, prompting everyone to snuggle beneath their blankets for warmth. Nestled together, Nicole found her personal heater in Sam's comforting arm, wrapping herself in his embrace.

"Let me show you something amazing," Sam whispered to Nicole, a touch of excitement in his voice.

Nicole chuckled softly, her hand exploring beneath the cozy blanket. "I'll just feel for it."

Sam chuckled in response, whispering playfully, "Behave, you pervert. Don't worry; you'll feel it as soon as the children go to sleep. For now, just look up and enjoy."

Nicole's gaze shifted upward, and a soft gasp escaped her lips. "Wow, look at all those stars."

Tara, the eldest of the children, couldn't help but chime in, "Is Dad talking about his stars again?"

Cameron joined in, his laughter dancing in the night. "Oh my god, he's gonna tell the story of your first kiss again."

Underneath a moonless sky, their rural home, far from the bright city lights, welcomed a majestic canvas of stars, shimmering like diamonds in the night. Sam, the dedicated stargazer, embarked on a celestial tour, beginning with the easiest constellation to find – the Big Dipper. As usual he soon traced a path leading to the Stars of Delphinus, using the bright guiding star of Altair as their celestial guide.

Cameron spoke up, a glint of curiosity in his voice. "Hey Dad, you know how you gave me one of the stars of Delphinus? I want to give it back and pick my own stars."

Nicole, intrigued, inquired, "Why's that, sweetheart? Don't you like your star, right across from Tara's and nestled between mine and your dad's?"

With a heartwarming smile, Cameron explained his reasoning. "I want to have a bunch of stars, so when I grow up, I'll have enough for my wife and children too."

Nicole's laughter echoed in the night. "That's adorable, sweetie. I don't think the sky's running out of stars anytime soon, so pick as many as you want."

Sam chimed in with a touch of whimsy. "The sky may be full of stars, but we have the cutest group. It's so gorgeous that it took your mom two kisses for each star."

Cameron couldn't help but tease his dad, saying, "Didn't I say you'll end up talking about your first kiss again?"

With a playful tone, he added, "Actually, I'll just keep my star. I'll sell it to my future wife for the same price."

As the night continued to unfold, a luminous half-moon, escorted by the two largest planets in the solar system, peeked through the mountains and graced the eastern horizon and began its ascent into the night sky. Its glow resembled a big shining yellow bowl, pouring light across the heavens. The Milky Way, like a gracious guest, allowed its glistening beams to dissolve in the moon's radiant glow and disappeared. While Saturn and Jupiter pulled the moon's chariot across the celestial canvas, switching off more and more stars, the celestial trio painted a mesmerizing and majestic scene in the night sky, one that would be etched in their memories forever.

Under the enchanting embrace of the starry night, as the children drifted into slumber, Sam and Nicole found their own celestial connection, deepening the intimacy of their shared moments. As they held each other close, their passion ignited, their love making unfolded beneath the blanket of stars.

Chapter 23

In the peaceful embrace of the morning, the Larabi family gathered around the breakfast table, where Naneh, a beloved and cherished figure in their lives, had thoughtfully prepared their meal. Known to everyone as "Naneh," a term synonymous with "mother" in Farsi, she held a unique place in the hearts of Larabi family. In the quiet corners of their hearts, she was a mother to them, providing the warmth and care they needed.

Though her given name was "Pari," she had come to be known as Naneh to the family. The bonds between Naneh and the Larabi family were forged through shared hardships and deep connections that transcended mere titles. Dr. Larabi's path had crossed with hers during a fateful visit to the hospital's infertility clinic. The couple, Pari and her husband, Javad, hailed from a humble village on the outskirts of Shiraz, known for its strong Lorr tribal presence.

Married for four years, Pari remained unable to conceive, a source of concern in a culture bound by tradition. Javad's family, supported by the village chief, had begun to pressure him to take a second wife in hopes of bearing children. The chief even suggested Pari's younger cousin for the role. While the idea of multiple wives was not uncommon in their village, Javad was averse to it. In a desperate and clever move, he appealed to their religious beliefs, claiming that he had dreamt of Shahe Cheragh, a holy figure. In the Shiite sect of Islam, the twelve Imams held profound significance, with Shahe Cheragh being one of their descendants. It was believed that these holy figures could grant miracles and fulfill wishes.

To secure their safety and deceive their family, they set out for the holy shrine of Shahe Cheragh in Shiraz, embarking on a journey of faith. As a holy relic, they offered their respects by kissing the shrine's golden door handle, and Pari fervently prayed for the miracle of bearing a child. She held a heart-to-heart conversation with Shahe Cheragh, pouring out her desires, explaining the gravity of the situation, and making a solemn promise to name her child "Ahmad" after Shahe Cheragh's first name and raise him as a devout Muslim.

Javad eventually urged her to leave, assuring her that they were headed to a place where miracles were a daily occurrence. Though Pari continued her silent prayers, she obediently followed her husband to a bus that would take them to Namazi Hospital. Javad, despite his limited education, held an open-minded approach. He had orchestrated this journey not to rely on superstitions but to seek the assistance of skilled doctors, an act he kept concealed from their village. Pari underwent necessary tests, and the doctor's verdict was unexpected: there was nothing wrong with her; the issue lay with her husband. This revelation left Pari devastated, fearing the judgment that would befall Javad in their village.

Pari resisted the doctor's suggestion to conduct tests on Javad, concerned that the knowledge of his infertility would irreparably damage his pride. Desperation overcame her, and she expressed her anxieties through tears, worried that the village would perceive Javad as less of a man. Overwhelmed by emotions, she ran out of the doctor's office, unintentionally colliding with Dr. Larabi. He offered a helping hand, and the doctor summoned her back into the office.

Unaware of Pari's deception, Javad was waiting for her outside the office and after seeing what happened followed them to the doctor's office. Pari continued her act, claiming that she was the one who couldn't bear children, fabricating a story about infertility to protect Javad's honor. As her confession unfolded, she shifted the weight of the situation to her own shoulders, shielding her husband from disgrace. "I can't bring children for you," she confessed, her eyes searching Javad's face for a reaction.

Javad's heart sank, but he remained silent, a testament to the complexity of emotions he was grappling with.

Pari continued, her voice steady but laced with fear. "I don't want to return to the village, Javad. And I don't want you to marry someone else. But if we go back, your family will insist, and who's to say she wouldn't face the same challenges?"

Javad's reply came after a heavy silence. "But I have no other skills. Farming is all I know. How will we survive here in the city?"

Inside the doctor's office, Dr. Larabi and his colleague listened to their conversation, both moved by Pari's brave front and her efforts to protect Javad's dignity.

Dr. Larabi, feeling a wave of empathy, decided to step in. "May I suggest something?" he offered, capturing Javad and Pari's attention.

Eager for any semblance of hope, they both nodded in unison.

Dr. Larabi proposed, "We might have a solution for you. There's a position available in the hospital that could suit you, Javad. And for Pari, my wife is looking for a nanny for our children. We also have a small guesthouse where you could live."

The offer ignited a spark of hope in Javad and Pari. The possibility of a new life, one where they could stay together and be of service, was more than they had dared to hope for. They accepted the offer with gratitude, a new chapter beginning to unfold before them.

Javad found a new purpose working as a security guard at the hospital, a role he embraced with dedication. Pari, as a nanny to Sam and Ariana, discovered a newfound joy in caring for the children, treating them with the same love and affection as if they were her own.

Despite the pressure from his family and the unspoken truths between them, Javad's loyalty to Pari never wavered. He remained faithful, respecting and supporting her through their shared journey. Pari, in turn, kept her secret close, focusing on the love and care she could provide to the children in her charge.

In their new roles, Javad and Pari found not only a means of survival but also a sense of belonging and purpose. Their lives, intertwined with Dr. Larabi's family, became a testament to the power of compassion, understanding, and the unexpected turns that life can take.

Chapter 24

The breakfast table buzzed with an unexpected revelation. Sam had anticipated sharing the morning meal with Farhad, but Jacqueline's words shattered his expectations. She revealed that Farhad and Ariana had set off for Farhad's parents' home, emphasizing the family's eagerness to reconnect with Ariana.

Bijan chimed in with fatherly wisdom, attempting to soothe Sam's disappointment. "Remember, son, when you first introduced Nicole to us, her brother wasn't part of the initial invitation either."

Sam's playful retort carried a tinge of humor, though his jest held a kernel of truth. "So, it's not merely breakfast, but a scheme to trade me in for my own sister?" he teased.

Nicole, grinning in response, offered a light-hearted observation, "Don't take it too personally, love. I simply don't think you're Farhad's type."

Following breakfast, Sam and Nicole embarked on a captivating journey to explore the bustling heart of Shiraz – the Bazaar. With a sense of adventure in the air, Nicole decided to leave the children under Naneh's watchful gaze, allowing them to enjoy their playful activities in the cozy alley.

As they ventured forth, Sam and Nicole embarked on a picturesque three-mile walk, their path guiding them through the lively expanse of Zand Boulevard. This remarkable boulevard, one of the longest and most vibrant streets in Shiraz, served as a vital link connecting the modern downtown area to the city's historic quarters. Named in honor of the visionary founder of the illustrious Zand Dynasty, this eighteenth-century reign brought an era of prosperity and cultural flourishing to Shiraz.

Chosen as dynasty's capital, the foundations of Shiraz's heritage were solidified, giving birth to significant historical landmarks such as the grand Vakil Bazaar, the regal Vakil Palace, the welcoming Vakil public bath, and the majestic Vakil Mosque. These structures stood as a testament to an era marked by architectural grandeur and cultural refinement.

However, the city's fortunes shifted in 1794 when the despised Qajar Dynasty ascended to power. The Qajar founder, in a brutal display of authority, ousted the Zand Dynasty, moving the capital to Tehran. The last Zand ruler, a tragic figure, was subjected to unimaginable torment. He endured both blinding and castration, followed by a cruel imprisonment in Tehran. It was within the grim confines of his cell that his life eventually met a tragic end, choked away by the relentless grip of history.

Stretching gracefully through time and space, Vakil Bazaar stood as an enduring testament to commerce in the heart of Iran. Established in the annals of history in 1760, this labyrinthine shopping center played a pivotal role in the economic lifeblood of the region. It functioned as a vital trading nexus, serving as the distribution hub for a plethora of treasures that adorned its bustling aisles. Among its prized wares were exquisite handmade carpets, resplendent fabrics, aromatic spices, intricate handcrafts, and priceless antiques.

For Nicole, the bazaar was an overwhelming sensory tapestry, a vibrant symphony of human interaction and commerce. Its vibrant spirit was reminiscent of the cacophony that enveloped the trading floor of the New York Stock Exchange. Here, the resonance of paper money ruled, as credit cards remained but a distant echo. In this bustling marketplace, haggling reigned supreme. Customers, driven by passion for the best deals, engaged sellers in animated negotiations. Amidst the whirlwind of transactions, store owners meticulously counted the notes with their trusty automated money-counting machines, securely storing them in their well-worn cash drawers. Remarkably, in this labyrinth of wealth, the absence of security guards cast a curious shadow. There was an unwavering trust that the honor among merchants prevailed, safeguarding the riches within.

Within this sea of treasures, an exquisite painting drew Nicole's gaze. It depicted an elderly man, masterfully rendered with a level of detail that breathed life into the canvas. Each wrinkle etched upon his visage, every line etched into his hands, stood as a testament to the artist's craft. Nicole was drawn to this captivating portrait, her eyes locked upon the captivating image. She couldn't resist the urge to share her discovery with Sam.

Upon seeing her interest, Sam approached the storefront, his curiosity piqued. Together, they examined the artistry before them. With a gentle encouragement, Sam invited Nicole to experience the artwork in its full tactile glory. An exquisite piece like this was meant to be appreciated not only with the eyes but also through the fingertips. Yet, a moment of hesitation gripped her, a touch of fear that her fingers might inadvertently disrupt the serene masterpiece.

Sam couldn't resist the allure of the framed artwork. He pulled Nicole into the store, eager to explore this newfound gem. Turning to the owner, he asked, "Haj-agha, may she touch this?"

The store owner, ever gracious and considerate, immediately responded, "No problem. Consider it yours."

Nicole's fingers delicately caressed the intricate tapestry before her, and her awe was palpable. "Oh my god, is this a carpet? The workmanship is astonishing."

The owner, proud of his wares, chimed in, "Not just any carpet. It's a Tabriz silk carpet, boasting a remarkable thirty-three knots per inch and requiring over six months of meticulous hand weaving."

Nicole stood enchanted by the masterpiece. "It's truly remarkable," she whispered in admiration.

The owner, who clearly held a deep affection for his inventory, couldn't help but share his passion. "This is Persian carpet craftsmanship at its zenith. Look at it; it captures nature's essence more vividly than oil on canvas paintings."

Curious about the price, Nicole inquired, "How much is this?"

The owner, ever the courteous merchant, replied with a customary display of modesty, "It's not worthy of you. Normally, it's 575,000 tomans, but for you, esteemed guests in our city, only 550,000 tomans."

Turning to Sam, Nicole inquired about the cost in dollars. Sam swiftly did the conversion, explaining, "About $600, but I'm confident that haj-agha will offer us an even better deal."

Haj-Erfaan, the store owner, lamented, "I'd be at a loss if I went any lower. There's simply no room for further discounts."

The price, to Nicole's surprise, seemed reasonable considering the craftsmanship and the fact that just the frame alone would have cost over $300 back in the United States.

Sam, with a sly grin, decided to employ the art of bargaining. While bargaining was customary in these bustling markets, Nicole was unfamiliar with the practiced dance of haggling. Sam initiated with the standard tactic of feigning disinterest, telling the owner, "We don't really need it. Besides, we can't fit its frame in our suitcase. Why don't you keep the frame, and I'll offer $350 for the carpet."

A good-humored chuckle escaped the owner. "That's quite impossible."

Undeterred, Sam made his counteroffer with a smile, "Let's meet in the middle at $450, and we'll both find ourselves quite pleased." He extended his hand in a gesture of agreement.

The owner, amused by Sam's tenacity, decided to indulge him. "You're a shrewd negotiator. Let's settle at $475." They shook on the deal.

Sam, displaying a dash of humor, added, "Then the frame shall be included."

The store owner readily agreed. Sam, however, presented a minor complication. He explained that he currently lacked the necessary cash but was willing to leave a $100 deposit.

As the store owner began to prepare a receipt, he inquired, "To whom should I make the receipt?"

Sam replied, "Saam Larabi."

Upon hearing Sam's name, the store owner had an unexpected reaction. He stopped in his tracks and, with an air of delight, questioned Sam about his relation to Dr. Larabi.

Sam responded, "He's my father."

Instantly, the store owner's face lit up with recognition. He eagerly dialed a number on his phone. "Hello, Mr. Doctor," he began the conversation. "This is Haj-Erfaan, how are you? Guess who's in my store right now?"

The store owner, now deeply engrossed in conversation with Bijan, turned to Sam and assured him, "Don't worry, Mr. Doctor, he's almost as good as his mother in bargaining."

As their encounter continued, Haj-Erfaan expressed his nostalgia for the close-knit neighborhood of their youth, when everyone in the town knew each other. Over time, the city had grown, and distances had widened between old friends. Yet, the warmth in their hearts still burned strong.

Sam, as a token of appreciation, placed the deposit on the counter. However, Haj-Erfaan, genuinely moved, refused to accept any money, insisting, "I don't need a deposit from you. Just take it. I'm sure I'll see Mr. Doctor around soon."

Sam politely informed the owner that he lacked a vehicle that day and asked if he could leave the carpet in the store, promising to return for it at a later time.

With an amiable smile, Haj-Erfaan assured them, "Go ahead and finish your shopping. When you're ready, come back, and I'll see if I can arrange a ride for you."

Sam and Nicole, their hearts warmed by the kindness and camaraderie of the market, extended their gratitude to Haj-Erfaan and made their exit, leaving the beautiful Tabriz silk carpet behind, for the moment.

Nicole couldn't help but express her amazement. "Is he really going to let us take the rug home without paying?"

Sam offered an explanation, shedding light on the unique dynamics of the market. "He knows my father. Most of the transactions in this place are based on people's word. Merchants extend credit to people with good reputation. This eliminates the use of credit cards or bank loans and their high interest rates."

Nicole playfully mused, "I wish Neiman-Marcus had the same policy."

Sam couldn't resist a tease. "It's not like you need another pair of shoes."

The entire scene unfolding around Nicole felt utterly novel and intriguing. An elderly man energetically pushed a wheeled cart, advertising his freshly picked sweet apples. A young boy, no more than eight years old, tugged at her sleeve, entreating her to buy a pack of chewing gum. Another man, carrying a wooden toolbox, vocally offered instant shoe repair and waxing services. Her attention was captivated by an antique store with a small display of old jewelry and ornaments, luring her inside.

The antique shop was manned by a wise, white-bearded proprietor who greeted them warmly. Sam and Nicole began to browse and select items they intended to purchase when the loudspeakers resonated with the call to the midday prayer, "azan." The elderly shopkeeper began the process of turning off the lights and lowering the security shutters halfway.

Noticing the sudden transition, Sam commented, "It looks like you're closing down."

The shopkeeper explained with gentle patience, "Do you hear the noon azaan time? It signifies that it's time to return home."

Sam responded, "Alright, we'll make our selections quickly."

A few moments later, the shopkeeper gently tapped Sam on the shoulder while indicating his wristwatch, signaling his desire to conclude their visit. "Why don't you return in the afternoon?"

Perplexed, Sam inquired, "Don't you want our money? It's frustrating to be rushed out like this."

The wise shopkeeper responded, unruffled by Sam's frustration, "I appreciate your intention, but if you don't purchase these items, someone else surely will. However, the time I'm sacrificing to rest and unwind is invaluable, and no one can buy that back."

"You make a valid point," Sam conceded, and they left the store without making a purchase. The shopkeeper promptly secured his shop and departed.

They retraced their steps toward the carpet store, where they found Haj-Erfaan waiting outside his locked shop.

"Here's the carpet," Haj-Erfaan announced warmly. "Congratulations; it's a fine piece. I'll be happy to give you a ride home."

Sam expressed his gratitude but hesitated, not wanting to impose. "Thank you, but I don't want to trouble you."

Haj-Erfaan dismissed his concerns with a warm smile. "Don't taarof. Your house is on my way."

Chapter 25

Following lunch, Sam decided to give Shervin a call in Dubai, hoping for some reassuring news. The persistent intrusion of work matters had made it challenging to set aside his concerns and fully embrace his vacation.

Shervin provided some insights into the situation and, though it didn't appear particularly promising, tried to offer a silver lining. He began, "I believe there is some good news. It seems that someone has contacted the sheiks and informed them that you bribed your way into securing the contract. They claim to have a paper trail, indicating a money transfer to our contact person involved in the deal."

Sam, somewhat exasperated, responded, "I thought you said you had good news."

Shervin went on to elaborate, "The positive aspect here is that these transfer records clearly show that you're not the one behind the money transfer. You can easily deny any involvement. Even if there's evidence of bribery, they can't connect it to you."

Sam's irritation simmered, and he retorted, "I'm more interested in discovering who the rat is than in proving my innocence. By the way, who made the money transfer?"

Shervin reassured him, "I personally arranged the transfer through numerous intermediaries, so not only will they be unable to trace it back to me, but even if they did, they wouldn't be able to link you to me. So the good news is that you're safe, and I won't have to take any drastic measures to protect myself since I'm just a freelance worker. Give me another three days to investigate further, and I'll call you with more information."

Sam sat silently, lost in thought, contemplating the perplexing situation and how his email account had been compromised. He wondered, "Is this personal?" As the revelation of bribery was not beneficial to anyone, he pondered who might benefit from his downfall when Jacqueline gently reassured Sam with a touch on his shoulder. "Everything will be alright; have faith."

Sam, feeling her comforting presence, responded, "Thanks, Mom." He was about to inquire further but stopped himself, understanding that his mother had her own plans for the day.

Farhad and his mother were on their way. After Farhad had dropped off Ariana at home and returned, his mother had phoned, seeking the traditional khastegari meeting—a formal step toward uniting their families.

Khastegari is a time-honored proposal mtradition, a formal step toward seeking a daughter's hand in marriage. It marks the initial stage of making their union official. Historically, khastegari was an integral part of prearranged marriages, where it was not uncommon for the bride and groom to meet for the first time at this event. In those days, the future bride might not lay eyes on her groom until they were legally wed. The families would gather, and the elders would discuss important matters, such as the dowry, the wedding date, and the couple's future residence.

Although the era of prearranged marriages has largely passed, there are instances where the initial meeting between the prospective bride and groom still occurs during khastegari. The bride-to-be typically serves tea and fruit, engaging in small talk with her suitor. If the young couple and their families find themselves amicable to the union, the courtship continues with supervised interactions. Once both parties consent to marriage, elders from both sides convene to plan the wedding, including decisions about the dowry. The dowry is the financial and material support the husband must provide to his wife should she request it, offering her a means to support herself after marriage, particularly in the event of divorce.

Virginity is a point of pride for the bride's family, and it's customary for some families to arrange for a doctor to certify the bride's virginity before her wedding night. The certificate is then proudly handed to the groom's family. In earlier times, close relatives would wait outside the newlyweds' room on their wedding night, and it was the groom's duty to provide tangible evidence of the bride's virginity.

Leading up to the wedding, the bride selects a jewelry set, which the groom purchases. She wears this set during the wedding ceremony. The wedding expenses are typically covered by the parents, and guests often gift gold, which can amount to a substantial sum. Some couples sell this gold if they need to raise funds for starting a business. Depending on the families' financial situations, they provide the newlyweds with as many of life's essentials as possible, to help them begin their life together. Some fortunate couples may even start their married life with a fully furnished home, a car, and all the necessary clothing and furnishings for their future children, all completely paid off.

Typically, the groom provides the residence, and the bride's family contributes her "jahaaz," which includes furniture and rugs for every room, along with appliances and kitchenware. Essentially, it encompasses everything needed to set up their new household. Some families begin assembling the jahaaz for their daughters over several years to ease the financial burden.

In more recent times, khastegari serves as a symbolic gesture, taking place after the couple has already met and decided to marry. It signifies respect for parents and elders in this changing landscape of modern relationships.

In recent years, a longing had brewed within Farhad, a yearning to create a family of his own. However, the complexities of the society around him had given him pause. He hesitated to embrace the idea of parenthood in this increasingly perplexing culture. The Mullahs had made Iran a depressing world where values were shifting, and Farhad was determined to safeguard the purity and sincerity of the past, which seemed to be slipping away. The girls he encountered often appeared more interested in his wealth than in him as a person.

And then he met Ariana. Her spirit was like a breath of fresh air, a link to a time before the societal upheaval. She was the embodiment of fun, down-to-earth, and direct, but most importantly, she was real. Farhad couldn't help but feel that he had finally found the one he had been waiting for, the missing piece in the puzzle of his life. Ariana had the potential to take him to America, a place he had always considered the ideal environment for his future children.

Ariana, on the other hand, had initially seen Farhad as an old friend. They had enjoyed each other's company, sharing laughter and friendship. As the days passed, she couldn't help but notice the subtle shift in his demeanor, revealing a depth of emotion he hadn't expressed before.

Farhad knew he couldn't delay his feelings any longer, and as he tried to find the right words, his face turned several shades of crimson. The weight of his unspoken emotions pressed on him, leaving him at a loss for words. Ariana, witnessing his struggle, found it endearing, a testament to his sincerity.

Unable to resist her amusement, Ariana decided to ease his burden. With an affectionate smile, she peered into his eyes, silently encouraging him to continue. When he faltered, she extended her hand and admitted, "I like you too."

Farhad was taken aback, his surprise mingling with relief. "How did you know what I wanted to say?"

With a hint of playfulness, Ariana responded, "I'm not a little girl anymore, Farhad. It couldn't be any more obvious."

Their connection deepened as they shared their feelings and dreams. The more time they spent together, the more they yearned to be in each other's company. Eventually, Farhad gathered the courage to ask the question that had been weighing on his mind. He inquired if Ariana would be open to the idea of her khastegari—taking their relationship one step further. Her response was a radiant smile and a resounding "yes."

Chapter 26

Farhad and his parents arrived at Dr. Larabi's house one crisp afternoon. The two families had been estranged for well over two decades, and yet the atmosphere felt more like a heartwarming reunion than the traditional khastegari they had gathered for. As is customary in Iran, conversations inevitably veered into political territory, but Mrs. Kamali, Farhad's mother, was a masterful diplomat. With finesse, she skillfully steered the dialogue back to the primary purpose of their visit.

Taking a sip of tea, she turned her gaze to Ariana and remarked, "It feels as if you left Iran just yesterday."

Bijan nodded in agreement. "Time has a way of slipping through our fingers, regardless of our wishes."

After a brief pause, Mrs. Kamali resumed, her tone sincere and heartfelt. "Mr. and Mrs. Doctor, it's with great pleasure that I must tell you, Farhad has fallen deeply in love with Ariana. We've come today seeking your permission and blessings to unite them in marriage."

With a genuine smile, Bijan replied, "They are both mature, responsible individuals, and they have my wholehearted blessing."

Mr. Kamali rose from his seat, his eyes brimming with joy. He approached Ariana and Farhad, embracing them with warmth and enthusiasm. "Congratulations to you both."

Jacqueline, too, joined in the jubilation. She hugged Farhad and expressed her delight. "Welcome to our family."

Amid the felicitations, Sam's voice finally broke through the mirth. "I don't want to be left out," he declared with a grin. "Let me join in the hugging festivities with my little sister and my dear old friend."

As they dove into wedding plans, their discussions occasionally veered into the ever-present abyss of political discourse. There's a saying in Iran that aptly captures the national sentiment: 'Every person in Iran is a politician, overflowing with criticism but bereft of solutions.'

With the impeding political discussions pushed aside, Farhad proposed having the wedding soon, assuring everyone that a spectacular celebration could be orchestrated in just two weeks. In reality, Farhad and Ariana had already harbored intentions of marrying before her vacation concluded. Her plan was to stay in Iran until Farhad's U.S. visa was approved, so they could embark on their American journey together. Meanwhile, Farhad would be in the process of liquidating some of his assets, ensuring he'd have the capital necessary to establish a construction company in San Diego. In the lead-up to their departure, Ariana eagerly embraced the idea of bidding farewell to her overnight shifts at the twenty-four-hour pharmacy, instead relishing the idea of being attended to by Farhad's diligent butler around the clock.

Amidst this whirlwind, Bijan proposed holding the wedding in his brother's garden, the same beautiful location that had hosted their welcome party. With time being of the essence, they decided to embark on a jewelry shopping spree that very day. Mrs. Kamali, Jacqueline, Farhad, Ariana, Nicole, and Sam promptly left the house, en route to the bustling shopping district.

Chapter 27

Hope meticulously documented her findings in a detailed email addressed to Sam. With each passing day, she delved deeper into the workings of the department, scrutinizing every detail for clues. While her investigation didn't uncover anything particularly suspicious, she couldn't shake the feeling that something was amiss. Damien appeared to be doing his best to manage the department, yet the underlying tension remained palpable. It was as if a shadow loomed over the entire office, and no one seemed willing to divulge the truth about what had befallen Sam. Hope's curiosity intensified, driving her to continue her search for answers.

Chapter 28

The dazzling display of jewelry stores on Molla-Sadra Street seemed to cast a spell over Nicole. Her eyes glistened as she took in the shimmering gold and precious stones. She turned to Sam, her voice filled with a mix of wonder and playfulness, "Why didn't you bring me here sooner?"

Mrs. Kamali, with her discerning eye, pointed to a captivating jewelry set in a display window and led the entourage into the store. As the group made its way inside, Sam's gaze was momentarily drawn to the sign of the neighboring store. "Has Mr. Safavi moved his store here?" he inquired, curiosity lacing his words.

Farhad, ever the source of insider knowledge, responded, "No, this is his son's, Bahram." Memories of their high school days, of youthful camaraderie and shared dreams, flooded back. Bahram, one of Sam's old classmates, had ventured into the family business after fulfilling his two years of compulsory military service. In no time, he had honed his craft, and with the support of his father, he now ran his own store.

Excitement coursed through Sam as he walked into Bahram's store. Farhad joined the group in the other store. Inside, women were engrossed in the delicate dance of choosing the perfect jewelry set. The patient salesman shuffled between them, presenting one exquisite piece after another. Ariana, Jacqueline, and Mrs. Kamali were in the midst of a careful selection process, with Ariana trying on each set to find the one that resonated with her the most.

In the adjacent display case, Nicole's eyes locked onto a mesmerizing bracelet that seemed as if it had been crafted to perfectly complement the necklace she had recently received for her wedding anniversary. The cunning salesman, keen to seize the opportunity, delicately took the bracelet and placed it alongside a pair of matching earrings, creating an ensemble that was simply enchanting.

Concerned about Sam missing this find, Nicole turned to Farhad, her voice tinted with anticipation, "Where is Sam?"

Farhad reassured her with a warm smile, "He's in the next store, catching up with an old friend of ours."

Intrigued and wanting to share her discovery, Nicole suggested, "I want him to see this set. I'll be right back."

Sensing an opportunity to reconnect with Bahram, Farhad ventured out with Nicole as well. Farhad made a promise to the salesman, "We'll be right back, please set these pieces aside for her."

A playful remark from Ariana reached their ears as they left, "Where are you taking my husband?"

Nicole flashed a reassuring smile and quipped, "Don't worry, I'll bring him back in one piece."

Chapter 29

Sam entered the Safavi jewelry shop, his eyes locked onto Bahram behind the counter. It was clear that his old friend had not recognized him, and a mischievous idea crossed Sam's mind. He crouched low over the counter and adopted a mysterious tone, his words laden with intrigue, "Excuse me, sir. I am here to take the package."

Bahram, now thoroughly puzzled, narrowed his eyes and responded, "What package?"

The suspense hung thick in the air as Sam continued, "Don't play dumb. Just bring the bag of ancient coins. They are getting smuggled out tonight."

Bahram's fists tightened, and he leaned in, a defiant glare in his eyes, "You are clearly in the wrong part of the town and for sure the wrong store."

Sam pressed on, his voice dripping with veiled menace, "I've never been more certain about where I am. You don't wanna mess with us. So, like a good fellow, give me the package, before I . . . ."

Bahram cut him off, his temper flaring, "Before you what?"

A tense silence enveloped the store as Sam grinned, trying to maintain his façade. "Take it easy, Bahram Khan," he laughed, attempting to defuse the situation. "I was just kidding. I didn't mean to get you upset."

As Bahram's gaze lingered on Sam, a puzzle of confusion etched into his brow. He squinted, piecing together the familiar yet distant image before him. Suddenly, like a light flicked on in a dark room, recognition dawned on his face, his eyes lighting up with a mixture of surprise and joy.

"Is that really you, Saam? How long has it been?" Bahram's voice, thick with emotion, broke the silence as he limped forward. His hearty punch to Sam's stomach was a playful reminder of their old camaraderie. "Tell me, what tall tales have you been spinning now?"

In response to Sam's curious glance at his limp, Bahram recounted a somber tale of a war wound from the conflict with Iraq, adding a layer of depth to their reunion.

Their exchange was suddenly interrupted by a woman's voice, unexpectedly slicing through the air. "Hello, Mr. Safavi."

Bahram's reaction was instantaneous and unsettling. His color drained, his body tensed, and his eyes flickered in alarm between Sam and the woman. Mustering his composure, he stuttered, "Hello, Mrs. Khalili. Welcome."

A chill, icy and foreboding, crept down Sam's spine, prickling his skin as the name echoed through the air. It was a name that conjured ghosts, stirring the dust of long-buried memories. Every instinct in his body howled in protest, warning him not to turn, not to face the specter of a past he had struggled to leave behind. But this wasn't just any name; it was a whisper from a different time, a siren call he found himself powerless to ignore.

With a heart that pounded like thunder against his ribs and a breath that seemed to catch in his throat, Sam felt an inexplicable pull, a gravitational force that compelled him to confront what lay behind him. It was as if the threads of his past had woven themselves into a noose, tightening with the mere mention of her name, leaving him gasping for the air of the present.

Each muscle in his body tensed, fighting an internal battle between the logic that screamed for him to maintain his course and the deep, unyielding desire to look back. The world around him seemed to blur, the sounds and sights of the room fading into a hazy background noise. His movements were not his own as he slowly, almost mechanically, began to turn. It felt like moving through water, every motion heavy with the weight of a thousand moments, a thousand 'what ifs.'

As he turned, time seemed to dilate, stretching the moment into an eternity. With each degree that he rotated, years peeled back, like layers of paint being stripped away to reveal the raw, unvarnished truth beneath. His heart raced, a frantic drumbeat in his chest, a herald to the impending revelation. Sam's mind was a whirlwind of emotions, caught in the eye of a storm that had been brewing silently for years.

And then, he faced her. The world snapped back into sharp focus, the background noise rushing back in like a tide. But none of it mattered. There she stood, a figure from another chapter of his life, suddenly and irrevocably altering the narrative of his present.

Their eyes met. Her gaze settled on the man before her, a stranger with an unsettlingly intense stare that sent ripples of discomfort through her. She stood there, perplexed and slightly unnerved, wondering who this man could be, why his eyes bore into hers with such an unspoken fervor. The air around them seemed charged, thick with an unspoken question that hung heavily in the space between them.

At first, her expression was a mixture of unease and guarded curiosity, her brow furrowed slightly as she tried to place this mysterious figure in the tapestry of her life. As seconds ticked by, laden with a silent intensity, her mind raced through the corridors of her memories, seeking a connection, a clue to this puzzle. Then, quite suddenly, the dam of recognition burst. Roxana's eyes widened in sheer astonishment, her hand instinctively flew to her mouth, muffling a gasp of disbelief. It was as if a dormant part of her past had been abruptly awakened. There, standing before her, was Sam – a ghost from a life she thought had long since faded into the shadows of time.

In that moment, they both stood frozen, caught in a silent exchange that transcended words. Their shared gaze was a bridge across years of separation, a conduit for emotions unspoken, for a history that had never truly been forgotten. Unaware of Nicole and Farhad's entrance, the pair remained suspended in their own bubble of time, oblivious to the world around them.

For Sam, the encounter was like stepping through a portal into another era. The past two decades, with all their victories and challenges, seemed to dissolve around him. The years melted away, leaving him face to face with a chapter of his life he had thought closed forever. In Roxana's eyes, he saw not just the woman she had become, but the echoes of the girl he once knew, the dreams they once shared. It was a reunion that was as unexpected as it was profound, a moment where time itself seemed to bow in reverence to the power of their rekindled connection.

Chapter 30

Everyone has a reason to remember their last day of high school. Some recall it as the threshold to adulthood, while others cherish it as the night of wild celebrations. For many, it's the bittersweet farewell to lifelong friends. But for Sam, that fateful day was etched into his memory for a different reason. It marked a day of joyous revelry that transitioned into an unexpected reunion with a long-lost friend since the fifth grade.

On June 15, 1978, at precisely 3:30 in the afternoon, the hushed ambiance enveloping the Razi High School courtyard was shattered by the exhilarating cheers of the graduating seniors. With their final exams behind them, summer break had officially begun. It was a moment they had anticipated since their first day of elementary school. They had successfully navigated the challenges of high school, a mix of excitement and melancholy swirling within them. Graduation meant the prospect of new adventures, but it also signaled a tearful farewell to the friends they had grown up with.

Yet, the last day of school felt different this time, there was no return after the summer break. The school's authorities in Iran make no plans for a grand celebration. No prom, no school-sponsored festivities, not even a formal graduation ceremony. The only acknowledgment of their achievement was the list of names and final results posted behind a glass window for all to see. "Pass" indicated success, a silent graduation ceremony of sorts, while the word "Fail" next to a name painted a harsh reality, necessitating a repeat of the entire year.

In the absence of official celebrations, it was up to the students to craft their own memorable evening. Each group of friends devised their unique ways to commemorate the occasion. Sam and his friends, however, settled on an unforgettable night of dancing and pulsating music at the International Discotheque.

As the sun sank below the horizon, enveloping the city in the darkness of night, a distinct feeling of excitement permeated the air. The promise of the future loomed large, and the rhythm of life's music seemed to grow louder as they stepped into the world beyond high school. It was a day that set Sam on a path he would never forget, a day when memories were etched deep into his heart and soul.

Amidst the fervent anti-Shah sentiments that swept the streets, sporadic "death to the Shah" slogans sprouted on the city's walls before the vigilant security police could erase them. Yet, in the more affluent district that housed the International Disco, life carried on calmly. Young men, adorned with Jason King size mustaches and afros, flush with cash, reveled in their exuberance, dancing and mingling with the young ladies to the pulsating disco anthems of the late '70s. The dance floor was a spectacle of vibrant colors, oversized collars, and bell-bottom pants, a synchronized tableau moving to the harmonious beats of the Bee Gees. It felt as if one had stepped into scenes plucked from the legendary movie, Saturday Night Fever. The space was packed to the brim with fresh-faced graduates, bumping into one another as they celebrated.

Sam, his energy spent and his breath ragged, navigated his way through the lively dance floor to reach the bar. There, he ordered a cold bottle of beer to replenish his vitality.

"Welcome to Shiraz, Mr. Travolta," a melodious voice chimed in.

Startled, Sam turned his attention to the source of the voice, locking eyes with a young woman in a chic, loose-fitting mini dress that accentuated her graceful legs. Her playful reference to his three-piece white suit, reminiscent of John Travolta's iconic outfit from Saturday Night Fever, left Sam slightly baffled. He couldn't discern if she was poking fun at him or extending a friendly overture.

"Thank you," Sam responded, intrigued. "I've heard Shiraz enjoys delightful weather this time of year."

"I hope it meets your expectations," she replied, a playful glint in her eyes as she traced the rim of her glass with a manicured finger.

Sam, slightly taken aback by her charm, leaned in a bit closer, the warmth of her smile catching him off guard. "Of course," he answered, a hint of curiosity in his voice. "Especially with its friendly people like you."

Her smile remained, but a tinge of mystery surfaced in her gaze. "Saam, you don't remember me, do you?" she asked, her words carrying an air of nostalgia hinting at a shared history.

Amid the hum of the bustling disco, Sam's eyes widened as he pondered how this stranger could know him so well. He studied her face, his curiosity now fully awakened. "Well," he started, lifting his beer bottle, "this brew must be something special. How else could I forget a striking face like yours?" He playfully asked for a clue.

A knowing smile adorned her lips, hinting at secrets of the past. Her eyes twinkled as she mentioned their shared history as elementary school classmates, the nostalgia palpable.

Intrigued, Sam's mind raced through the corridors of memory. He ventured a guess, "Sarah?" attempting to unveil her true identity.

She shook her head, amusement dancing in her eyes. "Wrong."

Undeterred, Sam tried once more, "Niloufar?" seeking a connection to their shared past.

With a gentle laugh rippling through her voice, she playfully revealed the inaccuracy of his assumption with a light-hearted tone. As she teasingly winked and walked away, Sam's sense of misery and frustration swept over him. He had lost the opportunity for a rekindled connection with an old friend.

"Damn it," Sam muttered, a sense of misery washing over him. Then, as if struck by a sudden revelation, he leaped to his feet and tapped her on the shoulder.

"Roxana Khalili," Sam declared confidently, a spark of recognition lighting up his eyes. "See, I remember."

With a nod, Roxana acknowledged the accuracy of his guess.

"Roxana," Sam repeated, his admiration now unmistakable. "You've changed so much, and, may I add, all for the better."

Roxana met his gaze with a mix of amusement and warmth. "You've changed too," she noted, her eyes twinkling, "and like any other boy here, you've grown to look like John Travolta. But the resemblance stops at his wardrobe."

"Wow, that was very frank," Sam said with a chuckle, taking the last sip of his beer.

Roxana responded with a laugh, her mood light and carefree. "It's okay, Saam. We know nobody can move like him."

With a twinkle in his eye and a sense of newfound confidence, Sam extended his hand, inviting her to join him on the dance floor. The DJ had just started playing Gloria Gaynor's 'I Will Survive,' setting the stage for a night of unforgettable memories.

The remainder of the night slipped by, an unbroken thread of shared laughter and rekindled camaraderie. As the early morning light threatened to paint the sky, they vowed to stay in touch, to let their rekindled friendship flourish.

Yet, the path they treaded was fraught with clandestine steps. In a society where dating was strictly prohibited, particularly for young girls, discretion was their trusted ally. They knew they had to keep their bond concealed from Roxana's parents, shielding it from watchful eyes and prying questions.

To navigate these treacherous waters, Sam devised a secret code, a phrase that would act as their lifeline. When he needed to call her, a simple phrase would be the key to ensure her family's unawareness. In a society still bound by traditional values, especially when initiating the khastegari process, parents were resolute about one thing - ensuring their son's future bride had a spotless past, untouched by previous relationships. In such an environment, one couldn't fault parents for their strictness. They were motivated by the need to preserve their daughters' reputation and protect their futures. In a world that clung to these age-old customs, maintaining the delicate balance between tradition and personal desire was a challenge they were determined to meet.

Roxana Khalili was born into the lap of luxury, an heiress to the Khalili family, one of Shiraz's most prominent and opulent households. Their roots lay deep in the fertile soil of the province of Fars, where her father and uncle reigned as the undisputed citrus kings. Generations had nurtured this thriving enterprise, an inheritance that had been passed down, carefully cultivated, from father to son. When their father breathed his last, it was her father and uncle who assumed the mantle, guiding their empire of orchards and groves into a new era.

From the earliest days of her youth, Roxana's destiny was etched in her mind - an arranged marriage to her cousin Nader. The refrain of her predetermined fate rang out repeatedly, like a somber yet inescapable melody. An oft-repeated saying echoed in her ears, an Iranian proverb that encapsulated her existence: "Your umbilical cord was cut with Nader in mind." It had been decreed from her very birth, a pact formed in the cradle, binding her to Nader until he was ready to take a wife. He was four years her senior, a man of the world when she was still coming of age.

As they journeyed through the landscape of their shared childhood, Nader's heart quietly cherished Roxana. He was a reserved and sensitive young man, a quiet observer of her life's daily tapestry. At times, he would shadow her from a discreet distance, ensuring her safety from boisterous boys who sought to engage her in conversation. Such chivalrous protectiveness was an age-old ritual, a rite of passage for enamored young men in their strict society.

Family gatherings provided an opportunity for Nader to engage in brief exchanges with Roxana, their conversations orbiting around mundane matters. Yet, their last encounter had been markedly different. An uncommon boldness overtook the usually bashful Nader, infusing his cheeks with a deep crimson hue. "You know," he stammered, barely meeting her gaze, "the union of cousins is believed to be a match ordained in the heavens."

The candidness of his declaration caught Roxana off guard. She had sensed his affection but never had he ventured into such intimate territory. As the weight of his words settled in her heart, the gravity of their past talks gradually crystallized into an impending reality. The specter of her khastegari, the traditional process for proposing marriage, loomed nearer, as she realized her uncle's family would soon come knocking at their door.

Dancing with Sam that enchanted evening marked a turning point in Roxana's life. It was a dance that drew her into an irresistible whirlwind, a closeness to a man like none she had ever experienced. At first, Sam was just a familiar face from the past, a friend reappearing after a long absence. Little did she know how profoundly her feelings for him would change, or how quickly he would occupy her every thought.

Now, Sam was an uninvited guest in her mind, occupying a space she felt guilty about. Her heart should belong to another, her future husband, Nader, the man she was intended to marry. But as the days turned into nights and her connection with Sam deepened, she couldn't help the pull of emotions that led her astray from the path she had always known. She longed to see Sam again, to dream about a future she had never envisioned before, with a man she had known for just a few fleeting hours.

Summer had begun, promising a season of freedom and leisure, but Roxana chose to remain at home, waiting in anticipation for Sam's promised call. Every ring of the telephone sent her heart into a flurry, and each time, she answered eagerly, hoping to hear the secret phrase that bound their clandestine connection.

Finally, the call they had both been yearning for came. "Is this the Aslani's residence?" the voice on the other end inquired, uttering their secret phrase with a touch of mirth.

With a joyful giggle, Roxana confirmed, "Yes, it is." It was their unspoken code, the key to their hidden world. Their conversation flowed, the precious minutes they shared slipping away until her father returned for lunch, forcing her to reluctantly end the call. Their secret encounters became a regular occurrence, clandestine moments that solidified their platonic connection, growing more potent as time passed. With each stolen phone call and each hidden rendezvous, the bond between them deepened, an affection that refused to be ignored.

As the scorching summer sun bore down on the city, coaxing its residents into the comforting embrace of the afternoon siesta, Roxana found herself navigating the oppressive heat. The plan, veiled under the pretext of a leisurely day at the Cyrus Hotel pool with her friend, took an unexpected turn as she stepped into the shimmering waves of heat.

In the midst of this torrid lethargy, a sudden disruption shattered her thoughts. The abrupt screech of a Suzuki motorcycle echoed through the languid air, and a helmet was thrust into her hands by its enigmatic rider. A gasp of disbelief escaped her lips as the familiar voice reached her ears. "Saam, are you crazy?" Roxana's eyes darted around, ensuring the clandestine conversation remained hidden from prying eyes. With a sense of urgency, she hastily donned the helmet, ready to embark on this unexpected escapade.

The motorcycle roared to life, carrying them away from the watchful eyes of the city's siesta-bound residents. Roxana fervently hoped that their mysterious rendezvous had gone unnoticed, dreading the idea of this secret adventure finding its way to her father's ears. The subtle hum of the engine became a symphony of secrecy as they navigated the streets, leaving the city's afternoon slumber behind.

The warm embrace of the afternoon sun painted a hushed ambiance around them, casting elongated shadows as they explored the town on Sam's motorcycle. The air, thick with the scent of summer, bore witness to a connection deepening with each passing moment. Roxana, nestled against Sam, felt the subtle intertwining of their stories against the backdrop of the sun-soaked streets.

Passing by familiar landmarks, including the International Disco where their paths first converged, stirred a cascade of emotions. The vibrant memories of that moment danced in the air, a silent testament to the journey they were embarking upon. The motorcycle, a vessel of shared secrets and unspoken promises, carried them through the tapestry of the town's hidden corners.

As the afternoon unfolded, the innocent joy of exploration became a canvas for the budding affection between them. The motorcycle's gentle hum served as a backdrop to the unspoken dialogue of hearts growing fonder. In the simplicity of shared glances and quiet moments, a connection blossomed, untouched by the complexities of the world.

Yet, as the afternoon waned, a subtle awareness crept in—the impending separation that awaited Roxana. The innocence of their connection, unmarred by the world's intricacies, stood vulnerable against the ticking clock. In the soft moments leading to Roxana's return home, the unspoken ache of parting lingered, casting a shadow over the otherwise radiant afternoon.

Finally, as they approached Roxana's home, the motorcycle gently rolled to a stop, and the embrace of the afternoon's magic reluctantly gave way to the reality of responsibilities. Roxana dismounted, and as she turned toward her home, a poignant silence settled between them. The depth of their connection, unspoken yet profoundly felt, painted the air with a bittersweet hue.

With a tender farewell, Roxana walked away, knowing who she wanted to spend the rest of her life with and it wasn't her cousin, Nader. Sam, watching her silhouette disappear into the heat-laden horizon, carried the warmth of the afternoon's magic—the innocent dance of two hearts entwined, captivated by the simplicity of pure love.

In the relentless blaze of that summer, Nader found himself drawn to his uncle's house like a moth to a flame, each visit fueled by an unspoken desire to capture Roxana's heart. Determined to secure a positive response before initiating the formal khastegari proposal, he rehearsed his words relentlessly, sculpting each sentence with precision. One fateful day, as the summer neared its twilight, Nader made a decisive stop at Roxana's residence, spotting her in the backyard. His practiced lines, carefully crafted on the journey over, stood ready on the tip of his tongue, a symphony of hope and anticipation echoing in his heart.

"Do you know what you want to do now, that you're done with school?" Nader inquired, a subtle depth to his words implying more than a mere career question. "You know what I mean."

Roxana met his gaze, understanding the unspoken subtext. "I know what you mean," she replied. "Let me spend this summer with my friends before asking your mom to come for my khastegari."

"You know I'll wait as long as it takes," Nader assured, his commitment evident.

A fake smile played on Roxana's lips, though beneath it, a silent hope lingered. By the summer's end, she wished, perhaps against reason, for Sam to step forward for her khastegari. Yet, she acknowledged Nader's unwavering determination.

"I saw you with him," Nader abruptly confessed, his revelation casting a sudden chill over the warm day. Roxana felt her mouth parch, words frozen in the summer heat. When she finally spoke, the admission stumbled out, "I wouldn't blame you if you hated me for that," her gaze avoiding his.

"At first, I wished I hadn't seen it," Nader admitted, his voice heavy with regret. "The way you laughed, the way your hair danced freely, the joy that lit up your face. You've never been that carefree around me. It felt like I'd lost you to him. Just tell me if..."

"Stop," Roxana interrupted, her face covered as tears spilled. "I don't know what I've entangled myself in. Please, don't shame me further. The guilt is suffocating. If fate ties us, nothing will alter that."

Nader, caught in the crossfire of love and empathy, tentatively reached out to hold her hand. Yet, just as he had done so often in the past, he halted, stopping himself just short of the gesture. "I didn't want to upset you, maybe it's best if I go. Remember, words echo swiftly in Shiraz."

With tear-streaked cheeks, Roxana retreated to the house, the blistering summer air heavy with the weight of unspoken words.

"How come Nader didn't come in?" her mother inquired, noticing the tear stains on her daughter's face. "What did he want?"

"You know what he wants. The same thing you all expect of me since the day I was born." Roxana's voice trembled with a mix of frustration and resignation. The weight of tradition and familial expectations pressed down on her shoulders, a burden she had carried for far too long.

Her mom stayed quiet, absorbing the heavy atmosphere that hung in the air. In that moment, their silent exchange spoke volumes, a conversation conducted through the language of shared emotions. She reached out, pulling Roxana into a loving hug, a gesture that sought to comfort and shield her from the weight of societal norms.

"Mom, when did you know you were ready to marry Dad?" Roxana asked, seeking solace and understanding in the midst of her emotional turmoil.

"It was not for me to decide. The elders decided for us. Your father was nineteen and I was only fourteen. Businesswise the union of the two families made good sense." Her mother's words carried the weight of years gone by, a narrative of a different era where love often took a back seat to practical considerations.

"Are you saying Nader and I should get married because it's a good business decision?" Roxana questioned, a glimmer of defiance in her eyes.

"He's a good boy and a hardworking businessman, but I would never make you marry someone you wouldn't want." Her mother rose from her seat and walked to the window, casting a nostalgic gaze into the lush yard. Memories of her own teenage years played like a movie in her mind. "One day we had some people over at our house. Later that day, my mother told me that I was getting married. That was the routine back then. We got married without knowing anything about love or each other. I guess love came afterwards. Unfortunately for some, love never came. They were cheated out of the most precious thing in life. Now, do you think I want such a life for my daughter? I want you to marry for love and nothing else." Turning toward Roxana, she continued, "I want you to get married to someone you know is the one and only. The one you know you can't live without. I've seen this kind of love only in the movies, but that's the kind of love I want for my daughter."

"How can a girl find that in this society without being labeled all sorts of things?" Roxana asked, her vulnerability laid bare.

"I'm sure there are ways." Her mom narrowed her eyes, holding Roxana's hand and gazing into her eyes. It seemed she was conveying, 'I know everything about you and Sam.' "But a girl should be smart enough to know not every boy is worth falling in love with, and make sure the families measure up."

Surprised and confused by her mom's remarks, Roxana's pondering was interrupted by the phone's ringing. Mrs. Khalili answered, listened, and then announced, "Yes, it is. Hold on... it's for you, Ms. Aslani." With a wide smile, she left for the backyard, revealing that she had known about the secret encounter for a while and leaving Roxana to contemplate the mysteries of her mother's wisdom.

Humming softly, "Gole goldoone man, Maahe eyvoone man," Mrs. Khalili carefully selected roses, weaving them into a floral arrangement. Her melody was a gentle whisper, a tune that seemed to dance with the petals. Lost in her task, she was startled when Roxana's voice suddenly intruded, breaking the rhythm of her song. "How long have you known?" Roxana inquired, her question hanging in the air, laden with unspoken implications.

"I'm surprised you hung up so quickly. Do you want to tell me who he is?" Mrs. Khalili asked.

"It's Saam Larabi," Roxana said conceitedly.

Mrs. Khalili paused, her eyes narrowing as she studied Roxana's expression. "Saam Larabi," she repeated, a mix of curiosity and concern in her voice. "Why is that name so familiar? Is he the one you went to elementary school with? The principal's son?"

Roxana nodded, her eyes sparkling with a hint of excitement. "Yes, he is."

A shadow of worry crossed Mrs. Khalili's face. "He's from a good family, but he's your age, only eighteen. Is he ready to commit and settle down at that age? I mean, have you two even talked about your future together?"

Roxana's cheeks flushed a delicate shade of pink, her emotions a swirling mix of embarrassment and eager anticipation. "Talking to you about him feels so strange," she confessed, her voice tinged with vulnerability. "Just moments ago, I was keeping him a secret, and now you're asking me to open up as if we're best friends."

Her mother, embracing her with a warmth that melted away years of distance, spoke with heartfelt regret. "We've not been as close as we should have been. I realize now I've built walls, just as my mother did, creating a distance between us. I regret not being there for you, not as a mother should." She loosened her embrace, looking deeply into Roxana's eyes, her gaze filled with an earnest plea. "Let's start afresh, as best friends. I'm here to listen, truly listen, whenever you're ready."

Roxana's voice rose, laced with a blend of frustration and readiness to open up, as her mother began to walk away. "We haven't planned anything for the future," she called out, her words echoing her internal turmoil. "But I want to tell you, my friend, everything about him."

Her mother turned, her expression inviting. "Does he treat you well? How does he make you feel?"

Roxana's response was heartfelt and genuine. "Yes, he treats me wonderfully. When I'm with him, it feels like I'm the only person in his world. My heart skips a beat every time I see him. He lifts all my worries away, making me feel as if I'm floating on air. I hope this makes sense to you."

Mrs. Khalili's eyes softened, her face reflecting understanding and compassion. "It makes perfect sense," she replied, her voice gentle. "It sounds like a love story from the movies. I hope it has a happy ending."

Roxana's voice wavered with a mixture of hope and uncertainty. "But do you really think we can be together?" she asked, seeking reassurance.

Her mother's response was a blend of motherly love and wisdom. "Only time will tell, my dear," she said, offering both hope and a gentle reminder of the complexities of love and relationships.

"Why do you say that? Don't you think we can be together?" Roxana's voice, tinged with a mix of hope and apprehension, sought affirmation.

Her mother's response came with a note of practicality, laced with a hint of concern. "I can't predict that, my dear. These questions are for him and his family. What are his plans for the future? How does he intend to support a family?"

Roxana, her voice heavy with the weight of looming change, shared, "He's been accepted to Tehran Medical School. He'll be leaving Shiraz in just two weeks." Her words trembled slightly, revealing the inner turmoil of her heart, torn between the joy of his success and the impending distance their relationship would endure.

"Another Dr. Larabi," her mom remarked, a note of nostalgia laced with pride. "With his father's storied reputation, establishing a successful practice won't be an issue. While we're not concerned about his future, time is not on your side with his imminent departure."

Acknowledging the complexity of the situation, Roxana admitted, "I know all of these things. I'm confused and don't know what to do or what to say," her words hanging in the air like unspoken dilemmas.

Her mother, a stalwart source of guidance, responded, "Again, I can't exactly tell you what to do. But I think after the start of his second year of medical school, I can convince your dad to let you marry him over his nephew if he comes for your khastegari."

Curious, Roxana questioned, "Why wait so long?" The uncertainty echoed in her voice, a longing for answers evident.

"Because next year, he can say he has successfully finished the first year and is serious about his ambitions. You can be engaged then and marry after he graduates from medical school. At that time, you'll be marrying a doctor, not just the son of a doctor. I'll cleverly put it in that context for your father. I'm sure he would love for you to marry a doctor."

Expressing her uncertainty, Roxana admitted, "I wish I knew what his plans were. I know girls are not supposed to ask that from boys," a vulnerability coloring her words.

"But this is about your future. You are entitled to know what his plans are," her mother reassured, a comforting presence in the midst of uncertainty.

"Thank you, Mom. It's such a relief not to have to keep him a secret anymore," Roxana said, her voice a blend of relief and slight trepidation.

Her mother's response was a comforting mix of encouragement and maternal care, her smile conveying understanding. "I'm glad too. I've heard you as a friend, and now it's time for some motherly advice," she said gently.

Roxana, with a shy smile, responded, "I think I can guess what's coming," her cheeks flushing with a hint of embarrassment.

"You're smart and I trust your judgment," her mother said with heartfelt sincerity. "I believe you have the grace and wisdom to preserve yourself for your wedding night," she added, the pride in her voice clear and unwavering.

Roxana nodded, her voice a mixture of assurance and a hint of shyness. "I understand, Mom," she said softly, her gaze dropping slightly, reflecting a mix of respect for her mother's wisdom and her own internal contemplation.

"I'm proud of you. Now go on and call him and get your answers." The words carried a poignant mix of encouragement, maternal support, and the inherent complexity of navigating love and life's decisions.

In the vibrant evenings of late 70s Shiraz, Thursdays were akin to the Saturday nights of the Western world—a prelude to the cherished Friday, the official weekend and the lone respite in Iran. Those were the golden days, a time when a family could lead a comfortable life on a monthly income of $300, a time when the streets of Shiraz transformed into bustling picnic grounds.

Families, their spirits as high as the towering cypress trees that adorned the boulevards, would gather alongside the streets or find solace on the grassy realms of boulevards' center dividers. Laughter would mingle with the tantalizing aroma of kabobs sizzling on grills, creating an ambiance of joyous revelry.

That particular summer carried an extra layer of cheerfulness, an effervescence that bubbled from the hearts of the people. For the first time in history, Iran's national soccer team had secured a spot in the prestigious World Cup, an event set in the vivid landscapes of Argentina. The collective pride and anticipation painted the city in hues of jubilation.

As the sun dipped below the horizon, signaling the end of the day, different groups of picnickers would emerge, each with their own melodic contribution. Boom boxes blared, and the rhythmic beats of percussion instruments set the stage for spontaneous gatherings. Strangers, connected by the shared pulse of music, would dance and sing together, transcending the boundaries of familiarity.

It was a symphony of unity, a celebration of life and shared dreams. In those enchanted Thursday nights, the spirit of Shiraz soared, echoing the joyous notes of a nation united by the love for soccer and the simple pleasures of communal revelry.

Under the soft glow of Farah Park's lampposts, Sam and Roxana found themselves in a quiet enclave. Sam, sensing a subtle shift in the air, decided to bring a touch of sweetness to the moment. He bought two bowls of Persian mulberries from a street vendor for one toman each, the plump berries glistening like drops of ruby in the dim light, and offered one to Roxana.

As they settled on a weathered bench, the ambiance carried a weight of the unspoken. Sam, observant as ever, noticed the uncharacteristic quietude in Roxana's demeanor. A gentle concern crept into his thoughts, wondering if everything was truly okay with her.

The air, pregnant with the unspoken tension, surrounded them like a delicate veil. Roxana, torn between the desire to broach the topic at hand and the shyness that held her back, found herself caught in the intricate dance of hesitation. The mulberries, their flavors bursting with the richness of the night, became a silent witness to the unspoken commitment that lingered between them—a commitment that needed no words to convey its depth and significance.

In the quiet embrace of the night, Sam drew Roxana closer, wrapping her in the warmth of his arms. Sensing the perfect moment, she gathered the courage to voice the rehearsed thoughts that had lingered in her mind.

Sam slid tighter to her and took her into his arms. "Tell me what's on your mind?"

Roxana, poised to reveal her innermost reflections, was momentarily interrupted by Sam's gaze turning upwards. "Look at those stars," he mused with a playful glint in his eye. "I'll show you mine if you show me yours."

Roxana playfully chided him, "Oh, you're such a pervert," as she gently nudged him. Her eyes then scanned the night sky, searching for her special star. "There it is," she said, pointing to a trio of stars. "The bright one in the middle, that's my star."

Sam, with a look of mock surprise, responded, "No way! Our stars are nearly side by side!" He tenderly held her hand, linking them together under the vast cosmic canvas.

"Ever since I was little, I've whispered wishes to that star every summer night before falling asleep," Roxana shared, her voice laden with the tenderness of nostalgia.

Sam, eager to deepen their shared moment, suggested, "Let me show you where my star is. It's a bit more elusive."

Sam guided her hand skywards. "Look there, draw a line from your star going left. That cluster of four stars, that's my own little piece of the sky."

Roxana, following his direction, observed, "They form a shape like a kite."

In that intimate moment of introspection, Sam's heart swelled with a profound realization. "It's amazing to think that your star has always been the beacon guiding mine," he shared, his voice rich with emotion. The notion that her star had unknowingly served as his celestial guide, steering others toward his own constellation, enveloped him in a sense of awe. Compelled by this newfound understanding, Sam leaned in closer, his lips meeting hers in a tender kiss that silently acknowledged the extraordinary bond they shared under the expansive night sky.

Roxana's voice, soft and laden with dreams yet to be voiced, floated through the air. "What if I let go of my star, and we both claim yours? That way, we'd each have two stars," she suggested, her words weaving a tapestry of shared dreams and possibilities.

Sam's heart responded with a warmth that radiated through his being. "I want you to remain my guiding star," he whispered back, enveloping her in an embrace that spoke volumes of his deep-seated emotions.

Her eyes, brimming with a blend of vulnerability and hope, met his. "Promise me you'll think of me every time you look at my star or when you're showing yours to someone else?" she asked, her voice a gentle echo of her heartfelt plea.

"I promise," Sam replied, the sincerity in his voice resonating in the stillness of the night.

Roxana, her voice barely above a whisper, sought reassurance. "Will we be like our stars, together till eternity? I need to know how you truly feel about us," she said, her arms tightening around him, a symbol of her trust and affection.

Sam, caught in the tide of emotions that this conversation had stirred, paused, his thoughts navigating the unexplored depths of their relationship. "Roxana, you're the only girl I've ever felt this close to, but to be honest, I haven't given much thought to what lies ahead," he admitted, his voice tinged with a mix of affection and uncertainty.

Roxana's voice was tinged with a deep yearning, resonating with a heartfelt desire. "I wish we were in a world where others couldn't dictate our future."

Sam, with gentle care, drew back slightly to look at her, delicately wiping the tears that had formed on her cheeks. "Why do you say that?" he asked, concern lacing his words.

Roxana took a deep breath, her heart heavy with emotion. "My cousin is planning to come for my khastegari. But I've fallen so deeply for you, Sam. The thought of being with someone else is unimaginable to me."

Sam's resolve was firm, his voice steady with conviction. "I won't let you go. I love you too much to lose you," he declared, the sincerity in his voice unmistakable.

Roxana's heart fluttered at his words, a mixture of surprise and happiness washing over her. "You've never said you love me before," she whispered, a smile breaking through her tears.

"It's the first time I've ever said it to anyone," Sam admitted, his own emotions evident.

Her confession was heartfelt. "I couldn't bear a life without you," Roxana said, her words sealed with a gentle, loving kiss.

Sam's eyes met hers, shining with a promise. "We'll be together till the end of time, like our stars," he vowed. "I'll speak to my parents, see what advice they have."

Roxana sighed softly, a sense of impending separation looming over them. "Summer is nearly over, and soon you'll be leaving for Tehran. I'll miss you more than words can say," she said, finding comfort in his embrace, their hearts beating in unison against the backdrop of the Farah Park's quiet.

The following day, Sam strolled alongside his father toward Namazi Hospital, divulging the intricate details of his heart's desires. "You want to marry the only daughter of one of the richest men in Shiraz, who is destined to receive the most opulent jahaaz. In return, the expectation is for the groom to possess a home of his own and proffer at least a thousand gold coins for her dowry," Bijan expounded.

"I had hoped you'd handle the housing matter," Sam jested, and everyone knows the dowry is more symbolic."

Bijan contemplated the situation and advised, "Why not wait until you've completed medical school before embarking on her khastegari? You're both just eighteen. What's the rush?"

"Nader is the rush. He seems to tick all the boxes a suitor is expected to, except he hasn't captured her heart. That's precisely why we should get engaged as soon as possible, then plan our marriage for when I've completed my studies."

Bijan pondered Sam's earnest plea. "If your love withstands the test of distance, we can proceed with her khastegari when you start the second year of medical school."

Relief washed over Sam's face as he expressed, "That's all I wanted to hear."

Sam traversed the lengthy path from the hospital edifice to the main gate, meandering through the resplendent garden encircling the structure. It wasn't the enchanting roses or the stately slender Cyprus trees that diverted his contemplations. Instead, the resonant chants of a gathering seized his attention. Upon reaching the front gate, he beheld a substantial assembly of demonstrators brandishing signs and placards.

"Death to the Shah, hail to Khomeini," resonated their collective chant. This marked Sam's initial encounter with Khomeini's name during that summer. He surmised that the mullah depicted in the small black and white picture placards was none other than Khomeini. Standing amidst a sizable cluster of spectators, Sam observed the protestors' fervor. Before long, anti-riot police vehicles arrived, discharging shots into the air. Pandemonium ensued as everyone dispersed, protestors abandoning their placards in haste to evade arrest. Even the onlookers, overcome with fear, hurriedly retreated.

Chapter 31

Sam and Farhad's Tehran apartment transformed into a cherished haven, a magnet for their newfound friends seeking solace after the rigors of school. While Tehran boasted a plethora of enticing activities, Sam's heart remained tethered to Shiraz, with most of his free moments spent immersed in conversations with Roxana over the phone. In the turbulent backdrop of the Iranian Revolution, the streets of Tehran echoed with both fervent cries for change and the ominous footsteps of martial law. As the political landscape shifted, Sam found himself caught between the swelling tide of protests and the overpowering love he harbored for Roxana.

The nights at the university turned into a battleground of ideologies, where students, armed only with their voices, clashed with the forces loyal to the Shah. The air was thick with tension, yet even in the face of impending violence, Sam couldn't shake the longing for his beloved Roxana, miles away in Shiraz.

The once vibrant cityscape transformed into a canvas of dissent, marked by burning banks, theaters, and government buildings. The unity among the people, referred to as brothers and sisters, created a profound contrast to a nation torn apart by revolution.

With each passing week, the protests swelled, occasionally prompting the university's closure. In the capital, the number of demonstrators soared past the one million mark, a sea of people flooding the streets, clamoring for the Shah's departure and the establishment of an Islamic Government.

Army trucks, brimming with armed soldiers, lined the main roads to quell the protesters. Martial Law descended, imposing strict regulations that prohibited gatherings of more than four people and banned street presence after nine at night. Like clockwork, at nine o'clock, the city plunged into darkness, only to reverberate with eager shouts from rooftops—"Death to the Shah" and "Allah Akbar." Soon, the entire nation embraced a public strike.

The atrocities turned the entire country against the Shah and his regime, compelling everyone to pick a side. Neutrality ceased to be an option; one was either aligned with the Shah or with the people.

As the wave of unrest and protest swept through the nation, schools shuttered their doors for safety as teachers rallied in support of the public strike. The climax of aggression unfolded on December 7, 1978, when a group of soldiers, in a violent breach, attacked Tehran

University's main campus. Breaking through locked gates, they left a tragic toll of students killed. The shockwaves reverberated across the entire country as university students, in a unified stand, adamantly refused to return to classes, prompting the closure of universities nationwide. The National Oil Company of Iran joined the strike, leading to a significant decline in oil and gas production, bringing the wheels of the economy to a grinding halt. It became increasingly evident that the figurehead of the people's aspirations, Khomeini, harbored no intentions of relenting until the Shah was ousted.

As the universities locked their gates, a contingent of impassioned students opted to remain in Tehran, fortifying the ranks of the revolution. Their collective vision: a nation akin to Switzerland, independent and free. However, for Sam, love trumped the call of the revolution, prompting his departure for Shiraz as soon as the university closed its doors.

Roxana and Sam's reunion unfolded not in the serene embrace of romantic settings, but amidst the dedication of demonstrations. Their hands locked in a tight grip, the other defiantly raised in a clenched fist, they echoed anti-Shah and pro-Khomeini slogans. Khomeini's staunch critique of the Shah's pro-Western stance resonated, condemning the exploitation of Iran's resources by powers like America, England, and France. Yet, paradoxically, these same Western powers seemed aligned in their desire to oust the Shah.

France played host to Khomeini, aiding in the dissemination of his messages. The BBC and Voice of America stood resolutely pro-revolution and anti-Shah. The nightly ritual of tuning in at 8:30 to BBC Radio became a nationwide tradition, eagerly awaiting Khomeini's announcements and details of the planned demonstrations for the next day. The motives behind the superpowers' opposition to the Shah remained elusive, challenging the belief that their actions were driven solely by the people's welfare. The intricate dance of global politics unfolded against the backdrop of a nation in tumult, grappling with questions of allegiance, power, and genuine intent.

On January 16, 1979, the Shah and his wife departed the nation, the official narrative attributing their exit to a vacation and medical treatment. The reality, however, unveiled a clandestine political maneuver orchestrated by the newly appointed prime minister. This maneuver harbored the aspiration of a return through the echoes of history, envisaging a replay of the 1953 scenario when Prime Minister Mossadegh, propelled by popular support, compelled the Shah's departure.

Behind this complex political theater, a shadowy coup d'état unfolded, masterminded by the nascent CIA and bolstered by the unwavering support of the British government and British Petroleum Company. This covert orchestration not only reshaped the political landscape but also marked a pivotal moment in the country's history, casting a long shadow over the unfolding events and the fate of the Iranian people.

Khomeini's return to Iran on February 1, 1979, unfolded as a foreboding omen. When queried by a reporter about his emotions upon returning home after fifteen years of exile, his dispassionate response hinted at a man devoid of sentiment for Iran and its people, his response was a mere 'nothing'. Behind the facade of a religious leader lay a cold and unyielding figure, steering the nation towards a looming abyss, shrouded in the darkness of his ambitions. The color of his turban mirrored the shadows cast by his intentions, darker and more ominous than the black plague, echoing a malevolence that reverberated globally, in time claiming millions of lives.

Born the grandson of an Indian mullah, Khomeini's early years were shadowed by rumors of his grandfather's potential association with the British government, leading some to suspect espionage. His contentious relationship with the Shah came to the forefront when the latter granted women the right to vote, a move that Khomeini vehemently opposed due to his conservative beliefs rooted in centuries-old ideologies.

Khomeini's conservative stance extended beyond politics, as he openly criticized universities, viewing them as potential sources of moral corruption. His analogies, such as comparing music enthusiasts to heroin addicts, revealed a deep-seated resistance to modern cultural influences. His regressive policies regarding women continue to cast a long shadow over the nation. Prohibiting women from riding bicycles or participating in sports in the presence of male audiences, he enforced a draconian dress code, compelling women to wear coverings and hijabs. These measures not only altered their legal standing but also subjected them to seeking permission from male guardians for basic activities. Overnight, women found themselves relegated to second-class citizenship.

His aversion to vibrancy extended beyond mere aesthetics, permeating every aspect of life. Anything hinting at beauty or liveliness was systematically suppressed. Even the once lively and colorful clothing of the populace swiftly succumbed to a somber palette, as if draped in the shroud of a dark slumber.

As Khomeini and his group of mullahs solidified their control, dissent faced harsh suppression. The once-promising leader began enforcing his vision with an iron grip, stifling opposition and restricting freedom of expression. The consequences of these policies became apparent only after the populace realized the extent of the changes imposed by Khomeini and his cadre, leaving many questioning the path their nation had taken.

Upon his arrival at Tehran's Mehrabad airport, Khomeini's first destination was the hallowed grounds of the revolution's martyrs. There, amidst a captivated audience of millions and a nation tuned in via television, he delivered a speech that would shape the narrative for years to come. Skillfully leveraging religious commitment, Khomeini vehemently denounced the reign of the Shah, painting a distorted picture of a nation in ruins, with cities reduced to rubble and flourishing cemeteries.

In reality, under the Pahlavi Dynasty, Iran had experienced long periods of peace and economic prosperity, fostering a comfortable life for its citizens. However, Khomeini adeptly manipulated these facts to craft a narrative that resonated with his audience, exploiting the emotional connection to the martyrs and stoking the flames of discontent. The impact of this masterful manipulation would later become evident as Khomeini's version of events took root in the collective consciousness of the Iranian people.

During that pivotal speech, Khomeini made sweeping pledges, including the commitment to hold free elections for a government truly representative of the people. He assured the nation that the clergy would not interfere in the democratic process. Bold and resonant, his words painted a picture of a future where homelessness would be eradicated, and Iranians would revel in the luxuries of free telephone services, heating, electricity, and bus transportation.

However, the stark disparity between these assurances and the subsequent reality revealed the hollowness of Khomeini's promises. Instead of prosperity, Iran plunged into decades of economic hardship, marked by the highest inflation rates in its history. Khomeini's once-promising vision gave way to a sinister presence that cast a long and ominous shadow over the nation, inaugurating an era defined by broken promises and unfulfilled prophecies.

To add another layer of intrigue, later on, Khomeini's speech was cunningly banned from broadcasting, and any mention of it mysteriously vanished from public discourse. This subtle act further obscured the stark contrast between his charismatic pledges and the harsh realities that unfolded, shrouding the true impact of his words in a veil of silence. The aftermath of that speech became a somber reminder of the challenges the Iranian people would face in the turbulent years to come.

How could an entire nation fall so easily under the spell of Khomeini's false promises? He wove a cunning enchantment over the populace, enthralling them to unquestioningly believe every deceitful utterance and blindly follow his every command. Some fervent supporters went to extreme lengths, deifying him, convinced he was a godsend or even the Messiah, asserting that he maintained direct communion with the Prophets and Imams.

A twisted belief even emerged, claiming that Khomeini's image adorned the moon—an alleged divine sign attesting to his righteousness. Remarkably, he never denied or spoke against such assertions, allowing the myth to persist and further solidify the mystique surrounding his persona. The atmosphere of blind faith and mythical reverence cast a surreal shadow over the nation, contributing to the perplexing phenomenon of a charismatic leader who could sway the beliefs and convictions of an entire people.

With his silver tongue, Khomeini declared that they should not rest until the regime was overthrown, promising a guaranteed place in heaven for those who died in his cause. In response, waves of riots spiraled out of control. The nation, ensnared in the web of his malevolence, exhibited a shocking level of blind devotion. Ordinary citizens, swept up in the fervor, dared to block the path of army tanks, confronting gunfire not with fear but with flowers. It was as if they sought to pacify violence with misplaced symbolism.

The haunting chant, "We gave you flowers, but you answered us back with bullets," resonated, underscoring the absurdity of their predicament. This chant became a chilling reminder of the twisted manipulation orchestrated by a man whose malevolent intentions would not only plunge the country into chaos but also cast a dark shadow over the entire region, setting the stage for an unseen and uncertain future.

The unyielding wave of popular discontent left no room for compromise; it demanded nothing short of the complete dismantling of the old establishment. The tipping point arrived when even the military, acknowledging the feeling of the people, underwent a profound shift. Soldiers, reluctant to turn their weapons against their fellow citizens, defected to join the people's cause. These transformative events culminated in the collapse of the government on February 11, 1979. The armed forces united with the people, and the Shah's last prime minister fled the country in the face of an irreversible tide of change. The convergence of these forces marked a historic turning point, symbolizing the triumph of the people's will over the existing order. A new era dawned upon Iran, ushering in a wave of exuberance among its people. They believed they had triumphed, claiming a well-deserved victory for democracy. Streets witnessed an unprecedented spectacle as elated drivers abandoned their vehicles to join the jubilant throngs in dance. The conclusion of a monarchy that spanned two and a half millennia was celebrated with passion.

The architects of the old regime faced swift and harsh justice, gathered and executed without the due process of trials. Their lifeless forms openly displayed on the front pages of daily newspapers, a stark testament to the unforgiving aftermath. No clemency was extended to those associated with the deposed Shah, and the count of executions rose inexorably. Fearing persecution and death, many chose to abandon their possessions and escape the country, echoing the upheavals witnessed in the French and Russian revolutions. These massacres, it seemed, were the inevitable fruits of a revolution deemed successful.

In the sinister hands of this malevolent figure, tens of thousands of innocent Iranians faced execution simply for daring to speak the truth. The nadir of this reign of terror was marked by the audacious occupation of the US embassy in Tehran and the subsequent hostage crisis. Carter, perceived as a weak American president, remained conspicuously silent on the matter, inadvertently emboldening the regime and paving the way for even more egregious atrocities over the decades. The repercussions of this silence are even palpable today, resonating in the escalating menace of international terrorism.

A year later, he recklessly steered the nation into an eight-year war with Iraq, a conflict that claimed over a million lives. The justification? The bizarre claim that Iraq was a mere stepping stone in the grandiose plan to destroy Israel and liberate Palestine. Ironically, even as Palestinian leaders publicly sided with Iraq against Iran, it was a deceitful charade. The knowing grip of Iraq, a sworn enemy of Israel, became just another propaganda tool, skillfully deployed to deceive the masses.

As the dust settled, the lingering effects of this tumultuous era continue to reverberate, casting a shadow over international relations and contributing to the ongoing complexities of the Middle East.

As the interim government settled into place and a semblance of normalcy returned to Iran, Sam found himself compelled to return to Tehran and resume his studies. However, this choice weighed heavily on his heart, as it meant once again being separated from Roxana. The trials of the revolution had forged a profound bond between them, and the idea of distance posed a formidable test to the resilience of their connection.

Undeterred by the uncertainties that loomed ahead, Sam embarked on the journey back to Tehran, fully aware that the road ahead held the dual promise of rebuilding and the poignant ache of being distanced from the one he held dear. The blend of hope for a renewed future and the bittersweet pang of separation infused his journey with a complex mix of emotions, marking a poignant chapter in their shared story.

Chapter 32

Roxana skillfully maneuvered the intricate dance of evasion, a clandestine ballet designed to avoid the frequent visits of Nader to his uncle's house. The persistent worry of Nader inadvertently unveiling her covert interactions with Sam haunted her thoughts like a lingering shadow, a constant undercurrent of anxiety coloring her every move. Yet, unbeknownst to her, Nader was no malicious force; he was a benevolent soul, genuinely fond of her. Oblivious to the depth of Roxana's concealed affair, he remained committed to safeguarding her secrets.

Amidst this delicate web of secrecy, Roxana clung to the passionate hope of a future with Sam. She eagerly anticipated the day when he would come to seek her khastegari, marking the start of a new chapter in their shared journey. The looming tension and concealed passion of their forbidden romance infused each moment with a thrilling sense of anticipation, weaving a tale of love entangled in the threads of secrecy and impending revelation.

In that pivotal year, the much-anticipated summer break was abruptly curtailed to make up for the lost time during university closures. Seizing the chance to elongate his time with Roxana, Sam ingeniously concocted a ruse, feigning the need to stay home while his family embarked on a visit to his grandparents in America. As soon as he wrapped up his finals, he swiftly made his way back to Shiraz.

For Roxana, every passing moment with Sam became a treasure, and she dedicated all her free time to nurturing their clandestine connection at his house, knowing that their stolen moments were all the more precious with his parents away. The backdrop of this covert rendezvous painted their summer with a palette of secrecy, infusing their time together with the thrill of forbidden romance and the sense of an intimate world carved out from the constraints of reality.

In the soft glow of Sam's room, the forbidden strains of Western music filled the air, creating a secret melody that echoed the clandestine nature of their love. The impending separation lingered in the room like a poignant note, and Roxana, overwhelmed with sorrow, found solace in the familiar tunes that danced around them.

As the final day of summer break unfolded, the inevitability of Sam's departure hung in the air, casting a shadow over the intimate space they had shared. The melodies became a soundtrack to their stolen moments together, each note a testament to the defiance of their love against the constraints of their world.

With the weight of impending separation pressing on her heart, Roxana's eyes shimmered with unshed tears. In that vulnerable moment, Sam, attuned to her emotions, reached for her hand and gently pulled her into the circle of his embrace. Their bodies formed a seamless connection, a silent promise etched in the tenderness of their touch.

"The wait is almost over. Once my parents return, we'll finally come for your proposal," Sam declared with unwavering assurance, coaxing a hopeful smile to grace the corners of her lips.

"I've seen you leave countless times, and each time it gets more difficult. I can't shake off the fear that in the end, we..." Roxana faltered, her eyes brimming with tears, unable to continue. The weight of unspoken fears hung heavy in the air, creating a distressing moment charged with both anticipation and the haunting specter of an uncertain future.

In a tender gesture, Sam ran his fingers through her cascading locks before gently guiding her down onto his bed. With his arms securely wrapped around her, he pressed his chest against hers, savoring the closeness, eager to explore every contour of her body. His hand, a delicate dance of nerves and smoothness, slid under the soft fabric of her blouse, tracing intricate patterns as he tenderly massaged her back. Continuing the subtle exploration, his hand traced a path over her breast, gently lowering and nudging aside the shoulder straps of her blouse. As he lowered the blouse, he smoothly unclasped her bra. Roxana's eyes instinctively sprung open as she held on to her bra, the unspoken words lingering in the air. Slowly, she closed her eyes again, allowing the moment to continue in the quiet intimacy they shared.

The room was imbued with a hushed intimacy, each caress a silent testament to the unspoken connection between them, a dance of sensations that unfolded in the quietude of that shared moment. Sam, seemingly oblivious to the previously set boundaries, persisted in his tender gestures, perhaps hoping that the approaching engagement would alter her limit and the dynamic between them. The dance of their connection continued with lingering kisses, a silent exploration of the uncharted territories between them.

Roxana appeared at ease, her breath deepening as the room grew warmer. Her hands, initially guarding her boundaries, now moved from protective restraint to embracing and exploring. As he kissed her neck, Sam's movements became deliberate, slowly navigating downward, leaving a trace of warmth in his wake. She shyly pulled off his T-shirt, her eyes kept shut. As his hands moved down her chest, they delicately stroked her breasts, all while they engaged in a passionate kiss. In the heat of the moment, they swiftly shed each other's clothing until she felt the need to pause and momentarily halt their fervent exchange.

She clutched his hand as he attempted to remove her underwear. "Please stop," she gasped. Deep down, a desire to continue pulsed within her, but the societal limits that bound her held sway, causing her to pause despite her inner yearning.

"What is it? You know that I love you," Sam whispered, his voice laced with a blend of concern and affection.

"I know you do. I'm just not ready yet. Please understand, if you really love me," Roxana replied, her words carrying the weight of vulnerability.

"I understand. I'm sorry if I made you uncomfortable," Sam responded, his tone softened with remorse.

"I know it's not easy for you. It's hard for me too," Roxana admitted, her voice tinged with a mixture of apprehension and sincerity.

"I said I understand. You don't have to explain," Sam retorted, frustration and heat seeping into his words.

"It doesn't have to be dull either; we can make it pleasurable without going all the way." Roxana's hand ventured below his waist, her words infused with a subtle promise that hinted at a shared journey of exploration and intimacy.

Chapter 33

Sam and Roxana eagerly anticipated a future where they could cast away the cloak of secrecy that shrouded their feelings and revel freely in each other's company. With determination, Sam initiated conversations with his parents, crafting a plan that would bring the day of their unmasked connection closer. They envisioned a time when they could openly embrace their love, starting with the traditional proposal for Roxana.

In the midst of Sam's first midterm exams, a small window of opportunity presented itself, and he seized it. A one-week break was secured, and on the first of November, he embarked on a journey to Shiraz. The airport reunion was a quiet celebration, with both his family and Roxana welcoming him back into their midst.

Amidst the backdrop of autumn, as the days grew shorter and the sky transformed into a canvas of yellowish-red hues, Roxana found solace in observing their enchanting garden through the family room window. Leaves, painted in the vibrant colors of the season, gracefully descended with each passing wind, creating a tapestry on the ground beneath.

On that particular Friday afternoon, as the sun dipped low, casting a warm glow that bathed the landscape, Mr. Khalili emerged from his bedroom. The air buzzed with a sense of anticipation, and the allure of that autumn afternoon held the promise of a momentous event in the making.

Jacqueline's morning call to Mrs. Khalili carried the sweet promise of excitement. "Can we come for Roxana's proposal on Sunday afternoon?" she had asked. As anticipation filled the air, Roxana, attuned to her father's daily routine, knew he never slept in that late. Usually, by 3:30, he would be sipping his tea.

She prepared a fresh pot, the fragrant aroma wafting through the air, and patiently waited for her parents, sensing they might be engrossed in a discussion about Sam, his family, and the forthcoming proposal.

As Mr. Khalili entered the room, a playful glint in his eye, he teased, "Let's have the tea that the bride-to-be has made." Roxana blushed, a radiant smile gracing her face as she hurried to the kitchen. With each cup poured, she indulged in daydreams of her impending wedding day, the joy of the moment reflected in her sparkling eyes. Placing the tray adorned with tea and sweets on the table, she turned to leave, the air alive with the promise of an enchanting journey about to unfold.

Mr. Khalili gently took hold of his daughter's hand with a touch of reassurance. "Your mom says Saam is an old classmate of yours, and he'll be a doctor soon," he shared, guiding Roxana to sit beside him. The air tinged with a mix of curiosity and apprehension.

"Please have your tea before it gets cold," Roxana murmured, her voice carrying a blend of emotions that danced between excitement and an unspoken anticipation. Words eluded her in the face of the momentous conversation unfolding, leaving a delicate silence hanging in the air.

Much like his contemporaries, Mr. Khalili was steeped in the traditions of his upbringing. A man of the old school, he had no inkling that his daughter had been in a relationship for over a year. The mere notion of Sam, someone familiar from Roxana's school days, unsettled him in a way he couldn't quite express. A hardworking provider, he had crafted a life of comfort for his family and, in return, expected unwavering respect and obedience from each member.

His children understood that his word was final, and challenging him was not an option. Behind the stern façade, however, lurked a softer side, a facet of his personality he preferred to keep concealed. While he projected an image of unyielding authority, in truth, his wife held the subtle power to influence his decisions. With a gentle voice and well-chosen words, she could navigate his convictions, allowing him to believe he was steering the ship while gently guiding him toward the path she desired.

"You're my only daughter. I want you to have the best life and lifestyle. I know Nader will give you such a life, but your mom insists that Mr. Dr. Larabi's son can make you happy and comfortable as well," Mr. Khalili expressed, his words laden with paternal concern and a desire for Roxana's happiness.

"Of course, we can see him and his family," Mrs. Khalili interjected, subtly glancing at Roxana. "Your father will decide whether he's the right man for you or not."

Roxana remained silent, her reserved nature in the presence of her father preventing her from expressing her thoughts or emotions. She listened attentively, a portrait of restraint in the face of familial decisions.

The following day, Nader arrived home with his uncle for lunch, and Roxana sensed that her father had already shared the news about Sam's upcoming proposal. After the meal, as Mr. and Mrs. Khalili retired for a nap, Nader approached Roxana, seeking a private conversation.

"Your father told me what's going on," Nader began. "My uncle has no idea that you two see each other."

"And I'd like to keep it that way unless you..."

"I can't make you like me," Nader gently interrupted. "I've told you before that I'm not going to hurt you by being a tale-teller."

"I know how you feel about me," Roxana asserted firmly, a newfound confidence in her voice. "When I was younger, I saw you as my future husband and giggled with the other cousins about it. But then I met him, and we fell for each other. Please don't hate me."

"Hate you?" Nader responded. "I love you too much to be able to hate you, no matter what you do." It was the first time he had ever expressed his feelings so openly, leaving Roxana momentarily speechless. Overwhelmed, she turned away, wiping away her tears, feeling the weight of traditions and expectations pressing on her.

"I wish you a happy life," Nader said, expressing a mixture of sadness and resignation. "I hope you will understand if I couldn't make it to your engagement party."

"Couldn't or wouldn't?" Roxana questioned, sensing his hurt. "Nothing is final yet anyway."

"You don't have to make me feel hopeful. I don't have the strength to see another person put a ring on your finger. I can't pretend to be happy."

"Does that mean you are going to abandon your cousin forever?" Roxana asked. "Please be there with the rest of the family and be happy for your cousin."

Nader gently held her by the arms, locking eyes with her. "I hope you have found happiness, Roxana," he said, his eyes welling up with tears. "I am going to bank on that little hope you left me with. Just know I'll still want you if it didn't work out with him or if you had a change of heart."

Roxana saw the pain in his eyes, making it difficult for him to continue. "I'm letting you go in the hope of returning to me on your own," Nader said before leaving her house.

Roxana, torn between blaming him for her guilt and feeling pity for his broken heart, retreated to her room. The encounter with Nader intensified her certainty about her love for Sam, realizing how much she had missed Sam even in just the brief conversation with Nader.

Sam was immersed in a game of pong on their old black and white TV when the phone's ring cut through the air. "Hello," he answered.

"You're right here in Shiraz, yet it feels like we're worlds apart," Roxana lamented over the phone, her voice tinged with longing. "I miss you more than you can imagine."

"I feel the same," Sam replied, his words echoing her sentiment. "What if I come to see you this evening?"

"That would be nice, but I have plans with my mom. We're going dress shopping for the khastegari. Can we meet tomorrow morning instead?" Roxana asked, hope coloring her voice.

"Absolutely, I'm here till Friday. How does nine sound for tomorrow?" Sam suggested, eager to see her.

"Are you planning to come on your bike? That might not be the best idea. How about I pick you up instead?" Roxana offered, a playful note in her voice.

Sam chuckled, agreeing to her plan. "Okay, that works for me," he said, the thought of their impending meeting infusing a sense of joyful expectation into the conversation. The promise of the next morning hung between them, a cherished prospect they both eagerly awaited.

Chapter 34.

Sunday, November 4, 1979, dawned with a sense of transformative promise, a day destined to be etched in Roxana's memory as a pivotal moment in her life. Amidst the backdrop of a nation on the brink of monumental change, Roxana awoke with a heart brimming with anticipation and a mind racing with thoughts of the day ahead.

As she prepared herself with meticulous attention, her reflection in the mirror revealed more than just a carefully curated appearance. Each brush stroke in her hair, each dab of dark red lipstick, was not only a testament to her excitement but also a silent act of defiance against the tightening grip of conservatism in the Islamic Republic. The backless halter-top blue dress she chose was not just an emblem of her personal style but also a subtle rebellion against the emerging restrictions of her time.

The anticipation swirled around her as she spritzed perfume with precision, the fragrance a whispered promise of the day's potential. Stepping into her high-heeled shoes, she felt a surge of independence, a feeling amplified by her new red BMW 320 to Sam's house. The car, a symbol of her autonomy, glided through the streets of Shiraz, each turn bringing her closer to the man who occupied her every thought.

Upon arriving, Roxana's heart skipped a beat. She rang the bell as Sam was stepping out of the shower, her pulse quickening as she anticipated his reaction. The air crackled with the significance of the day, each moment shaping the course of their lives in ways they were yet to comprehend.

"Come on in," Sam called out, buzzing her in. His voice, still slightly muffled, echoed from inside, "You're early. It's not even nine yet."

Roxana chuckled lightly. "What are you up to?" she asked, her voice laced with playful curiosity.

"Just getting ready. Come up," Sam replied, his tone light and inviting.

As she entered, she found Sam sitting on the floor, clad in his bathrobe, absorbed in the task of putting on his socks. Roxana leaned against the doorway, a teasing smile playing on her lips. "Do you always dress in such a unique order? Socks before pants?"

Sam looked up at her, his task momentarily forgotten. "It's my little ritual. I start with the socks – always have." His eyes roamed over her, taking in her appearance. "You look absolutely stunning," he remarked, his admiration clear.

Roxana, basking in the compliment, spun around gracefully. "I'm glad you noticed. This dress isn't exactly motorcycle-friendly," she said, her laughter filling the room.

Sam, still in awe, joked, "I think I need to pick my jaw up off the floor."

Roxana's eyes sparkled with playfulness. "So, my future husband, where are you taking me today?" she asked, blowing him a kiss.

Caught in the moment, Sam abandoned his sock, swiftly getting to his feet to embrace her. Their kiss was passionate, full of the promise of the day ahead. "Right now, the best place to be is right here," he whispered, guiding her gently toward his bed.

Roxana's voice was light, flirtatious. "And what do you have in mind, Mr. Bad Boy?"

Instead of responding, Sam simply smiled and carefully laid her down on the bed. He reached over to the cassette player, and the room was soon filled with the soft, melodious tunes of the Ambrosia, creating a romantic ambiance. The music, like a soundtrack to their emotions, set the tone for a day that would be remembered forever in their hearts.

"Could you at least give me a moment to take my shoes off?"

"Allow me." Sam's hands delicately slid down her toned legs, removing her shoes with a touch both gentle and sensual. His lips traced a path over her soft skin, planting kisses along each leg until they reached the hem of her short dress. His hand slipped under the fabric as he moved upward, placing kisses on her neck.

"It's your lips," Sam confessed, his gaze fixated on her luscious mouth. "It's these lips that drive me wild every time I see you." He stole another kiss. "God took his time crafting these perfect outlines," he murmured, trailing his finger along the border of her lips. "It took him five days to fill them with the most aphrodisiac color in the heavens, a hue more intoxicating than any known to the celestial realms. On the sixth day, he created you around these perfect beauties. He rested on the seventh day to admire his flawless creation."

Roxana smiled. "Some people wait their entire lives for a love like this. Some never find it," she reflected. "How lucky I am to find you when I wasn't even looking or aware that such a love existed. Promise to love me the same forever."

"I promise." Sam sealed the promise with another kiss, slowly sliding down her dress.

She pulled the bed covering over her exposed top, not due to the cold but because her hands trembled as she untied his robe and tossed it to the floor. Sam gradually lowered her dress until it was completely off.

"You're shaking, are you cold?" Sam observed.

"Not really. I don't know why."

"Let me warm you up," Sam suggested, pressing his warm body against hers. He started by kissing her neck, making his way under the sheet to her bare breasts, savoring the taste of her silky skin. His hand ventured to the rim of her undies, where he lingered for a few seconds. His fingertip gradually slipped under her panty line.

Roxana pressed tighter against him, swallowing hard. Although she knew the words she wanted to say, they eluded her.

"What is it?" Sam inquired, tenderly rubbing around her panty line.

"We're almost married," Roxana finally whispered. "It's OK. Take it off."

Sam's hand froze. "Are you sure?" he asked, immediate regret coloring his words.

At nineteen, brimming with hormones and the eagerness of youth, Sam had no intention of denying himself this moment, his first foray into the realm of sexual intercourse.

"Aha," Roxana moaned, "as long as you'd still consider me pure and immaculate on our wedding night."

As Sam lay on top of her, their bodies entwined in a dance of passion, Roxana's heart pounded with a mixture of fear, uncertainty, and nervous anticipation. It was her first time uniting with a man, and as she slowly opened her eyes, she found assurance in the deep love and passion reflected in her lover's gaze. With a calm resolve, she closed her eyes again, surrendering to the moment.

In the cocoon of their shared intimacy, they lingered in bed, making up for lost time, lost in the tender exchange of emotions and desires. Sam and Roxana's emotions swirled in a delicate dance of vulnerability and elation as they lay side by side, their bodies still tingling from their first intimate encounter. Their hearts beat in unison, a rhythmic reminder of the profound connection they had just forged.

In the quiet aftermath, Sam stole a glance at Roxana, his eyes filled with a mixture of awe and tenderness. He marveled at the beauty of her bare soul, now laid bare before him. The intimacy they had shared had transcended mere physical pleasure; it had awakened a profound understanding of one another's desires and insecurities.

Roxana, too, gazed at Sam, her heart aflutter with a newfound sense of completeness. She felt a warmth enveloping her, a sense of belonging she had never known before. Their shared vulnerability had opened a door to a deeper, more profound love than either of them had imagined.

As they lay there, fingers gently tracing the contours of each other's skin, they knew that this moment would forever define their relationship. It was more than just a physical union; it was a union of two souls, navigating the intricate path of love for the first time. And in that shared intimacy, they found not only passion but also a profound connection that would shape their future together.

Roxana finally pointed to the clock on the wall, breaking the enchanting spell. "It's almost 12. We must leave before your parents get home."

Sam, soon draped in his robe, left the room to afford her some privacy. A few minutes later, Roxana descended the stairs. Their eyes met, and in that moment, it was as if a new, profound connection had been forged between them. Unable to look away, they were captivated by each other's presence.

"I'll be back in a second," Sam whispered, breaking the spell as he hurried to his room to get ready. The air was charged with a newfound intimacy, the residue of their shared experience lingering as they prepared to face the world beyond the confines of their shared moments.

As the two navigated the streets on that fateful Sunday afternoon, an eerie tension gripped the air. The rhythmic honking of horns, accompanied by shouts of "Death to America," echoed through the city. While such slogans had become almost commonplace since the revolution, the spontaneous outbursts from passing cars and pedestrians sent a shiver down their spines.

"It must be disheartening to endure that on a daily basis," Roxana observed, sensing Sam's frustration with the unsettling display, cursing everyone that chanted the slogan.

"You don't have to be American or half-American for those words to cut deep," Sam retorted, his frustration palpable. "How can any decent human wish for the total annihilation of a nation? I know they might argue it's aimed at policies and leaders, but I bet they wouldn't tolerate hearing 'Death to Iran' in return, no matter the interpretation."

Roxana nodded in agreement, her expression mirroring his concern. "It's not just offensive; it's a troubling sentiment."

"America is a far more democratic country than any in the Middle East will ever be. They should be wishing death to dictators and governments not elected by the people instead," Sam asserted passionately.

"These same people would trade half their lives for a chance to live in America. Just ignore them," Roxana suggested, trying to ease the tension.

"Soon, I'll take you to America. We'll start in San Diego, where my grandparents live, and then we'll traverse the entire country," Sam envisioned, his eyes gleaming with a distant dream.

"That sounds like a dream, but for now, I must return home," Roxana said, conscious of the approaching afternoon, bringing with it the anticipation of her proposal with Sam's parents.

Chapter 35

As the first rays of morning sunlight bathed Shiraz, Roxana prepared to see Sam, oblivious to the unfolding events in Tehran. Little did she know that, at the same time, a group of audacious ringleaders had orchestrated a chilling spectacle. Hundreds of students, fueled by a passion that bordered on fanaticism, converged on the U.S. Embassy, their march punctuated by the clinking of chain cutters discreetly concealed under the flowing chadors of some female participants.

With ominous determination, they breached the compound, their chants of "Don't be afraid" and "We don't mean any harm" a deceptive guise for the inhumane act unfolding. The embassy, a sovereign outpost on foreign soil, fell prey to this orchestrated invasion. The occupiers, exploiting the reluctance of the Marines to employ deadly force, overpowered the defenses, seizing control of the entire compound.

Six fortunate embassy personnel, absent from the compound executed a clandestine escape plan, managed to slip away from the clutches of the hostage-takers. However, for the rest, the nightmare had just begun—a harrowing 444 days of captivity.

In the face of this brazen act, President Carter, paralyzed by fear and indecision, failed to respond decisively, inadvertently emboldening the perpetrators and their tyrant regime. The news of the embassy occupation reverberated globally, prompting a mix of shock, outrage, and disbelief.

While some individuals, appalled by the blatant breach of international norms, voiced their condemnation, a disconcerting wave of support echoed in the streets. The ominous chant of "Death to America" gained traction among those who disregarded diplomatic conventions and international laws. The State Department, compelled to prioritize the safety of its citizens, urgently called for the evacuation of all U.S. nationals from the country.

In the aftermath of this hostile takeover, diplomatic relations between the two nations crumbled, severed on that fateful day. The embassy, once a symbol of international cooperation, had become a grim stage for a prolonged and tragic ordeal, leaving an indelible mark on the pages of history.

Chapter 36

As Sam stepped into the house, a palpable tension hung in the air, signaling that something significant had unfolded during the brief hours he was away. The atmosphere crackled with urgency, and before he could fully comprehend the situation, Bijan's stern voice pierced the silence, demanding swift action.

"Where have you been?" Bijan's words hung heavy. "Pack your stuff. We have to leave quickly."

Confused and unaware of the unfolding events, Sam's attention was abruptly seized by a television program. The screen unveiled a distressing scene—American Embassy staff, blindfolded and bound, led by a group proclaiming themselves as "The Muslim Students Followers of the Imam's Line."

Jacqueline, Sam's mother, sat in front of the TV, tears streaming down her face. Bewilderment etched across Sam's features, he questioned, "What's going on?"

As Jacqueline explained the grim situation, the weight of reality crashed over Sam. "We have to leave Iran immediately," she sobbed.

Sam's mind raced, grappling with the sudden upheaval. "I can't leave. I don't want to. I have a life here. What about my school? And Roxana's proposal—we can't just abandon that."

"I've already spoken to her mom. We'll go for her proposal when we return," Jacqueline replied, her voice heavy with the weight of their predicament.

The day, once filled with anticipation for Roxana's special day, now blurred before Sam's eyes. A line had been crossed, and the reality of irreversible change loomed. "I can't just leave her behind. I'm staying," Sam declared, his voice unwavering.

Bijan, understanding the gravity of Sam's internal struggle, placed a comforting hand on his shoulder. "I know it's hard to leave someone you love. They will free the hostages, and everything will return to normal. Call Roxana, assure her of this."

Caught in a web of conflicting emotions, Sam hesitated. His heart, bound to Roxana through an intimate encounter that felt like an unspoken pact, propelled him to make a crucial decision. Turning away from the disarray, he headed to make the call, the uncertain future hanging heavy in the air.

As Khomeini's words resonated on national TV, casting a shadow of uncertainty, Bijan understood the gravity of the situation when Khomeini called the it the "second revolution", and the American embassy was branded as "the American's spy den." Realizing that this unfriendly act wouldn't be swiftly resolved, he felt the urgency to secure the safety of his wife and children in the face of a looming war.

With a heavy heart, Bijan, using his connections, managed to secure three tickets on the Pan Am flight departing Tehran the next day. However, this decision meant he couldn't accompany his family to America, opting instead to ensure their safe departure from Tehran.

Meanwhile, Sam, grappling with the tumultuous turn of events, reached out to Mrs. Khalili over the phone. Her voice trembled with anxiety as she inquired about their departure plans.

"I'm still in shock. I don't know what to do. All I know is that Roxana and I want to be together," Sam confessed, his voice laden with emotion.

Concerned for Sam's well-being, Mrs. Khalili responded, "I want you to be well and safe, so you can take care of my daughter." Passing the phone to Roxana, she acknowledged the depth of their connection.

After the call Roxana slammed the phone down in frustration, couldn't comprehend the betrayal of the gentle and tolerant Islam she had learned about at school. "What brand of Islam is this? To take guests as hostages and humiliate them like this?" she exclaimed, searching for answers.

Her mother, attempting to soothe her daughter's anguish, reassured, "Not even infidels do such a thing. Be strong. Things always work out for the best." Despite the optimism in her voice, Roxana found herself overwhelmed by the injustice of it all.

"He said he might have no choice but to leave," Roxana cried into her hands. "What great sin did I commit to be punished like this?"

Her mother, breaking away from the societal norms, offered rare solace, "Come here, my dear." In an unprecedented move in Iran, she hugged Roxana tightly, wiping away her tears. "Go to his house and stay with him as long as you want." It was a poignant gesture, a mother's understanding that love transcends the barriers of tradition and uncertainty.

As Roxana was leaving, her heart weighed heavy with a tumultuous mix of emotions. The events of the day had unfolded like a nightmare, and the news of Sam's impending departure from the country had shattered the fragile dreams they had woven together. The US embassy takeover by radicals in Iran had cast an ominous shadow over their budding romance.

Just hours ago, they had shared an intimate moment, a tender union that had been fueled by the belief that they would soon be married. Moments ago the world had seemed so full of promise, as if their love could conquer any obstacle. Now, as she drove toward Sam, she couldn't help but replay those moments in her mind.

Roxana had given herself to Sam with a heart brimming with hope and trust, believing that their love would lead them to a blissful future together. But the reality of the situation had intruded upon their passionate encounter, and the impending separation seemed cruel and unfair.

Tears welled up in Roxana's eyes as she neared is house, her heart aching with a profound sense of loss. She had opened herself up to vulnerability, to love, and to the possibility of a shared life with Sam. Now, it felt as though the future they had envisioned was slipping away, torn apart by the forces of politics and unrest.

Chapter 37

The doorbell's chime echoed through the house, heralding Roxana's arrival with eyes that betrayed the weight of impending separation. Bijan, wearing a mask of reassurance, opened the door and enveloped her in a hug, a gesture that spoke of paternal care and understanding. "Everything's gonna be OK," he whispered, the words both a comforting lie and a desperate plea for solace. Roxana, summoning a fragile smile, ascended the stairs with hope flickering in her eyes.

In Sam's room, the air was heavy with a poignant mixture of love and impending departure. Amidst the haunting truth of their situation, Sam, flipping through photo albums, remarked, "It's amazing how fast your life changes. I was on top of the world this morning, and now I feel the world has collapsed on me."

Roxana, perched on the edge of his bed, noticed the freshly changed sheets, a subtle but tender gesture that touched her heart. "Tell me you changed the sheets yourself," she implored, tears tracing down her cheeks.

Sam, with a gentle nod, confessed, "I changed them before leaving this morning," and, leaning in, kissed away her teardrops.

As Roxana sobbed, her head found refuge on Sam's shoulder. "It's hard to see you leave again. Promise you will come back for me. They can't make me marry Nader. I'll wait for you."

"Look, I'm only packing for two weeks," Sam reassured, presenting his half-packed luggage in a feeble attempt to ease her heartache. "I'll be back before you miss me too much, and we'll get engaged right away. Now let me see that seductive smile of yours."

"I miss you already," Roxana admitted, a bittersweet smile gracing her lips. "The way I shared my love with you was reserved for my husband only. I consider you as my husband already."

"And I consider you as my wife," Sam declared, holding her hand with a tenderness that transcended their fleeting time together. "I want you to keep my memories until I come back." With that, he handed her his cherished photo album, a tangible piece of their shared moments, a testament to a love that defied the imminent separation.

Jacqueline, Ariana, and Sam embarked on a somber journey, leaving behind the familiar, unsure of when they would return. The airport, a scene of tearful farewells, echoed with the heaviness of impending separation. Relatives gathered, faces etched with sorrow, as the announcement to board the plane drew near.

Sam's aging grandmother, a fragile figure of heartbreak, spoke through tears, "I'm not going to live long enough to see you again." Sam, with a brave façade, consoled her, unaware that it would be their last encounter. If he had known the length of his absence, he might have cherished each moment, especially with his cousin, Ali, who would later fall in the war with Iraq.

Most of his time was spent with Roxana, a love that blossomed in the face of uncertainty. They, for the first time, displayed their affection unabashedly, disregarding judgmental eyes. As Sam sought final farewells, every warm hug intensified the reality of departure. He tried to stay strong, but when he turned to Roxana for their last goodbye, his stoic resolve crumbled, tears flowing freely in front of everyone.

Bijan, understanding the gravity of the moment, hugged his son and whispered, "No matter what, I'll take care of her," leaving Sam and Roxana alone to navigate the heart-wrenching farewell.

"Now I know our love is eternal," Roxana declared, witnessing Sam's tears for the first time, a testament to the depth of their connection. Yet, in the public eye, their physical expressions of love were restrained, a painful concession. Choking back tears, they settled for holding hands, their final words laden with the hope of a swift reunion.

Jacqueline and Ariana hugged Roxana, their goodbyes exchanged with heavy hearts. As they walked toward the gate, Roxana, with a desperate scream, broke free from decorum. She ran to Sam, tears streaming down, and embraced him in front of everyone. In that moment, they reassured each other of their unyielding love before reluctantly letting go.

As Sam, the love of her life, passed through the security check, he gradually faded from view, leaving behind an emptiness that echoed through the depths of Roxana's soul. The bustling airport, once filled with the warmth of shared moments, now felt desolate and cold.

While everyone else departed, Roxana remained, unable to tear herself away from the forlorn scene. Her face pressed against the frigid window, she stared, unblinking, at the departing runway, each passing moment further etching the pain of separation into her heart.

The airplane, carrying away not just Sam but also the dreams they had woven together, moved slowly into the distance. As it gained altitude, her tears, now a torrential cascade, mirrored the weight of her grief. Waving goodbye with a mixture of love and anguish, she followed the plane's trajectory until it vanished into the vastness of the sky.

"Goodbye, my love," she whimpered, the words a fragile farewell that hung heavy in the air. The strength that had sustained her until then began to wane, and with a heartbreaking surrender, she slid down to the floor, overcome by the overwhelming burden of sorrow. The cold tiles offered a stark contrast to the warmth that once radiated from their shared laughter and embraces.

The airport, now transformed into a solemn space, bore witness to the echoes of a love left behind. The air, heavy with unspoken words and the residue of lingering emotions, painted a poignant picture of heartache. Roxana's grief, palpable in the quiet aftermath, lingered like an enduring melody, a haunting reminder of a love that had departed with Sam, leaving only the hollowness of aching silence.

The memory of this day would forever be etched in Roxana's heart, a bittersweet reminder of a love that might never fully blossom. She longed for the day when they could be reunited, when the world would be a safer place for their love to flourish. Until then, she could only hold onto the memory of that day and the love that had ignited in the midst of uncertainty.

Chapter 38

After departing from Shiraz, the Larabi family found themselves navigating a tumultuous scene at Tehran's Mehrabad Airport on that fateful Monday, November 5, 1979. Their journey to America necessitated a connecting flight from Tehran, where chaos reigned supreme. The airport was a maelstrom of desperation, particularly among Americans frantic for a way out. They scrambled over one another, vying for the slightest opportunity to secure a seat on any outbound flight, indifferent to the cost.

In the midst of this frantic crowd, Dr. Larabi acted with a blend of desperation and calculation. Understanding the gravity of the situation, he meticulously placed a substantial sum of cash amidst the pages of their passports. This unspoken gesture, a silent plea for safe passage, was his strategic move as he handed over their travel documents to the ticket agent. His heart pounded with a mix of fear and hope, as he sought to ensure his family's escape from the turmoil that had engulfed the nation.

The agent, unyielding and curt, snatched the passports. " I doubt if you can get on," he declared callously. Rather than engage in argument, Dr. Larabi chose patience, hoping for a favorable outcome.

A subtle transformation crossed the agent's face as he discovered the cash. "Your tickets have been reconfirmed," he stated, a forced smile accompanying the assurance. With a perfunctory efficiency, he checked in their bags and handed over the precious boarding passes.

Jacqueline, Sam, and Ariana bid a heartfelt farewell to Bijan and navigated their way through the bustling airport to board the colossal Boeing 747 aircraft. As they embarked on their journey, the hopeful chatter of fellow passengers lingered in the air. "I hope the hostages get freed by Thanksgiving," one optimist remarked, unaware that the arduous wait would extend to 444 days, culminating on the day of Ronald Reagan's inauguration.

As Sam stepped onto the aircraft, his heart weighed heavy with a blend of emotions that threatened to overwhelm him. The collective sigh of relief from the other passengers as the last Pan Am flight out of Tehran, under the command of Captain William R. McDougal, ascended into the sky, seemed distant, drowned out by the deafening drumbeat of his own conflicted heart. He stole a glance out the window, watching Tehran's city lights fade into the distance, and with each passing mile, it felt as though he was leaving a piece of his soul behind.

His gaze wandered around, a stark reminder of Roxana's absence. The memory of her tearful eyes and the promises they had made to each other haunted him. As the aircraft ascended into the night sky, Sam couldn't help but feel a mixture of fear, sadness, and determination. Sadness for leaving the woman he loved behind, uncertain of when they would hold each other again. And determination to escape the chaos and turmoil that had gripped their nation, hoping that one day, he would return to a different Iran, one where they could finally be together.

Chapter 39

Amid the uncertainty and chaos, Jacqueline and her two children found themselves seeking refuge with her parents, clinging to the hope that normalcy would soon return. Yet, as days stretched into weeks, the elusive resolution seemed increasingly distant, and Sam began to grapple with the unsettling realization that their temporary refuge might be morphing into a more permanent situation.

In the midst of this upheaval, Ariana, thrust into the middle of the school year, navigated the challenges of a new Middle School. Encouragement from Sam's mother and grandparents echoed, urging him to consider applying to UCSD's premed program. However, Sam hesitated, harboring an aversion to following the path of countless Iranians who had immigrated to Southern California, yearning for a return home that now seemed improbable. The specter of an exile he never envisioned loomed large.

Faced with this new reality, Sam sought counsel from an immigration lawyer, driven by a singular purpose—to expedite Roxana's journey to America. The following morning, a phone call at the ungodly hour of 5:30 a.m. shattered the stillness. It was Roxana, her voice tinged with sadness, questioning whether he would ever return.

The weight of Roxana's words hung heavy in the air, a heartbreaking revelation that left Sam grasping for understanding. As Sam spoke of the possibility of him being with her in six months through a fiancée visa, Roxana's tearful admission shattered the fragile hope that had sustained them.

"I don't have six months to wait. I don't even have one," Roxana cried, her voice echoing with a sense of urgency that sent shivers through Sam's core. Her next words, delivered with a desolate tone, landed like a heavy blow. "Maybe you should forget about me, and I should learn how to endure a life without you."

Confused and desperate for clarity, Sam pleaded, "Why would you say that? What's another four or five months? We've waited this long."

But Roxana, burdened by a reality, revealed, "Time is not on my side. Besides, don't you know my father? He would never let me leave before getting married."

The ambiguity fueled Sam's confusion. "What do you mean time is not on your side?"

"If we can't be together right away, then there is no point in explaining it," Roxana uttered, the weight of her unspoken pain palpable in the air.

Desperate for answers, Sam implored, "I'm confused. Please stop crying and tell me what's going on."

"It's more difficult than you think. Promise you'll do what I'm going to ask you."

Feeling a growing sense of unease, Sam reluctantly agreed, "What's on your mind, my love? Just tell me."

"You must promise first."

"You're acting so weird. OK, I promise."

And then, like a cruel twist of fate, Roxana unfolded a heart-wrenching request, asking Sam to forget her. The words, laden with a profound sadness, reverberated through the conversation. "I want you to remember that you were the first love of my life, and you will always stay in my heart. But now I want you to go on with your life and forget about me. Promise you'll do that."

Sam, caught between love and confusion, grappled with the enormity of her request. "I know I promised, but I'm not sure if I can do that. Why are you doing this? What about your promise when you said, 'I'll wait for you?'"

In the silence that followed, Roxana, her voice heavy with emotion, pleaded, "Please don't make it any harder. I want you to know that I'd choose death over a life without you, but I want you to have a normal life. Don't try to contact me anymore."

In the haunting aftermath of Roxana's wrenching request, the silence on the other end of the line echoed through Sam's soul. The weight of her plea hung heavy in the air, a painful admission that their paths were irrevocably diverging. Undeterred by the emotional abyss that yawned before him, Sam, fueled by a love that refused to be silenced, persistently called her in a desperate bid for a shred of clarity.

However, each attempt to bridge the growing chasm between them was met with the haunting ring of an unanswered call, intensifying the torment that gripped Sam's heart. The persistent echoes of his unanswered cries seemed to reverberate through the void, a stark reminder of the love that once thrived but now teetered on the precipice of irreparable loss.

The crushing finality of the situation reached its zenith when Sam's father, a reluctant bearer of painful truths, revealed the bitter reality: Roxana was set to marry Nader. This revelation struck Sam like a thunderbolt, leaving him in a state of disbelief and agony. The dream they had nurtured, the promises made in the shadow of uncertainty, now shattered like delicate glass, leaving behind a mosaic of heartbreak.

In that moment, Sam found himself suspended in a grief-stricken limbo, caught between the echoes of their shared past and the harsh reality of an unwritten future. The phone, once a lifeline to Roxana's voice, became a silent witness to the unraveling of a love that, against all odds, had slipped away, leaving Sam to navigate the wreckage of a shattered connection and the unfathomable pain of an unanswered call.

Chapter 40

Now, let's fast-forward to the latter half of 1999, where we find Sam engrossed in Bahram's jewelry store. In this momentous reunion, after two decades, Sam and Roxana locked eyes, blissfully unaware of the world around them. Little did they know, their reunion was about to become a focal point of unforeseen consequences.

As fate would have it, Nicole and Farhad entered the scene, their entrance timed with the precision of a playwright's pen. Nicole, brimming with eagerness and excitement, intended to whisk Sam away to the adjacent shop, eager to showcase a set of matching earrings and bracelet. However, as her eyes fell upon her husband, she was met not with the anticipated joy but with a strange and delicate stir of emotions between Sam and another woman.

Farhad, witnessing the unfolding scene, felt a surge of urgency and attempted to warn his friend. Shouting a cordial greeting, "Hello, Mr. Bahram!" he tried to capture Sam's attention, but the vines of the moment had already wrapped themselves around Sam and Roxana, binding them in a shared history.

A womanly instinct, sharp as a dagger, stirred within Nicole. The atmosphere crackled with unspoken tension, and the seed of suspicion, planted in that fleeting moment, began to take root. Little did they know, the threads of their lives were weaving into a complex tapestry, and the choices made in this encounter would reverberate through the chapters yet to unfold.

Farhad's call acted as a timely diversion, redirecting Sam's attention just in time to catch the uncomfortable stance of Nicole. The air hummed with unspoken tension as Sam, adept at navigating emotional currents, greeted them with a casual smile and a nonchalant wave. However, beneath the veneer of pleasantries, a subtle dance of trust and distrust was beginning to unfold.

Roxana, sensing the undercurrents, chose a quiet exit, her head lowered as she slipped away without bidding farewell to Bahram. Sam, acutely aware of her departure, tracked her with a sidelong glance. As Roxana reached for the door, a poignant twist of fate made her lock eyes with Nicole, tears painting a silent narrative of pain.

In that charged moment, Nicole, observing the emotional tableau before her, couldn't help but wonder about the mysterious woman who had captured Sam's attention. Was she the same woman he had spoken of, the one whose union with him had been thwarted by fate's capricious hand?

Farhad, the sage friend, attempted to diffuse the tension. "I'm sorry, but Nicole wants to put a dent in your wallet. She saw a set next door," he informed Sam, attempting to steer the conversation away from the palpable tension.

Sam, ever the loving husband, seized Nicole's hand, but the gesture felt different, tinged with an unfamiliar texture. "It's me who needs her permission," he declared, his grip on her hand tightening. "Everything I have is hers. I love you more than anything. You deserve anything you wish for," he whispered into her ear, attempting to drown out the echoes of memories resurfacing from his past with Roxana.

As they exited Bahram's store, promises to return echoing in the air, the atmosphere between Sam and Nicole had subtly shifted. Nicole, once captivated by the allure of a jewelry set, now seemed to keep a calculated distance from Sam, her demeanor a delicate dance of curiosity and guarded emotions.

Farhad, astute as ever, couldn't help but play the role of the candid friend. A swift smack to the back of Sam's head was accompanied by words heavy with both concern and reproach. "Oh my god, that was Roxana, wasn't it? What are you doing, looking at another man's wife? Whatever happened between you two and how it ended is in the past. Don't forget that she's married now, and so are you."

Sam, attempting to downplay the encounter, protested, "we didn't even say a word to each other. What are you talking about?"

"That's what I'm talking about," Farhad retorted, pointing discreetly to Nicole. "Are you that oblivious not to see how upset she is? She saw how you two were staring at each other."

In the tumultuous wake of emotions, Sam, seemingly lost in the memory of Roxana, admitted, "She's still so beautiful."

"You should forget about how she looks. Does Nicole know anything about you two?" Farhad pressed.

"I told her everything a long time ago. She probably doesn't remember it," Sam replied.

Farhad's response was laced with a mix of exasperation and wisdom. "Are you really that naive? Of course, she remembers. Women don't forget anything."

Feeling the urgency to address the brewing storm, Sam confessed, "I have to say something before she asks me who that woman was."

The tension lingered as they eventually settled on purchasing a necklace, bracelet, and earring set—a momentary distraction from the underlying currents. After giving Mrs. Kamali a ride home, Sam seized what seemed like the opportune moment to casually mention Roxana, hoping to alleviate Nicole's unease.

"Hey Mom, I saw an old classmate of mine at Bahram's store," Sam casually injected into the conversation. Jacqueline, Ariana, and Farhad occupied the back seat, their curiosity piqued. "I wouldn't have recognized her if Bahram hadn't said her name out loud."

"Who?" Jacqueline inquired.

"Khalili," Sam replied, mentioning only Roxana's last name.

Ariana and Jacqueline exchanged surprised and confused glances. Sam, attempting to downplay the encounter, continued, "however, she did not recognize me. How could she after so many years?"

Nicole, keeping her gaze ahead, interjected, "Oh honey, she knew exactly who you were. Her eyes said it all." She briefly turned to Sam, her hand resting on his on the steering wheel. "What was her first name again?"

In a subtle attempt to shift focus, Farhad interjected, "Who are you talking about?"

Ignoring the attempt to change the subject, Sam mentioned Roxana's first name casually, as if she were an inconsequential figure. "Do you remember Roxana?"

"Are you sure? How come I didn't see her? You're probably mistaken. You've been away for too long," Farhad interjected, attempting to deflect.

"Roxana," Nicole whispered almost reverently, the syllables carrying a whispered acknowledgment of a name etched in Sam's history. "Small world," she added, a wistful undertone hinting at the intricate tapestry of interconnected lives. In those words, a nuanced understanding unfolded, as if the past had woven its threads into the present, leaving a trail of untold stories and unexplored emotions.

A taunting silence draped over the car for the remainder of the way. Sam, now caught between the haunting memories of Roxana and the palpable hurt in Nicole's eyes, wished he had not turned toward his past love. The replay of Roxana's reaction after recognizing him echoed in his mind, gradually replacing the image of the teenage girl with the woman she had become. Mortified by the turmoil within him, Sam grappled with conflicting emotions—guilt over causing anguish to Nicole and the incessant curiosity about the unanswered questions from his past. Was it the intensity of their breakup that lingered, or did one never truly forget their first love? The turmoil within him mirrored the complexities of love, history, and the persistent echoes of a past that refused to stay silent.

Chapter 41

In the dimly lit corner of Bahram's store, an air of caution hung heavy as Bahram voiced his concern. "Are you certain you know what you're doing?" he inquired, his eyes narrowing with worry. "This is her phone number, but you should tear this paper and erase her from your thoughts."

Sam held the paper with her number, a tangible link to a forbidden connection. His gaze lingered on the digits, contemplating the weight of Bahram's words. The flickering light seemed to cast shadows on the precipice of a decision.

"You're playing with fire," Bahram cautioned, his words resonating with the gravity of the situation. "The punishment for entanglement with a married woman is death by stoning now."

A shiver ran down Sam's spine as the stark reality settled in. "You're right. I didn't return here to play with fire." With a decisive motion, Sam tore the paper into irreparable fragments, severing the tangible tie to a potentially perilous liaison.

"I knew you would have done the right thing," Bahram affirmed, a sense of relief coloring his words. "Not only for your sake and hers, but also for your families."

"I'm sure you won't breathe a word of this to anyone," Sam pressed, seeking assurance.

"Of course not," Bahram vowed, a solemn promise hanging in the air.

As Sam clasped his friend's hand and departed the store, he skillfully veiled the truth: despite the paper's destruction, her seven-digit allure had etched itself effortlessly into the recesses of his memory. An easy task for him, those digits became a clandestine secret, carefully concealed from Bahram's watchful gaze, a silent pact between Sam's consciousness and the remnants of a torn paper.

Chapter 42

On a nondescript Monday morning, the sun cast its golden hues on a seemingly ordinary day for Roxana. She went about her routine, preparing breakfast for Nader and their son, ushering them out the door with tender kisses, unaware of the clandestine observer across the street—Sam, hidden in the shadows of his car. Patiently, he waited for Nader's departure before summoning the courage to dial Roxana's number. The phone felt heavy in his hand as he hesitated, repeatedly disconnecting before the final digit was pressed. Eventually, resolve won over hesitation, and the phone rang in the stillness.

"Hello," a woman's voice responded, the echoes of time reverberating in the air. "Hello," she repeated, a soft acknowledgment of the connection spanning two decades.

Sam, overwhelmed by emotions, found himself speechless, gently disconnecting. Minutes passed, the weight of unspoken words pressing on him. Gathering all the courage he could muster, he dialed once more.

"Hello," Roxana answered, the familiarity of their secret code breaking the silence.

"Is this the Aslani's residence?" Sam uttered, the words etched in history, dormant for twenty years but rekindled in that moment. Roxana, swept by a torrent of emotions, struggled to respond, uttering, "I'm sorry, but…" The words hung in the air, her mind a whirlwind of memories, leaving her silent.

"Hi, Roxana. How are you?" Sam's voice, a lifeline to the past, made her catch her breath. With a voice trembling with emotion, she whispered, "Saam?"

"Yes, it's me. I hope I didn't catch you at a bad time."

"Does your wife know you're calling me?" Roxana's inquiry cut through the tender reconnection, revealing the complexities beneath the surface.

Caught off guard, Sam stammered, "I think the word you're looking for is no," she exclaimed.

"I'm sorry. I didn't mean to make you uneasy," Sam apologized, his shock palpable.

"How did you get my number anyway?" Roxana's question exposed the fragility of their clandestine conversation.

"I have my connections," Sam replied, attempting to lighten the mood.

Roxana, aware of the impending turmoil, cautioned, "Do you know what kind of mess you are putting me in? What if your so-called connection tells someone? You know how fast news gets around in this town."

"No one knows that I have your number or that I am calling you," Sam reassured, trying to calm the tempest within her. "I know you belong to someone else now. I also know it's not right, but you've been on my mind since the other day, and I had to hear your voice."

"Should that justify a married man calling a married woman?" Roxana's firm question echoed the moral complexities.

"Maybe I made a mistake calling you. I have some unanswered questions about us, and what was I supposed to do with all these memories that have rushed into my head?" Sam, caught in the undertow of emotions, revealed his inner turmoil.

"I don't know. But I know we should end our conversation right now. Old memories only bring more pain. Imagine that I answered all of your questions. How is that going to change your life now?"

"It probably wouldn't. Maybe it was just an excuse to see you."

"Now you want to see me? So cliché, just like a Hollywood movie, it always starts with talking, which leads up to their first meeting, and you know the rest. But they weren't supposed to talk in the first place. At the end, they'll end up not only hurting themselves but also the people around them."

"I know you're right. I should just say goodbye," Sam admitted, his heart heavy with the weight of reality.

"That was Nicole in the store, right?" Roxana's unexpected revelation caught Sam off guard. "How do you know her name?" he asked.

"I told you, the news gets around fast in this town. You are right, we should say goodbye." With those words, Roxana hung up, leaving Sam in the silence that followed. She had maintained composure throughout their conversation. However, the moment she ended the call, her strength crumbled, and tears streamed down her face. With eyes blurred by sorrow, she tenderly traced the outlines of framed family pictures adorning the room. Selecting one capturing a moment of maternal embrace with her infant son, she clutched it tightly to her chest. Approaching the window, she gazed into the distance, unaware that Sam, from across the street, witnessed the raw vulnerability etched across her features. Sam's heart ached with the realization that the echoes of their shared past had left indelible imprints on both their souls. He longed to call again, to comfort her in the midst of her tears, but he resisted, understanding that sometimes, letting go is the hardest part of love. He only drove away when it became evident that she wouldn't return to the window, leaving behind the fragments of a reunion that lingered in the air like a poignant melody.

Chapter 43

"Where did you go so early in the morning?" Nicole inquired as Sam stepped through the door. The scent of breakfast lingered in the air, a reminder of the shared family moments awaiting him.

"Just went out for a drive," Sam replied, the weight of a lie etching shame across his features. He hesitated, a fleeting doubt crossing Nicole's eyes, as if curiosity and suspicion danced on the edges of her thoughts. "I had to clear my head before calling Shervin to see what news he's got for me."

****

In the high-stakes realm of corporate maneuvering, Genesys Inc. found itself at the precipice of a game-changing contract with Emirates Genomics the prior year. The looming specter of a Dutch competitor, armed with a cutting-edge machine far superior to Genesys', cast an imposing shadow over their ambitious endeavors. Sensing the need for decisive action, Sam, a key player in Genesys, resolved to take fate into his own hands.

With the Dubai skyline shimmering on the horizon, Sam embarked on a journey to the heart of opportunity. His destination: a pivotal meeting with Emirates Genomics that could tilt the scales in their favor. Recognizing the power of personal connections in the intricate dance of negotiations, Sam reached out to Shervin, an old ally whose expertise had proven invaluable in navigating similar treacherous waters in the past.

As the plane touched down in Dubai, Shervin's reassuring presence at the airport offered a glimpse of orchestrated confidence. Amidst the bustling international hub, Shervin conveyed that every detail had been meticulously handled. The impending meeting with the sheiks, seemingly a mere formality, carried the weight of strategic finesse.

Shervin leaned in closer, his voice dropping to a whisper that carried a conspiratorial weight. As he unraveled the intricacies of their latest endeavor, he revealed the shadowy figure at its heart - an enigmatic middleman known only as 'The Broker'. The price for The Broker's influence was steep, a staggering six-digit sum, but the promise it held was immense. Shervin's eyes gleamed with a mix of excitement and apprehension as he spoke of the clandestine meetings and encrypted messages that had become their norm.

The atmosphere in the room grew thick with tension, both acutely aware of the risks involved. This was no ordinary business venture; it had evolved into a high-stakes gambit, teetering on the edge of legality. The revelation that Emirate Genomics had ties to powerful political circles only added to the gravity of the situation, the weight of potential consequences hanging over them like a sword of Damocles.

Their mission, initially a straightforward contract negotiation, had transformed into a complex web of intrigue and hidden agendas. Now, it was not just about securing a deal but navigating the treacherous waters of power and influence. The silent question on everyone's mind was clear: were the rewards worth the perilous dance they were about to perform?

A year had passed since that fateful conversation, yet the threads of their meticulously crafted plan now seemed to fray, each strand unraveling like a delicate house of cards. In the hushed stillness of his room in Shiraz, Sam's pulse echoed the frenzied beat of his thoughts. Outside, the tranquil view of their lush garden stood in stark contrast to the storm of confusion brewing within him—a clandestine dance of betrayal and suspense playing out against the backdrop of an otherwise serene morning.

The phone's ring sliced through the silence, a harbinger of impending revelations. "I hope you've had enough time to make sense of this mess," Sam said, his voice steady but laced with a tinge of urgency.

The air was thick with unspoken tension, their conversation loaded with the gravity of a secret now dangerously close to being exposed. Shervin, ever the master of composure, spoke with a calm that belied the chaos of the situation. "Well, first I must tell you, someone at Genesys harbors a deep animosity towards you. In fact, it's more than dislike; it's outright hatred. The Emirates have intercepted every detailed contact between us. Fortunately, you've never directly communicated with The Broker," he revealed, his words painting a picture of a treacherous landscape they were navigating.

Sam's response was tinged with frustration and a simmering sense of betrayal. "You wouldn't even tell me his name," he retorted, the undercurrents of anger palpable in his tone.

"Now you understand why. My profession demands such secrecy. Thankfully, the payoff came directly from me, leaving no trail back to you. But it's clear now, someone has been keeping a close watch over you. The sheiks are thirsty for blood, and as for The Broker, he remains as elusive as Keyser Söze, impossible to track. I've been informed that the informant had two conditions: ensure the deal with Genesys proceeds, and secondly, to exert pressure on Genesys to terminate your position," Shervin continued, methodically laying out the intricate web of deception and intrigue that now threatened to entangle Sam's professional life.

"That doesn't make any sense. They want me fired but keep the steady profits. It sounds personal," Sam thought aloud, his mind grappling with the conflicting motives at play.

"It also sounds like a good business manipulation," Shervin said, his voice carrying the weight of experience. "Figure out who would benefit the most if you left the company. I would imagine he is a high-ranking stockholder. See if anyone approaches you to acquire your shares or blackmail you into selling them," Shervin advised, his words a roadmap through the labyrinth of corporate machinations.

"Are you gonna be in any kind of trouble?" Sam asked, a thread of concern weaving through his words.

"What can they do? Fire me? Or refund my bribe money? No, I'm OK. Those sheiks had some money to burn, and we helped them do it. Do you really think they needed those machines anyway? They're just somewhere collecting dust," Shervin lightheartedly remarked, a touch of nonchalance masking the calculated risks they had taken.

"Then why are they so upset about this bribery thing? I thought they were upset about getting ripped off with the slower machines," Sam inquired, seeking clarity amid the murkiness of the situation.

Shervin recalled the iconic line from "The Godfather": "They don't want to look ridiculous, and you made them look ridiculous—now that they stand exposed," Shervin explained, a wry understanding of corporate dynamics coloring his words.

"I have to figure out who this guy is," a resolute determination seeping into Sam's tone as he faced the challenge head-on.

"Just deny everything. I personally think they would do you a favor if they fired you. Just relax and enjoy life. It's not like you need more money," Shervin's words offering a momentary respite, a glimmer of perspective in the midst of turmoil. "But I'll keep you posted," he assured, a silent promise of camaraderie in the face of the storm.

Chapter 44

On a crisp Wednesday morning, the 11th of August, the Sam Larabi family embarked on a journey to the enchanting city of Isfahan, drawn by the celestial allure of a total solar eclipse. Bijan and Jacqueline remained back devotedly engaged in orchestrating the impending wedding of Ariana in Shiraz.

Situated approximately 500 kilometers north of Shiraz, Isfahan stood as a picturesque haven perfectly aligned with the trajectory of the eclipse. An influx of spectators from every corner of the globe converged upon this historic city, eager to bear witness to the celestial spectacle.

Their journey to Isfahan became a tapestry of historical exploration, as the family paused to explore the remnants of ancient Achaemenid palaces in Pasargad and Persepolis. Pasargad, once the illustrious capital of Persia during the reign of Cyrus the Great and his son Cambyses, unfolded its storied past before their eyes. Intriguingly, Cyrus' tomb bore the local moniker "Prophet Solomon's mother's grave," a shrewd renaming, perhaps, to safeguard the site from potential desecration by Arab invaders. The echoes of bygone eras resonated with the family as they traversed the rich tapestry of Persian history on their celestial pilgrimage.

Persepolis stands as a testament to the magnificence of Iran's historical legacy, unrivaled in grandeur. Its genesis can be traced back to the ambitious vision of King Darius the Great in the sixth century BC, marking the commencement of a construction endeavor that would result in a sprawling complex spanning over 1.2 million square feet.

An architectural marvel, Persepolis boasts sixty-foot stone columns, colossal statues depicting both humans and animals, and intricately carved tombs of the kings nestled in the surrounding mountains. The sheer scale of the structures exudes an aura of grandiosity, reflecting the might of the empire that once flourished within its boundaries.

Surprisingly absent are fortification walls, an omission that serves as a silent testimony to the undeniable power wielded by the ancient empire. Intricate carvings of soldiers and immortal guards grace colossal stone blocks, with none depicted in a defensive stance, their swords and spears sheathed.

Inscribed narratives unveil the vibrant tapestry of the kingdom's unity, portraying members of diverse tribes offering gifts to their sovereign on the auspicious New Year's Day—a tradition rooted in antiquity, aligning with the arrival of spring.

Regrettably, the echoes of Persepolis' glory were marred by the ravages of history. In 330 BC, Alexander and his army, in a tumultuous act of conquest, plundered and set ablaze this majestic palace, forever altering the course of its storied existence.

Upon reaching Isfahan, Sam, Nicole, and the children immersed themselves in the rich history of the city, exploring its venerable landmarks. The clock approached 3:30 p.m., leading them to the breathtaking expanse of Imam Square—a place that once bore the name Shah Square in a bygone era, destined, perhaps, for another name transformation in the future.

Shah Square, encircled by historic palaces, mosques, and remnants of the Safavid Dynasty's bazaar, stands as the second-largest square globally, eclipsed only by Tiananmen Square in China. A place steeped in history, the square's grand arena was once a stage for spirited polo games, the king himself observing the athletic spectacle from the terrace of his palace.

On this particular day, the square pulsed with vibrant energy, throngs of visitors converging to witness the impending celestial event. At every turn, street peddlers seized the opportunity, offering specialized glasses to safely capture the beauty of the imminent eclipse, a modern contrast to the historic echoes resonating within the square's storied grounds.

"Be careful, don't gaze directly at the sun," Sam cautioned, handing tinted glasses to Nicole and the children.

"Look, it's already in front of the sun," Cameron exclaimed, his eyes tracing the celestial dance.

"Oh my god, he's right. They're overlapping," Nicole shared, her voice infused with genuine excitement.

"Why isn't it dark yet?" Tara inquired, curiosity tinting her words.

"You'll have to be patient until the moon completely veils the sun. That's when the magic unfolds—everything will plunge into darkness, and the stars will emerge," Sam explained, drawing from his experiences in far and near corners of the world where he had witnessed the same awe-inspiring phenomena.

As the dark side of the moon inched across the sun's face, a transformative hush settled over the surroundings. At 4:30 p.m., the majority of the sun's luminous surface succumbed to the lunar interloper. A gradual descent into darkness ensued, the air carrying a discernible chill, and the streetlights, unwittingly deceived, flickered to life.

Then, at the precise moment of 4:32:42 the culmination of celestial alignment transpired—the total eclipse. A profound silence enveloped the expansive square, each onlooker captivated by this extraordinary, once-in-a-lifetime spectacle. The moon, resembling a colossal obsidian disk, seamlessly cloaked the radiant sun, casting an otherworldly aura over the gathered multitude.

With a sense of reverence, Sam removed his glasses, allowing his gaze to ascend to the darkened expanse above. "That's Venus," he declared, tracing the arc of the bright celestial entity in the sky. "And there, on the opposite side of the veiled sun, is Mercury," he added, pointing to the distant planet. "These rare moments, gift us with this exceptional view."

While Sam unveiled the cosmic wonders, Nicole and the children remained transfixed by the sun's gradual reemergence. In a mere minute and a half, at the precise juncture of 4:34:15, the sun, seemingly in haste, pierced through the other side of the moon. It burst forth, its radiant beams dispelling the celestial darkness as if it were a mere ephemeral veil.

As the sun reclaimed its celestial throne, its rays, akin to a gentle breath, extinguished the stars in the firmament—each one succumbing like flickering candles in a breeze, dissolving into the backdrop of the rekindled day.

Amidst the celestial spectacle, Sam's phone chimed, pulling him from the enchanting eclipse. A shadow passed across his features as he answered the call, his eyes briefly clouded with concern.

"Hey Sam, it's Farhad. Listen, I don't want to alarm you, but your father's not feeling great." Farhad's voice carried a note of concealed worry.

Sam's heart skipped a beat. "What's wrong? Is he going back to the hospital?"

"No, nothing that dire. But you should come back if you can," Farhad urged, a hint of urgency threading his words.

Before Sam could respond, the call waiting tone beeped intrusively. "I have another call," he said quickly. "I'll call you right back."

Switching lines, Sam's voice trembled with apprehension, half-expecting to hear more bad news, perhaps from his mother or father. Instead, a soft, familiar voice floated through the line, "Did you see the kite stars when it got dark?"

Sam felt a jolt of recognition. He instinctively stepped away from Nicole, his gaze still fixed on the distant horizon. "Did your guiding star remind you of anyone?" Roxana continued, almost in a whisper. Unlike the last phone call her tone now friendly and warm.

"lately, I don't need stars to be reminded of you." Sam replied, his voice tinged with nostalgia.

"Still the sweet talker, huh," Roxana teased gently. "When are you returning from Isfahan?"

A playful smile curled at the corners of Sam's lips. "And what gives you the impression that I'm in Isfahan?"

"I remember everything about you, Saam. The boy I knew wouldn't miss this for the world."

Nicole's soft inquiry broke through his thoughts. "Who is it?"

Quickly covering the receiver, Sam lied smoothly, "It's Farhad, honey. Just checking in on us." He turned away, a knot of guilt tightening in his stomach.

Roxana's voice turned soft, yet probing. "I didn't mean to make you lie to your honey."

"Why are you calling now? After all this time? And how did you get my number?" Sam's tone was a mix of confusion and accusation.

"I have my connections too. So, when will you be back?" Roxana persisted.

Sam hesitated. "Why do you ask?"

"I have something of yours to return," she said cryptically.

"Where should we meet? I can make it back by tonight."

"Tomorrow. Do you remember my father's pomegranate garden?"

A flood of memories rushed back to Sam. "Of course, I remember. That's where I..."

"Easy, tiger," Roxana interrupted with a laugh. "A simple 'yes' will do. Let's meet at eleven."

Ending the call, Sam turned back towards Nicole, his mind racing.

The impending return to Shiraz bore the weight of unspoken truths, and as they retreated from the eclipse-lit square, the enigma of Sam's life unfurled in the shadows of fleeting celestial wonders. The journey back, both physical and emotional, promised revelations and challenges, weaving a narrative as intricate as the constellations above.

As the journey back to Shiraz unfolded, the oppressive silence between Sam and Nicole weighed heavier than the miles they traversed. Breaking the uneasy quietude, Nicole's voice cut through the air, laden with a mix of curiosity and an unspoken worry.

"Who was the first caller then?" she inquired, her eyes betraying a longing for reassurance. "I mean, before the call waiting?"

Sam, caught off guard by the unexpected question, fabricated a response with practiced ease. "It was Shervin," he lied, his words hanging in the air like a fragile illusion. The trust that once bound them now seemed to dissolve, leaving a palpable void. "He had some questions."

Nicole, her fingers gently running through Sam's hair, sought solace in the concocted tale. Desperation lingered in her touch, a silent plea for the deception to be real. Yet, beneath her hopeful exterior, an instinctual skepticism painted a darker narrative.

"How do you feel?" she asked, her touch a delicate dance between seeking comfort and probing truth.

"Not so sure," Sam replied tersely. A chasm widened between them, a tangible rift born from the lies he wove. The weight of deception hung heavy, and he sensed the fragile threads of trust snapping, leaving him ensnared in a web of his own making. As they neared Shiraz, Sam's mind fixated on the impending meeting with

Roxana, a battle between his desire for innocence and the unsettling awareness of the choices he was making. The internal struggle mirrored the quiet turmoil of the journey, leaving Sam adrift in the dissonance of right and wrong.

Chapter 45

The door creaked open, disrupting the heavy silence that clung to the house like an unwelcome guest. Sam's entrance brought a somber acknowledgment from Jacqueline, Ariana, and Farhad, their quiet greetings hanging in the air.

"How's Dad doing?" Sam inquired, his voice a fragile thread in the muted atmosphere.

"He's doing better now. He's sleeping," Jacqueline responded, her words carrying the weight of recent worry. "He ran out of breath this afternoon. His body was covered with cold sweat."

"That doesn't sound good," Nicole remarked, concern etching her features. "Did he have any sharp pain in his chest? Maybe I should take a look."

"No, it wasn't a heart attack," Jacqueline reassured, leading Sam and Nicole to the nook. "Dr. Mir stopped by earlier and examined him. His condition is worsening daily."

"Be hopeful," Nicole urged, her words a gentle offering of solace. "We must take him to the States. I guarantee he'll get the best treatment."

"His last wish is to see Ariana's wedding. He wants her to be happy and settled while he's still alive," Jacqueline revealed, the weight of unfulfilled dreams casting a shadow over the room.

"There is only one week left till the wedding, I assume everything is going as planned," Sam commented, his voice tinged with a mix of practicality and a desire for reassurance.

"Farhad's doing his best. He said the invitation cards will be ready tomorrow morning. We've already invited everyone by phone, and tomorrow we can send the cards out," Jacqueline shared, the preparations for joy contrasted against the impending sorrow.

"Everything is going to be OK. It's late. You should go to sleep and be with Dad," Sam gently suggested, a weary acknowledgment of the reality they faced.

Exhausted from their long journey, they sought solace atop the rooftop, allowing the fatigue to overshadow their customary exchanges about stars and constellations. As the night enveloped them in a silent embrace, they yielded to sleep's call, a collective surrender that left a tangible heaviness of unarticulated feelings and thoughts hovering in the quiet recesses of their minds, unspoken yet deeply felt. This unspoken emotional burden lingered, marking the night with a profound yet silent introspection.

****

The morning unfolded with Farhad's announcement carving a tangible marker in the day's narrative. "I just got off the phone from the print shop," he declared after breakfast. "Invitation cards are ready."

Sam seized the opportunity like a lifeline, volunteering to pick up the cards. His intentions were twofold—masked beneath the guise of a mundane task lay the desire to escape the house. Armed with the address, he navigated his way to the print shop. The cards, collected swiftly, became both a tangible burden and a gateway to the impending rendezvous with Roxana.

Before heading to the designated meeting place, Sam made a deliberate detour to a flower shop. A bouquet of long-stemmed red roses, carefully chosen, now sat beside him in the car. The crimson blooms held the weight of old memories, memories that had been dormant but were now rushing back as he approached the rendezvous spot. The very place where she once promised to love him for the rest of their lives.

As he reached the indicated address, the landscape seemed transformed. Where once stood clay walls and fruit trees, now loomed a large house at the garden's entrance. Sam parked the car in the middle of the alley, a momentary confusion settling over him as he surveyed the altered surroundings. It was a different scene from the one etched in his memories.

Amidst this uncertainty, his phone stirred to life, a call from Roxana breaking the silence. "Come in," her voice, a blend of invitation and enigma, resonated through the phone as the imposing gates of the garden swung open, ushering Sam into a realm where past and present collided with the weight of unanswered questions.

As Sam eased his car into the garden, the imposing figures of two large German Shepherds accompanied his every move. The atmosphere hung thick with anticipation as he cautiously parked, reluctant to step out while the vigilant dogs circled displaying their formidable canines.

The tension eased as the dogs bounded toward the building upon Roxana's call, their departure granting Sam the freedom to exit the car. He approached warily, thoughts racing about the choice of his first words. Roxana, unbound by the constraints of Islamic covering, stood before him, a vision of stunning elegance in her casual attire. Her hair, meticulously styled, framed a face that time had only enhanced, not diminished. Radiant beauty and an alluring figure, resolute against the passage of years, greeted him.

A friendly smile adorned her face, pulling him closer with an irresistible magnetic force. Sam walked toward her, each step a dance of uncertainty and longing, until he stood mere inches away. Their eyes locked, hazel meeting hazel, as a surge of unspoken emotions and the weight of emotions lay palpable between them.

Sam extended the bouquet, each flower a silent testament to the multitude of unvoiced emotions swirling between them. "These are for you," he murmured, his voice a soft undercurrent of nostalgia and yearning.

Roxana's eyes shimmered with a complex dance of feelings as she accepted the gesture. "Thank you, they're beautiful," she replied, her voice a delicate blend of warmth and restraint, their fingers lingering in a momentary waltz of touch.

"Step inside, I have something for you," Roxana's invitation was laced with an enigmatic formality, a veil draping the once-familiar intimacy between them.

"Truthfully, seeing you was my real anticipation," Sam confessed, his words tinged with a hopeful vulnerability, seeking to bridge the growing chasm of time and choices between them.

Roxana's expression tightened, a fortress rising in her gaze. "Please, let's not unravel old threads. I intend to return something of yours, marking an end to... whatever this is," her voice was a definitive closing of a chapter long read.

"I scarcely recognized this place," Sam remarked, eyes scanning the villa, echoes of a life they might have shared whispering in the corners.

"My father's gift for my wedding," Roxana revealed, her words unveiling slices of a life pieced together in his absence. "We escape here on Fridays, away from the city crowd."

Sam's laugh was a shadow of regret. "So, this could have been ours?"

"Many things could have been, if not for fears and faraway choices," Roxana's reply was a gentle yet piercing reminder of his escape.

"I never wanted your wealth, Roxana. It was you, only ever you," Sam's defense was a quiet plea, a flicker of the old flame struggling against the winds of change.

"We are not here to exhume past lives," Roxana's tone severed the growing branches of what-if's, her stance immovable as the history they shared settled around them like dust, a testament to what once was and what could no longer be.

Inside, Roxana gestured toward an enigmatic box perched on the table, its presence heavy with unspoken narratives. "There it is," she announced, her voice a mix of detachment and a subtle, untraceable emotion.

Sam approached the box, a simple container yet so laden with implications, a silent custodian of their shared history. Lifting the lid, he was greeted by an old photo album, its pages a mosaic of laughter, love, and lost dreams. It was the same album he'd left with Roxana, a parting gift filled with moments frozen in time, on a day when farewells felt like a temporary pause.

His fingers traced the edges of the album as he sank into the chair, each photograph a doorway to a past drenched in sunlight and innocence. Roxana watched him, her presence a blend of warmth and distance, as he was momentarily lost in the sea of memories.

"It's not that I grew tired of these faces, these moments," Roxana commented, her voice threading through the quiet room as she joined him. "But it's yours to revisit, to hold."

Sam barely registered her words, his focus tethered to the images that danced before his eyes. "Yes, thank you," he murmured, his mind echoing with the laughter and whispers of years gone by.

Roxana leaned closer, her gaze softening as she pointed to a particular photo. "It doesn't feel like it's been that long since you gave this to me," she murmured, her voice trailing off as she touched the picture of them together, young and unburdened, beside the motorcycle that had been their steed on countless adventures.

Sam paused at that photo, their smiles immortalized, their spirits entwined in a carefree embrace. "This was our last picture," he noted, the memory vivid and aching.

Roxana's smile was a wistful curve of lips, her eyes shimmering with an unshed melancholy. "Those days... they were the happiest," she confessed, her voice a soft whisper of longing and regret. The album lay between them, a bridge over a river of time, laden with the sweet, sorrowful weight of remembrance.

"Then why did you walk away from us, I think you owe me the answer?" Sam's voice broke the stillness, his question an ache in the silence.

Roxana's stance was resolute, yet a flicker of something indefinable passed through her eyes. "I owe you no explanations, Saam. It's best you take these memories and headed home before your wife gets worried."

Sam's frustration simmered beneath his words. "Why the bitterness towards Nicole? After all, it was you who left, who moved on first."

Roxana's gaze was unwavering, her voice steady yet not unkind. "My feelings towards Nicole are irrelevant. You've built a life, yet here you are, seeking... what, exactly?"

"I might ask you the same," he countered, his voice a mix of accusation and a deeper, unspoken yearning.

"This isn't about battling old ghosts," Roxana's voice softened, a quiet plea underlying her firm words. "Please, take the album and leave the past where it belongs."

Sam hesitated, his eyes lingering on the photo, their younger selves captured in a moment of unguarded happiness. "I don't think you just called me here just to return a few faded photographs. Look at us here, wrapped in each other's world. We were everything to one another. Don't pretend you've simply erased that."

With a heavy sigh, Sam closed the album, his touch lingering on the cover as if to imprint the feeling one last time. "If you want me gone, I'll go. But it's clear, despite everything, part of you is still with me, just as part of me lingers with you."

With those final words, he picked up the album and walked towards the door, his departure a silent echo of their shared past, leaving behind a heavy quiet filled with the things left unsaid and feelings still simmering beneath the surface.

Roxana's voice trembled, breaking the heavy silence, "You know how I mentioned not resenting Nicole? That wasn't entirely the truth." Her admission was a raw edge of vulnerability, her words thick with emotion, causing Sam to pause mid-step. "I don't resent her, but I envy her... her place in your life now." Roxana's steps were hesitant, yet drawn inexorably toward Sam. She stopped just behind him, her presence a tangible reminder of the love they once shared, now a ghost of whispers and sighs. "I know I was the one who left first," she began, her voice a fragile thread of sound, "but you never left my heart. Not until you're father told me about your marriage." Her words spilled out, a confession of the heartache she'd guarded so closely. "It was then that you even vanished from my dreams, the last place I held you close." Her voice faltered, the admission revealing the depth of her longing and the raw wound of feeling replaced, even in the imagined corners of sleep. The room seemed to hold its breath, enveloped in the poignant revelation of a love that lingered in the silent spaces of her heart.

Sam turned slightly, the surprise evident in his voice. "My father?" He was grappling with the revelation, the depth of their connection seeping into the space between them.

Roxana's eyes held a sea of unshed tears. "Yes, he was the bridge between our two worlds, even when you didn't know it. He was my son's pediatrician. I would often ask about you, sometimes pretending I'm there for my son, but it was you I was there for."

The confession halted Sam, his heart wrestling with what to do next. "Should I leave?" he asked, his voice a mix of hope and resignation.

"You're right, the photos were a pretense," Roxana admitted, her voice barely above a whisper. "I needed to see you, to confront the ghost of us that lingers in every corner of my memory. I tell myself you should leave, but every part of me is screaming for you to stay."

Sam turned fully now, facing her, his eyes reflecting the storm within. "I feel the same," he confessed. "We can't just erase what was, can we? Besides, what's wrong with two old friends meeting again?"

"You know we're not just old friends," Roxana said, her voice a testament to their tangled history. The room seemed to close in around them, the years of distance collapsing as they stood there, confronted by the undeniable truth of their enduring connection.

Sam shifted the conversation, seeking safer ground. "How's life been treating you? How many children do you have?" he inquired, attempting to navigate away from their emotional whirlpool.

"Just one boy," Roxana's reply was soft, "He's just turned nineteen. Time flies." She gestured towards the chairs, "Please, sit. I'll get us something to drink."

As Sam took his seat, his fingers absentmindedly brushed the album's surface, each touch stirring memories like ripples across a still pond. Roxana returned, setting down glasses of limeade, the tart scent briefly cutting through the thick nostalgia.

Sam, lost in the album, paused on a photo, his heart tightening. "I almost didn't recognize you that day in the store," he confessed, a gentle acknowledgment of time's relentless march. "But then I saw your Lips, those same magical lips from the past, and then I knew."

The air hummed with a silent symphony of what-ifs and remembrances. Roxana, catching the tender look in Sam's eyes, felt a familiar warmth bloom in her chest. Her face warmed, not just from the limeade's tartness but from the flood of memories his words unleashed.

Amidst the dance of past and present, Roxana, leaning slightly forward, curiosity tinting her voice, asked, "And what were you buying that day? Something special for Nicole?"

Their conversation meandered, a delicate ballet between the present and a past too potent to be left unspoken.

Sam, lost in the labyrinth of memories, began unraveling the threads of the past. "Actually, we were getting a wedding set for Ariana."

"Oh my God. Little Ariana is getting married. I wish I could tell her congratulations. Who's the lucky guy?"

"You probably won't believe it: Farhad, my old roommate. They just met ten days ago, and they're already getting married a week from today."

A wistful sigh escaped Roxana's lips as she entertained a fleeting wish against reality. "Maybe that's what we should have done. We wouldn't have to meet in secret now."

Sam, compelled by an unspoken yearning, admitted, "I was about to come for your khastegari that day." His fingers tenderly combed her hair back from her face, a gesture laden with the echoes of what could have been. The soft strands slipped through his fingers like the sands of time.

"Do you ever wonder how it would have been if we never separated?" Roxana's gaze held a depth of emotion as she entwined her fingers with his. "Would we still love each other as much as we used to?"

"I couldn't love you less if I tried. You stopped talking to me, remember?"

The weight of the unspoken hung in the air, a poignant reminder of the paths not taken. Roxana, caught in a moment of vulnerability, couldn't resist asking, "How about now?" Yet, almost instantly, her hands flew to his mouth, as if trying to retract the question before it could alter the delicate balance of their reunion. "No, don't answer that. Forget I even asked." The room seemed to hold its breath, teetering on the precipice of unspoken confessions and the lingering traces of a love that had weathered the test of time.

Sam's question lingered in the air, a poignant echo of all the years passed. "Are you happy with your life?" It wasn't just a question; it was a search for understanding, for closure.

Roxana's response was tinged with a sorrowful honesty. "I've built a life with Nader, a good one. But sometimes I wonder how much fuller my heart might have been if my path had never crossed yours." Her words hung heavy, a quiet admission of a heart divided, a love never fully relinquished. "You've become an indelible part of me, Saam, in ways deeper than you could ever imagine. And it's not fair to Nader; he deserves all of me, but a piece of my heart still beats rhythmically to the thought of you."

Sam's heart ached with the need to understand, to unravel the mystery of their parting. "Then why did you leave?" he persisted, the question a quiet plea in the space between them.

Roxana's face was a canvas of pain and regret as she implored him to let the past remain shrouded. "It's a maze of reasons, Saam, a tangle of circumstances. Digging up the past will only bring more pain."

"But I need some semblance of peace," Sam insisted, his voice a mix of desperation and longing.

Roxana, her tears a silent river down her cheeks, whispered, "Some truths are too heavy, Saam. I fear they would crush what little peace you have."

Understanding the torturous road this conversation could lead down, Sam relented, his voice softening to a whisper. "Alright, I won't ask again." With a step forward, he enveloped her in an embrace, a gesture of comfort and shared sorrow. Roxana, surprisingly, melted into the hug, her body acknowledging the bond that neither time nor circumstance could fully erase.

In that embrace, they found a silent communion, a bittersweet acknowledgment of a love that once burned brightly and still smoldered in the hidden chambers of their hearts. Roxana's embrace tightened, a silent plea for comfort in the storm of emotions swirling between them. Her tears were a testament to the depth of what remained unspoken, each one a poignant reflection of their shared past. "Why did it have to be this way?" she murmured, the question a soft echo of longing and regret.

Sam felt the full weight of her grief, his own heart echoing her pain. He soothed her with a gentle caress, his touch a balm to the raw edges of their shared wounds. Drawing back slightly, he looked into her eyes, his own eyes a mirror to the ache in her voice. "Seeing you cry breaks my heart," he whispered, his thumb tenderly brushing away her tears.

"I'm alright," Roxana managed, a fragile smile breaking through the clouds of her sorrow. It was a smile that carried the history of a thousand shared smiles, each one a fleeting defiance against the sadness of the moment.

Sam, seeking to lift the veil of gloom, complimented her smile, trying to recapture a glimmer of the lightness they once shared. "That smile is priceless."

Roxana, her eyes still glistening, let out a small laugh, the sound a rare music in the heavy silence. "Flirting after all these years?" she asked, a mix of amusement and melancholy in her voice.

"Is it working?" he responded, a playful lilt to his voice, an attempt to bridge the gap of years with the levity of their younger selves.

"It worked wonders back then. You don't have to try again," she replied, her voice a soft blend of affection and wistfulness.

Sam's hand lingered on Roxana's face, each touch a silent conversation between their souls. As if the years apart were just a brief pause, his touch around the border of her lips evoking memories of a time when they were inseparable.

Roxana's heart ached with the bittersweet truth of his words. "If only wishes were our reality," she whispered back, her voice a soft testament to the depth of her longing.

In the quiet that followed, they found themselves drawn together, a dance as old as time, their movements a testament to the enduring pull of a once-in-a-lifetime connection. Their lips hovered in the breathless space of nearness, a moment suspended between the past and the present.

But the spell was broken as Sam's phone pierced the silence, its ring a jarring reminder of the lives they led outside this room. Reluctantly, they parted, the bubble of their reunion burst by the call of the outside world.

Sam, with a heavy heart, answered the phone, Farhad's voice pulling him back to reality. "I'm on my way," he assured, his voice a mask of normalcy over the turmoil of emotions roiling inside him.

As he ended the call, the room felt immeasurably larger, a heartbreaking reminder of the paths they had chosen and the undeniable bond that, despite everything, refused to be forgotten.

As Sam declared the imminent call of his responsibilities at home, a soft sorrow underlined his voice, a reflection of the inner turmoil stirred by their meeting. "They're waiting for me," he said, the words heavy with more than one meaning.

Roxana, her own heart echoing the ache in his voice, nodded understandingly. "When will you leave Shiraz?" she asked, a hint of hope flickering in her voice for perhaps another chance, another moment.

"Two more weeks," Sam replied swiftly, his heart racing with the unspoken desire to stay in this moment forever. He opened his arms wide, inviting her for one last embrace.

She stepped into his arms, her body language whispering the words her lips couldn't form. As they held each other close, the world outside faded, leaving only the palpable beat of their hearts and the warmth of their shared past.

"Take care," Roxana murmured as they reluctantly parted, her voice a gentle caress, echoing the sentiment of their embrace.

Sam held her close, his lips grazing her cheek in a tender goodbye, each one reluctant to break the connection, to end the moment. Yet, as they stepped back, the reality of their lives, the commitments and paths they had chosen, settled back around them, a poignant reminder of the distances they must maintain.

Sam navigated the familiar streets, each turn taking him further away yet keeping him anchored in the web of emotions that their encounter had spun. His phone, a silent companion now, buzzed to life, Roxana's voice immediately flooding the space.

"You left the album behind," she said, her voice carrying a mix of urgency and an unspoken longing.

With a calm smile, Sam replied, "Perhaps I left them with you on purpose." Their conversation danced between earnest pleas and playful banter, a delicate balancing act of emotions and desires. "Maybe I wanted an excuse to return," Sam admitted, the truth of his words veiled in jest.

"What makes you think I'll agree to see you again?" Roxana's tease hung in the air, a playful challenge that sparked a familiar thrill in Sam.

"I guess I'm still the risk-taker I used to be," Sam replied, his voice light but earnest.

"You really haven't changed, have you?" Roxana's voice was a mix of amusement and affection, a smile audible in her words.

"Let's aim for tomorrow," Sam's voice held an optimistic tone, the very thought of it painting a hopeful picture.

Roxana, ever the realist, tempered the moment with caution. "Tomorrow's packed here, with it being Friday and all. Let's not rush this. Next week, perhaps?"

Sam's heart sank a little. "An entire week feels like an eternity now," he confessed, the longing in his voice unmistakable.

Roxana, understanding the stakes, reminded him gently, "Patience, Sam. We need to tread carefully. The garden's only safe on Thursdays."

A sigh escaped him. "Then wait, I shall," he conceded, though every fiber of him resisted the idea.

Roxana, sensing his disappointment, sweetened the deal. "How about I make it up to you? Breakfast, my treat, next Thursday. Be here at eight?"

The offer brought a small, hopeful smile to Sam's face, a glimmer of something beautiful amidst the tangle of their situation. "Breakfast it is," he agreed, the promise of another meeting, no matter how brief or fraught with caution, enough to fuel the anticipation in his heart.

Chapter 46

On Friday August 13th, much like any other Friday in Shiraz, the gardens bustled with families enjoying their day off. The Khalili family had gathered at Nader and Roxana's villa. Laughter and the sound of children playing in the pool filled the air, but Roxana's heart was elsewhere—entangled in the memories of the reunion with Sam the day before in the very house that now echoed with life. Every corner held a trace of him, and the kitchen, once a place of shared limeades infused with love and passion, now stirred bittersweet echoes.

"You're so quiet today. Is everything OK?" Roxana's mom observed, sensing the unspoken turmoil.

"I'm fine," Roxana softly smiled, attempting to mask the storm within.

"Have you forgotten that I'm your mother? I know you better than you think. Tell me what's on your mind," her mother gently prodded.

"Life is not fair," Roxana admitted, her gaze drifting to the window, where her son partnered with Nader in a card game against both grandfathers.

"Life was not meant to be fair," said her mom. "But we can and should make it enjoyable."

"Saam is in town," Roxana blurted out abruptly. "I saw him at the Safavi jewelry store the other day."

"Saam, Saam," Mrs. Khalili repeated. "The Larabi Saam? Is that where your mind is today? How could you even think about him when your husband and your son are right here?"

"Sometimes we're not in control of our thoughts, Mom. If it weren't for this damn regime, it could have been him playing cards outside," Roxana explained, her voice tinged with a mixture of vulnerability and nostalgia, hoping for a compassionate understanding.

"Why are you troubling yourself with him? How long has it been? I'm sure he's married with children too and not wasting his time thinking about you," her mom reassured, attempting to offer solace.

"Don't be so sure," Roxana said, her words shrouded in an emotional tapestry of uncertainty and yearning. "I mean, how can you be so sure?" Her heartache spilled into her voice, revealing the depth of her unresolved feelings.

Her mother's eyes held a mix of concern and wisdom as they met Roxana's. The room seemed to hold its breath, the weight of unspoken emotions hanging in the air, threatening to drown them both in the currents of the past. As the silence lingered, the ache of lost possibilities and the bittersweet longing for a different life echoed in the room, creating an invisible but palpable tension that neither could escape.

"Don't tell me you guys are talking," Mrs. Khalili said, hoping for a negative answer.

"He didn't even recognize me," Roxana lied, the words escaping with a heavy sigh, the lie hanging heavily between them like a fragile web, a protective shield for the complexity of their shared past.

"Thank God. You shouldn't bother yourself with the past," her mom advised, the caution in her tone reflecting the concern for her daughter's emotional well-being.

"I wish I could tell him why I left him," Roxana confessed, her voice trembling with the weight of unspoken emotions, the ache in her heart palpable.

"There is nothing to tell, my dear. He left you first, and you decided to marry Nader. It's just that simple," her mom tried to simplify, yet the complexities lingered beneath the surface.

"Mom, you know that he had no choice," Roxana pleaded, seeking understanding.

"I know. And you decided to marry Nader. Now, even thinking about another man is a sin, and God will burn you in hell," her mom warned, the sternness in her words revealing the societal norms weighing heavily on her.

"I think I've burned enough in this life to deserve a full pardon from God in the afterlife," Roxana whispered, her lips quivering with a mixture of defiance and resignation. "Don't worry. He'll only stay in my memories as he always has." She took a deep breath and put on a phony smile. "See, everything is OK," Roxana said before leaving the room, leaving behind the weight of emotions too heavy to bear, an unspoken ache echoing in the silence.

Chapter 47

On Tuesday morning, as the house emptied and a quiet settled in, Roxana stepped into her home gym. The steady rhythm of her feet against the treadmill beat a determined tempo, filling the room with the sound of persistence and focus. The digital counter on the machine climbed, marking the intensity of her workout at 168 BPM, each beat a small victory in her personal quest for health and vitality.

Immersed in the unfolding drama of her favorite soap opera, Roxana found a momentary escape, her mind adrift in the fictional world. But the real world broke through with the intrusive ring of the phone, a sharp reminder of life outside her controlled environment.

With a glance, Roxana decided to let the machine take the call, her focus unyielding, her breath steady. Yet the caller left no message, just a sudden silence that seemed to loom larger than any words might have. The unanswered call hung in the air, a mystery wrapped in the ordinary, leaving Roxana with a lingering sense of curiosity amidst the echoes of her continued workout.

The second ring was insistent, a loud and clear call that pulled Roxana away from her exercise routine. Her heart still racing from the workout, she quickly made her way to the source of the interruption. The voice that greeted her was achingly familiar, each word sending a wave of emotion through her.

"Is this the Aslani's residence?" The question was simple, yet charged with an underlying current of shared history and unspoken words.

Roxana's response was light, flirtatious, yet underscored with genuine happiness. "Just for you, it is," she said, her playfulness belying the rapid beating of her heart.

Sam's voice came through the phone, laden with affection and an unmistakable yearning. "Is it Thursday yet?" he joked, a reference to their planned meetings that seemed to hold all their unfulfilled wishes.

Roxana's reply was a soft exhale, a mixture of longing and realism. "I wish," she admitted, her voice a delicate balance between desire and the gravity of their situation.

Sam, ever the hopeful romantic, suggested, "Let's pretend it's already Thursday," his voice a tender brush against the stark reality of their circumstances.

Roxana, though tempted by the thought, held firm. "Maybe we shouldn't," she reminded him gently, aware of the risks and repercussions their meetings entailed, a tightrope walk between yearning and caution.

Sam's voice carried a mix of resolve and understanding, aware of the delicacy of their situation yet unable to resist the pull towards her. "Everyone's preoccupied with the wedding. It's the perfect cover to sneak away," he argued, his words a blend of logic and longing.

Roxana, caught between desire and the reality of their circumstances, played along with a hint of mischief. "Well, I've hidden your photos in the garden. They're not even with me," she teased, trying to infuse a lighter note into their heavy conversation.

"As if I needed an excuse to see you," he retorted, his amusement tinged with the deeper truth of his feelings.

Yet Roxana couldn't shake off the looming sense of what their meetings meant. "Each time we meet, it's only going to make your leaving harder," she confessed, the thought a heavy stone in her heart.

Sam's response was a candid reflection of his feelings, "I've never been one to think too far ahead. All I know is I want to see you now."

Roxana, ever mindful of the reality of their situation, held firm. "We can't risk being seen, and the garden isn't an option today. Thursday is our day, unless you think of somewhere else safe."

Undeterred, Sam proposed an immediate, if risky, solution. "Meet me in the alley down from your house in an hour," he said, his voice a blend of assurance and pleading.

Roxana's hesitation was clear in her voice, "I'm scared, Saam. This isn't easy."

"Just say yes," he urged gently, his request simple yet laden with the weight of their situation, a testament to the depth of his desire to maintain their connection, no matter the risk.

Roxana's movements were cautious and deliberate as she slipped out of her home, her senses acutely tuned to the environment around her. She felt the weight of her actions with each silent step, the fabric of her headscarf drawn a little closer, a symbolic barrier against the prying eyes she feared might be watching. Her heart whispered a continuous stream of prayers for invisibility, for the freedom to meet Sam without repercussions.

As she turned into the alley, the world seemed to narrow down to the path before her, the walls echoing her quickened heartbeat, the air heavy with anticipation and fear. She moved with a heightened awareness, every sound magnified, every shadow a potential witness.

The distant rumble of a motorcycle grew steadily closer, the sound reverberating off the alley walls, a discordant soundtrack to her nervous wait. As the bike halted next to her, Roxana's first instinct was to look away, to hide her face, to wish the rider would simply continue on. But the sound of the horn, a brief but insistent beep, drew her gaze reluctantly back.

The moment she saw the familiar face behind the visor, a mix of shock and relief flooded through her. "Oh my god, it's you," she gasped, the tension breaking in a sudden surge of emotion, the memories of their past riding adventures surging forward.

"Quick, put this on," Sam's voice was both a command and a comfort, urgency laced with the shared excitement of a forbidden adventure. Handing her the helmet, he beckoned her to join him, to escape, if only briefly, from the world's gaze.

Hesitation battled with desire in Roxana's heart, but the pull of the past, of the man waiting beside her, was too strong. With a trembling hand, she took the helmet, the symbol of their shared recklessness, and prepared to step into the unknown.

As Roxana settled onto the motorcycle behind Sam, a mix of nostalgia and exhilaration washed over her. "This bike... it's like a time machine," she said, her voice muffled by the helmet yet clear in its wonder. The familiar sensation of the bike's vibrations brought a flood of memories, each one a vivid snapshot of their younger, more carefree days.

Sam revved the engine, and they were off, weaving through the streets of their town. The world outside became a blur of colors and shapes, but inside her helmet, Roxana's mind was crystal clear, filled with the acute sensation of being alive, truly alive, perhaps for the first time in years.

Their reflection flickered in the windows they passed, two silhouettes against the backdrop of the town, a visual echo of their secret union. For Sam, the ride was a bittersweet symphony of emotions; the thrill of Roxana's proximity warred with the guilt of what they were doing. He felt the weight of their situation, yet he couldn't deny the pull of the moment, the intoxicating sense of being with Roxana, even under such fraught circumstances.

Regardless of the speed at which he maneuvered the bike, Roxana clung to him with unwavering intensity. Her body molded against his, and she rested her head gently on his back, enveloped in the warmth of their shared secret. In those stolen moments, she closed her eyes, allowing her imagination to paint a vivid picture of a life entwined with Sam. Terrified at the prospect of being discovered, she found solace in the safety of his embrace, tuning out the cacophony of street sounds that threatened to pierce their cocoon.

The sensation of the wind rushing past, coupled with the rhythmic beat of the engine, fueled Roxana's daydreams. In her mind's eye, she envisioned a future where Sam was hers openly, where their love wasn't shrouded in secrecy. Each curve of the road fueled the fantasy, and she only opened her eyes when the motorcycle came to a gentle stop, snapping her back to the reality of their covert rendezvous.

Sam's eyes took in the dilapidated grandeur of the old International Hotel, its silent facade a stark reminder of the vibrant life it once held. "This ruined place holds so many memories," he murmured, removing his helmet to better view the place where their lives had intertwined years ago.

Roxana, standing beside him, let her gaze wander over the ruins. "It's hard to believe this was the same place we danced the night away," she said, the nostalgia evident in her voice.

A smile touched Sam's lips at the mention of their first meeting. "I'll never forget that night, or the outfit that earned me the nickname Mr. Travolta," he said with a chuckle, the memory a welcome respite from the weight of their current reality.

"Have you ever thought about, maybe..." Roxana's voice trailed off as she walked toward the fence of the Hotel, her gaze lingering on the crumbling façade of the once-lively International Discothèque.

"Thought about what?" Sam pressed, his interest piqued by the wistful tone in her voice.

"Never mind. It's a foolish thought," she dismissed quickly, a fleeting shadow darkening her features.

"But now you've got me wondering," Sam persisted, stepping closer, his desire to understand her turmoil evident in his eyes.

Roxana hesitated, the weight of unspoken dreams and fears pressing down on her. "It's impossible, just forget I mentioned anything," she murmured, her voice barely a whisper.

"No, tell me. I need to know," Sam insisted, his voice firm yet gentle, coaxing her to reveal her hidden thoughts.

After a moment's pause, laden with the gravity of what she was about to disclose, Roxana exhaled a shaky breath. "Have you ever thought about leaving Nicole if I left Nader? Maybe then, we could be together again," she confessed, her words hanging between them, vulnerable and charged with possibility. Her eyes searched his, looking for an answer or perhaps an escape from the reality they were both entangled in.

The question crashed into Sam with the force of a tidal wave, leaving him reeling in a sudden vortex of disbelief and turmoil. The thought had never dared to skim the surface of his consciousness, let alone take root. The idea of leaving Nicole, the life they had built together, was unimaginable.

"I shouldn't have said it," Roxana's voice broke through his inertness, her words rushing out in a torrent of regret. "Just forget it, please. Let's pretend I never mentioned such madness." She turned away slightly, her silhouette framed against the decaying grandeur of the International Hotel, a poignant symbol of dreams and realities crumbling around them.

"I couldn't leave Nader either," she continued, her voice steadier but still laced with an undercurrent of what-ifs and if-onlys. Her words were a self-imposed sentence, spoken with a conviction that belied the pain of renunciation evident in her eyes.

"It's ok. Everyone dreams. Even the married people," Sam whispered, inching closer, his voice a gentle challenge to the silent air between them.

Roxana's eyes widened when she felt the touch of his hands on her back, as she instinctively retreated. "What are you doing?" she hissed, swiftly securing her helmet, her movements laced with urgency. "This isn't America, Saam. Here, even whispers can condemn us to death. We mustn't gamble with fate like this, not again." Her voice was a mix of fear and defiance, a delicate tremor betraying her resolve. "Let's just leave until Thursday."

"As you wish," Sam replied, a softness in his voice masking the turmoil beneath. He kick-started his bike, the engine's roar slicing through the tense air. He didn't take the direct route back to her neighborhood. Instead, he chose the winding, longer paths, as if each turn and alleyway could delay their inevitable farewell. His deliberate detour was a silent offering, granting her moments to escape into her thoughts, away from the prying eyes of their world.

The motorcycle's fading rumble left a tangible echo in the air, a blend of yearning and the harsh whisper of reality. Roxana stood there, enveloped in the fading vibrations, her heart a battlefield of desires and duties. The mingling scents of dust and dreams lingered, a poignant reminder of the delicate dance between what they longed for and what life demanded.

Chapter 48

"Are you gonna fall asleep on the couch watching TV again?" Nader asked, his voice carrying a mix of curiosity and concern as he prepared for bed.

"No, I'll be in right after this episode," Roxana assured him, her gaze fixed on the flickering screen. Lately, she found herself sidestepping any close encounters with Nader, an unspoken guilt lingering each time he touched her—a sensation akin to betrayal against Sam, whose forgiveness she silently implored. Besides the constant headaches she claimed, the allure of the TV became her refuge, a shield to ward off the intimacy she feared with her husband.

Seating himself beside her, Nader remarked, "You never watched this much TV before. Sometimes I feel like you are avoiding me."

Roxana harbored a storm of emotions, a secret turmoil of guilt and an inexplicable yearning for Sam's understanding. The forbidden nature of her emotions puzzled her, and she wished she could broadcast her inner conflict to the world, questioning why something so inherently wrong felt so undeniably right. Each passing moment became a countdown to the stolen rendezvous with Sam the next morning, and she had meticulously prepared the garden for their clandestine breakfast.

That night, Roxana's emotions toward Nader seemed to echo the early days of their marriage—the anticipation, the uncertainty, the shared moments that now felt like distant memories. Yet, she wasn't the excited bride eagerly awaiting her wedding night or the intimacy of a shared bed with her newlywed husband. Instead, her thoughts were consumed by a yearning to confide in Sam, to unravel the enigma of her departure. She harbored the belief that if Sam understood her reasons, he would harbor resentment for the rest of his days.

Despite the tangled web of emotions, Roxana acknowledged Nader's unconditional love, a devotion that persisted even in the shadow of her past with Sam. She vividly recalled how she had falsely assured Nader that Sam was a forgotten chapter, erased from both her mind and heart for all eternity. Roxana was certain that any inkling of her continued connection with Sam would shatter Nader's trust and potentially lead to the dissolution of their marriage.

While Nader anticipated an explanation for Roxana's consecutive nights of absentia from their shared bed, she had no inclination to extinguish the flames of her lingering feelings by surrendering to Nader's embrace, especially not on that particular night. She had to conceal the truth. Choosing her words carefully, she proposed, "Why don't you watch this episode with me?" Roxana was well aware that Nader would never indulge in such an activity, yet the suggestion hung in the air, a fragile bridge connecting her tumultuous emotions and the façade of normalcy she sought to maintain.

"I have to work early tomorrow morning and can't be late, because if your father won't fire me, my father will," Nader chuckled, heading towards the bedroom. "I haven't given up," he turned back with a playful glint in his eyes. "I'm still waiting for the day that I capture your heart."

"Stop saying that," Roxana replied, her words tinged with guilt. "You do have my heart."

"I meant all of it," Nader confessed, his eyes holding a knowing sadness. In that moment, he acknowledged the truth that lingered unspoken between them for decades— he was aware that, despite their marriage, a part of her heart remained tethered to someone else.

Chapter 49

The stage was set for Ariana and Farhad's impromptu wedding on that destined Thursday, August 19th. The family and friends had come together, each contribution weaving seamlessly into the next, creating a tapestry of festivity and love. Amidst the buzz of preparations, Sam found himself caught in the current of anticipation for his own clandestine meeting.

Nicole, ever intuitive, suggested he remain close, perhaps sensing the unusual flutter of his heart. Sam, cloaked in the guise of routine deception, mentioned a breakfast with an old friend. This half-truth, oddly comforting at first, soon became a heavy shroud as the reality of his duplicity sank in. "There's nothing left for me here," he said, attempting to mask his restlessness.

"Could you call a cab for me before you leave?" Nicole's request was simple, yet it tethered him momentarily to the domestic life they shared.

"Of course," he replied, the number rolling off his tongue as he called for a cab, a mundane act punctuated with a stolen kiss and a hollow farewell.

"Wait with me for the cab. Your friend won't mind a slight delay," Nicole suggested, unknowingly anchoring him in their shared space a moment longer.

"Sure, I can wait," Sam responded, his eyes flickering to his watch, the seconds ticking away like a silent alarm. With each lie, the chasm between him and Nicole widened, his ability to meet her gaze with untruths marking a disturbing milestone in their marriage. The thought of Roxana, entwined with the reality of his fading commitment to Nicole, stirred a tempest within him. He was haunted by the diminishing warmth of his feelings for Nicole, even as he gravitated irresistibly toward Roxana. The internal clash was relentless, a maelstrom of guilt, longing, and a deep-seated fear of the unknown future of his marriage.

"That must be your cab," Sam said, a sense of urgency veiled beneath his casual remark as the doorbell chimed.

Nicole moved gracefully towards the door, pausing only to suggest he might offer his help to Farhad. Sam nodded, a hollow promise hanging in the air. He watched from the window as Nicole slipped into the cab and disappeared down the street. Once she was out of sight, he made his escape, leaving behind any notion of consulting Farhad.

Soon enough, Sam found himself at the garden's entrance, the gates creaking open before him. There stood Roxana, a vision in the same halter top blue dress that haunted his memories. It was the dress from their last, passionate day in Shiraz, a symbol of both love and loss.

As he parked the car, the weight of the moment settled around them. "How are you?" he greeted, his voice a mix of warmth and underlying tension.

"I'm fine," Roxana replied.

"You sure are," Sam's voice carried a playful edge, a light remark to ease the heavy air. His eyes, however, held a deeper story, reflecting a tangle of desire and nostalgia.

Roxana's response was cut short as she stepped closer, the faint blush on her cheeks a testament to the myriad feelings coursing through her. Her hand found his, their fingers locking together in a moment that transcended the years apart. The dress wasn't just a dress; it was a portal to a past filled with longing and love, a poignant reminder of what once was and what could never be again. As they stood there, the world around them seemed to pause, acknowledging the gravity of their reunion.

The breakfast table was a canvas of care and affection, each dish and utensil placed with intention and thought. Roxana turned to Sam, breaking the comfortable silence between them. "Tea or coffee?" she asked, her voice steady but revealing a hint of anticipation for his preference.

"Tea, please," he replied, maintaining eye contact, an unspoken conversation flowing silently between them.

As they settled into the quiet rhythm of the morning, Roxana's curiosity surfaced, piercing the veil of casualness. "So tell me, Saam, what excuse did you use to leave the house this time?" Her question, casual on the surface, carried a deeper probe, her eyes searching his for the truth beneath the facade.

Sam hesitated, then with a strained casualness, he responded, "The truth. I said I'm meeting an old friend for breakfast." The admission, while partially honest, felt heavier than the most intricate of lies.

Roxana's response was a mixture of appreciation and wistfulness. "I like your honesty. Do you think you may someday move back to Shiraz?" Her question hung in the air, a delicate thread of hope tethering her to the possibility of a different reality.

The question caught Sam off guard. "I, I don't think so," he stammered, the conflict within him spilling into his words. The reality of their situation, the impossibility of what she hinted at, filled the silence that followed with a tangible heaviness.

"I know. I'm just getting used to seeing you on a regular basis," Roxana conceded with a gentle resignation, her words a soft echo of the longing they both felt. The desire for a more open, less clandestine relationship was clear, yet so was the understanding of its impossibility.

Sam's gaze lingered on Roxana, taking in the vision she presented in the halter top dress that accentuated her elegance and grace. "I clearly remember turning around and seeing you in that dress," he began, his voice a soft murmur of remembrance. "You were standing in the doorway, as mesmerizing as you are this moment."

Her response was a dance of words left unfinished, her smile carrying the weight of memories. "And then I spun around to..." she trailed off, the sentence hanging in the air, a symbol of moments paused in time. "It was so long ago. How I wish we could revisit that day," she whispered, her voice a delicate mixture of regret and yearning. Roxana felt the sting of nostalgia and the bitter sweetness of memories that lingered like the fragrance of a forgotten garden.

Sam's eyes softened as he took in Roxana's words, the compliment on her dress now deepening into something far more significant. "It's not just a dress to me. I intend to keep it forever," she whispered, her voice a fragile thread weaving through the air, laden with love and a tinge of sorrow. Her hand in his felt like a lifeline, a tangible connection amidst the ethereal nature of their bond.

Her confession continued, each word infused with the depth of her feelings. "You left my real world, but in my dreams, you never did. In those dreams, I'm always wearing this dress when we're together." Her admission revealed the dress as more than fabric and thread; it was a symbol of undying hope and cherished memories, a testament to a love that refused to wilt in the harsh light of reality.

"I only wore it for you," she continued, her breath catching as emotion surged within her. "Like girls keep their wedding gowns, this is mine. And I feel luckier than them all because I wore mine twice for the same man." The metaphor of the wedding gown imbued the dress with a sacredness, elevating it to an artifact of their love, a silent witness to the depth of her commitment. As she spoke, tears began to trace her cheeks, each one a crystal testament to the profound emotions stirring within her. The moment held them, a delicate bubble of past, present, and the hauntingly beautiful might-have-beens.

"It didn't have to be our last day," Sam's voice barely rose above a whisper, his words heavy, laden with the unresolved emotions and unanswered questions that still haunted him.

"Don't. You promised," Roxana's plea was soft yet firm, her voice trembling on the edge of breaking, a testament to the fragility of the peace they had built over their past.

"I know, I'm sorry," Sam's voice cracked, the admission of his feelings exposing the raw edges of his own wounds. "It just felt like...like you had instantly forgotten me."

"How could I forget you, Saam?" Roxana's voice was thick with emotion, her words resonating with the enduring pain of a love that had never truly faded. "You were my first love. And after...after I broke your heart, I lived every day with that weight, the fear that you might hate me for leaving you so abruptly."

Sam reached out, his touch gentle as he wiped away her tears. "It's OK. Come here," he murmured, drawing her into an embrace, a safe harbor amidst the storm of their past. She nestled against him, her tears dampening his shoulder, as he ran his fingers through her hair, each stroke a silent vow of comfort and understanding.

"I've told you before, I could never hate you," he reassured her, his words wrapping around them like a blanket, soft and comforting. His heartbeats, steady and strong, seemed to cradle her in their rhythm.

"Then you forgive me?" The hope in Roxana's voice was fragile, a delicate thing threatened by the weight of their history.

"I'm sure you had a good reason," Sam replied, his forgiveness not fully articulated, yet hanging in the air between them, a bittersweet gift tinged with the aches of the past. Their embrace, a silent testament to the complexity of their feelings, held them close, a moment of solace in the eye of the storm.

"You've always been on my mind. Your memory never let me fully love Nader the way I love you," Roxana confessed, her gaze locked with Sam's as she gently traced the contours of his lips with her fingertips. "Your thoughts never allowed me to let him kiss my lips the way you kissed them."

The air hung heavy with the bittersweet blend of forgiveness and regret, the room echoing with the heartbeat of a love that had endured, suffered, and emerged from the shadows of the past. In that tender moment, they were suspended in the delicate dance of healing, the unspoken words and shared heartaches creating a symphony that resonated with the pulse of a love that refused to be forgotten.

Their breaths intertwined, creating a delicate melody of longing and reconciliation. Their eyes, mirrors of emotions too profound for words, gazed into each other's souls, seeking solace and understanding. The weight of years melted away as their lips, parched and yearning, drew closer in an unspoken pact of shared longing. Finally, their mouths met in a soft collision, a union of lips that spoke a language only they understood. It ignited a long, passionate kiss, a communion of souls that had weathered storms and found each other once again in the calm that followed. In that embrace, somehow, the world felt smaller, less complicated, as if the universe had conspired to grant them this moment of solace amidst the chaos.

Chapter 50

Nicole's curiosity was piqued when Sam returned on Tuesday after the bike ride with Roxana. "Where were you today?" Nicole's casual inquiry was a thin veil over the torrent of suspicion brewing inside her. Sam's too-quick dismissal, "Just rode around for a while," did little to quell the rising tide of doubt. The sight of the extra helmet was like a spark to kindling, igniting a flame of suspicion that she couldn't shake off.

"Alone?" she pressed, the word heavy with unspoken accusations.

"Of course, honey, alone. Why do you ask?" Sam responded, his tone attempting normalcy.

Sam's quick affirmation and evasive gaze only fanned the flames of her suspicion. She halted her inquiry about the second helmet. "You know, you should take me for a ride one day." She donned the helmet with a grace force, her voice betraying none of the storm raging within.

As the helmet settled onto her head, Nicole's world shattered with the sharp scent of another woman's perfume. It wrapped around her like a ghostly embrace, a cruel revelation of betrayal that knocked the breath from her lungs. Her vision blurred with tears, a mix of hurt, anger, and disbelief. The ground seemed to sway as she crouched by the door, the weight of her discovery anchoring her to the spot.

Inside her, a battle raged between intuition and denial, a war of emotions that left her reeling. The sting of betrayal was acute, a physical ache that mirrored the turmoil in her soul. "Had there been others?" The question echoed in her mind, a relentless drumbeat of suspicion and fear.

With a monumental effort, Nicole took the helmet off and pulled herself together, wiping away tears and gathering the shards of her composure. She couldn't let this moment define her; she wouldn't allow the pain to be her undoing. Stepping toward the family room, her resolve was a shield against the chaos, each step a march toward an inevitable confrontation.

Yet, as fate would have it, her path was intercepted by Ariana, who, unaware of the maelstrom she had stepped into, halted Nicole's determined stride with a simple hang-up of the phone. The pause was momentary, but in the eye of the storm, it felt like an eternity. Nicole stood there, the weight of the truth heavy on her shoulders, the scent of betrayal still clinging to her skin, and the tempest of her emotions swirling dangerously close to the surface.

"That was the tailor," Ariana's voice cut through the heavy silence, a vibrant burst of excitement that contrasted sharply with Nicole's inner turmoil. "My wedding gown is ready. Would you come with me for the final try-on?" Her eyes sparkled with the joy of a bride-to-be, unaware of the storm raging in her friend's heart.

Nicole was caught in the throes of Sam's betrayal, each beat of her heart a painful reminder of the love she feared was lost. The joyous occasion of Ariana's wedding gown fitting clashed violently with her own world, crumbling under the weight of doubt and suspicion. She was torn, a part of her longing to escape into Ariana's happiness, another part sinking deeper into the quicksand of her despair.

"What do you say?" Ariana pressed, her smile fading a touch at the sight of Nicole's strained face. "Is everything alright? You seem...off."

Nicole stood there, a war waging within her. Should she let the shadow of her personal agony darken Ariana's light? With a monumental effort, she summoned a smile, a fragile facade to mask the agony within. "Nothing's wrong," she lied, her voice a soft echo of her former self. "I'd love to come with you. Really, I would."

"Great!" Ariana beamed, her excitement undimmed, turning away to continue her day, blissfully unaware of the depth of Nicole's pain.

Once alone, the smile that Nicole had so painstakingly held in place shattered like glass. She retreated to her room, a sanctuary of solitude, and collapsed onto the bed. The room spun around her, a maelstrom of doubt, betrayal, and a lingering scent that was not her own. She closed her eyes, wishing for the oblivion of sleep or a dream, any dream that could whisk her away from the cruel reality of her waking life.

Her thoughts drifted, unbidden, to the days before this catastrophic vacation, a time when her life seemed unblemished and full of promise. She cursed the moment they decided to embark on this journey, mourning the loss of the sweet veil of ignorance that had once enveloped her marriage. Yet, despite the overwhelming evidence, a stubborn flicker of love and hope urged her to cling to the possibility of Sam's innocence. It was a desperate grasp at the straws of her crumbling reality, a silent prayer that maybe, just maybe, her heart was wrong.

As the wedding day approached, Nicole watched Sam with the guarded eyes of a woman betrayed, studying him like a stranger. The intimacy they once shared had morphed into an unbearable chasm, her heart wincing at the thought of being alone with him. Nightfall no longer brought solace, only intensifying the relentless echo of her doubts and fears.

Thursday's light crept through the curtains, offering a sliver of hope as no further signs of deceit marred the dawn. Gripping onto this fragile optimism, Nicole braced herself to confront Sam, to lay bare her fears and perhaps seek his forgiveness for her suspicions. But as she approached the precipice of reconciliation, she watched in silent horror as the tenuous threads of trust disintegrated with his every move.

The casual announcement of his plans to meet an old friend sent icy tendrils of doubt spiraling down her spine. Her mind raced with the haunting question: who was this old friend? Driven by a need for clarity, she orchestrated a plan, her voice trembling as she ask Sam to call her a cab, her entire being tensed for the looming confrontation.

"Salam," she greeted the cab driver, her voice a mix of politeness and tension. Struggling with her limited Farsi, she urged him to hurry, "Boro. Lotfan. Zood. Boro." Her repeated pleas were a desperate mantra, each word heavy with the urgency of her mission.

The driver, sensing her distress, inquired gently about her destination, his tone laced with concern. "Koja?" he asked, but she could only repeat her urgent plea.

"Yes, ma'am," he finally complied, pulling away with a swift motion that mirrored Nicole's racing heart. "By the way, I speak English, ma'am?" he offered, a small comfort in the midst of her turmoil.

A sigh of relief escaped her as she asked him to park discreetly at the corner, her eyes glued to the house, searching for any sign of Sam. The driver, now acutely aware of the tension, stole glances at her through the rearview mirror, sensing the gravity of her situation. As Nicole crouched low in her seat, the weight of her mission, the fear, the hope, and the desperation of what she was about to do, cloaked the car in a heavy, anticipatory silence.

As Sam's car approached, Nicole leaned forward, her voice a hushed urgency. "You see the car that's coming toward us? I want you to follow it." The driver glanced at the side mirror, his eyes briefly meeting hers in the rearview mirror, a silent nod sealing their unspoken pact.

As Sam's car glided by, a bubble of awkward silence enveloped them, only punctured by the driver's tentative inquiry, "Do you have any idea where he's going?"

Distracted, Nicole shot back, "How come you speak such good English?" trying to divert her turbulent thoughts. "And stop calling me ma'am, please."

The driver, with a hint of a smile, explained his academic background and the economic hardships pushing him into this line of work. His words, a story of unfulfilled dreams and resilience, barely registered with Nicole, her gaze locked on the car ahead, a beacon leading her deeper into the maze of her fears.

The streets narrowed and twisted, each turn a mirror to the growing tension inside the cab. Finally breaking the silence, Nicole asked, "Is this normal for you?" seeking some solace in shared uncertainty.

"Following someone? Not really," he replied, his eyes meeting hers in the mirror, reflecting an odd blend of empathy and curiosity.

As Sam's car turned down a secluded road, Nicole's heart thudded against her chest, each beat a drumroll to the looming revelation. The vehicle came to a halt by a gate, and Nicole instinctively ducked down, her breaths shallow and rapid.

She prayed for a benign explanation, for her suspicions to be proven wrong. "Are you sure you want to go through with this?" the driver asked, his voice a gentle nudge back to reality.

But Nicole was past the point of return. The gate creaked open, revealing Roxana in a dress that left no room for doubt. As Sam stepped out to greet her, the last vestiges of Nicole's denial crumbled away. The closing gate felt like a closing chapter, each inch a tightening noose around the life she thought she knew.

Nicole's world, once so secure, was now a swirling vortex of betrayal and heartache. As the gate shut, her breath hitched, a suffocating wave of realization crashing down upon her. The finality of the closing gate, the image of Sam with another woman, it all coalesced into a painful epiphany. She was far from the blissful ignorance that once colored her life; now, all that remained was the raw, jagged edge of truth.

In that heart-wrenching moment, as the gate to the unknown closed, Nicole felt the very essence of her world disintegrate. The trust she had tenderly nurtured with Sam shattered irreparably, leaving her amidst the debris of what once was. The figure by his side was no mere acquaintance; she was the embodiment of Nicole's deepest fears, a rival, a stark threat to the life and love she had cherished.

The betrayal was a palpable force, pressing against her chest, stealing her breath in silent gasps. Her hands, once steady and sure, now shook uncontrollably, grasping for the remnants of a reality that no longer existed. The gate's final clang was a resounding echo of the chasm that had opened between them, leaving Nicole isolated in a cocoon of desolation, her heart splintering quietly in the backseat of the cab.

Tears clouded her vision, each one a silent testament to the agony of her disillusionment. The pain of Sam's infidelity was a relentless ache, settling heavily in her soul. Her sobs, though quiet, were a cacophony of anguish in the stillness, a poignant melody of a love lost and a future forsaken.

Faced with a crucible of decisions, Nicole teetered on the edge of an abyss. To confront them would mean facing the raw, jagged edge of betrayal, to witness firsthand the unraveling of a shared life. To flee was to choose a path of self-preservation, to preserve what remained of her dignity and hope for a brighter tomorrow.

The man she once saw as a beacon of love and stability had become a stranger, a ghost of the past that haunted the hollows of her heart. The present was a landscape of sorrow too vast to navigate.

With a resolve born from the depths of her despair, Nicole whispered her command to the driver, "Just drive away." Those words were a liberation and a sentence all at once, severing the final ties to a love story that had turned into a poignant tragedy.

As the car pulled away, each mile was a step further from the life she had known, a widening gulf between her and the remnants of a shared past. Ahead lay a road fraught with uncertainty, a path she must tread with the fragments of her broken dreams and the silent strength of a woman reborn from the ashes of despair.

This was not just an end but a beginning, a somber yet determined journey toward healing and newfound independence. It was the close of a chapter written in shared memories and silent tears, a painful farewell to a love that had withered in the shadows of deceit. Nicole's eyes, once filled with tears, now gazed forward with a fragile determination, ready to embrace the dawning of a new day and the promise of a future crafted by her own resilient spirit.

Chapter 51

Tara and Cameron, their laughter echoing through the house, chased each other from room to room, leaving a trail of joy in their wake. The whirlwind of their play abruptly ceased when they burst into Nicole's room, finding her nestled in a quiet corner, tears betraying the turmoil within.

"Why are you crying, Mom?" Tara's concern etched on her face as she settled beside her mother. Cameron, sensing something amiss, perched himself on Nicole's lap.

Nicole, summoning a fragile smile, brushed away the evidence of her silent tears. "It's nothing. I just miss home."

The innocence in Tara's eyes mirrored a child's inability to grasp the complexities of the grown-up world. "Don't you like it here, Mom?" she inquired, sincerity coloring her words. Cameron, with a purity that only children possess, echoed the sentiment, "It's so much fun."

Nicole, torn between the joy in her children's laughter and the weight of her own emotions, urged them gently, "Play a bit longer and then take showers and get ready for tonight."

As the door closed behind the fleeting figures of her children, Nicole, alone with her thoughts, began the task of packing. The decision, unspoken yet resolute, had solidified within her. She had made up her mind to take the children and leave on the first flight the next day.

In the quiet solitude of that room, each item she placed in the suitcase carried the weight of a heavy heart. It wasn't just about missing home; it was about reclaiming a sense of belonging, a sanctuary where the echoes of laughter weren't haunted by the shadows of unspoken pain. The clothes folded with meticulous care held the essence of a decision fueled by a mother's love and the unyielding desire to shield her children from the storms that raged beyond their youthful understanding.

The haunting scene of the garden door swinging open, revealing Roxana in her alluring dress, played on an endless loop in Nicole's mind. Seeking refuge, she submerged herself in the bathtub, shutting her eyes in a desperate attempt to erase the vivid images etched in her memory. As the water embraced her, she grappled with the unsettling questions that echoed in her mind. Is this his first time? Was I too blind to notice it before? The answers remained elusive, shrouded in a fog of disbelief and heartache.

Nicole's gaze was locked onto her own reflection, her eyes searching for the strength she needed in the mirror. The puffiness beneath her eyes was a cruel testament to the recent silent cries. The sound of the door creaking open startled her from her reverie, as Sam entered, his presence immediately suffocating the room.

"Hi sweetie. How was shopping?" he asked, his voice casual, as if the fabric of their life hadn't been irrevocably torn.

Nicole's hands tightened around her robe, the fabric a meager barrier against the deluge of emotions threatening to break. "How was breakfast?" Her question was a thin veneer over the churning suspicion.

"It was great," Sam replied, his nonchalance fanning the flames of her indignation.

"I bet it was. Is she married too?" Nicole's words slipped out, sharp and accusing.

"I think you mean he, and yes, he is," Sam corrected, his voice steady but a flicker of unease passing through his eyes.

"No, I mean she," Nicole's voice cracked, the weight of her hurt and anger no longer containable. "Stop lying to me, you pig. It's over." Her words were a tempest, unleashing all the pent-up fury and heartbreak. Sam's presence, once a source of comfort, now felt like an intrusion, a reminder of the betrayal that had seeped into the very core of their marriage.

As the accusations hung between them, the room was charged with the electricity of a relationship at its breaking point. Nicole, her heart in shards, stood defiant, a portrait of a woman pushed to the edge, ready to reclaim her life from the deceit that had overshadowed it.

Sam, taken aback, stood in stunned silence, confronted with the wreckage of his deceit. The weight of his actions bore down on him, the gravity of the betrayal leaving no room for excuses. As Nicole laid bare the shards of their fractured trust, the room became an arena for the clash of emotions — anger, heartbreak, and the irreparable breach of a love that had once felt unbreakable.

"I saw her, Sam," Nicole's voice trembled with the weight of her revelation. The strength to stand deserted her, and she collapsed onto the bed, her tears a testament to the shattering of her world. "I saw her. And I saw you going into that house, going back to your old love. Tell me, Sam, has she always been on your mind all these years that we've been together?"

"Now, that's not fair . . ." Sam attempted to interject, his words faltering in the face of Nicole's anguish.

"You're not in a position to lecture me about fairness," Nicole's cry cut through the room like a jagged blade.

"Let me explain." Sam, compelled to bridge the chasm between them, cautiously took a seat beside her.

"Don't you dare touch me," Nicole recoiled at the mere brush of his hand on her shoulder. "I tried to make sense of this. Believe me, Sam, I did. I asked myself, is he tired of me, or is our romance gone? Maybe I was too busy with the kids and work. But then I didn't see you with just any woman. I saw you with Roxana, the woman you almost married and apparently still love. Then I realized how naïve I was trying to blame myself instead of seeing you as the two-faced bastard you really are." Each word dripped with a mix of pain, betrayal, and a raw honesty that severed the final threads of illusion holding their relationship together.

The silence in the room was palpable as Sam struggled to hold Nicole's piercing gaze, the burden of his betrayal pressing down like a physical weight. Nicole, her voice laced with a blend of pain and incredulity, implored for an explanation, her words echoing the agony of a shattered heart. "How could you do this to us?"

Sam's admission was slow, his voice a mere whisper, as if speaking louder might fracture the fragile hope he clung to. "I know you saw me," he confessed, his eyes averted, unable to face the reflection of his deceit. "But please, it's not what you think, Nicole."

"Stop lying! Just stop!" Nicole's plea broke through the room, her voice trembling on the verge of despair. The walls seemed to close in around them, each syllable of denial adding to the claustrophobia of the moment.

Sam's plea for understanding was desperate, his face a mask of regret and helplessness. "I know I've broken your trust, but give me a chance to mend things. Let me explain," he implored, his voice barely above a whisper, laden with the weight of his mistakes.

Nicole's resolve was unyielding, her words cutting through his pleas like a knife. "You're only sorry because you were caught. This is the end," she declared, the finality of her decision reverberating like a death chime for their relationship.

Sam's desperation grew as he begged her to reconsider, his face contorted with the agony of impending loss. "Please, don't say that," he murmured, his voice raw with emotion.

"How many times did you see her?" Nicole demanded, her need for the truth overcoming the dread of its implications.

"Three times," he confessed, his voice breaking with remorse. "I swear, that's the truth, and nothing happened beyond . . ." His voice trailed off, leaving the sentence hanging, a tacit admission of the pain he had inflicted.!

Nicole's disbelief permeated the room as she cut him off, "Only three times?" Her voice was heavy with scorn and disbelief. "And did you fuck all three times?" The question itself was a venomous arrow aimed straight at the heart of their marriage.

"No, she wouldn't..." Sam's response was immediate, almost reflexive, but the implications of his words hung heavily between them.

"Get out!" Nicole's command was sharp, unequivocal. She pointed towards the door, her gesture a dismissal of their shared history. "So it was your intention. It doesn't matter what actually happened. I can't stay with you. We're done."

Sam, a mixture of regret and panic etched on his face, opened his mouth to protest, to explain, but Nicole cut him off with a wave of her hand.

"You've said enough," she declared, her voice cold and steady. "I can't even look at you anymore. Just leave. I'll be here through the wedding, but the kids and I are leaving first thing in the morning." The resolve in her voice left no room for negotiation, her words severing the last ties of their frayed bond.

"Don't involve the kids," Sam pleaded, the desperation clear in his voice.

"They were involved the moment you chose to fuck around," Nicole shot back, her voice trembling with a barely contained rage.

Resigned, Sam nodded. "I'll make arrangements for your departure tomorrow," he said quietly, not daring to incite further wrath.

As he turned to leave, he paused, a last flicker of hope in his eyes. "I won't give up on us. I know I've hurt you, but deep down, I believe you know I never meant for any of this to happen." His plea was a whisper of a once-strong love now crumbling.

Nicole remained silent, her focus on the task of packing, her movements deliberate and final. The click of the suitcase signified more than just a trip; it was the closure of a chapter in their lives. Her expression, once soft and loving, was now a mask of determination and sorrow, a reflection of the journey she was about to undertake - a journey to find a new sense of home and healing, driven by the indomitable spirit of a mother's love and the resolve to protect her children from the storm that had toppled their lives.

Chapter 52

On the sacred canvas of a wedding day, Iranian traditions unfold like delicate petals, each carrying the weight of symbolism and the promise of a shared destiny. Before the sun casts its golden glow, the groom embarks on a journey to fetch his bride, a voyage painted with the hues of love and adorned with the blossoms of hope. The "Bride Car," draped in a tapestry of flowers, becomes a carriage of dreams, navigating the streets as witnesses to a union in bloom.

At the heart of the ceremony, the bride and groom perch on a stall, elevated above an intricately adorned table. Symbols of luck and prosperity weave a tale of their new life—a life sweetened by crystallized sugar and honey, and embellished with trays of Persian delights, a confectionary ode to the sweetness that love bestows.

A congregation of close female friends and family forms a protective cocoon, holding a silk scarf above the couple. Two sugar rocks collide above the fabric, their fine granules cascading like a gentle rain. A visual poem, it narrates the fall of sweetness onto the canvas of their intertwined destinies.

In the dance of light and fire, life's energy finds expression through a mirror and candelabras. Prosperity unfolds, manifested in traditional flat Persian bread adorned with calligraphic verses, alongside a small jar harboring the alchemy of coins and rice. Fertility is heralded by the presence of painted eggs, almonds, and walnuts—a bountiful tapestry of life's beginnings.

Heavenly fruits, the ruby allure of pomegranates, and the crisp embrace of apples, stand testament to the sanctity of union. A tray of colored wild rue incense, aromatic and mystical, is a guardian against the malevolent gaze, casting a protective veil over the couple's shared journey.

In this rich tapestry of tradition, the wedding ceremony unfolds, a symphony of symbols that transcends regions, religions, tribes, and families, echoing the timeless resonance of love and commitment.

As the couple takes their seats, a moment of anticipation envelops the air. The groom, a veil between him and the bride, lifts the delicate fabric, revealing the face of his destined companion in the mirror. Vows, ethereal promises whispered in the sacred space, weave an invisible thread between their souls.

In a tender ritual, the groom, a sculptor of sweetness, anoints his beloved's lips with the golden nectar of honey. A kiss follows, sealing not only the shared sweetness but also the covenant of love. In a mirrored dance of reciprocity, the bride, in turn, bestows the same enchanting gesture upon her groom. A symphony of exchanged sweetness, a prelude to the harmonious duet of their lives.

Guests, adorned with offerings of gold coins and jewelry, cast their tributes into the treasury of wishes, announced and gathered in a vessel of dreams. Finger foods, delectable whispers of culinary delight, grace the tables, a prelude to the grand feast awaiting at the nighttime reception.

As the sun takes its bow, guests, enchanted witnesses to the unfolding tale, retreat to rest and change, preparing for the symphony of celebration set to ignite in the nocturnal hours. The reception, a celestial gala, concludes with the bride and groom embarking on a journey illuminated by the soft glow of the Bride's Car, a vessel of dreams adorned with the whispers of flowers.

The caravan of well-wishers, a procession of joy, trails behind them, the rhythmic symphony of honking horns echoing the harmonies of celebration. The Bride's Car leads the way, navigating a labyrinth of roads that unfold like the pages of a fairy tale, guiding the couple to the doorstep of their new home—a threshold where dreams intertwine and love finds its eternal abode.

Chapter 53

As Farhad and Ariana alighted from the resplendent Bride's Car, their arrival at Dr. Larabi's house marked the commencement of a ceremonial journey. With grace and elegance, they walked hand in hand, Tara and Cameron trailing behind, delicately holding the train of Ariana's gown. A retinue of joyous cousins accompanied them, transforming the path into a floral carpet with the scattered confetti of rose petals.

In a ballet of symbolism, a little cousin led the procession, strewing fragrant rose petals as offerings of love and purity. Following in their wake, another cherubic figure carried a brazier, flames dancing in harmony with the rhythmic beats of celebration. Wild rue, whispered into the fiery embrace, sought to bless the unfolding union and shield it from the envious gaze of the evil eye.

Farhad, entranced by the vision of his radiant bride, stole glances in the mirror that adorned the wedding table. A canvas of familial love and tradition, the tableau unfolded with each step, a tale painted with the hues of cultural richness.

A tapestry of women assembled over their head. Like sorceresses weaving spells of sweetness and fortune, they unfurled a silk scarf, its paisley embroidery a testament to the intricate artistry of tradition. In a dance of ritual, sugar rocks emerged, guided by tender hands, as whispers of blessings swirled in the air, drawing the essence of sweetness to enshroud the couple in a tapestry of joy and prosperity.

In the midst of the ceremonial sweetness, Jacqueline observed Sam with tears seemingly born of joy glistening in his eyes, unaware that they were instead the crystalline droplets of remorse. She gracefully handed the sugar rocks to Farhad's mom, orchestrating the next chapter of the tradition by beckoning Nicole to join.

"Your turn," Jacqueline announced, a twinkle of merriment in her eyes. "Traditionally, only the chosen ones get the honor of rubbing the sugar rocks. The belief is that the bride inherits the luck of the one wielding the rocks."

Nicole, hesitant, responded, "Then, she probably wouldn't want me doing it."

Jacqueline chuckled, dismissing Nicole's uncertainty. "What nonsense are you talking about? I can only hope Ariana gains as much luck as you possess."

If only you knew, Nicole mused.

"Ariana would insist you do it more than anyone else," Jacqueline assured as Mrs. Kamali passed the sugar rocks to Nicole. The grains began their dance, swirling in the air like tiny fairies, as Nicole, with a heavy heart, pressed them together. In that moment, she offered silent wishes of boundless luck and an idyllic life for Ariana, reminiscent of the life she once shared with Sam before this ill-fated journey. As she glanced at Sam, his gaze fixed on her, a genuine smile graced his face. In response, Nicole involuntarily mirrored the smile, but it swiftly faded into a furrowed brow of inner turmoil.

As the festivities dissolved into memories and guests departed to prepare for the upcoming reception at Sam's uncle's garden, an air of melancholy enveloped Nicole. Alone in her room, she began the ritual of changing, attempting to shed the emotional weight of the day.

Amidst the solitude, a hesitant knock echoed through the room. "Who is it?" Nicole's voice, tinged with certainty that it was Sam, concealed a wellspring of sorrow.

"Can I come in?" Sam's request lingered behind the closed door, a plea for permission before intruding into the fractured sanctuary of what remained of their intertwined lives.

Nicole, now enveloped in a bathrobe, reluctantly opened the door just enough to maintain a barrier. "What do you want?" Her question cut through the air, a frigid gust of emotions.

"I was going to rest a bit," Sam's words hung in the space between them, carrying the weight of unspoken truths.

"Let me get my stuff then. I can't stand being in the same room with you," Nicole's response was a stark declaration, a testament to the chasm that had grown between them.

"Don't worry then. I'll find somewhere else." The door was almost shut when Sam pivoted and dropped a bombshell. "You're all set. Your plane leaves tomorrow at noon."

Time stood still for Nicole. His words, heavy with finality, echoed in the room. A life without Sam unfolded before her eyes, a daunting prospect. The possibility of closure tugged at her, a desire for him to offer an explanation. With closed eyes, she placed her hand on the door, sensing a mirrored gesture from Sam on the other side. Summoning her courage, she grasped the door handle, took a deep breath, and swung it open. Instead of Sam, she was met with an empty corridor, the echo of his retreating footsteps on the stairwell fading into the profound silence. The door, a symbolic gateway to her fractured reality, swung shut with a soft, heartbreaking thud.

Chapter 54

In the grandeur of Farhad and Ariana's extravagant ceremony, the opulence of the setting belied the turmoil within Nicole. The air buzzed with anticipation as the guests, adorned in their finest, gathered before the arrival of the bride and groom. Farhad and Ariana, a vision of love, entered in with the Bride's Car, greeted by the thunderous applause of their guests. They gracefully circulated among the tables, expressing gratitude for the attendees before settling into their seats.

As the band played a soulful melody, inviting the newlyweds to share their first dance, the atmosphere brimmed with celebration. However, a shadow loomed over Nicole as Sam rose from his seat, extending an invitation to the dance floor.

"I know the way," Nicole muttered, her steps heavy with reluctance, passing Sam on her way to the center of the stage.

Sam's hands enveloped her, a feeble attempt to bridge the emotional chasm between them. The dance floor, usually a space of joy, became a battleground of unspoken pain. The light flickered across Nicole's face as she removed one of Sam's hands, holding the other with a fragile grip. His eyes pleaded for forgiveness, but Nicole's gaze remained elusive.

"You broke my heart," Nicole moaned, her voice carrying the weight of shattered dreams. "You broke my heart, Sam."

"For what it's worth, we were not going to see each other again. We realized it was a big mistake from the beginning. Please give me a chance to mend everything," Sam implored, desperation etched on his face.

Nicole, locking eyes with him for the first time, questioned the feasibility of healing wounds so deep. "How do you mend a broken heart? Tell me, Sam, how do you do that?"

"You're the heart doctor," Sam attempted a feeble jest. "Tell me how, and I'll do it."

A pause lingered, the music a distant hum in the background. Nicole, having halted in their dance, revealed the harsh reality. "Even then, it would leave a scar forever," she declared, her voice resonating with the wisdom of a heart doctor intimately acquainted with the permanence of scars. The dance floor, once a symbol of unity, now bore witness to the irreparable fractures between them.

In the tender embrace of the slow song, Sam clung to the fleeting moments, praying that the music would play on, freezing time in the sanctuary of the dance floor. His heart quivered with the fear that, perhaps, he only possessed her until the final notes echoed through the air.

As the last strains of the song hung in the atmosphere, she released his hands, severing the fragile connection that bound them in the dance. With each step she took away from him, Sam felt the gap widening, an unbridgeable gulf expanding at a pace that echoed the crushing gorge of light years.

He watched her silhouette recede, the distance becoming an insurmountable expanse. In that agonizing moment, Sam questioned whether he would ever again have the privilege of holding her in his arms, the warmth of their shared past slipping away like grains of sand through desperate fingers. The fading song's echoes resonated through the garden, a poignant reflection of the dissonance between Sam and Nicole, leaving Sam enveloped in a somber reverie of better times. Each note seemed to linger, a mournful accompaniment to the shards of their once harmonious life, now scattered around him like fragments of a forgotten melody. The silence that followed was heavy, filled with the unspoken grief of what had been and the haunting realization of all that was lost.

Chapter 55

The next morning unfolded like a bittersweet tableau for Sam. Awaking with a hollow ache in his chest, he found solace in the presence of the children nestled beside him. Nicole's parting words, uttered with the tender concern of a loving mother, echoed in his mind: "They should stay with you on their last night here. I'll sleep in their room."

Checking the time, Sam discovered it was almost nine, and the weight of the sleepless night clung to him. In silent reverence, he treaded lightly towards Nicole's room. The door, slightly ajar, invited a hesitant peek. The sight within struck a chord in his heart — a neatly made bed adorned with two sets of carefully placed clothes for Tara and Cameron, and five suitcases standing sentinel by the door, silent witnesses to an imminent departure.

Descending the stairs, the murmurs of conversation reached him. Nicole and his mother shared a moment in the family room, their exchange carrying a weight that hung in the air. Peeking into the kitchen, Sam found his father seated at the table, immersed in a book with a glass of tea by his side. As he stepped into the room, the morning salutation escaped his lips, "Good morning." Yet, the ache in his heart spoke louder than his words, a silent anthem to the imminent departure.

"Good morning." Bijan said, setting aside his reading glasses.

Sam poured a glass of tea, the ritual of a familiar routine offering a thin veil of normalcy. "What are they talking about?" Sam asked, gesturing towards the living room.

"Women," Bijan chuckled. "They never run out of things to talk about. They're probably gossiping about last night. Who wore what and who said what."

Sam wished that was the case, a simple chatter about trivial matters. But he knew the undercurrents were more profound. He walked towards the family room, hoping to catch the drift of their conversation. As he intruded with a tentative question, "Am I interrupting something?" his presence was met with silence.

Turning toward him, their eyes held an unspoken weight, and Jacqueline's gaze bore into Sam's soul. Nicole clasped Jacqueline's hand, exchanging a look that conveyed a myriad of emotions, and without a word, she left the room, a ghostly presence passing by Sam.

The room was immersed with a stifling tension as Jacqueline's words shattered the silence, "Nicole is leaving today and you're the one who should explain why."

Sam, overcome with a tide of guilt, collapsed into the nearest chair, his entire being heavy with the burden of his indiscretion. His confession was a mere whisper, "I wronged her, Mom." a fractured admittance of the pain he inflicted on the woman he vowed to cherish.

"Who's the other woman?" Jacqueline's voice cut sharply through the thick air, her accusation pinpointed to an old flame, "Roxana?" Sam's nod was heavy, laden with the weight of his betrayal, an unspoken confirmation that sent ripples of disappointment and anger through Jacqueline. The atmosphere became charged with an almost tangible disapproval from Jacqueline. Her words were like daggers, each one laden with frustration and disbelief at the folly that had unfolded.

"I know it was wrong to see her, but we just talked, nothing else." Sam's feeble attempt to downplay the affair did nothing to quell the rising storm within Jacqueline. Her voice escalated, a crescendo of indignation and urgency that filled the room.

Jacqueline's anger was more than emotional; it was rooted in the harsh reality of their society's unforgiving laws. She reminded Sam of the severe repercussions of his actions, not just on a personal level but legally as well. In their land, an act as seemingly benign as a clandestine meeting could lead to draconian punishments, death by stoning. The gravity of the situation was palpable, the weight of Sam's mistake hanging over them like a dark cloud, threatening to burst and drown them in its shadow.

As he sat there, the full magnitude of his recklessness bore down on him, a burdensome realization that what started as a whispered conversation had spiraled into a life-altering scandal. "I know it was a mistake, and I want to make it right. But Nicole... she just won't give me a chance." Sam uttered. His heart aching to reverse the irreversible. Every fiber of his being vibrated with the desire to make amends, yet the cold, hard truth was that Nicole remained unreachable, her heart sealed off from his pleas.

Jacqueline watched her son, her own heart heavy with a mother's sorrow and wisdom. Her question to Sam was more than words; it was an invitation to introspection, a nudge to consider the enormity of his betrayal from Nicole's perspective. "What would you do if you were in her shoes, Sam?"

The silence that followed was thick, filled with the weight of unspoken truths and the gravity of a trust broken. Sam, with his eyes cast down, was the picture of contrition. The realization of what he had done, the utter disbelief at his own capacity to inflict such pain, washed over him. "I can't even imagine her doing something like this," he admitted. It was a moment of stark clarity, a painful acknowledgment that he couldn't even begin to imagine the roles reversed without feeling a deep, unsettling churn in his gut.

"And that's precisely why it's so hard for her," Jacqueline said softly, yet with a firmness that underscored her words. "She trusted you, Sam, and you shattered that trust. I can't tell you how to fix this, but the path to forgiveness, if there is one, starts with you proving that you're worthy of her trust again." She didn't need to raise her voice; the truth of her words cut through him sharply. Her eyes, filled with a mix of pain and resolve, fixed on Sam, reminding him of the long and uncertain road to redemption that lay ahead. It wasn't just about saying the right words or making grand gestures; it was about the slow, painstaking process of rebuilding trust, step by step, day by day.

A vulnerable curiosity flickered in Sam's eyes. "Mom, would you have forgiven Dad if he..."

Jacqueline's expression tightened, clouded with memories and what-ifs. "The quick answer is no. But life... life isn't always about quick answers. People endure and stay together through storms much worse than this. When a woman stands to lose so much, she might find reasons to reconsider. So, the real answer? Maybe I would forgive, if I had absolute assurance it wouldn't happen again."

She reached out, her hand gently squeezing his. "Nicole loves those children immensely, Sam. She wouldn't want to tear their world apart. If you want any chance of mending this, show her, genuinely show her, how much your family means to you. Let her see your remorse, not just hear it. Actions, in this case, will speak louder than any words you can offer."

Naneh's voice held a tinge of sadness as she announced the readiness of breakfast, her eyes flickering with unspoken concern. Jacqueline's request for Javad to fetch Nicole's luggage hung in the air, a heavy prelude to the impending departure.

"I didn't know you were leaving today," Naneh confessed, her tone carrying the weight of unexpected separation. "Be daste Khoda," she whispered, a silent plea for divine protection, her hands forming an unseen shield around Nicole and the children.

In the midst of this quiet farewell, Jacqueline's footsteps echoed with a sense of urgency as she ascended the stairs to help Nicole. "I don't blame you for doing this," Jacqueline gently conveyed, her words a bridge between understanding and sorrow. "I can't tell you what to do. I wish you would give him a chance to make everything right again."

Nicole's response, laden with the weight of unspoken struggles, hung in the air like the fragile threads of a decision unraveling. "How would he do that? And even if by some miracle he did, will our life ever be the same again? I need some time apart from him to decide what to do."

"We must wake the kids now," Jacqueline declared, her voice a bittersweet reminder that life, despite its trials, marched on.

The sound of hurried footsteps echoed through the house, carrying the energy of youth and innocence. Tara and Cameron descended the stairs like a whirlwind, their voices a symphony of excitement and urgency. "Dad, Dad!" they called, a chorus of young hearts seeking comfort.

"I'm here," Sam reassured, his voice a steady anchor in the midst of their exuberance. "Why are you guys screaming?"

"We don't want to go back yet. We have so much fun here," Tara and Cameron chimed in, their words a plea laced with the pure joy of childhood.

Sam knelt down to their eye level, his gaze reflecting a mixture of love and responsibility. "But you guys must stay with your mother and take care of her. I promise to get you lots of gifts when I get back."

Tara's eyes, pools of innocence, welled up with emotion. "I will miss you, Dad," she whispered, her small hand reaching out to grasp his.

"I'll miss you both too," Sam replied, enveloping them in a heartfelt embrace. The weight of impending separation hung in the air, and in that tender moment, Sam found solace in the warmth of their shared affection.

"I still have some stuff to do here. Meanwhile, I want you two to be the best kids and don't give Mommy any trouble. Now go on and have some breakfast. We are leaving for the airport soon," Sam instructed, his voice a blend of parental authority and a yearning for a smooth transition in their absence.

In the somber ambiance of the airport, Sam checked them in, the mechanical process a stark contrast to the emotional turmoil brewing within. With the boarding passes in hand, he approached Nicole, their connection tethered by unspoken words. She swiftly took the passes, an unspoken farewell in her movements, leaving Sam with a silent ache.

"Is there anything I can do to change your mind?" Sam's voice quivered with the weight of desperation as Nicole distanced herself. Her response was a simple shake of the head, a gesture that spoke volumes, a heartbreaking silence that echoed through the departing corridors.

Bijan, a silent witness to the unraveling scene, stepped forward with a fatherly concern. "Do you have everything, my dear?" he inquired, his voice a gentle undercurrent of support.

"I think so," Nicole whispered, her words carrying the burden of uncertainty. "When you live with someone for so long, you think you really know him. I guess I was wrong," Nicole admitted, her voice carrying the weight of shattered illusions and the ache of a love gone awry. The words lingered in the air like an unresolved melody, haunting the spaces between them.

Bijan, the wise observer, responded with a mix of empathy and understanding, "I'm certain no one knows him better than you do, and I'm sure you know how much he loves you and the children. He made a terrible mistake, and he knows it. A lot happened after he left that he never found out about. If I had told him everything, he wouldn't have to look for the answers himself." Bijan's tone held a subtle knowing, a revelation that hinted at the depth of unspoken truths, as if he carried burdens of untold stories.

Nicole, in her quest for understanding, ventured into the shadows of the past. "What did you keep from him?" Her question, a plea for clarity, opened a door to the concealed chapters of their past lives.

"It doesn't matter now," Bijan replied, his words a delicate dance around the gravity of the undisclosed. There was a nuance in his tone, a suggestion that the passage of time had transformed the significance of those hidden truths. A silent wonder lingered in the spaces between his words, contemplating whether Roxana had unraveled the secrets to Sam.

As the announcement for flight 637 to Tehran reverberated through the sterile corridors of the airport, it cast a poignant backdrop to the unfolding emotional tableau.

"Have a safe trip," Bijan's well-wishing words carried a depth of sincerity as he enveloped Nicole in a farewell hug. Their embrace, a silent exchange of support, whispered of unspoken emotions and the gravity of departure.

"Come home soon, Dad," Cameron's voice, laden with the sorrow of separation, echoed like a melancholic refrain. It was more than a farewell; it was a son's plea for the swift return of normalcy, a hope that hung in the air like a delicate promise.

"I'll be home before you know it," Sam's assurance, though resolute, bore the weight of the uncertainty that lingered between departure and reunion. His words, a tether connecting the present to an imagined future, sought to anchor the family in the face of impending change.

"Remember that you're the man of the house now and must take care of your mother and sister," Sam hugged Cameron.

"I will, Dad. What time should I make them go to bed?" Cameron's attempt at humor, a fleeting moment of levity, carried a bittersweet undertone. It was a son's way of navigating the uncharted waters of familial responsibility, a jest that masked the vulnerability beneath.

"I'll leave that up to you," Sam's response, while seemingly casual, hinted at the profound shift in the family dynamic.

Turning toward Tara, Sam's attempt at humor injected a fleeting moment of lightheartedness into the heavy atmosphere. "Oh look, here's my favorite daughter."

"I'm your only daughter, Dad," Tara's retort, wrapped in playful defiance, carried the echo of a deeper truth. It was a daughter's way of asserting her unique place in the familial tapestry, a gentle reminder of the bonds that tied them together.

"It makes me love you even more," Sam's confession, delivered with a soft smile, added a layer of tenderness to the moment.

He met Nicole's teary gaze, their eyes locking in a silent exchange pregnant with unspoken longing. "We'll be together soon," Sam's promise, delivered against the backdrop of imminent separation, wove a thread of hope through the fabric of farewell.

As Nicole and the kids disappeared beyond the confines of the security check, leaving a palpable void in the terminal, Sam turned to his mother with a heavy heart. "You and Dad go home. I'll come a bit later," he murmured, his voice carrying the weight of unspoken burdens.

Pressing his face against the vast, cold glass pane that separated him from his family, Sam became a silent observer of their departure. His breath fogged the surface as he watched their plane taxiing away from the terminal. In that moment, the glass transformed into an invisible barrier, a metaphorical wall that mirrored the emotional distance growing between them.

His longing manifested in a silent wish, a desperate desire to breach the boundaries of reality. He yearned to step onto the runway, to halt the departure of that airplane, to freeze time and keep intact the fragile threads of family. The scene played out in his mind like a scene from a movie, where love triumphs over separation, and endings are rewritten with the power of sheer will.

The deafening roar of the airplane engines shattered his reverie as the metallic beast took flight, carrying with it the essence of his world. In the thunderous tumult, Sam felt the tearing of invisible threads connecting him to Nicole and the kids. Their ascent into the vast expanse of the sky mirrored the widening chasm of the unknown, leaving Sam standing alone, grounded by the weight of unspoken truths.

As the plane disappeared into the distant heavens, Sam wished he could unravel the tangled strands of their recent past. There was a longing to share the untold story, to convey the complexities that had woven themselves into the fabric of their lives. The garden held secrets, words left unspoken, and Sam yearned for the chance to rewrite the narrative, to bridge the gap before the distance became irreversible.

The weight of unspoken truths pressed heavily on Sam's shoulders as he yearned for the courage to confess the tumultuous events that had transpired in the garden. It began with a kiss, a kiss that ignited a cascade of memories, pulling Roxana back to a time when the same man had kissed her with the same fervor. However, the once-delightful aura of innocence that enveloped those moments had now been replaced by a suffocating cloud of guilt and impurity. It felt as though the man she kissed now was a different entity altogether, a stark contrast to the boy who had departed two decades ago.

As Sam replayed the scenes in his mind, he could almost taste the bittersweet echoes of that passionate kiss. It was a haunting reminder of a connection that transcended the present, echoing the echoes of an intimate history. The very essence of love and betrayal seemed to dance in the shadows of that stolen moment, casting a complex web of emotions over the garden where the boundaries of fidelity blurred.

Roxana's visceral reaction, a gentle yet firm push, marked the turning point in the story. As she halted the progression of his hands – one caressing her back and the other daring to explore the terrain beneath her short dress – the atmosphere shifted. The touch, once laden with shared secrets and stolen intimacy, now became a catalyst for the awakening of guilt and the realization of crossing lines that were never meant to be breached.

In the silent resistance of Roxana's push, the unspoken language of boundaries asserted itself. It was a quiet plea for restraint, a line drawn in their soils, a moment where innocence was tainted by the irreversible stain of indiscretion. Sam's heart ached as he grappled with the contrast between the past and the present, between a love that once flourished in the garden and the guilt-laden reality that now enveloped it.

As Roxana spoke, the weight of unspoken emotions hung in the air, the room heavy with the complexity of their past. "My heart belongs to you, Saam, but not my body, not anymore," she confessed, turning slowly to face him. Her words were a delicate unraveling of the intricate threads that bound them, a revelation of a love confined to the sanctuary of her heart.

A tender ache enveloped Sam as he combed his fingers through her hair, a silent gesture of understanding and acceptance. "I'm happy just to be here with you. You know how much I care for you," he expressed, his touch a silent reassurance in the face of the unspoken.

Yet, Roxana, with a vulnerability that echoed in the depths of her gaze, continued to lay bare her soul. "I know. I also know that you can't say you love me," she asserted, preempting any response from Sam. "Please don't say anything. I don't want you to make something up."

A swirl of confusion and unspoken truths danced in the air. Sam, grappling with the weight of his own emotions, attempted to bridge the growing distance. "Why would you think..."

"It's not that complicated," Roxana interrupted again, her voice a mixture of sorrow and acceptance. "I shared my true feelings with you when I said I love you. If you felt the same, you would have said the same thing."

Sam, with a vulnerable admission, acknowledged, "You're right, I couldn't say it."

"It's OK, Saam," Roxana lifted his chin, her touch gentle but filled with a sad knowing. "You're lucky that you can love your spouse so much that you couldn't say it. I wish I could feel the same way."

"I don't know what to say," Sam confessed, his own vulnerability laid bare in the face of Roxana's raw honesty.

"She is lucky to have all of your heart," Roxana acknowledged, her words carrying the weight of both resignation and longing.

"How lucky is she when I'm here with you, and if you hadn't stopped..." Sam's words lingered in the air, a sentence left unfinished, the unspoken implication casting shadows over their existence.

"I yearn to feel the same way about my husband," Roxana's admission reverberated with the echoes of unfulfilled desires. "Recall when I expressed loving you more than him. The sorrowful reality is that I know you could never love me as profoundly as he does." Her words carried the weight of experience, hinting at confessions made to her , adding an intricate layer to the fabric of their long journey.

"I loved you so much, Roxana, but you shut me out of your life. He was given a chance to show his love. I wasn't," Sam's voice echoed with the bitterness of unspoken pain, the echoes of a love that had slipped through his fingers.

"Actually, he proved how devoted he was before we got married. I told him everything that happened between us, and he still wanted to marry me," Roxana revealed, her words carrying the weight of a tumultuous past. As she defended her choices, memories of troubled times played across her face, underscoring the significance and vitality attributed to virginity in their culture.

"So you made sure you had someone before dumping me. But why? Was it because he had more money?" Sam unfairly accused, the sting of betrayal coloring his words.

"How dare you judge me like that? You don't have the slightest idea what I had to go through. But Nader did," Roxana retorted, her frustration bubbling to the surface. The wounds of her past, now exposed, were raw, and Sam's judgment only intensified the ache.

"How about what I went through? At least you had him," Sam's words held the echoes of a love lost, the bitterness of abandonment.

"Stop it, Saam," Roxana implored, her plea laced with the vulnerability of a heart laid bare. "It really hurts when you talk like that."

"I was hurting too. Did you even think about that before choosing the easy way out? At least now I know why you left," Sam softened his tone, a glimmer of understanding dawning.

"No, you don't," Roxana cried, the weight of her secret pressing on her shoulders.

"Then tell me," Sam insisted, his need for the truth cutting through the emotional fog.

"You don't want to know," she hesitated, the burden of the truth heavy on her soul.

"I do," Sam pressed, a desperate yearning in his voice. "I really do."

"I died that day. Believe me, it was more difficult for me..." Roxana hesitated, the weight of the unspoken truth casting shadows on her face. The air hung heavy with the unspoken, the silence echoing with the pain of concealed secrets. Sam, undeterred, kept insisting until Roxana's resistance crumbled, and she shouted, "I was pregnant with your baby." The words, heavy with the weight of revelation, tumbled into the room, leaving a palpable sense of relief and an added burden on her shoulders.

The news hit Sam with the force of a moving train, freezing him on the spot. The gravity of the revelation sank in, reshaping the landscape of their lives, together and apart.

"I'm sorry, Saam, but you made me say it. Please say something, please, Saam. I should have kept my mouth shut," Roxana pleaded, her vulnerability laid bare. "We never wanted you to find out. You can tell me you hate me, but please, just say something."

Sam was speechless. He leaned against the wall, his back sliding down to the floor next to her. The weight of their intertwined past remained heavy in the air, the room filled with the silence of broken revelations and the palpable ache of two hearts trying to navigate the wreckage of what once was.

Chapter 56

As we journey back to the waning days of 1979, a year marred by the consequences of a nation's own missteps, we encounter Roxana in the sanctum of her room, a haven where her innocent prayers resonate with the heartache of a soul entangled in the tragedies of her time.

Kneeling in the dim light, Roxana directs her fervent pleas to God, grappling with questions only the divine could unravel. She confides in Him, seeking understanding as to why, at the cruel hands of fate, Sam was wrested from her during the darkest hours of her life. In the solitude of her sanctuary, she confesses her perceived sin, a love so pure that she only surrendered to its depths when the promise of marriage lingered on the horizon.

Tears stream down her cheeks as she implores for God's forgiveness, her words a poignant melody of innocence seeking redemption. Roxana reasons with the Almighty, laying bare the sincerity of her love and the careful steps taken to preserve the sanctity of their union. She pleads for the torment to cease, beseeching God not to unravel the fabric of her life with relentless punishment, a desperate call to the divine to spare her from the repercussions of a world stained by the misfortunes of its own making.

About three weeks had elapsed since Sam bid farewell to Iran, and Roxana found herself five days overdue for her menstrual period. With each passing day, the shadow of her worst nightmare loomed larger. Alone in her distress, she sought refuge in the only solace she knew — her prayers. Yet, as the weight of her unease grew within, she recognized the imperative need to confide in the one person she believed could offer solace and understanding.

Under the sprawling canopy of an ancient tree, Dr. Larabi parked his 1950 Oldsmobile Futuramic 88, its vintage charm a stark contrast to the modern facade of Namazi Hospital. As he secured the vehicle, the parched leaves above whispered secrets of the past, setting a stage for the impending encounter. The air was thick with the scent of impending rain, a subtle reminder of the changing tides of life.

As he turned, a silhouette approached, her form shrouded in the hospital's fluorescent shadow. "Hello, Mr. Doctor," came the quivering voice of Roxana, her words floating like a feather on a gentle a breeze. Her eyes, wide and brimming with unshed tears, betrayed a vulnerability that tugged at Bijan's heartstrings.

"Hello, my daughter. I'm surprised to see you here." Bijan's voice was a soft balm, his words carrying the weight of a thousand comforting embraces. He noted the tremble in her lips, the way her hands clasped and unclasped in a rhythm of anxiety.

"I... I need to confide in you. May we speak privately?" Her request hung between them, a delicate thread of hope stretched taut with urgency. Bijan nodded, sensing the gravity of her words yet to be spoken.

Within the sanctuary of his office, the world outside faded to a murmur. Bijan closed the door, enveloping them in a cocoon of confidentiality. "Saam says you two talk every day, weaving dreams of a future reunited," he began, hoping to ease her into revelation.

Roxana's eyes fluttered shut for a moment, as if gathering the shards of her courage. "But when? When will these dreams weave into reality?" Her voice was a whisper, each word a petal falling from the blossom of her hope.

"Saam seeks counsel with legal advisers, to hasten the day when dreams and daylight merge," Bijan revealed, his tone a mixture of reassurance and solemnity. He observed the play of emotions across her face, a canvas of worry and wistful longing.

The room seemed to close in around them, the ticking of the clock a reminder of the fleeting nature of time. Roxana, unable to meet his gaze, stared at the floor in a heavy silence. Sensing there was more beneath the surface, Bijan pulled a chair and sat beside her. Gently, he raised her chin, discovering tears silently streaming down her face. In that tender moment, he acknowledged the depth of her pain, reassuring her that tears alone couldn't dissolve the hardships she faced. With a steady hand on her shoulder, he spoke words of hope, promising that, one day, the souls divided by distance and circumstance would be reunited, their love standing resilient against the trials of separation.

Roxana hesitated, each syllable escaping her lips with measured weight, an attempt to convey that her purpose extended beyond the obvious. Dr. Larabi, sensing the depth of her unspoken sentiments, gently clasped her hand, a silent reassurance that he was there to listen, not to judge. His comforting touch spurred her to vocalize the emotions that had long lingered in the shadows.

"I... I want to talk," she finally managed, the words fragile and laden with unspoken feelings. Yet, a veil of embarrassment and shame clouded her admission. The fear of judgment and the vulnerability of exposing her innermost struggles made the confession almost unbearable.

Dr. Larabi, unwavering in his support, encouraged her to share her burden, assuring her that he was not a mind reader, but a compassionate listener. Roxana, grappling with the intensity of her emotions, acknowledged the potential magnitude of her revelation. She confessed that the weight of her words, once spoken, might render her unable to meet his gaze again.

Bijan, with genuine compassion, reassured Roxana that his role was to help people, encouraging her not to be too hard on herself. He hoped to lift the weight of her troubles, coaxing her to open up. Recognizing her struggle, he proposed a considerate gesture: closing his eyes to create a safe space for her to share.

Grateful for his understanding, Roxana lifted her head to find him with closed eyes, offering her a sense of privacy. "I'm listening," he assured her.

Overwhelmed with hesitation, Roxana began, "Oh my god. I don't know how to start."

"Talk as though God is the only one listening," Bijan gently suggested, releasing her hand, allowing her to imagine a sacred conversation between her and her Creator.

Roxana, turning her chair away, folded her hands in prayer, confessing the intimate details of her relationship with Saam. She pleaded with God, acknowledging the depth of their love and the fear that gripped her as she faced a potential reality. Bijan, maintaining the integrity of his closed eyes, braced himself for the revelation that unfolded.

As Roxana revealed her fears of being pregnant, the room grew silent, the weight of her words lingering in the air. Bijan, sensing her vulnerability, kept his eyes closed, understanding the gravity of her confession.

When Roxana finished speaking, she broke the silence, hearing her own heartbeat. Despite her initial trepidation, she looked at Bijan, who still had his eyes closed, and declared him the only person she could turn to. Pleading with him to open his eyes, she sought connection and reassurance.

"You'd be surprised if you knew how often these things happen," Bijan responded, his words carrying a mist of promise, reassuring her that she was not alone in society. He emphasized that it wasn't a time for a lecture but urged caution for the future.

"I'm sorry, Mr. Doctor. You're right. We were stupid. We weren't thinking," Roxana admitted, acknowledging their lapse in judgment.

Bijan, understanding the weight of the situation, advised her to focus on the present and take the necessary steps, beginning with a test. Fearful of the potential repercussions, Roxana voiced her concerns about the news spreading.

"You have no choice," Bijan responded, dialing a number on his office phone, signaling the beginning of the journey to navigate the challenges ahead.

The room began to blur around Roxana as the weight of her situation pressed upon her. In an attempt to steady herself, she leaned back in the chair, her mind spiraling with worry.

Dr. Larabi, recognizing her distress, held her hand in a gesture of comfort. He conveyed his empathy, acknowledging that he could only imagine the turmoil she was experiencing. With a solemn promise to help in any way he could, he suggested starting with a blood test and asked her to return the following day for a more in-depth discussion. Encouraging her to take some time to clear her head, he initiated the process of drawing blood.

"Did you tell Saam you were coming here?" Dr. Larabi inquired, preparing for the blood test.

"Oh no, Mr. Doctor. He doesn't know anything about this," she replied.

"Maybe it's best to keep it that way for now," he suggested, recognizing the delicate nature of the news and unsure of how Sam might react.

Roxana did not feel the needle penetrated her soft skin, preoccupied with worry, found solace in reciting prayers from the Koran. Grateful for the doctor's assistance, she expressed her appreciation amid the quiet room.

"I'm glad you didn't leave with them," Roxana said, her curiosity piqued. "By the way, how come you didn't leave the country? You're the only person I know who can go to America but didn't."

Dr. Larabi explained that his deep connection to the country and its people compelled him to stay. He couldn't simply abandon his responsibilities, even in the face of challenges. Roxana, acknowledging his dedication, believed he had more than fulfilled any obligations owed to the people.

"Put some pressure here," Dr. Larabi instructed as he placed a Band-Aid on her arm. He delved into the reasons behind his decision to stay, sharing that the country had sponsored his education. Despite changes in regimes, he emphasized that his moral responsibilities extended beyond politics. Reflecting on the Shah's initiative to send students abroad, Dr. Larabi expressed the belief that educated individuals should return to contribute to the betterment of their homeland, especially in times of need.

The following day, Roxana returned to the hospital, her heart pounding with anxiety, eagerly praying for a negative test result. Surprisingly, the door was unlocked, and she timidly entered. Dr. Larabi, sensing her distress, motioned for her to come in, offering her a seat as he greeted her at the door.

"You came early to work today," Roxana smiled nervously. "I hope there is some good news."

Dr. Larabi, with a heavy sigh, began expressing the harsh reality that life was not meant to be easy, but somehow, we manage to survive. In that moment, Roxana sensed the weight of his words, and her eyes welled with tears.

"I can't change the facts," Bijan said, his eyes filled with sympathy and care. He tried to comfort her as she struggled to catch her breath. Roxana sobbed, feeling as if her life were over, searching for answers in the doctor's demeanor.

"What else can I do besides killing myself?" she responded when asked about her thoughts on the situation. Dr. Larabi assured her that, although not easy, she would live through this ordeal.

"Unwed and pregnant," Roxana cried, fearing her father's reaction. She envisioned being disowned, marked as a reject in society, unable to raise her head amongst friends and family. Despite the doctor's reassurances that these things happen, she declared that it didn't happen in her family. Dr. Larabi understood her distress but encouraged her to explore her options, leaving Roxana in tears with no clear path in mind.

As Dr. Larabi paced his office, he proposed an option: talking to her father and convincing him to allow her to go to Turkey, where she and Sam could get married. Roxana, aware of her father's traditional values, knew this suggestion was impractical.

"No one can blame him either," Dr. Larabi acknowledged, aware of her father's influential position in society. Testing the waters, he gently suggested, "What if he knew about the situation?" Roxana's sigh indicated that this was not an option.

"I'm not out of my mind," Roxana cried. "First, he would kill me, and then Saam whenever he gets the chance. No, that's not even an option."

Bijan continued to pace, exploring solutions. Roxana, with hesitance, mentioned the abortion option, only to be confronted by the doctor's acknowledgment that it was both illegal after the revolution and morally complex, considering it would be his first grandchild. Despite this, he confessed that the idea had crossed his mind, and if it were the only viable option to rescue her from this predicament, he would arrange it.

"It may be my only option. I'm running out of time. You're the only one who can help me," Roxana declared.

Dr. Larabi advised her to go home, take time to think, and assured her that he would respect her final decision.

Chapter 57

On her way home, the weight of Roxana's choices bore down on her like a heavy burden. Each step felt more laborious, echoing the internal struggle within her. The streets of Shiraz, once familiar and comforting, now seemed foreign and unwelcoming. Her mind raced with conflicting thoughts, and the reality of her situation weighed heavily on her heart.

The sun obscured by ominous dark gray clouds casted dark shadows across the city, mirroring the uncertainty that loomed in Roxana's future. With every passing moment, she grappled with the implications of her decision. The bustling streets became a backdrop to her inner turmoil, and the once vibrant colors of the marketplaces now appeared muted and somber.

As she reached her doorstep, Roxana hesitated before entering, a mixture of fear and resignation in her eyes. The threshold symbolized a crossing into an uncertain chapter of her life, one she had never imagined. The quietude of her home embraced her like a shroud, and the echo of her footsteps reverberated with the weight of impending choices.

In the solitude of her room, Roxana sank into contemplation, grappling with the harsh reality of her predicament. The weight of impending decisions hung heavy in the air, and she found herself standing at the crossroads of choices that would irreversibly alter the trajectory of her life. As tears streamed down her face, each drop seemed to carry the weight of the uncertainty that clouded her future.

Amidst her quiet despair, a soft knock on the door disrupted the stillness of her solitude. Roxana hastily wiped her tear-stained face, and the knocks persisted, growing in intensity. Nader's voice reached her, seeking permission to enter, and she reluctantly granted access.

As she faced Nader, he implored for a moment of her time. With a nod, she stepped aside, allowing him to enter the sanctuary of her room—an intimate space she had never shared with him before.

Nader, navigating the uncharted boundaries of her solitude, nervously accepted the offered seat on her bed. The weight of the unspoken situation lingered in the air, and he attempted to diffuse the tension with a casual remark about the 'Grease" movie poster on her wall. "I finally watched that movie." Roxana, feigning a smile, recognized the diversionary tactic but played along.

After a palpable silence, Nader broached the real reason for his presence. He mentioned Sam's departure and his uncertain return, probing Roxana's willingness to wait for him. Sensing an underlying motive, she responded with a vague assurance of waiting a lifetime but acknowledged the unpredictable nature of life's twists.

In a hesitant attempt to convey his feelings, Nader apologized for any distress caused, assuring Roxana to take all the time she needed for Sam. However, he also expressed his unwavering commitment to patiently wait for her in case she reaches the conclusion that he would never return.

In the somber atmosphere of her room, Roxana recognized the sincerity reflected in Nader's eyes and body language. She grappled with conflicting emotions, sensing the depth of his admiration and unwavering dedication to her. Contemplating her own harshness, she acknowledged his kindness but stressed the complexities of her situation, implying that if he knew the full story, he might not desire her.

Nader, undeterred, declared his unconditional love, vowing to stand by her side regardless of the circumstances. Roxana, taken aback, urged him not to wait for her, believing he deserved someone more deserving of his kind heart. Despite her protests, Nader insisted on making his own decisions and respecting her privacy. The looming difficulty of revealing her secret to him weighed heavily on Roxana.

As they delved into the painful recollections, Roxana's words were like stepping stones across a tumultuous river of memories. With a quivering voice, she unveiled the hidden chapter of her life with Sam, sharing his bed with him, her sentences steeped in regret and a longing for what might have been. "It happened only on his last lingering hours in Shiraz. We were young, foolish, and believed we're getting married soon." The soft timbre of her voice seemed to reach back in time, touching the remnants of a bond that had once felt unbreakable, now fractured by the relentless passage of time and the weight of decisions.

Nader, his face a mask of disbelief, recoiled as if the words were physical blows. "I can't reconcile this image of you," he stammered, his voice a mixture of shock and hurt. "You, him, entwined in such a way...I never saw you like that."

"Saw me like what? A sinner? A lover?" Roxana's retort was sharp, her tears shimmering with defiance. "You promised me understanding, not condemnation," she reminded him, her plea wrapped in a shroud of despair.

The room felt smaller as Nader began to pace, each step a testament to his inner conflict. "But to sleep with someone outside of marriage... How will you explain that on the judgment day?" His words, though uttered in turmoil, pierced the air with the gravity of societal and spiritual judgment.

Roxana's defense was a flood of raw emotion, her tears a testament to the deep scars left by love and loss. "Yes, I embraced love with all its consequences," she affirmed, her voice trembling. "If my past renders me unworthy in your eyes, then perhaps it is best you leave," she declared, her sorrow turning to a quiet resolve.

In that moment, the room became a crucible of conflicting emotions, with each word and tear reshaping their understanding of love, faith, and forgiveness. Roxana's admission and plea, set against the backdrop of their shared life, hung in the air – a poignant reminder of the complexities of the human heart.

Nader quietly opened the door, the sight of Roxana's trembling form etching a deep line of conflict within him. As her sobs echoed through the sparse room, something within him shifted, a silent war between his bruised beliefs and the unyielding pull of his heart. With a sigh that seemed to carry the weight of the world, he closed the door and returned to her side, his movements hesitant yet determined.

He sat beside her, the bed dipping gently under his weight. Reaching out, his hand brushed her hair with a tenderness that belied his earlier turmoil, each stroke a silent vow of his enduring presence. The room was thick with the gravity of their shared past and the uncertainty of the future, yet in that moment, there was only the two of them, enveloped in a fragile bubble of intimacy.

Nader's voice broke the heavy silence, each word a tremulous note of raw honesty. "My heart aches with what you've shared, not out of judgment, but out of a love so deep it's woven into my very being," he murmured, his voice barely above a whisper. "To love is to risk the agony of betrayal, yet here I am, tethered irrevocably to you. You've always been the melody of my life's song, Roxana. My first, my only."

He paused, his hand lingering in her hair, the connection a tangible comfort between them. "I wish our hearts beat in perfect harmony, that your love mirrored mine. But even in the face of our divergent paths, my love remains unshaken. Please, forgive my initial recoil. It was the shock speaking, not the man who has cherished you since our first breath of shared air." In the dim light of the room, his admission hung between them, a testament to the complexities of love and forgiveness. Roxana, taken aback by his unexpected admission, understood the cultural significance of purity in the eyes of the men in her world.

"I will always love you," Nader whispered again, his hand tenderly tracing the contours of her hair, a silent symbol of his enduring affection. His heart ached with a paradoxical blend of selflessness and longing; he wished for her happiness, perhaps with Sam, yet harbored a quiet plea to the heavens that somehow, fate would intertwine her path with his.

Roxana, amidst her tears, looked up at Nader, her eyes a swirling pool of uncertainty and sorrow. She gently chided him, insisting that he needn't bind himself to comforting her, especially when her heart was a tangled mess of past and present. But as she spoke, a deeper truth trembled on the edge of her lips, a revelation that her tears were not just for Nader's shock or her own regret but for something more profound and aching within her.

"What burdens your heart so much?" Nader asked softly, his fingers delicately tucking a strand of her hair behind her ear, his gaze searching hers with a mix of concern and earnest yearning to understand. The sight of her so utterly forlorn stirred a deep protectiveness in him, an urge to shield her from the tempest of his own emotions.

Roxana's grip on his hands tightened, a physical testament to her turmoil. It was a touch that spoke volumes, a silent acknowledgment of his kindness, yet it also revealed the depths of despair that threatened to engulf her. Her tears were the surface of an ocean of unsaid pain, a pain that seemed to devour her from within.

"Please, let me be your anchor," Nader implored, his voice a soft but firm declaration of support. "Whatever storm rages within you, don't face it alone."

In the heavy air of the room, Roxana felt the oppressive weight of her secrets, the fear that sharing them might only deepen her isolation. Yet, Nader's unwavering gaze, filled with genuine concern and an unspoken promise of steadfastness, offered a glimmer of hope. As she hesitated on the precipice of confession, the silent tension between them was a bridge over the chasm of their past and a testament to the possibility of a shared future, however uncertain it might be.

Suppressing the whirlwind of dread and despair inside her, Roxana teetered on the brink of silence and confession. The compassion and understanding Nader had shown ignited a flicker of hope and trust amidst the darkness of her fears. With a voice quivering with vulnerability, she began to unravel the tightly wound fears that had haunted her since that fateful day. As she spoke, the strokes of Nader's hand in her hair slowed, each movement laden with the dawning realization of the impending storm.

Roxana's breath hitched as she approached the crux of her turmoil, the words heavy as stones on her tongue. "I just found out that I'm pregnant," she whispered, the admission falling into the room like a thunderclap. The weight of her confession was palpable, filling the space with a tension that was almost suffocating.

Nader's hand retracted almost reflexively, as if the words had physically pushed him away. His face, a canvas of shock and disbelief, mirrored the internal chaos that raged within him. Such situations were things of fiction to him, tales spun on the silver screen, not the harsh reality confronting him now, especially with the woman he envisioned a future with. The societal stigma of an unwed mother loomed over them, a dark cloud of judgment and shame.

Yet, as he watched Roxana, her face awash with tears, her body trembling with the burden of her secret, something within him shifted. Her vulnerability, the raw openness of her confession, reignited the promise he made to himself – to be her support, her steady rock in the tumultuous seas of life. His love, deep and unyielding, was not easily swayed by societal norms or personal fears.

Nader grasped for a thread of hope, murmuring about the possibility of a mistake, perhaps clinging to the cinematic trope of a mistaken pregnancy as seen in movies like 'Grease.' But the stark confirmation from Roxana, underscored by the authority of a doctor's diagnosis, shattered that fragile hope.

In a whirlwind of panic, Nader's mind raced through the potential ramifications—the involvement of a doctor, the risk of the news spreading, and the haunting question of who she had named as the father. Roxana, sensing his anxiety, soon unraveled the details, revealing that only Nader and Doctor Larabi held the weight of this secret, shielding it even from Sam's knowledge.

In that moment, Nader grappled with conflicting emotions, feeling both burdened by the weight of the revelation and privileged over Sam by the intimacy of the shared secret. With a heavy heart, he broached the delicate topic of Roxana's plan, recognizing that Sam's return was uncertain, leaving her with limited options. A tense pause hung in the air as Roxana hesitated, choosing to leave the details unspoken.

Undeterred, Nader pressed, sensing the gravity of her unspoken decision. Roxana, succumbing to the weight of his insistence, finally declared the painful truth—she had resolved to undergo an abortion. The room fell silent, enveloped in the heaviness of a choice.

Nader laid bare his convictions, expressing with a heavy heart that, in his belief, abortion was a grave sin. His sincere prayer echoed through the room, a desperate plea for Sam's swift return—wishing against the odds, yet willing to endure the pain if it meant saving the life of the innocent child growing within Roxana. Teary-eyed, he confronted the harsh reality of their situation, grappling with the moral complexities that now defined the secret they endured.

Nader stood solemnly before the window, his eyes fixed on the skeletal branches of the garden trees cloaked in the soft embrace of the season's first snowfall. The quiet descent of snowflakes outside mirrored the heavy contemplation within him. The reality of the situation weighed heavily on Nader's shoulders.

In the depths of his thoughts, Nader grappled with the knowledge that Roxana's father, his own uncle, would never consent to her leaving the country for a swift, private union. The patriarch would insist on a grand, traditional ceremony in Shiraz, preserving the family's honor and showcasing the union of his only daughter in a manner befitting their stature.

Yet, a flicker of a solution sparked in Nader's mind—a delicate balance to secure the future, preserving the unborn child and ensuring Roxana's hand in his marriage. A plan formed, delicate and intricate, offering a glimmer of hope in the face of their mutual turmoil.

Nader settled beside Roxana, his hand gently cradling hers as he unveiled his solution. In a heartfelt admission, he emphasized that he'd never force her into a choice between him and Sam, fully aware of the unfavorable odds stacked against him. With a tenderness in his voice, he posed a question: would she entertain the idea of marrying him if Sam couldn't return promptly? A pact, hidden from the world, where they'd embrace the impending arrival of their child, shielding this secret even from Sam.

Roxana stood in stunned silence, her emotions swirling in a whirlwind of shock and surprise. The revelation of Nader's unexpected proposal left her speechless, and the unspoken thought echoed in her mind: she never thought he would want to marry her after learning her secret. Grappling with this unexpected twist, she found herself at a loss for words, uncertain of how to navigate this revelation and its profound impact on their lives. She remained silent, contemplating the complex web of emotions entangling their lives.

"Promise you'll think about it," Nader urged gently, sensing her silence. With sincerity in his eyes, he laid bare his feelings, expressing that he had already bestowed upon her the entirety of his heart. He sought only a fraction of hers in return, a commitment to allow him to work tirelessly to win the rest, even if it took a lifetime.

In a touching moment, he embraced her, marking a first in their adult lives. As he departed, he left behind a heartbreaking declaration, "Just know that I'll help you in any way possible, even if your answer is no."

****

In the quiet of that evening, Roxana couldn't bear the weight of unspoken decisions any longer. Despite the vast expanse of an eleven-and-a-half-hour time difference, she mustered the courage to dial Sam's number at 5 p.m., rousing him from his slumber at 5:30 a.m. San Diego time. The distance between them felt insurmountable, and Sam's words, though sincere, offered no immediate solution. He spoke of a future together, of bringing her to America in about six months. Yet, for Roxana, time had become an unaffordable luxury.

In the hushed tones of heartbreak, she knew the intricacies of their intertwined world would shatter any hopes of a future. Abortion, a desperate option, loomed in the periphery, but she couldn't bring herself to ask Dr. Larabi to partake in such a clandestine act. The path ahead, though painful, became clear – to protect her secret, her unborn child, she had to sever ties with Sam, the love of her life, and embrace a marriage with Nader.

Summoning the strength to utter the words, she delivered the crushing blow over the phone. "Forget about me," she pleaded, her voice breaking, before abruptly hanging up. The weight of those final words settled on her shoulders like a heavy cloak, and as the receiver rested in her trembling hand, the reality of a world without Sam crashed over her like a wrecking ball.

Roxana collapsed, the weight of the world dragging her down to the cold, unforgiving floor. She wrapped her arms around her knees, her body curling into a tight ball as if to shield her from the storm of emotions raging within. The sobs that wracked her body were the visceral expression of a soul in torment, each cry a testament to the devastating crossroads she faced.

The phone's insistent ring pierced the heavy silence, each chime a stark reminder of the love and life that lingered just beyond her reach. Sam's attempts to bridge the distance between them felt like salt in an open wound, a poignant reminder of what once was and what could never be again. With each ring, the chasm within her seemed to deepen, swallowing any remnants of hope or solace.

Desperate to escape the relentless tide of despair, she rolled across the floor, her movements erratic and pained, as if physically trying to distance herself from the agony that clung to her. The world outside her cocoon of misery ceased to exist, the only reality being the flood of tears that streamed down her face and the raw, hollow feeling of loss that echoed through her being.

Eventually, the tempest of her cries subsided into quiet, fitful gasps, the physical and emotional exhaustion pulling her into a restless slumber. There, on the floor, Roxana lay adrift in a sea of sorrow, the dim light of the room casting long shadows over her still form. The haunting echoes of a fractured love story whispered around her, a lullaby of regret and longing that accompanied her into the dark embrace of unconsciousness.

****

In the quiet solitude of his room, Nader traversed the corridors of his thoughts, dwelling on the day's revelations. Steeped in the traditions of his conservative upbringing, where religious values and family customs held sacred sway, he grappled with a dilemma that tugged at the very fabric of his beliefs.

In the sacred tapestry of his dreams, he had envisioned the sanctity of his wedding night countless times. A vision where he, guided by tradition, would delicately lift the veil from her face, placing a symbol of commitment on her finger before sealing their union with a tender, first-time kiss. Yet, as his mind painted this romantic tableau, a dissonance crept in. The pristine white of her wedding gown, reserved for the purest of brides, now carried a weight of uncertainty, tarnished by the echoes of a love she once shared with another.

Regret gnawed at him, questioning the earnest promise he made to make her his. The clash between the deep-rooted values of his upbringing and the overpowering love he felt for her intensified, a relentless battle within his soul. In this tempest of conflicting emotions, the intrusive ring of the phone cut through the turmoil.

"Hello," he answered, his voice carrying the weight of his internal struggle.

"Hi, it's me, Roxana."

The moment her voice graced his ears, doubt dissipated like morning mist in the sun. Her presence on the other end, the embodiment of a decision crystallized, became a solid rock in the tumultuous sea of his thoughts. Regardless of her complex past, she emerged as the one he longed to spend his life with, an ethereal being untouched by her troubled history.

"I was thinking about you. I'm glad you called. How are you feeling?"

"Can I see you tomorrow?" she asked, her plea reaching across the invisible line, carrying with it a desire for solace and understanding. The sincerity in her words echoed in his heart, and in that moment, he knew, without a shred of doubt, that his love for her transcended the cultural barricades that sought to divide them.

Chapter 58

The soft chime of the doorbell echoed through the quiet halls of Dr. Larabi's home, a gentle herald of Roxana's much-anticipated arrival. Bijan, his interest momentarily tucked away with the closing of his book, rose to greet the bearer of heavy news. Naneh's voice, warm and inviting, announced Roxana's presence as she stepped into the threshold of their home.

In the living room, a sanctuary of comfort and conversation, Bijan ushered Roxana to a seat, his gestures a silent offering of refuge. Naneh, ever the gracious hostess, soon arrived bearing a tray fragrant with the scent of freshly brewed tea and the sweet allure of delicate cakes. The arrangement on the table, a tableau of hospitality, sought to ease the tension of the impending dialogue.

As they settled into the velvety embrace of the couches, Bijan, with a cup of tea cradled in his hands, broached the subject that hung like a heavy cloud over their heads.

Roxana, her gaze lowered, found solace in the warmth radiating from her own cup. The tears that welled in her eyes glistened like fragile pearls, each one a silent harbinger of the pain and conflict that roiled within her. With a voice quivering like a delicate leaf in the wind, she unfolded the layers of her tormented heart. She spoke of the impossibility of her situation with Sam, her voice a tremulous thread weaving through the silence of the room.

She confessed that while abortion loomed as a dark possibility, the life burgeoning within her was the sole, tangible thread connecting her to Sam. This revelation, a confession of both love and despair, filled the room with a profound sense of gravity.

Dr. Larabi, a silent sentinel of empathy and wisdom, absorbed her words with an attentive ear. His eyes, reflecting a deep well of understanding, never wavered from Roxana's face. He recognized the immense burden of her choice, the weight of societal expectations against the fierce, protective love of a mother.

"I know I'll start showing soon," Roxana interjected softly, her voice trailing off. "That's why we need your help, Mr. Doctor."

"We?" Bijan's confusion was evident. "I was under the impression Sam didn't know."

Roxana's voice cracked as she held back tears. "He doesn't. Nader and I... we've decided to marry. He's willing to raise the child as his own, swearing to cherish them as if they were birthed from our love."

Bijan's response was tinged with a mix of disbelief and rising anger. "I'm at a loss for words, Roxana. But why do you need my help in this?"

Her voice faltered, the weight of her situation rendering her speechless for a moment. "Please, don't look at me like that, Mr. Doctor."

Bijan sighed, his voice softening despite his frustration. "I'm not here to upset you, but Saam's not going to easily forget someone like you."

A bitter smile touched Roxana's lips. "Forgetting him will be harder for me. His child is growing within me, a constant reminder of what could have been. It's a sad fate, but it's mine to bear."

Bijan understood the gravity of the situation. Nader's decision to marry Roxana was not just an act of love but a sacrifice to protect her honor and their family's reputation. As much as he wished it was Sam standing by her side, he knew this was the only viable path under the circumstances.

"You are making a significant sacrifice, Roxana. But even with a swift marriage, the baby's arrival will raise questions," Bijan pointed out.

"That's where we hoped you could assist," Roxana said hesitantly. "Could you... could you tell everyone the baby was born prematurely?"

Bijan raised an eyebrow. "So you need me to bend the truth? Remember, I'm a pediatrician, not an obstetrician."

Roxana nodded. "We're aware. But with your influence, perhaps a colleague might be persuaded to corroborate our story."

Dr. Larabi sat back, his mind racing. The plan was fraught with ethical dilemmas, a tangled web of lies. Yet, he couldn't see another way out. Despite the deceit, it seemed the only path to protect his grandson and Roxana from the harsh judgments of society. Despite the chaos of emotions, he recognized Nader's profound love and commitment, a glimmer of hope in an otherwise bleak scenario. Perhaps, under different stars, it would be Sam standing beside Roxana, but fate had woven a different tapestry.

Meanwhile, undaunted by the moral labyrinth they were navigating, Roxana and Nader meticulously laid out every aspect of their impending nuptials. The wedding unfolded with an unexpected opulence, a testament to the groom's family's wealth and perhaps a balm to soothe the undercurrents of deception that pulsed beneath the surface.

Dr. Larabi, burdened by the secret and the well-being of all involved, sought counsel and aid from Dr. Kadivar. Her expertise in obstetrics and gynecology was crucial to the execution of their plan. After much persuasion and understanding the direness of Roxana's predicament, Dr. Kadivar reluctantly conceded, her acquiescence a heavy decision borne of compassion rather than conviction. The plan took shape - Roxana's labor would be announced as prematurely, a charade to safeguard the secret they held close.

The months rolled by, each day a step closer to the culmination of their carefully constructed deception. Finally, in a hospital room charged with unspoken narratives, Roxana brought a new life into the world. The baby boy, healthy and unaware of the maelstrom of emotions around him, became the unwitting centerpiece of their charade. Dr. Larabi, now the guardian of this delicate secret, oversaw the necessary arrangements, ensuring the illusion remained intact.

As the child was heralded into the family, Nader's embrace was one of genuine love and acceptance, his affections untainted by the origins of his son's birth. His dedication was a silent vow, a promise to provide a loving father's care, irrespective of the biological truths that lay buried.

Roxana's journey was one of profound emotional complexity, each day a navigation through a maze of love, regret, and resilience. Her gaze, often lost in the distance, reflected the tumultuous journey of her heart — sorrow for the love lost and hope for the future she was determined to build.

Thus, in the vibrant city of Shiraz, a story unfolded quietly, its chapters filled with the silent sacrifices and unspoken bonds of those entwined in the tale. A narrative complex in its morality and poignant in its humanity, leaving an indelible mark on the lives it touched, woven discreetly into the fabric of everyday existence.

Chapter 59

As we traverse the familiar path back to the garden where their story once bloomed, Sam and Roxana found themselves again, seated together yet worlds apart, each lost in a maze of unspoken thoughts and silent regrets. The air around them was thick with the weight of untold stories, the kind that hung heavily between heartbeats. It was here, against the backdrop of whispering leaves and the fading light, that

Sam, his voice a mixture of confusion and hurt, shattered the silence that enveloped them.

Roxana, her eyes a mirror to her soul, faced him with a resolution born from the deepest wells of her pain. There was a tremor in her voice, a fragile strength as she chose to lift the veil of secrecy that had clouded their past. She confessed the heart-wrenching truth, the hidden catalyst behind her sudden departure — a life conceived in a fleeting moment of love that bound her to a future she had never envisioned, a future without Sam.

As she spoke, the reality of his own connection to the child dawned on Sam, a mixture of astonishment and a profound sense of loss washing over him. The narrative unfolded further, revealing Nader's remarkable act of love and sacrifice — a commitment to raise Saamaan as his own, forsaking his desire for biological children to ensure the child never felt anything less than wholly loved.

"Saamaan! His name is Saamaan?" Sam's voice broke, his emotions spilling over as the significance of the name — a tribute to him — became clear. It was a revelation that bore the sweetness of honor and the sting of separation, a name that etched his legacy into the life of a child he might never know. A testament to the depth of their connection and the sacrifices made for the sake of a child named after his father.

Roxana, with a gentle firmness in her voice, confirmed the homage, a bittersweet acknowledgment of a bond that, while severed by circumstance, would forever linger in the essence of the child they both loved. "You may not walk beside him, but your spirit will always be a guiding star in his journey," she shared, her words a delicate tapestry of love, regret, and unyielding respect for the paths they had chosen.

Roxana lifted herself gracefully from the ground, her movements a testament to the resolve that had carried her through years of hidden truths. She reached for the photo album, its cover worn with the passage of time but holding within it the imprints of a past both cherished and mourned. As she flipped through the pages, the images gazed back at her, each a frozen moment of joy, hope, and the inevitable shadow of a father's absence.

With each turn of the page, Roxana recounted the stories behind the photographs to Saamaan, her voice weaving a tapestry of memories. She filled the silent gaps with laughter and tears, crafting a narrative that connected Saamaan to Saam, the father he had never known. The story telling sessions had become Roxana and Saamaan's sacred ritual, a bridge spanning the chasm between past and present, a way for Roxana to keep Sam's spirit alive in the heart of their son.

Yet, as the relentless march of time reshaped their world, a poignant day dawned. Saamaan, his fingers tracing the outlines of the photographs, his eyes wide with the innocent curiosity of childhood, pointed to a picture of Sam and uttered a single word, "baba." The simplicity of the utterance held a universe of meaning. It was a recognition, a calling out to a figure who was familiar yet unknown, a name that had danced in the stories but had never echoed in the hallways of their home.

That single word was a profound turning point, marking the end of an era of stories and the beginning of a new chapter of understanding. It was a moment suspended in time, capturing the poignant realization of a young boy and the deep, abiding love of a mother. Roxana, holding back a swell of emotions, knew then that the tales of Sam had woven themselves into the fabric of Saamaan's being, shaping his identity in ways both visible and hidden.

Sam poured out his heart, confessing the bittersweet memory of standing outside her house the first time he called her, unknowingly witnessing his own son leaving. The revelation of having a nineteen-year-old son weighed heavily on him. In the midst of their conversation, he dared to ask how Saamaan would feel if he were to learn the truth.

"That is not even an option," Roxana's voice cut through the air, sharp with anger, as she implored Sam to grasp the profound repercussions of his words—a Pandora's box that, once opened, would cast shadows over lives and burden Saamaan with indelible labels. Sam, realizing the gravity of his thoughtless remark, acknowledged its foolishness but remained adrift in the uncertainty of the situation. Roxana, her gaze heavy with the weight of the secret she bore, emphasized the necessity of silence, underlining the protection it offered to everyone entangled in their intricate web of truths and lies. In a poignant moment, Sam pleaded with Roxana to deliver a heartfelt embrace to Saamaan on his behalf—a simple request that carried the weight of unspoken sentiments. Roxana, touched by the plea, vowed to convey the message through the warmth of her embrace.

In the room, where shadows danced with the remnants of daylight, Sam's voice broke the heavy silence, his words laden with the ache of unresolved feelings. "How about us?" he murmured, a vulnerable plea hidden within the question. His eyes, earnest and searching, met Roxana's, seeking in them the answer to a question that had lingered through the years.

Roxana, her posture steady and her gaze unwavering, responded with a decisiveness that sliced through the haze of nostalgia. "There is no 'us' anymore," she affirmed, her voice resonant with the finality of her words. She reached out, enveloping Sam in a hug that was both a comfort and a closure, a physical manifestation of the distance that time and circumstances had imposed between them.

The years had woven their separate tales, tales that had diverged from the shared path they once walked. They now belonged to others — to families and commitments made in the wake of their parted ways. Roxana's conviction was a testament to her growth and the acceptance of her present life. With a gentle firmness, she implored Sam to embrace the future, to let go of the past's whispers and fully commit to the path he had chosen.

"It's time for me to give all of my heart to my husband. It's overdue, and he truly deserves it," Roxana stated, her words a reflection of her commitment and love for the life she had nurtured. It was an overdue acknowledgment, a recognition of the love and patience that had been bestowed upon her.

Sam, his heart a tumult of emotions, felt the poignancy of her words. The warmth of her embrace lingered, a bittersweet reminder of what once was and what could never be again. Relinquishing the tender memories and the hope of rekindled love was a task daunting in its emotional depth. Yet, he understood the imperative of moving forward, of honoring the lives and loves that had filled the spaces once occupied by their youthful dreams.

In the dimming light of the room, as they parted from the embrace, a silent understanding passed between them. It was an acknowledgment of the journey they had traveled, the love they had shared, and the separate futures they must embrace.

In a poignant exchange, Roxana, with a tenderness that bespoke years of shared history, advised Sam to leave and return to his wife before any irreparable damage occurred. It was time to safeguard not only their individual futures but also the sanctity of his feelings for Nicole and the vows of his marriage.

The weight of unspoken farewells hung heavy in the air. "I'm finally letting go of you," Roxana whispered, her arm slowly falling from its embrace. She admitted that she would linger, tears streaming down her face, once he departed, mirroring the heartache of their separation two decades past. The echoes of the past lingered, but she resolved to return home to Nader, determined to be the same loving wife to him that she could have been to Sam.

Sam, sensing the impending departure, acknowledged the bittersweet nature of their encounter. As he readied himself to leave, he expressed gratitude for this unexpected reunion. Roxana, in a poignant gesture, handed him the photo album, a repository of memories. "Don't forget it again," she urged, her voice carrying the weight of shared history. With a tender smile, she revealed, "You'll find some baby pictures in there," a subtle reminder of the threads that still bound them together.

As they embraced for the final time, Sam tenderly traced his finger over her lips, etching a bittersweet memory. Roxana summoned the strength to walk to the window, silently witnessing him exit the garden and vanish from her life forever. After the door closed behind Sam, sealing the final chapter of their shared past, Roxana stood motionless by the window, her gaze lingering on the empty path where he had disappeared. The garden, once a symbol of their love, now bore witness to the definitive end of their story. The tender touch of Sam's finger on her lips haunted her, a poignant reminder of what they once had and what could never be again.

The overwhelming torrent of emotions she had held at bay broke through her defenses. Her legs, once firm and resolute, gave way beneath her, sending her collapsing to the floor. There, amidst the silence of the room, Roxana allowed herself to mourn the loss fully. Her sobs were deep and consuming, each one a release of the pain, the love, and the dreams that had intertwined her life with Sam's. It was a catharsis, a necessary outpouring of grief for the years they spent apart and the finality of their farewell.

Yet, within her was an unyielding core of strength, a resilience forged through years of navigating life's complexities. Slowly, with a resolve that spoke of her inner fortitude, Roxana began to collect herself. Her breaths became steadier, each one a step towards reclaiming the composure she had momentarily lost. She meticulously adjusted her appearance, smoothing out the creases in her clothes, wiping away the tears that had streaked her face. Each action was a reaffirmation of her decision to move forward, to honor the life and commitments she had made since Sam's departure two decades ago.

Exiting the room, Roxana closed the door on the echoes of her past, her heart heavy yet hopeful. She walked back into the world, back to Nader and the life they shared, carrying with her the indelible marks of her journey. In her heart, she knew that the pain of goodbye was also a testament to the depth of what they had shared, a bittersweet symphony of life's relentless march forward and the enduring capacity of the human heart to love, lose, and ultimately, endure.

****

As the door creaked open, the lively tune of a melody greeted Nader and Saamaan, leading them to a jubilant Roxana lost in dance and song. With a fluid motion, she approached Nader, her eyes twinkling with happiness. "Welcome home," she chimed, planting a tender kiss on his cheek before handing him a cool glass of limeade.

Saamaan watched, a smile creeping onto his face as his mother turned to him with a playful glint. "Your turn for some refreshment, but first, a hug!" she declared, waving a glass enticingly.

Saamaan looked towards Nader, his eyebrows raised in amusement. Nader, with a chuckle, nodded in approval. "Go on, her hugs are the best part of coming home," he encouraged.

As Saamaan wrapped his arms around Roxana, she whispered softly into his ear, "This one's special, Saamaan." The hug was a silent testament to the love she harbored, a message meant for Sam carried through the embrace of his son.

Later that evening, as the night drew in, Roxana's voice filled the room with a light-hearted command, "I'll be taking a shower. When I come back, I expect to find you waiting," she teased, a mischievous sparkle in her eyes.

Nader, with a theatrical groan, retorted, "I Guess the TV is losing to me tonight." His words were playful, belying the anticipation that bubbled beneath.

Roxana's laughter rang clear as she replied, "Definitely."

The house settled into a comfortable silence, punctuated only by the soft sounds of Roxana's movements. Nader lay in wait, the dim light casting a serene glow over the room. When Roxana emerged, the sight of her, fresh and radiant, struck a chord within Nader. In that fleeting glance, he recognized the profound journey they had traversed together, the challenges they had overcome, and the deep, abiding love that anchored their life. In that moment he realized that, in every sense, he had indeed conquered every corner of her heart.

Chapter 60

In the hushed embrace of the night, Sam's agony resonated through the silence. He grappled with the weight of his own folly, the betrayal of Nicole's trust a haunting melody in his conscience. As dawn approached, the first echoes of the day manifested in three short knocks on his door. Wearily, he allowed entrance, "come in", his voice a weary invitation.

His father, discerning the shadows etched across Sam's face, inquired about his well-being with genuine concern. In a shattered whisper, Sam uttered the painful truth, "She's gone, Dad. She's gone." His father, a seasoned navigator through life's tumultuous seas, reminded him that the journey is seldom a tranquil voyage. Seated beside his desolate son, he imparted invaluable advice to ride the waves, persisting through the storm to find tranquility. Yet, Sam, burdened by the wreckage of his own choices, confessed to having nothing left to fight for—no job, no family.

Bijan acknowledged the depth of Sam's despair but refused to let him succumb. "You won't give up that easily," he declared, recognizing his son's resilience. He urged Sam to toil earnestly, for in hard and honest work lies the path to redemption and the reclamation of everything he had lost.

"Honesty? A funny advise coming from you," Sam chuckled bitterly, the tone of his words casting a shadow of rudeness, a stark departure from their usual exchanges—a biting comment that sliced through the air like a sharp blade.

Bijan's brows furrowed in response, the unexpected edge in Sam's voice catching him off guard. "What is that supposed to mean?" he asked, bewildered by the sudden change in demeanor.

Sam, evading the direct question, acknowledged his awareness of the long-hidden truth, the secrets of two decades laid bare. His demand for an explanation echoed through the room, a reason for the withheld truths. Bijan, resolute, clarified that it wasn't his decision to share those revelations. Caught in the crossfire, Sam grappled with conflicting loyalties, asserting that a father deserved to know.

Bijan, staunch in his defense, spoke like a physician bound by an oath. He disclosed that Roxana had chosen this path, seeking refuge in the shadows, and he had honored his patient privacy and wishes.

"How could you do that to me? I am his father," Sam lamented, the anguish of the unspoken question lingering, a palpable ache.

"Nader is his real father," In a harsh retort Bijan asserted Nader's role as the true father—a role he embraced with unwavering dedication. He demanded Sam to accept the stark reality, dismissing his paternal claim as that of a mere sperm donor in the grand tapestry of Saamaan's life.

Sam lowered his head, remorse flooding him for the sharpness of his words to his ailing father.

"No one meant to hurt you, my son," Bijan comforted, drawing Sam into a protective embrace.

"Things would have been so different if you had told me. I'm not saying better, just different," Sam confessed, his voice tinged with regret.

"Think about it, son; what else could she do? Nader came up with the plan, and he raised Saamaan with all his heart. Don't you see? You were destined to be with Nicole," Bijan explained, a gentle encouragement in his tone.

"I know I should get my life back," Sam admitted, the weight of the task ahead settling heavily on his shoulders.

Bijan offered a warm smile and patted him on the back, a silent reassurance.

"I can't believe Nader let her name him Saamaan," Sam said, the wonder and a hint of gratitude evident in his voice.

"He's a kind man," Bijan replied, his thoughts on Nader filled with respect and admiration. "He has a heart that understands beyond the ordinary."

"You saw him growing up. Tell me about him," Sam urged, his voice thick with a yearning to know the son he had never had the chance to raise.

Bijan placed a comforting hand on Sam's back, offering solace through his touch. "Every time I saw Saamaan, it was like looking back at you at that tender age." His voice, tinged with nostalgia, filled the room with echoes of the past. "He's always been special, reminding me so much of you — the way he walks with a determined tilt, just like you did as a youngster, or how he squints when he's deep in thought, mirroring your own reflective gaze."

Bijan smiled, a warm, affectionate expression that seemed to embrace the room. "Like you, he's got a keen mind for math, always solving problems with an enthusiasm that bridges our conversations. And oh, his first little romance was quite the tale, beating you to the punch in the love department, a kiss on the cheek of the neighbor's girl when he was in the third grade."

Sam listened, a mix of emotions playing across his face as Bijan continued. "He's grown into a remarkable young man, Sam. While he follows in Nader's footsteps in the family business, his spirit, his drive, it's all you."

"I wish I could talk to him, even just once," Sam expressed with a profound yearning, his voice laden with the weight of missed years and unfulfilled paternal dreams. Each word was a testament to his longing to connect with Saamaan, to experience the simple joy of his laughter, to partake in the father-son moments that had eluded him for two decades.

Bijan, deeply attuned to the ache in Sam's heart, gently steered the conversation towards a focus on mending the present rather than dwelling on the what-ifs of the past. "Now come downstairs, and after breakfast, let's plan for your departure home," he advised, emphasizing the importance of reconciling with Nicole and rebuilding the life that awaited him.

As Bijan moved to leave the room, Sam's voice, soft yet urgent, halted him. "Dad," he called out, a simple word heavy with emotion and meaning. In a swift motion, Sam rose and embraced his father, his actions speaking louder than words, conveying an apology and a deep-seated regret for any hurt he might have caused. "Please forgive me," Sam implored, clinging to the embrace, a premonition gnawing at him about the finite nature of time they had left together.

Bijan, enveloping his son in a tighter hug, offered words of unconditional love and reassurance. "You've always been the best son anyone could wish for," he consoled, his voice a soothing balm to Sam's troubled soul. He affirmed that any fleeting moments of upset were insignificant in the grand tapestry of love and pride he felt for his son.

As Bijan exited the room, his steps faltered, a sudden wave of dizziness overwhelming him. Each stair felt like a mountain, his body heavy as lead. He clung to the banister, his knuckles white, as an unrelenting exhaustion wrapped around him like a shroud. His breaths came in labored gasps, a silent battle raging within as beads of sweat traced the worry lines on his forehead.

From the corner of her eye, Jacqueline caught the harrowing scene. Her heart skipped a beat at the sight of Bijan's agony. She dropped what she was holding, the clatter of the object hitting the floor lost in the urgency of the moment. "Bijan!" Her voice, filled with a raw fear, pierced the stillness of the home.

As Bijan succumbed to his fate, his body seemed to lose all strength, collapsing like a marionette whose strings had been abruptly severed. The eyes that once sparkled with gentle understanding now dimmed, veiled with a sheen of pain as they fluttered closed. The robust figure, long revered as a bastion of resilience and vigor, now lay surrendered to gravity's unyielding embrace. Vulnerable and eerily still, he resembled a fallen oak, its might momentarily forgotten. The thud of his descent onto the ground reverberated through the space, a stark, resounding echo that spoke to the transient nature of existence and the sobering reality of our mortal coil.

Jacqueline's cries for help were a desperate plea, a call to the universe to undo the cruel twist of fate unfolding before her. "Help! Somebody, please!" Her voice broke, each word soaked in dread and disbelief.

Sam, upstairs, felt a chill run down his spine as his mother's terror-stricken voice reached him. His feet moved of their own accord, propelling him down the stairs, two, three steps at a time. His mind raced, images of his father interspersed with flashes of fear and uncertainty. As he reached the bottom, the sight that greeted him halted his breath.

There lay Bijan, his father, the man who had taught him about strength and love, now a fallen hero in the hallway. Sam's knees buckled as he fell beside him, his hands shaking as they reached out to Bijan. "Dad! Dad, please," he begged, his voice choked with tears, the realization of his father's mortality crashing into him like a tidal wave.

Jacqueline, alongside Sam, knelt, her hands fluttering over Bijan, unsure how to revive the rock of their family. The room filled with the sound of their combined grief and fear, a poignant reminder of the bonds that tie a family together, even in the face of the unimaginable.

In that critical moment, their lives paused, suspended in a vortex of emotions — love, fear, desperation — all converging around the man who lay motionless before them. It was a scene that would forever be etched in their memories, a stark testament to the profound impact one life has on another, and the unspoken vows of family to hold on, to fight, and to love, even when faced with the darkest of trials.

Chapter 61

"Look, it's Uncle Luke and Brenda," Cameron exclaimed, his voice filled with excitement, and he eagerly waved at them as they descended the stairs in San Diego Airport. The anticipation in the air was palpable, the atmosphere buzzing with the promise of long-awaited reunions.

As Luke and Brenda approached, warm smiles adorned everyone's faces, and embraces ensued, each hug a manifestation of the pent-up affection that had accumulated during their separation. The air was filled with the delightful chaos of joyful greetings.

Brenda, her eyes gleaming with curiosity, inquired about Nicole's well-being. Sam's detailed explanations during the call had left her concerned, and now, face to face, she sought reassurance. The bond of shared history and friendship radiated in Brenda's genuine concern for Nicole.

With genuine and familial warmth, Luke efficiently collected the suitcases from the carousel, maneuvering through the bustling airport crowd. The clatter of luggage wheels on the polished floor merged with the hum of airport activity.

Tara and Cameron, exuding youthful energy, eagerly offered to assist with the luggage carts. Luke, with a playful smile, accepted their offer, "as you wish". The scene unfolded like a choreographed dance, family members moving in harmony toward the exit.

As Luke walked hand in hand with Brenda, the entwining of their fingers spoke volumes. Nicole, trailing behind with a mix of emotions, observed the locked hands and couldn't help but wonder if there was something left unsaid. The unspoken tension lingered in the air, and Nicole couldn't shake the question that hung heavy in her heart, wondering if, once again, history was repeating itself.

As they navigated the familiar streets on the way home, the soft purr of the car engine provided a rhythmic undertone to the conversation inside. The fading sunlight cast a warm glow through the car windows, creating a serene atmosphere.

Luke, his voice laced with concern, ventured into the delicate territory of Sam's return and his ordeals at work. The words lingered in the air, carrying the weight of unspoken expectations and a shared history. The distant hum of traffic outside the car blended with their conversation, creating a backdrop of urban quietue.

Nicole, however, abruptly severed the discussion, her voice cutting through the evening air like a sharp blade. The atmosphere inside the car shifted, charged with unspoken tension. "Next time he calls you, you can ask him yourself". The scent of tension mixed with the cool evening breeze.

"Why are you so mean to Uncle Luke?" Tara's whispered inquiry added a layer of innocence to the charged atmosphere. The hushed quality of her voice resonated, punctuating the silence that followed.

Nicole, recognizing her abruptness, felt a pang of remorse. The emotional texture of her regret was palpable, an intricate dance of vulnerability and contrition. "Sorry, Luke," Nicole conceded, the lament in her voice echoing the complexities of her emotions.

Luke, with his characteristic charm, brushed off the tension. "No worries. I understand."

Brenda, injecting humor into the scene, delivered a playful smack to Luke's head. "I don't think you do. You're a man. How could you? You're all pigs." Her words, laden with humor and a hint of exasperation, reverberated in the confined space of the car. The laughter that followed created a momentary break in the emotional intensity.

The children, succumbing to the fatigue of the day, dozed off in the back seat. Their rhythmic breaths, accompanied by the distant sounds of the night, created a soothing symphony of rest.

Nicole, upon reaching home, tenderly arranged the slumbering children in their beds. The rustle of sheets and the faint murmurs of the kids, though usually comforting, now carried a weight that pressed heavily on Nicole's heart. The house, once a sanctuary of familial warmth, now echoed with the absence of Sam, casting a profound shadow over the familiar spaces they had once shared. Each creak of the floor and hushed whisper seemed to amplify the void left by his departure, intensifying the solitude that enveloped Nicole in the silent aftermath of the day.

As Brenda and Luke bid Nicole goodnight, their hugs held an unspoken understanding. The tactile sensation of the embrace carried the weariness of the day and the attachments between friends. The closing of the door marked the end of the evening, leaving Nicole to ponder the echoes of the night and anticipate the dawn of a new day.

Chapter 62

In the urgency of the moment, Sam swiftly assessed Bijan's vital signs, relief washing over him as he confirmed, "Thank god, he's breathing and has a pulse."

"The ambulance should be here soon," Jacqueline, her hands now cradling her face, responded with a mixture of worry and hope.

"Help me get him off these cold tiles," Sam directed his mom, determination etched across his face.

Together, Sam and Jacqueline carefully lifted Bijan's fragile body, the coolness of the tiles clinging to his skin. As they moved him to the family room, a silent exchange of glances spoke volumes about the gravity of the situation.

Bijan, slowly opening his eyes, was greeted by the sight of Jacqueline. A genuine smile brightened his face, a silent reassurance of their shared strength.

"How are you feeling?" Jacqueline inquired, her voice a soothing presence in the tense atmosphere.

Naneh, with a heartfelt plea, offered Bijan a glass of water. "Khoda komakesh mikoneh," she prayed silently, seeking God's assistance.

Sam, gently supporting Bijan's head, assisted him in sipping water. Naneh, placed a pillow under his head as she dried her tears with the corner of her headscarf, an emotional portrayal of her quiet prayers for his well-being. The room, filled with the collective concern and care of the family, became a sanctuary of hope amidst the uncertainty that lingered.

"Everything's gonna be OK," Jacqueline assured Bijan, her voice a comforting melody in the midst of uncertainty.

"Have I told you lately that I love you," Bijan managed to say, a smile gracing his face despite the weight of the moment.

"You always do. But now you should save all your energy so you can say it again in the years to come," said Jacqueline, her words carrying a mixture of hope and resignation.

In the quiet of the room, Bijan's words hung heavy, a solemn admission of the finite nature of his existence. "I don't have years left. It's different this time," he spoke, the weight of his realization etched into each syllable.

Sam, desperate and clinging to a thread of hope, begged his father, "Listen to Mom and stay positive." His plea echoed through the room, a raw expression of love and fear intertwined.

Bijan, with a lifetime of emotions in a single gesture, reached out and clasped Sam's hand. His touch conveyed gratitude and pride, a silent acknowledgment of the son he cherished. "You're the best son anyone could wish for. Now promise me this. Never let your mom feel lonely."

Amidst the heavy air of impending loss, Jacqueline interjected, her voice trembling with fear, "Stop talking like that. You will be here for me. I want you to believe it. Now say it. Say you'll be here for me."

"Even if I have said it lately, I want to say it again. I love you so much. Even my enlarged heart wasn't big enough for all of my love for you." Bijan, with a touch as gentle as his words, wiped the tears from her face. It was a poignant moment, a profound expression of enduring love and the stark reality of the limits imposed by mortal existence.

The door opened and Ariana rushed in, her eyes filled with worry, and ran towards her father, a cascade of questions pouring from her lips about how he felt. Bijan, basking in the warmth of his family's presence, declared, "Everything just became okay now that my whole family is with me." His gaze lingered on each face, savoring the joy of these precious moments while a twinge of pain marked his uncertainty about how much longer he had with them.

Expressing gratitude for his life, he spoke with a twinkle in his eye, "Best wife, best children, and a life filled with love." Ariana, unable to contain her emotions, pleaded with her dad not to talk that way, assuring him he'd be around for another hundred years.

In a moment of tenderness, Bijan turned to Ariana, caressing her teary face, and asked about her love for her husband. Ariana, tearfully, affirmed her love but redirected the focus to his well-being. Bijan, with a father's pride, expressed joy in witnessing her happiness.

Turning towards Sam, Bijan shared his wisdom, emphasizing the importance of family. He urged Sam to do whatever it takes to reunite his family, extracting a promise to bring peace to his mind.

Overwhelmed, Sam collapsed into his father's arms, sobbing uncontrollably. In his raw vulnerability, he confessed his fear of losing his father, unable to fathom life without the man he had always relied on. The weight of the impending loss bore down on him, and he pleaded for guidance on how to navigate a world without his presence.

The distant wail of the ambulance siren sent Sam and Ariana dashing to the front door, their hearts pounding in tandem with the urgency of the moment.

Bijan turned to Jacqueline, his eyes reflecting a well of emotions. From his side pocket, he retrieved an old pen, a relic from the day they first met. "Do you remember giving this to me on the day we met? You used it to write your phone number for me."

Jacqueline, overcome with nostalgia, couldn't suppress her tears. "How could I ever forget? You were so sweet, wouldn't even let me pay at the café. It was many years ago, and I would repeat everything again in a heartbeat."

Bijan, a small smile playing on his lips, continued, "I only used this pen for writing our anniversary cards until the ink dried up. Perhaps now is the right time I give it back to you." He delicately placed the pen in her palm, closing her fingers around it.

In the midst of this intimate exchange, paramedics hurried into the room, a whirlwind of urgency. With his eyes fixed on the family picture, Bijan managed to utter, "It's been a wonderful journey," just before the oxygen mask was gently placed over his nose and mouth, the weight of his words lingering in the air.

As he was being carried away on the gurney, Bijan's weakened eyes moved from Ariana's tear-streaked face to Sam's trembling gaze and finally rested on Jacqueline's pained expression. In those fleeting moments, he sought to etch the image of their faces into his memory, a desperate attempt to carry their essence with him.

The weight of his wearied eyelids grew heavier, and, like the closing curtain on a poignant scene, his eyes slowly shut. In that tender moment, there was a quiet surrender, a peaceful departure that left an indelible mark on the room.

Every second in the waiting room felt like an eternity, a cruel stretch of time where despair hung heavy in the air. Jacqueline and Ariana, overwhelmed by grief, quietly wept as Sam, though crumbling inside, tried to be their pillar of strength. The creaking of the waiting room door became a heart-wrenching symphony, each opening raising hope that was mercilessly dashed.

Minutes morphed into agonizing hours, and the door finally swung open. Dr. Mir, with a grave countenance, approached the family waiting on the edge of despair. The room plunged into a dense silence, pregnant with the weight of impending news. When the words finally left the doctor's lips, the silence shattered, replaced by a guttural, anguished scream – the raw expression of a family left broken in the wake of their profound loss.

In the aftermath of Dr. Mir's somber revelation, the once vibrant room now echoed with a profound emptiness. Jacqueline, Ariana, and Sam stood frozen, their world shattered, their hearts heavy with the weight of irreplaceable loss. The reality of a life without Bijan, a husband and father who had been the bedrock of their existence, sank in with brutal force. Grief, a torrential wave, engulfed them, leaving behind a desolate landscape where joy once bloomed. The family, now fragmented and forever changed, grappled with the void left by a man who had filled their lives with love, laughter, and unwavering support. The room, once filled with anticipation, now bore witness to the inconsolable sorrow of a family thrust into the depths of mourning.

Chapter 63

Regrettably, in Iran, the ritual of mourning eclipses the celebration of life. The nation observes nine official holidays dedicated to commemorating the departed, while birthdays are marked by only three. Even the birth anniversary of Khomeini goes unrecognized, whereas the day of his demise, June fourth, stands as a national holiday. The mourning period spans forty days, during which close relatives wear somber black attire. Men abstain from shaving, and women forgo the adornment of makeup. The cultural norm eschews open-casket viewings or wakes, with burials typically conducted on the third day. Until then, close relatives suspend their business operations, converging daily at the deceased's residence.

Excessiveness permeates this cultural fabric, manifesting in various forms of ostentation. Whether it's extravagant parties, opulent cars, the educational achievements of their offspring, sartorial choices, hairstyles, residences, cosmetic surgeries, or linguistic prowess, individuals go to extremes to showcase their status. Mourning is no exception. Each day witnesses gatherings where individuals vie to exhibit their grief, shedding copious tears and occasionally fainting. Even in sorrow, the propensity for ostentation remains unbridled. The scenes, replete with unrestrained wailing and fainting spells, are so disheartening that children are deliberately kept away.

Memorial services follow a structured pattern, occurring on the third, seventh, tenth, and fortieth days, culminating in an annual remembrance. For prominent figures, these gatherings in mosques can swell to thousands. Attendees bring flowers, seizing yet another opportunity to outshine one another in their displays of grief. Close kin of the deceased stand stoically at the entrance, offering gratitude to each visitor, transforming an occasion of collective sorrow into a subtle competition for societal acknowledgment.

****

The news of Dr. Larabi's passing swept through the town like an uncontainable wildfire. That night, their home overflowed with a sea of friends and family—hundreds of individuals who regarded him not just as a physician but as a cherished friend, a family member, and one of Shiraz's most revered philanthropists. Each face carried the weight of sorrow, a testament to the profound impact he had on their town and their lives.

As the night wore on, Sam's uncle and his family lingered, the final threads of companionship linking them to the departed. "The crowd proved how much he is missed," Sam's uncle whispered to Jacqueline, his voice heavy with grief. "Many people in this town loved him like a brother or a father." He embraced Sam and Ariana tightly before departing, tears tracing a silent path down his cheeks.

"We'll see you tomorrow," Sam assured, escorting his uncle to the door.

After bidding farewell, Sam returned to Jacqueline, who clung to a pen, lost in her thoughts. "I can't believe he's gone," she murmured, her mind swirling with memories. "With this pen, I wrote my phone number for him the first night we met. That was forty-four years ago. The Passage of time only deepens the pain of loss. He never let me feel lonely in this country where I had no one. Now I feel abandoned without him." The weight of her grief hung heavy in the air as Sam struggled to find words, and Jacqueline, overwhelmed, sought solace in the tangible traces of their life together.

Sam solemnly disclosed that there was another matter to attend to—he had spoken to Farhad to coordinate the transportation of Bijan's body to San Diego. He inquired if Jacqueline was comfortable with this arrangement. Her response was immediate, a resolute "Of course," emphasizing that Bijan's wish was to rest where his entire family lay.

Reassured by her acceptance, Sam continued, revealing that Farhad believed he could expedite all the necessary paperwork in less than a week. With a compassionate gaze, he suggested to his mother that she should try to get some sleep. Jacqueline, her thoughts likely consumed by the daunting reality of a room that would forever lack Bijan's presence, nodded and began the slow journey to her bedroom. In the silent echoes of grief, she must have contemplated how to return to a space that would never again be graced by Bijan's comforting presence.

Sam spent a restless night tossing and turning, unable to find solace in sleep. The prospect of navigating a world without his father weighed heavily on him, and he half-expected to wake up from the nightmarish reality that had befallen his family. The mere thought of stepping out of his room, confronting the stark absence of his father's presence, was a daunting prospect he struggled to accept. The weight of grief permeated every corner of his consciousness, casting a somber shadow over the dawn of a new day.

Sam heard his mom's voice pierce through the early morning stillness, with groggy eyes, he glanced at the nightstand clock. Its red digits declared the ungodly hour—5:18. Instantly, he catapulted out of bed, a surge of urgency propelling him downstairs to unravel the reason for this untimely summons.

"Sam's here. Hold on," Jacqueline's voice relayed to the caller. Ariana, too, emerged hastily from her room. Jacqueline extended the phone to Sam, revealing that it was Nicole on the line. As Sam uttered a tentative hello, he instinctively distanced himself from his mom.

Nicole offered her condolences, expressing disbelief over the loss, recounting how Jacqueline had shared the tragic details. "I can't believe he's gone," Sam lamented, conveying the collective shock that enveloped everyone.

Nicole, sensing the profound connection between Sam and his father, gently probed into his emotional state. Sam, opening up about the internal turmoil, acknowledged the difficulty but underscored the importance of maintaining resilience for his mom. He shared the poignant details of Bijan's last request, emphasizing the commitment to fulfill his father's wish by ensuring Jacqueline never felt the weight of loneliness, and the plan to bring her home with him.

Nicole, grasping the depth of Sam's emotional turmoil, listened as he poured out his heart, revealing the overwhelming sense of losing everything and everyone he loves. While offering genuine sympathy for the pain caused by his father's passing, she delicately introduced a touch of reality, gently suggesting that for losing his family the responsibility lay solely on his shoulders. In a conversation marked by strained emotions, Nicole, asserting that she didn't intend to argue, requested to speak with Ariana. Sam, seeking solace in the well-being of his children, inquired about them and conveyed his imminent return. However, Nicole's response was chilly as she declared that the kids were fine but made it clear that Sam wouldn't be staying with them.

"I don't want to argue either." Sam passed the phone to Ariana and retreated to his room, leaving the weight of unspoken tensions hanging in between them.

On the third day following Dr. Larabi's passing, the atmosphere in the Namazi Hospital Conference Hall was filled with a mix of sorrow and defiance. Despite the objections from Sam's uncle and other relatives, Sam stood firm against the traditional choice of holding the memorial service in a mosque. He couldn't reconcile the essence of his father's beliefs with the hypocrisy he saw in the mullahs who, in his father's eyes, masked their crimes under the guise of religion. To honor his father's stance, Sam, with the assistance of Dr. Mir, secured the conference hall for a memorial service that would reflect the man Dr. Larabi truly was.

"In the hallowed halls of Namazi Hospital, a place sanctified by the pursuit of healing, we gather for a purpose it has not known before," began Dr. Mir, his voice resonating through the solemn air. "It is an honor for us, the dedicated faculty and staff of this institution, to pay tribute to Dr. Larabi, a man whose lifeblood flowed into the very foundation of this place, becoming an inseparable part of its identity."

Sam stood at the entrance, a silent observer to Dr. Mir's heartfelt speech, welcoming the influx of mourners with a solemn nod and a heartfelt handshake. Each handshake held a depth of shared grief, a silent understanding passing between them as they navigated the collective sorrow filling the air. In contrast to the customary segregation in mosques, this hall allowed men and women to share the same space, albeit through separate entrances. The room gradually filled, becoming a sea of grieving souls. The air was thick with the fragrance of numerous floral arrangements, some so opulent and immense that they required a truck for transport, their weight and significance carried by a collective effort of mourners.

From the doorway, Sam found himself engulfed in the fitting words of Dr. Mir honoring his father. The weight of the moment pressed on him until a gentle touch on his shoulder broke his concentration. Startled, he turned, only to be met with the unexpected sight of Nader and Saamaan standing before him. "My condolences," Nader offered, extending a hand for a handshake, while Saamaan stood quietly by his side. Sam, caught between shock and gratitude, expressed his thanks for their presence, desperately seeking words to prolong the interaction, yearning to engage with his son for the first time, and perhaps the last.

Nader shared a few words about Dr. Larabi, acknowledging the goodness that defined him and the significance he held for their entire family. As the handshake concluded, Nader made his way into the auditorium.

Saamaan extended his hand, a gesture that transcended mere formality, carrying beneath its surface a current of unexplored emotions. "Dr. Larabi was my pediatrician," he disclosed, the words hanging in the air like a delicate veil concealing the intricate tapestry of their turbulent family history. As Saamaan excused himself and made his way to join his waiting father, the air seemed to shimmer with the echoes of untold stories and severed connections.

In the somber setting of the funeral session, Sam stood at a distance, his gaze fixed on the young man who unknowingly embodied the intersection of two separate lives—his own and the son he never had the chance to raise. Saamaan, oblivious to the complex tapestry of relationships surrounding him, was engaged in conversation with others, his voice resonating in the air like a distant echo of mysterious stories.

As Sam observed his son from afar, a whirlwind of conflicting emotions surged within him. Each expression on his face, was a poignant reminder of the missed years, the unspoken connections, and the profound absence of a father-son bond that fate had denied them.

Sam's heartache was concealed beneath a stoic exterior, masked by the shared grief over the loss of the grandfather they both mourned. He longed to reveal the truth, to bridge the chasm that separated them, but the weight of circumstances held him back. The funeral hall became a theater of silent agony as Sam grappled with the complexities of his emotions.

Witnessing Saamaan, unaware of the paternal presence lingering in the shadows, stirred a bittersweet cocktail of regret and longing within Sam. Each word exchanged, every shared memory of the deceased grandfather, was a missed opportunity to speak the unsaid, to mend the fractured threads of their common lineage, watching his son without being able to claim him, feeling the weight of a secret that echoed through the hallowed halls of grief. In the midst of mourning, Sam's silent monologue resonated with the ache of a father's unexpressed love, a symphony of emotions woven into the fabric of this sad, clandestine encounter.

As Sam turned to greet others, his attention was unexpectedly drawn to a subtle spectacle near the women's entrance. Across the room, his gaze collided with Roxana's. In that brief moment, their eyes locked in an unspoken exchange that transcended the mere act of acknowledgement. The curve of her lips formed a meaningful smile, and her nods, accompanied by nuanced body language, conveyed a depth of understanding. It became evident to Sam that Roxana, with her orchestrated subtleties, had played a pivotal role in bringing him face to face with Saamaan. Grateful for this orchestrated encounter, Sam reciprocated with a subtle nod of acknowledgment.

Meanwhile, Ariana, positioned by the entrance to welcome the women, observed the unfolding scene with keen awareness. As the realization dawned upon her, she recognized Roxana, adding a layer of intrigue and emotion to the unspoken dynamics between the characters.

"Oh my god, Roxana." The instinctive hug between them spoke volumes, carrying the weight of their common world. Despite Ariana's awareness of the inappropriate encounter between Roxana and Sam, a sense of cherished connection lingered between the two women. Roxana, clasping Ariana's hands, expressed a wish for a meeting under better circumstances, and Ariana, with a subtle tug, led her away from the bustling crowd.

"Congratulations," said Roxana mentioning that she had heard about Ariana's marriage to Farhad. Ariana, in response, bluntly asked if Saam had been the one to tell her. Ariana's response cut through the air with a sharp edge, "I didn't think you would waste time with small talks in that garden all alone." The words hung in the moment, carrying an unspoken weight of unanticipated revelations and complicated emotions.

Roxana, overcome with embarrassment, lowered her head and blushed. She finally found the words to explain, "It seems you know everything, but I hope you know nothing happened. I just gave back his old photo album that he had left behind with me." The admission carried a mix of relief and a plea for understanding.

Ariana responded firmly, "You don't have to convince me, but Sam's wife took the kids and left, it jeopardized Sam's future with his family." Her words carried a weight of concern and understanding, acknowledging the gravity of the situation.

"Oh my god," those words slipped from Roxana's lips as her eyes met Sam's intense gaze. Tears welled up in her eyes. "We never intended to hurt anyone." The weight of regret hung in the air, and Ariana, with a mix of compassion and caution, declared, "You may get burnt playing with fire." Roxana, desperate to convey their innocence, likened it to a reunion of two old friends. However, Ariana, firm in her stance, asserted, "It lost its innocence the moment you hid it from your spouses."

Ariana enveloped Roxana in a warm embrace, holding onto a friendship that had weathered various storms. The memories of the past lingered as Ariana reassured her, "You have nothing to worry about. It's not about retaliation. No matter what's happened in the past, we all still love you. I wish I had seen you under better circumstances too. Just calm down and go inside." The hug served as a bridge between the tranquil past and the tumultuous present, offering solace and understanding amidst the chaos.

"Hard to imagine I'm getting advice from little Ariana. Farhad's a lucky man," Roxana said, recalling Ariana from her teenage years, as she walked inside.

As Sam stood at the entrance of the hall, his eyes immediately found Roxana. The sight of her, surrounded by the warmth of her family, struck a deep, resonant chord within him. It was a vivid, painful contrast to the void left by his own family's absence, each smile and touch among them a reminder of what he had lost or perhaps never fully reclaim.

The crowd, dressed in mourning, moved like shadows around him, their voices a low murmur against the backdrop of his spiraling thoughts. It was Jacqueline's voice, however, that sliced through the din, her words a sharp reminder of the day's significance. "I hope you're thinking today is the day she forever walked out of my life." The remark, unexpected and poignant, reverberated in his mind, adding a deeper hue to the sorrow of the day.

As Sam's gaze drifted from Roxana to the architecture of the hall around him, a flood of memories washed over him. The high ceilings, the grandeur of the space, it all mirrored the lecture hall where he had first spoken to Nicole. He could almost smell her perfume in the air, see the flash of her smile, remember the way she played with her hair in that quintessential eighties style. Each detail of that defining moment was etched in his mind, a vivid recollection that now mingled with the bitterness of loss.

"I remember every bit of that moment," he murmured to himself, his voice barely audible above the hum of the gathering. "And yes, today is the day she forever walked out of my life." His admission was a quiet surrender to the tides of change and regret that had shaped his life. The hall, with its grandeur and echoes of the past, now held the weight of his reflection, a poignant backdrop to the tapestry of memories and lost opportunities that he carried with him. As he stood there, lost in the past yet fully present in the heartache of the moment, Sam grappled with the complex weave of emotions that defined his journey — a path marked by love, loss, and the enduring hope of redemption.

Chapter 64

Let's embark on a journey, one that spans across the expansive meridian lines and vast oceans, charting a course to the farthest reaches of the globe. Our path unwinds and weaves through the world's hidden nooks and crannies until it gently guides us to the coastal sanctuary of La Jolla, a gem often hailed as the Jewel of California. Here, amidst the serene elegance of this picturesque locale, we find Nicole and Brenda. They are comfortably seated on the balcony of Nicole's house, a vantage point offering an unobstructed view of nature's grand display.

As the day gradually concedes to the gentle embrace of evening, the western sky becomes a canvas painted with the vibrant colors of the San Diego sunset. Nicole and Brenda, with their gazes locked onto the horizon, are momentarily lost in the beauty that unfolds. It's a scene that transcends time, a daily ritual of the sun that never fails to enchant its audience. The balcony, a modest stage set high above the ground, offers them front row seats to this exquisite end-of-day ceremony, a spectacle of light and color that dances across the sky and water, bidding the day goodbye with a promise of tomorrow's return.

Brenda's tequila sunrise cast a soft, amber glow in her hand as she took a thoughtful sip, her eyes full of concern for the friend beside her. "Do you miss him?" she ventured, her voice a gentle nudge into the depths of Nicole's heartache.

Nicole let out a sigh, heavy with the weight of memories and loss. "Everywhere I look, I'm reminded of him," she confided, her voice barely more than a whisper. "Every little thing we touched, every dream we built together... it's like living in a house haunted by the ghost of our love." Her gaze drifted, lost in the silent echo of his absence that permeated every corner of her life. A raw, unspoken agony lingered in her words, a silent scream of, "How could he ruin our life like that?"

Brenda reached out, her hand a warm presence against the cold swell of sorrow. "I know it's not easy what you're going through," she murmured, her empathy a soft blanket around Nicole's trembling shoulders.

Nicole's eyes, brimming with the tumult of betrayal and confusion, met Brenda's steady gaze. "He says nothing happened, but I saw them, Brenda. I saw Roxana with him," she admitted, the admission a crack in the dam holding back her tears. "Sometimes, I wonder if ignorance would have been a blissful amnesty."

Brenda, ever the rock in the stormy seas of Nicole's life, offered words steeped in understanding and comfort. "Nicole, don't blame yourself. The fault lies with him, not with you. The extent of their betrayal doesn't change the fact that he stepped outside your marriage."

Nicole nodded, a fragile smile playing on her lips as she absorbed Brenda's words, a mantra to soothe the relentless ache. She confessed to shutting Sam out, unable to reconcile the man she loved with the betrayal that had unfolded before her eyes. "It's hard to accept that the person who gave you the best memories has become just a memory," she reflected, the bitter irony not lost on her.

Their intimate conversation, a fragile thread of healing and understanding, was shattered by the shrill ring of the phone. The sudden intrusion jolted them, a stark reminder that the world outside continued its relentless march, indifferent to the maelstrom of emotions swirling within. As Nicole hesitated, Brenda gave a supportive nod, a silent pledge of her unwavering presence, no matter what the call might bring.

Nicole's fingers hesitated for a moment before lifting the receiver, the room suspended in a moment of anticipatory silence. As she pressed the phone to her ear, Sam's voice, a familiar yet distant sound, emerged, laden with an urgency that seemed to fill every corner of the room.

"What is it?" Nicole's voice was steady, yet her eyes flickered towards Brenda, signaling the undercurrent of anxiety that the call had stirred. Brenda, sensing the shift in atmosphere, leaned in with a questioning look.

"Sam," Nicole mouthed silently, her eyes locked with Brenda's, sharing the identity of the caller. A shared history and understanding flowed silently between them.

"Mom is coming back with us," Sam continued, his voice threading through the air with a vulnerability that seemed almost tangible. He spoke of his hopes for his mother's comfort, his concern evident even through the distance.

Nicole listened, her expression a mask of calm, but her eyes— a tempest of conflicting emotions. The room, once filled with the light-hearted banter and warmth of friendship, now seemed to bear witness to the complexities of past and present intertwining.

Brenda's expression, a mix of curiosity and concern, prompted Nicole to divulge the gist of the conversation. Covering the receiver, she whispered, "He's coming back with his mom." The words hung between them, a new layer added to the unfolding situation.

"Pig," Brenda exclaimed, her voice a blend of jest and genuine frustration, close enough for Sam to hear. A smile tugged at Nicole's lips, a momentary relief from the tension. Sam, well accustomed to Brenda's spirited personality, let the comment slide without offense.

Reassuring Sam, Nicole's voice became a soft balm of assurance. "We'll make sure she's comfortable," she promised, her words a bridge of empathy and care.

Yet Brenda couldn't resist another playful jab, her "Pig" ringing out again, a testament to the enduring bond and the lightness they tried to maintain even in the midst of life's complexities. Sam, his patience evident, then asked for the children, a request that brought a new layer of sadness to the conversation.

Nicole, feeling the weight of the moment, glanced at Brenda, a silent communication passing between them. As she prepared to summon the children, the room seemed to breathe again, the tension momentarily lifted, but the undercurrent of what was to come lingered, a silent prelude to the next chapter of their intertwined lives.

Chapter 65

As Northwest flight 729 began its descent toward San Diego, the city's sprawling lights greeted Sam like a bed of twinkling starry constellation, a familiar yet distant welcome from the place he had once woven into the fabric of his life. The aircraft gently descended through the layers of the evening sky, the hum of the landing gear unfolding beneath him like a soothing lullaby, albeit one that couldn't fully quiet the thrum of apprehension in his heart.

As the plane touched down, the screech of tires against the tarmac punctuated the night air, a stark reminder of the reality that awaited him beyond the airport's gates. Each vibration through the cabin floor seemed to echo the tumult of emotions Sam harbored about his imminent reunion, a blend of longing, apprehension, and unresolved sentiments that hung heavy in his chest.

Meanwhile, in the bustling airport lobby, Nicole stood surrounded by Tara, Cameron, Brenda, and Luke. Their collective gaze was trained on the arrival gate above, a mix of anticipation and anxiety etched on their faces. They represented a patchwork of the life Sam was returning to — a life filled with complexities, love, and the inevitable confrontations that lay ahead.

As footsteps began to echo down the corridor, signaling the arrival of passengers, their hearts collectively tightened. This was more than just a homecoming; it was a threshold to new beginnings, or perhaps necessary endings.

As Sam made his way down the escalator, the familiar sights and sounds of the airport came rushing back to him, a blend of nostalgia and anxiety. But it was Cameron's voice that cut through the din, a beacon of joyous reunion in the crowded space. "Dad!" Cameron yelled, his excitement sending him dashing towards the stairs, his young legs barely keeping up with his eagerness.

Nicole, ever the protective mother, called out to Cameron, her voice a mixture of warmth and caution, "Cameron, wait!" Her eyes followed her son, a smile tugging at the corners of her mouth despite her worries.

Luke, with Tara's hand securely in his, moved quickly to keep up with Cameron's enthusiastic pace, their faces lit with the anticipation of reuniting with Sam. The air was charged with the electricity of imminent family reunion, a moment they had all been waiting for.

As Jacqueline, Ariana, and Sam finally reached the bottom of the escalator, Cameron, unable to contain his excitement any longer, leaped into his father's arms. "I missed you so much," he declared, his words muffled against Sam's shoulder.

"I missed you too, buddy," Sam responded, his voice thick with emotion. He hugged Cameron tightly, his gaze drifting over to Nicole, who was watching them with a complex expression. With a deep breath, he gently set Cameron down and turned to Tara, lifting her into a hug and kissing her cheek. "Are you coming home with us?" Tara asked. "Of course, I'm coming home," he laughed in response to her innocent query, but her next words, "I thought mom was mad at you," struck a chord deep within him.

Sam looked into Tara's eyes, a mix of love and remorse swirling in his own. "Let's talk about that later, okay? Look, Grandma's here too!" he said, shifting her attention to Jacqueline's approach.

Underneath the surface of the happy reunion, Sam felt the weight of his past actions, the understanding of how deeply his choices had affected his family. The laughter and hugs couldn't fully mask the undercurrent of tension and the silent questions that lingered in the air. As he held Tara close, he knew the road to healing and forgiveness would be a long one, but the first steps were being taken right there, in the embrace of his children, under the watchful eyes of the woman he had hurt and the family waiting to mend.

In the midst of heartfelt reunions, the tension between Sam and Nicole was palpable. As they stood facing each other, the air thickened with the weight of past mistakes and unsaid apologies. Their eyes met, a silent conversation taking place in the brief moment before Nicole's cold nod and subsequent turn away shattered any illusions of a quick reconciliation. The space she put between them, both in steps and in the withdrawal of her gaze, spoke louder than any words could, leaving Sam with a profound sense of regret and the daunting realization of the long road ahead to possibly mend their bond.

As if bearing the physical manifestation of his grief, Sam followed the airline baggage handler to retrieve the coffin that held his late father. Each step felt heavier than the last, the sight of the somber casket before him a stark reminder of the finality of death and the unspoken conversations left hanging in the balance. Nicole's distant, sorrow-filled eyes, a mirror to his own heartache, only deepened the sense of loss and longing that enveloped him.

After the grim procession to secure his father's remains, Sam returned to find Nicole had taken Jacqueline and the children home, a gesture that underscored the chasm that had formed between them. Left waiting outside the terminal were Ariana, Luke, and Brenda, their presence a small solace in the overwhelming tide of emotions. After ensuring Ariana was comfortably settled in her residence, Sam rejoined Luke and Brenda, their silent support a testament to the bonds of family and friendship that still held, despite the turbulence of recent events.

However, as soon as Sam climbed back into the car, Brenda's pent-up frustration and protective instincts found an outlet with a resounding smack to the back of his head. "That was for hurting my best friend," she declared fiercely, her voice laden with indignation and concern. Her questions poured forth, demanding answers and accountability for the pain inflicted on Nicole. Her sharp words and stern demeanor reflected not just anger but also a deep-seated worry for the friend she had seen suffer.

Sam, still nursing the sting from Brenda's smack, tried to inject some humor into the tense situation. "Could've asked more gently, you know," he quipped, rubbing the back of his head.

Brenda, unmoved by his attempt to lighten the mood, shot back sharply. "Sure, I could have. But it wouldn't have made the point clear, would it? No subject changing," she asserted, her voice brooking no argument.

Sam glanced towards Luke, hoping for some form of reprieve or at least a slight intervention. However, Luke, well aware of the dynamics at play, raised his hands in a gesture of surrender. "Dude, I'm staying out of this one," he declared, offering a wry smile that did little to hide his intention to remain neutral.

Attempting to deflect once more, Sam pointed out the apparent rekindling between Luke and Brenda. "I see you two hooked up again," he said, a note of tease in his voice, hoping to shift the focus.

Luke, amused and curious, leaned into the banter. "I'll tell you our details if you tell me yours," he replied with a grin, eager to hear more about the situation between Sam and Roxana.

Brenda, having none of it, slapped the back of both their heads, her actions punctuated by her calling them "pigs." Her determination to keep the conversation on track was evident. "I said, no changing the subject!"

Sam, realizing the futility of evasion, sighed deeply. "What can I say? It was a mistake, and nothing happened. I just hope Nicole can find it in her heart to forgive me." He then looked at Brenda with a mix of irritation and appeal. "By the way, ever consider helping us patch things up?"

Brenda, noting the genuine remorse in Sam's voice, softened slightly. "I hope she forgives you," she said, her tone less combative than before.

Luke chuckled at the sudden shift in Brenda's demeanor. "See, she can be nice too," he teased, lightening the mood in the car.

Sam offered a grateful nod to Brenda. "Thanks, I know you're just looking out for Nicole," he acknowledged, the tension between them easing slightly.

The car ride continued in a heavy silence, each person lost in their own thoughts until they reached Sam's house. As he got out, Sam thanked them for the ride and expressed his hope to see them again under better circumstances. With a small wave, he turned and walked towards the house.

As the door swung open and the familiar chorus of "Daddy's home!" filled the air, Sam's heart swelled with a mixture of joy and sorrow. Tara and Cameron's exuberant sprint toward him was a brief reprieve from the heavy cloak of guilt that he wore. Lifting each child onto his shoulders, he made his way to the family room, their laughter a temporary balm for his aching soul.

There, the somber figures of Jacqueline and Nicole sat deep in conversation, their quiet exchange punctuated by the occasional shimmer of tears on Nicole's cheeks. The jovial mood of the children's welcome contrasted sharply with the tension that hung between the adults. As Nicole excused herself with a subdued goodnight, avoiding Sam's hopeful gaze, the chill of her departure seemed to permeate the room, leaving behind a haunting silence.

Sam motioned for the children to head to their room, promising to join them shortly to tuck them in. As they scampered off, he joined Jacqueline, sinking into the adjacent chair as if the weight of his world rested squarely on his shoulders. "I messed up, Mom," he murmured into the stillness, his admission hanging heavy in the air. The words, filled with remorse and a desperate plea for understanding, seemed to echo off the walls, amplifying the sense of desolation that filled the room.

Jacqueline's response, steeped in disappointment yet laced with a mother's inherent concern, was a stark reminder of the pain Nicole was enduring. "She's devastated, Sam," she said softly, each word a testament to the raw emotional toll of his betrayal. The air thickened with the truth of his indiscretions, and as Jacqueline's gaze met his, the unspoken agony of the situation was palpable.

In a last-ditch effort to find some solace, Sam pleaded his case, insisting on his love for Nicole and his regret for the hurt he had caused. Yet, Jacqueline's response was unyielding, a necessary dose of reality amidst the confusion and hurt. "What you did was wrong, Sam," she said firmly, a declaration that left no room for excuses or justifications.

"What can I do now?" Sam's voice broke the silence that had settled over them, his question a reflection of the turmoil churning within. Jacqueline's eyes softened, but her words remained firm. "It's late. Go put the kids to sleep," she advised, her suggestion a gentle nudge toward taking responsibility and facing the consequences of his actions.

As he made his way upstairs, the weight of the day's events bore down on him, each step a reminder of the long journey of redemption that lay ahead. The dimly lit hallway seemed to stretch on endlessly, a metaphor for the path he must now navigate to rebuild the trust and love he had shattered.

Pausing outside Cameron's room, Sam's resolve faltered as the muffled sounds of his children's conversation seeped through the door. Tara's comforting whispers and Cameron's quiet sobs were a stark reminder of the ripple effects his actions had caused. The realization that his mistakes had not only broken his marriage but also wounded the hearts of his children was a sobering moment, one that would haunt him in the days to come.

With a deep breath, Sam gently opened the door, his expression a mask of fatherly affection as he prepared to face his children. The task of soothing their worries and mending their spirits loomed large, yet it was a step he knew he must take.

"Sweetheart, what wrong?" Sam's voice trembled, laden with a melancholy weight as he nestled between Tara and Cameron. With the gentlest touch, he dabbed at the tears streaking Cameron's cheeks, jewels of sorrow glistening under the room's soft light.

"I'm... I'm okay," Cameron murmured, a valiant but futile attempt to stifle the sobs, his little chest heaving with every silent cry. The whirlwind of emotions tangled within him, too complex and heavy for his young mind to navigate.

Sam's gaze shifted, seeking solace or perhaps an answer in Tara's eyes. After a moment laden with unspoken words, she whispered, her voice barely a sigh, "It's Grandpa. He's heartbroken."

Sam wrapped Cameron in a warm hug, trying to comfort him. "I know you're really sad, buddy. Grandpa loved you a lot, and he still does, even though we can't see him anymore. He's like a big hug around us all the time, even if we can't feel it. And he wouldn't want us to be too sad for too long, okay?"

Yet, as Cameron nestled closer, his words, raw and unguarded, pierced the still air. "But you, Dad, the thought of never seeing you again..." His voice cracked, a testament to the profound fear of loss only innocence can feel. "Promise me, no matter what, you won't leave us like Grandpa did," his plea, adrift in this vast, scary world.

As Sam held them both, a fortress against the encroaching shadows of the unknown, he whispered, "I promise, with every beat of my heart, to stay as long as the stars will allow." His voice, a steady rock amidst the storm of uncertainties, masked his own trembling fears.

Unbeknownst to Sam, Nicole had silently approached the children's room, intending to check on them. She lingered in the muted shadows of the hallway, her presence a silent whisper against the soft murmur of the room. As the hushed tones of her family's tender exchange drifted to her, a profound stillness settled within her, as though the world had paused, acknowledging the gravity of the moment.

The words, each laden with love and fear, seeped into her, weaving a tightness around her heart. She felt a visceral ache, a mix of admiration and sorrow for the strength and vulnerability her loved ones displayed. The innocence of her children's concerns, paired with Sam's gentle reassurances, painted a bittersweet tableau of the family she cherished deeply.

Her eyes, glistening in the dim light, reflected a tumult of emotions. She grappled with the realization of the inevitable—of how time, indiscriminate and relentless, would one day reshape their family portrait. The thought of a future without Sam, the unwavering pillar of their small world, sent a shiver through her, as chilling as the thought was paralyzing.

Yet, amidst the swell of fear and uncertainty, a fierce resolve began to kindle within her. Nicole understood that while the future was a mystery woven with threads of fear and hope, the strength of their family bond, the laughter and tears shared, would be the guiding light through any darkness. She decided to face the tides, come what may.

The following morning, just as the first rays of sunlight touched the sky, Sam quietly slipped out of the house. The car's engine purred to life as he turned the ignition key, a familiar ritual from his younger days that offered a brief moment of solace. Nicole was stirred from her restless sleep by the telltale sound of the garage door.

As the morning sun struggled to break through the window, Nicole lay in bed, grappling with the weight of her emotions. The room, once filled with warmth and shared dreams, now echoed with the haunting silence of shattered trust. "It's going to be hard on the kids, but how can I forget about what you've done?" Her thoughts, a desperate plea, as if Sam stood before her, listening to the unspoken words. The question lingered, unanswered, as she relived the painful choices that led them down separate paths.

With a heavy heart, Nicole rose from the bed, compelled to witness Sam's departure. The familiar rumble of his car engine echoed through the emptiness of their separated lives. "Why did you make us go our separate ways?" The air hung heavy with unanswered questions, and as Sam's car turned the corner, it marked the end of an era, disappearing from her view, out of sight and seemingly out of her life.

Returning to the solitude of her bed, Nicole grappled with the indelible image of Sam entering the garden, where Roxana waited as a silent witness to their unraveling bond. The ache in her chest mirrored the tangled mess of emotions, as she attempted to force forgetfulness upon the unforgettable.

Sam guided the car off the freeway onto Mira Mesa Road, a route etched in the routine of his daily commute to work. Yet, at Scranton Road, he defied the familiar and made a right turn instead. A few miles down the road led him to El Camino Memorial Park – a solemn destination, now his father's eternal resting place. Here, amidst the stillness of the cemetery, Sam orchestrated the arrangements for the funeral and burial, scheduled to unfold on Monday.

As he navigated the winding paths, memories of his once-perfect life unraveled before him, now tainted by the choices that had effortlessly dismantled it. The echoes of his own undoing reverberated through the serene surroundings, each headstone a silent testament to the permanence of decisions made.

In the midst of this contemplative journey, his cell phone interrupted the somber melody. The caller ID displayed a simple word that carried a complex weight – "Home." The pulsating uncertainty of what awaited him on the other end lingered in the air, a poignant reminder of the fractured life he was trying to navigate.

In the anticipation of hearing Nicole's voice, Sam answered the call, only to be greeted by his mother's concerned inquiry about his early departure. Sam reassured her that he was okay and explained the reason for his early morning venture – arranging the funeral details for his late father.

Jacqueline, on the other end of the line, informed Sam that she intended to stay with Ariana and was waiting for her to come. Sam, desiring her comforting presence, urged her to stay with them as she always had. He questioned why she felt the need to leave, asserting that nothing had changed.

Jacqueline, however, laid bare the stark reality. She acknowledged that things had indeed changed, and he needed to face the truth. She disclosed that she had discussed the situation with Nicole, emphasizing that the couple needed space to confront and resolve their issues. With a mother's straightforwardness, she insisted that he had to admit his mistakes, express genuine remorse, and prove to Nicole that he understood the gravity of his actions.

Sam, his demeanor heavy with regret, confessed that he doubted anything could make amends at this point, as Nicole seemed resolute in her decision for him to move out.

"Be hopeful," Jacqueline encouraged, her words carrying the weight of a mother's hope and a son's redemption.

Chapter 66

The sanctum of their home, once a haven of laughter and shared dreams, now hung heavy with the weight of unspoken truths. Nicole's voice barely broke the thick air as she called out for dinner, each word heavy with a reluctance born of the impending storm she harbored within her heart.

Cameron, with the earnestness of youth, pleaded for her to call Sam, his voice a mix of hope and impatience. Tara echoed her brother's urgency, their united front a poignant reminder of the family's fragile unity. Nicole felt the delicate balance tipping as she stood at the precipice of change, the truth of their separation looming like a shadow ready to eclipse the light of their togetherness.

Her heart, a tempest of love and dread, throbbed painfully against her ribs. She knew the moment was near when the veil would be lifted, revealing the rending of what once seemed unbreakable. Fear gripped her, the fear of watching her children's faces crumble with understanding, the fear of their love wavering under the weight of disillusionment.

As Tara's voice, tender with concern, cut through the silence, "why are you so sad lately?" Nicole felt the thin veneer of her composure crack. "How can I be sad when I have you two?" she whispered, her words a fragile shield against the onslaught of her own emotions. She pulled them close, a desperate embrace seeking to fortify them against the coming storm.

Cameron's soft accusation, "We heard you cry the other night," sent a shiver down her spine. His words, so innocent yet so revealing, threatened to unravel her. The rumble of the garage door was a pardon, a brief respite from the inevitable. As the children's cries of "Dad's home!" filled the air, Nicole felt a momentary relief wash over her, a fleeting sense of normalcy in the chaos.

Sam's return, the familiar rituals of bedtime stories and gentle goodnights, offered a temporary solace. As he tucked the children into bed, their faces peaceful in sleep, he lingered in the doorway, the image of their innocence a balm to his weary soul.

In the dimly lit corridors of their once vibrant home, Sam moved like a ghost, his footsteps a silent echo of the life they used to share. As he approached the living room, his gaze fell upon Nicole, a solitary figure of contemplation and sorrow. Her hair, a cascading testament to the years they'd woven together, lay around her like a veil of whispered memories. Each strand seemed to hold a story, a shared laughter, a whispered secret, and the ache to reach out to her was a palpable force within him. Yet, the chasm of their strained silence lay vast and insurmountable between them.

He settled into the love seat, an island of space between them, as the air grew thick with the unsaid. Nicole sat with a poise that belied the storm within, her eyes holding a universe of hurt, betrayal, and fading hope. The tension stretched thin, a fragile silence that begged to be broken.

Breaking the tension, it was Sam who dared to address the unspoken turmoil. "Are we gonna talk about the big elephant in the room?" His words hung in the air, a gentle invitation to unravel the complexities that had woven their lives into an intricate tapestry of joy and sorrow.

The air hung heavy with tension as Nicole, her gaze steely, delivered a blunt and cutting statement. "You should move out," the words sliced through the room, leaving an uncomfortable silence in their wake. Nicole, perceptive to the undercurrents of Sam's expectations, couldn't resist a touch of sarcasm. "What were you hoping to hear? Good job scoring with your old girlfriend. Is that what you expected?"

The scene intensified as Sam, burdened by the weight of his mistakes, tried to interject with a term of endearment. "Listen, my love..." His words hung in the air, fraught with the weight of regret. But before he could finish, Nicole sharply cut him off, her voice dripping with scorn. "How could you call me 'my love'? Did you call her the same thing when you guys fucked?" She fought hard against the rising tide of tears, determined not to let her emotions overcome her. The room crackled with unspoken pain, the fracture in their once-unbreakable bond now laid bare.

"Stop with that shit, I told you we didn't …" Sam halted. His words hung in the charged atmosphere, but Nicole remained unmoved. The trust, once unbreakable, now shattered into irreparable fragments.

Sam, grappling with the consequences of his actions, acknowledged Nicole's justified anger. "You have every reason to be mad at me," he admitted, the weight of responsibility heavy on his shoulders. "I single-handedly ruined our beautiful world, and I want to rebuild it." The plea lingered in the air, a fragile hope for redemption amid the wreckage of their fractured relationship.

Nicole unleashed her recurring nightmare to him—the haunting scene where Roxana awaited him at the gate, and as the gate closed, it symbolized the shuttering of their marriage. She implored, "How can I ever wipe that memory away?" Sam, faced with the weight of his actions, had no choice but to lower his head in shame.

Choking back tears, Nicole continued, expressing disbelief that he could treat her in such a way. In her mind, he had seemed incapable of hurting his family, but witnessing him in the garden shattered her world. With a mix of pain and desperation, she demanded honesty, asking, "Were there others?"

"Of course not, you have every right to make me feel like shit. I know I shattered your world," Sam admitted, his voice tinged with remorse. "But I want to put the pieces back together and make your world whole again." The room hung heavy with the echoes of broken trust.

"What was lacking in your life that made you run to another woman?" Nicole's voice held a mixture of pain and accusation. Caught off guard, Sam abruptly replied, "Nothing," denying any deficiency in his life. However, he quickly shifted the focus, expressing a desire to understand why Roxana had suddenly left him.

Nicole, her hurt radiating in her face, posed a poignant question, "What difference would it have made to know or not to know?" The weight of unspoken implications hung in the air, their conversation fraught with the tension of unresolved issues.

"We had a relationship, and she just let go. Wouldn't you want to know?" Sam's words hung in the heavy air, each syllable digging his grave deeper.

"Not at this point of my life, I wouldn't," Nicole's voice, a mix of frustration and hurt, echoed through the room. "You weren't even twenty years old back then. You have to learn to let go sometimes. I saw Tony White at our last high school reunion. We had a relationship, and one day he too just let go. Should I have slept with him to find out why?"

Sam met her gaze, his eyes revealing the struggle within. The weight of lost trust loomed large, and he knew she wouldn't believe him, no matter how vehemently he swore that nothing had happened. Under his breath, he grunted, "You'd never do that." The unspoken plea for understanding lingered in the charged atmosphere.

"We need some time away from each other," Nicole declared with a cold finality, rising from her seat and making her way towards the bedroom. Pausing at the doorway, she added that Sam should spend the day with the kids tomorrow, finding a delicate way to break the news to them, but he was not to return home after the funeral.

"Is this truly what you want, deep down?" Sam pleaded, a desperate sense of loss permeating his words, realizing he might be losing her forever.

"I was content with what I had," Nicole cried, the weight of her emotions evident. "Maybe it's time to see what you truly want, deep down."

Sam stood before the closed door, an invisible force pulling him toward it like a magnet. As if seeking solace, he pressed his face and palms against the wood, closing his eyes, letting his imagination transport him to a time when they were together on the other side. The haunting sound of her tears reached his ears, snapping his eyes open. A wave of shame washed over him, and he sluggishly stepped away, leaving the closed door standing as a barrier between them.

The next morning, Sam planned to take Tara and Cameron out to breakfast, a small attempt to create a sense of normalcy amid the tumultuous emotions that gripped their home. As they sat in the car, the kids couldn't help but ask, "How come Mom isn't coming with us?"

Sam, choosing his words carefully, told them to go and ask her, hopeful that the rift between them could be bridged, even for a brief moment. The children, with their innocent curiosity, ventured back home, their steps echoing through the quiet house.

However, the anticipated joy of having a family breakfast together was shattered when Tara and Cameron returned alone to Sam's waiting car in the garage. Their small faces carried a mix of confusion and disappointment as they relayed their mother's message: "Mom said she has things to do and can't make it." The thinly veiled excuses hung in the air, leaving an unspoken tension between Sam and his fractured family dynamics.

Sam posed a simple question to Tara and Cameron, "Where would you like to go for breakfast?" The response, harmonious and filled with childhood delight, echoed through the car as both kids exclaimed, "Pancake house!"

The scent of syrup lingered in their memories as they indulged in pancakes, but the warmth of the moment couldn't entirely dispel the shadows that loomed over their fractured family. Despite the hearty breakfast, an unspoken yearning for completeness lingered beneath the surface.

In a bid to weave threads of joy into their strained reality, Sam surprised the kids with a trip to Belmont Park on Mission Beach. The vibrant sights and sounds couldn't quite mask the palpable absence of Nicole, leaving Sam to navigate the roller coaster of emotions within and around him.

As Tara and Cameron eagerly queued for the roller coaster, Sam's gaze wandered to the remnants of the Red Onion nightclub, now an empty space resonating with memories of shared laughter and dancing with Nicole. A wave of nostalgia washed over him, carrying him back to happier times when the world seemed more intact.

Peering through the window, lost in the echoes of the past, Sam's eyes involuntarily closed, replaying the dance of love they once shared. The laughter of yesteryears intermingled with the distant sounds of the amusement park, creating a symphony of both joy and sorrow.

"What are you looking at, Dad?" Tara's curious voice cut through his reverie. The once lively nightclub now stood empty, a silent witness to the passage of time.

"We wanna go to the beach," Cameron declared, breaking the spell. Eager eyes filled with anticipation begged for approval. "Can we get some swimming trunks and go swimming? Please. Please. Please," he pleaded.

In that vulnerable moment, Sam couldn't deny his children's simple request. A visit to a beach store ensued, where they traded memories of a once-whole family for swimming trunks and towels. With sand between their toes and the ocean's embrace ahead, Sam, Tara, and Cameron sought solace in the rhythmic waves, hoping that, for a moment, the sea could wash away the complexities that clung to their lives.

****

Nicole lingered in bed longer than her usual morning routine, the weight of impending change settling in the air around her. Eventually, she sought solace in the comforting embrace of her morning coffee on the porch, a routine disrupted by the echoes of uncertainty. As the steam curled from the cup, her thoughts meandered to Sam and the kids, pondering the impact of her decision on their young hearts.

With a determined resolve, she promised herself strength, vowing to staunch the flow of tears that threatened to escape. The porch, once a haven, now bore witness to the silent contemplation of a mother navigating the labyrinth of emotions.

Returning to the bedroom, a sense of purpose eclipsed the sadness that lingered. Nicole embarked on the somber task of packing Sam's belongings, a ritual she had undertaken countless times before. Yet, this occasion bore a different weight, as if she were encapsulating half of her life and a myriad of shared memories within those two small suitcases.

Each folded garment, each cherished memento, carried the echoes of a life she once knew, a life that now teetered on the precipice of irreparable change. As she carefully arranged his belongings, the act of packing became an emotional journey, a symbolic representation of a future rewritten.

Dragging the laden suitcases to the garage, Nicole left them conspicuously in sight—a visual testament to the unspoken rift that now divided their shared space. Each suitcase stood as a silent plea, a visual metaphor for the unspoken chasm that had emerged between them, waiting for Sam to confront the tangible manifestation of their shattered union.

****

The darkness of the evening had already enveloped Sam and the kids as they returned home. Guiding the car into the familiar confines of the garage, Sam's eyes were drawn to the suitcases, their presence casting a solemn shadow over the space. As he lifted the weighty cases, their tangible reality served as a confirmation—an unspoken acknowledgment that the imminent separation was now an undeniable truth.

The gravity of the moment settled upon Sam, a weight he could no longer evade. He knew the time had come for that long-dreaded conversation with the kids, a conversation that would unravel the fabric of their shared family life. With a plan in mind, he aimed to broach the topic during dinner, but the right moment eluded him, and courage faltered in the face of impending sorrow.

Another attempt was made during the shared joy of ice cream for dessert, yet the words remained lodged, unspoken, as Sam grappled with the emotional avalanche that awaited. On the journey home, he teetered on the edge of disclosure, yearning to shelter his children from the impending storm. Perhaps a flicker of hope lingered, a hope that Nicole had reconsidered, only to be extinguished as he lifted the tightly packed suitcases once more. The visual testament of their fractured reality stood as an unwavering reminder.

The children's jubilant voices filled the air as they rushed inside, eagerly calling out to their mom to tell her about the fun day they had. Meanwhile, Sam took deliberate care in placing the suitcases within his car, a deliberate pace that mirrored the weight of his impending revelation. With a sense of detachment, he proceeded to the room that had become his temporary sanctuary, each step a measured approach to the inevitable.

In the solitude of the shower, Sam found himself rehearsing the delicate words he needed to share with the children. The weight of the truth he was about to unveil hung heavily over him. Emerging from the bathroom, Sam somberly navigated to Cameron's room, where the boy eagerly hopped onto his back, their laughter momentarily drowning out the impending heaviness.

As they made their way to Tara's room, Cameron, with an innocence that heightened the impending difficulty, expressed how much he had missed Sam during his stay in Iran. The reality of the task ahead weighed on Sam, and he gently dropped Cameron onto Tara's bed, the gravity of the moment palpable.

Expressing fatigue, Sam acknowledged Cameron's growth, his attempt at levity clouded by Tara's evident sadness. Her blunt question pierced the room—how long would you and Mom not talk to each other? Seating himself beside the bed, Sam recognized the perceptive nature of children, acknowledging their ability to discern underlying tensions.

"Did you break something?" Cameron's curiosity was met with a metaphorical explanation from Sam, who confessed to breaking something precious and the arduous journey required to mend it. Tara, hopeful for a quick resolution, suggested buying a new one for Mom. Sam, wrestling with the complexity of the situation, gently revealed the irreplaceable nature of what he had broken.

"I don't know how long Nicole's going to stay mad at me," Sam admitted, a thread of vulnerability woven into his words. The room remained draped in a heavy silence, the unknown duration of

Nicole's anger casting a shadow over their shared reality. The children, though young, were becoming witnesses to the intricate dance of emotions that shaped their family's future.

Cameron's hopeful tone, expressing the belief that Mom's anger is always short-lived, echoed through the room. Feeling the weight of the moment, Sam seized the opportunity to convey the difficult truth to his children. "I hope one day she will forgive me, but until then, I can't stay here," he explained, his gaze moving between Tara and Cameron, who were becoming unwitting spectators to the unraveling complexities of their parents' relationship.

Tara, grappling with the sudden emotional turbulence, sought clarification in desperation. "What do you mean? Are you getting a divorce?" she cried, her voice carrying the fear of an uncertain future. The mention of divorce from Tara hovered in the air, a specter that Sam quickly dispelled. "No, we're not getting a divorce," he reassured, attempting to anchor the conversation in a semblance of stability.

However, the impact had already taken root. Cameron, tears streaming down his face, recalled Sam's promise from the previous night, adding another layer of emotional weight to the unfolding scene. "You promised that you would never leave us," Cameron sobbed, his plea echoing the profound impact parents have on the security of a child's world.

Sam, recognizing the depth of their distress, explained, "Sometimes adults need to be apart to solve their problems," attempting to rationalize the complexities of adult relationships in terms the children could comprehend. He reassured them that everything else would remain unchanged, promising, "I'll still come and see you every day."

Tara, unyielding in her desire for familial unity, insisted, "We don't want you to leave, and we want you and Mom to start talking to each other." Her plea mirrored the innate longing for a harmonious family, a sentiment that resonated with the vulnerability of youth.

Sam, concluding the difficult conversation, acknowledged, "When you're older, you will understand," leaving the door open for a future reconciliation. As he uttered his commitment to return soon, the children grappled with the profound shifts reshaping their world.

Tara, with genuine concern for her father's well-being, asked the question that had yet to cross Sam's mind: "Where are you going to live?" Sam, momentarily taken aback by the inquiry, rallied to provide a reassuring answer. "Wherever I go, I'll be just a phone call away," he assured them, attempting to inject a sense of stability into their uncertain future. Acknowledging the toll of the day, Sam gently suggested it was time for them to go to sleep.

However, the children, eager to prolong the fleeting moments of connection, pressed on with another request. Yearning for a comforting story, they reminded Sam of the tale he had promised to share. With a warmth that masked the internal turmoil, Sam inquired about the story they wanted to hear. Cameron, with a hint of playfulness, suggested, "Tell us the story of how you and Mom met."

Excitement lit up Tara's face as she concurred, "Oh yeah, let's hear that again." Obliging their request, Sam began the familiar narrative, "On a clear evening on top of Soledad Mountain…". Yet, as he wove the story of their serendipitous encounter, a subtle shift in his tone betrayed an underlying heaviness. Unlike the countless times he had recounted the tale before, this time, an unspoken realization hung in the air—a realization that the story, this time, might lack the once-inevitable happy ending.

Chapter 67

The morning air held a hushed reverence as Sam stepped into the light of a new day, a day fraught with the weight of final goodbyes. The dawn's early light was a soft caress, a contrast to the heavy reality awaiting him. His movements were deliberate, each item placed in the duffle bag a symbol of his journey, not just to the chapel but into a future reshaped by loss.

Donning his suit, he moved with a solemn grace, an outward armor to fortify him against the day's emotions. The drive to the chapel was a quiet pilgrimage, each mile bringing him closer to the inevitable confrontation with grief and the collective mourning of a family united in sorrow.

Upon entering the chapel, the sight of Jacqueline and Ariana, pillars of strength and sorrow, greeted him. The air was still, punctuated only by the soft whispers of those gathered to pay their respects. The white casket, a stark reminder of the finality of death, lay adorned with flowers, symbols of love, remembrance, and the beauty of a life once vibrantly lived.

Jacqueline, the very picture of composure and grace, stood vigil by the casket, her connection to Bijan transcending the barrier of death. Ariana's gentle touch, a silent testament to their shared loss, offered a semblance of comfort. As Sam approached, the reality of his mother's profound loneliness struck him—an emptiness that the presence of family and friends could only momentarily alleviate.

Sam's approach was hesitant yet necessary, a son coming to stand beside his mother in a moment of shared vulnerability. The proximity to the casket, to the tangible representation of Bijan's departure, was a stark confrontation with the finality of life. In the silence of the chapel, filled with hushed tones and quiet sobs, Sam prepared to navigate the complex landscape of farewells and the remembrance of a life that had left an indelible mark on all who were gathered. The ceremony ahead was not just a farewell to Bijan but a moment of reflection and unity for a family navigating the tides of grief together.

"How are you holding up?" Sam's voice was gentle, his embrace a cocoon around his mother, embodying the care and concern that filled him. His gaze searched hers, looking for signs of the unspoken grief that he knew must be burrowing deep within her soul.

Jacqueline's response was a graceful nod, her smile tender yet tinged with the sorrow of her immense loss. As she dabbed at the tear that dared escape, her voice held a steady calm. "I'm okay, dear," she reassured him, her resilience a testament to her strength. Yet, her maternal instincts remained attuned to Sam's unspoken troubles, her inquiry about Nicole not just a question but a gentle push for him to face his own challenges.

Sam, however, wasn't ready to delve into his own tumultuous life, not today. His deflection was swift, yet Jacqueline's knowing glance spoke volumes. She understood more than she let on, her wisdom guiding her to give him the space yet reminding him of the importance of reconciliation and family unity.

The arrival of Nicole and the kids marked a moment of bittersweet reunion. Sam's smile at the sight of his family was a flicker of light in the somberness of the day. Nicole's interaction with Jacqueline was one of mutual comfort, a shared understanding of loss, and a communal grieving for the patriarch they had all loved.

Jacqueline's affectionate gesture towards Nicole, Tara, and Cameron wove a sense of continuity and love that transcended the grief of the moment. Her words to the grandchildren about their grandfather's love for them were a gentle reminder of the legacy that remained, a legacy of love and family bonds that would outlast the pain of their current sorrow.

The soft whispers of memories filled the chapel as Sam and Ariana stood together, their conversation a delicate weaving of words to honor Bijan. Amidst this somber exchange , a moment unfolded that seemed out of place amidst the grief. Sam hardly noticed the persistent tug at his hand. It was a small, determined pull, one that spoke volumes without a single word. When the warmth of another hand slipped into his, a jolt of recognition surged through him. Without thinking, he clutched it tightly, the familiarity of its touch igniting a flood of memories.

He turned sharply, half-expecting, half-hoping, only to find Cameron looking up at him with eyes wide with a mix of hope and innocent scheming. The realization dawned on him; Cameron, in his childlike wisdom, had been orchestrating a silent plea for unity in the midst of their shared loss.

Nicole, engrossed in a conversation with Jacqueline, hadn't seen their son's subtle maneuver of pulling her hand and placing it in Sam's. But the sudden silence and the shift in energy caught her attention, prompting her to turn. Her eyes met Sam's, a silent exchange passing between them, still holding hands. In that brief interlude, Sam's thumb brushed against her hand, a gesture so familiar yet so distant now, laden with the tenderness of what once was and what still might be.

But the moment was fleeting. Nicole, her heart a battleground of emotions, withdrew her hand as gently as the situation allowed. The touch, brief as it was, left a lingering warmth, a silent testament to the intricate dance of their relationship, now poised at the precipice of farewell. In the eyes of their son, however, lingered a flicker of hope— a wish unspoken, that perhaps, amidst the finality of goodbyes, there was room yet for reconciliation.

Nicole's voice, sharp with surprise and confusion, cut through the quiet of the chapel. Her eyes, wide with the sudden jolt of their hands touching, fixed on Cameron, seeking an explanation, "what are you doing?"

Sam, ever the peacemaker, quickly tried to diffuse the tension. "He was just playing," he offered, a gentle attempt to shield Cameron from her sharp gaze. Yet, Cameron's tearful eyes and the earnestness in his small voice betrayed the truth. "I wasn't playing. I want you to be friends again. I don't want Dad to leave us." This wasn't a mere child's play; it was a heartfelt attempt to heal a rift he could neither understand nor accept. His words, simple yet profound, resonated with the fear and longing only a child could express so purely.

As Cameron's emotions overwhelmed him, leading him to flee the scene, Nicole's maternal instincts surged to the forefront. Her reprimand faded into a heart-wrenching realization of the impact their separation had on their children. The sight of her son's retreating back, coupled with the tension of the moment, cracked the composed façade she had maintained. With a hurried, "Excuse me," she chased after Cameron, her movement a mix of desperation and care, leaving behind a trail of unshed tears and unsaid words.

Tara clung to Sam's leg, her small hand a plea for reassurance. "I don't want you to leave us either," she voiced, vulnerability in her eyes.

Sam gently lowered himself to Tara's eye level, ready to offer comfort, when he noticed the presence of Nicole's parents. "Today, we're here to comfort Grandma. Look, your grandparents are here. Let's say hi to them, and we'll talk about this again."

Approaching with condolences, Nicole's parents expressed sympathy for Sam's loss. Grateful for their presence, Sam acknowledged their condolences, and Nicole's mother, sensing Tara's distress, embraced her in a comforting hug and bestowed a tender kiss.

Nicole's father, ever genial, winked at Tara and planted a gentle kiss on her head. "Let's say hi to Mrs. Larabi," he suggested, leading the way toward the casket.

As the interactions unfolded, Nicole's mother offered a remark to Sam. "Welcome back. I'm sure you all missed each other so much."

In that moment, a subtle revelation dawned on Sam. Nicole hadn't informed her parents of their current situation. Another layer of complexity added to an already delicate and emotional day.

Sam was taken aback by the unexpected arrival of Hope. "My condolences, Sam," she offered sincerely.

Hope gracefully stepped aside, directing Sam's attention down the hallway where Mr. Phillips and Damien led a procession of Genesys employees. "I'm so sorry for your loss," Mr. Phillips conveyed, his voice resonating with genuine sympathy as he firmly shook Sam's hand.

Expressing gratitude, Sam greeted each person from work, acknowledging the significance of their presence on this difficult day. Mr. Phillips, emphasizing Sam's role as a friend to all, particularly pointing out Damien, conveyed the collective sense of mourning shared by the Genesys team.

Damien lingered behind the group, offering Sam a comforting pat on the back. "Welcome back, buddy. I can't express how sorry I am," he conveyed empathetically. Sam, still grappling with the reality of his father's passing, shared his disbelief.

Sensing Sam's need for support, Damien sincerely offered assistance. "Let me know if there's anything I can help with."

Contemplating the uncertain path ahead, Sam glanced toward Nicole, realizing that the possibility of reconciliation seemed distant. Summoning courage, he broached a challenging subject. "Actually, there might be," Sam admitted, gazing at Nicole from afar. The realization that the bridge between them might be irreparably burned prompted him to ask the daunting question. "I might need a place to crash for a couple of days."

Damien, without hesitation, responded with enthusiasm, "Of course, man. Stay as long as you want."

Sam shook Damien's hand, appreciative of the lifeline extended in the midst of his emotional turmoil, before proceeding to greet other friends and family gathered for the solemn occasion.

The chapel was a sea of somber faces, every seat almost entirely filled. Sam stood resolute behind the podium, his gaze fixed on the casket, a vessel containing the remains of the man who had shaped his existence. As he addressed the gathered mourners, gratitude mingled with pain in his eyes, teary and heavy with the weight of loss.

With a deep breath, Sam embarked on his speech, a eulogy painted in the hues of emotion. His words took the form of a poignant poem:

> In the voyage of years, your shoulders stood strong,
> A haven to cling to, a refuge lifelong.
> As I aged, they remained my steadfast embrace,
> The highest peak in love, a celestial space.
>
> Now, an emptiness, a void profound,
> Nothing can fill where love once crowned.
> "I miss you, Dad," whispers in the air,
> Your absence, a weight my heart must bear.

As the burial concluded, Luke approached Sam with a compassionate embrace, acknowledging the profound grief that now enveloped his friend. Encouraging strength, Luke offered silent support in the face of the tumultuous emotions Sam grappled with.

Sam's gaze shifted, settling on Nicole and Brenda, the women who had played pivotal roles in his life. In this moment of reflection, memories of their initial encounters flooded his mind, each recollection etched with significance.

Approaching him with genuine concern, Brenda extended her condolences to Sam. However, the sincerity soon took a turn as Brenda, known for her frankness, addressed the complexities of Sam's relationships. "My condolences, Sam," she began, her tone shifting. "Why couldn't you be as good a husband as you were a son?"

Sam, caught off guard, sought clarification. "Is that meant to be a compliment or an insult?"

Brenda, without offering a clear answer, gestured to Luke, signaling their departure. In her departure, Brenda left behind a lingering acknowledgment of the hurt inflicted upon Nicole, a tangible consequence of Sam's actions.

Sam turned back toward Nicole. She hastily turned around and started to walk away. Sam hurriedly followed her and pleaded for her to listen, even if she wouldn't look at him.

Nicole's hurried strides soon came to a stop.

Sam cautiously began to speak, his words akin to a delicate approach toward a beautiful bird, mindful not to startle it into sudden flight. He admitted his wrongdoing, emphasizing that he never took her for granted. Acknowledging his colossal mistake, he expressed a genuine willingness to go to the ends of the earth to make things right. With sincerity in his voice, he implored Nicole to share how he could keep her in his life. Sam recognized the gravity of his actions but remained hopeful, stating that her silence about their situation with her parents indicated that she hadn't given up on them completely. "I know you hate me but I'm begging for a second chance."

Nicole took a short step back, her eyes reflecting a storm of emotions. "Do you think I want you to leave because I hate you?" she questioned, her voice tinged with a mix of sorrow and frustration. "It would have been so much simpler if I could just hate you," Nicole whispered, her voice barely audible over the weight of her emotions. "These days, my life feels like a relentless nightmare. I grew accustomed to seeing you, inhaling your scent, holding you close. There are moments when I despise myself for loving you so intensely, and that's why the pain cuts so deep. I'm faced with a choice: adapt to a life without you or somehow awaken from this haunting nightmare."

Her tears, glistening like unshed raindrops, did not allow her to carry on. With a heavy heart, she concluded, "Goodbye, Sam," barely managing to get the last words out before turning away, leaving the weight of her unspoken feelings hanging in the air.

Sam's gaze lingered on Nicole's retreating figure, a heavy ache settling in his chest. The weight of unspoken words hung between them like an invisible barrier. He turned away reluctantly, his steps leading him back to the solitude of his car, where Damien and Mr. Phillips awaited.

Expressing gratitude for their presence, Sam conveyed his intention to return to work the next day. Mr. Phillips, brimming with enthusiasm, revealed the necessity for a crucial discussion, urging Sam to visit his office after work. The looming specter of handling the sheiks' affairs demanded Sam's attention, and Mr. Phillips stressed the importance of preventing any potential fallout and safeguarding the substantial surplus.

After departing from the cemetery, Sam maneuvered his car to a halt near Damien's condo. Seeking solace, he reclined the seat, closed his eyes, and attempted to escape the tumult of his life in a brief reprieve. The quiet sanctuary of his dreams was shattered when Damien rapped on the car window, rousing him back to reality. With a helpful gesture, Damien assisted Sam with his suitcases, leading him to one of the bedrooms.

Opening the closet, Damien, apologetic for the space constraints, suggested rearranging the boxes in the closet to make room. Sam halted him, expressing gratitude and refusing to be a burden. Unfazed, Damien, with a spark of excitement, unveiled one of the boxes filled with old photos and VHS tapes. Proposing a nostalgic journey, Damien insisted they delve into these cherished memories.

Stretching out on the couch, Sam and Damien sifted through the photos. Amid laughter and shared memories, Sam broached the subject of work, seeking Damien's candid opinion on why Mr. Phillips wanted to meet him first upon his return. Damien, admitting his lack of insider knowledge, fetched a bottle of tequila and two shot glasses from the kitchen.

Pouring the shots, Damien inquired about Sam's mysterious conduct with Emirates Genomics. Sam, taking a shot, responded, "I just did my job and secured the contract, whatever it took." As the tequila warmed their spirits, Damien, with a reassuring demeanor, advised Sam not to overthink it. Encouraging him to face Phillips and promising a swift move-out from his office, Damien signaled a camaraderie that transcended the turbulent uncertainties of Sam's life.

Sam downed the shot, the warmth of the tequila coursing through him as he delved into the trove of old pictures. He shared a snapshot with Damien, reminiscing about their youth, and humorously requested a refill.

Another shot was poured, and Sam downed it eagerly, signaling for more. The room was filled with the nostalgic hum of a VCR as Damien inserted a tape. The flickering images on the screen unveiled a bygone era — a shaky camera, the familiar cadence of Damien's voice, and the echo of Luke's voice resonating through the years. "I think it's on," Damien's voice reverberated from the television, a gateway to the past and a portal to a time they all wished they could revisit.

The camera steadied on Luke in his graduation gown. Sam, captivated, emptied another shot. Luke bantered about graduation day, his eyes playfully wandering every time a girl passed by. "I am graduating today with no idea of whom I'm doing next. All I know is, she is among this crowd," he quipped, maneuvering the camcorder through the sea of graduates.

Amid innuendo-laden jokes, Sam finally came into view. "There I am," he declared, raising his shot glass for another sip, the bittersweet taste mingling with the memories of a time when the future was an open gift waiting to be unwrapped.

The camcorder swayed to the left, capturing Nicole in its lens. She smiled and waved, mouthing a silent "Hi." Sam, immersed in the memories unfolding on the screen, confessed that he would give anything to return to that moment, a time when life felt simpler, filled with youthful exuberance and untold promises.

As the tape continued its journey through time, Luke turned the camera towards Brenda. "Finally found my graduation gift," he declared with a mischievous grin. Brenda, in her playful response, told him to shut up and delivered a light smack. Suddenly, a loud sound reverberated as Luke had ducked, and Brenda's playful hit landed on the camera instead sending it hurtling to the ground.

The television screen displayed a rapid descent, the ground rushing closer, accompanied by a cacophony of undistinguished voices exclaiming, "Oh shit." Another resounding noise, and then darkness enveloped the screen.

"Stupid guy broke my camera that day," Damien said with a chuckle.

Sam laughed heartily, the memories flooding back. Sam refilled the shot glasses, his gaze fixed on the vintage tape playing. "On this tape, I see everyone who matters to me," he announced, the weight of alcohol making his head heavy. "I've been blessed with the best friends in the world. Thanks again for being there, Damien. I really love you, man."

The ritual continued, a blend of old pictures, vintage home videos, and the warmth of shared drinks. As midnight approached, Damien woke up in the living room, the TV static whispering of the night's revelry. Sam lay passed out, surrounded by the remnants of their evening—a drained tequila bottle and scattered bags of chips. Despite Damien's attempts to rouse him, Sam remained in a deep slumber. With a sigh, Damien turned off the TV and retreated to his room.

The next morning greeted Sam with a punishing headache, a reminder of the night's indulgence. Opening his eyes, he struggled to make sense of his surroundings. A glass of water offered some relief, and he stumbled into the shower, letting the running water wash away the lingering traces of the night.

Hungry and disoriented, Sam checked the time and realized it was nearly noon. Opting for a pizza delivery, he contemplated the hours ahead before his return to work at 5:30. With time to spare, he sought solace in another box of memories. However, upon opening the closet door, he discovered Damien had rearranged the boxes before leaving for work, a subtle but meaningful gesture that didn't go unnoticed.

Sam pondered, "Poor guy thinks I need more space." With that thought, he ventured into Damien's room in search of the boxes. Stacked neatly in a corner of the closet, the boxes awaited him. A keen eye noticed that Damien had made room for them by temporarily relocating some of his own clothes onto the bed.

Feeling a mix of gratitude and a hint of melancholy, Sam moved the boxes back to the other room and carefully rehung Damien's clothes in the closet. The unspoken realization lingered—"at our age everybody needs their space," Sam mused. "I should give him his. I'll just pack my stuff and check into a hotel after my talk with Phillips."

As Sam opened the first box, he discovered it held only documents. Slightly disappointed, he pushed it aside and unveiled the second box, revealing a treasure trove of pictures and videotapes. Lost in the nostalgia of old memories, something in the peripheral vision caught Sam's attention in the first box. Intrigued, he shifted his gaze, and what he saw left him stunned. "What the fuck?" Sam uttered to himself, reaching for a stack of papers that held an unexpected revelation.

Chapter 68

In Damien's office, the palpable tension thrummed like a taut string, the clock's relentless march towards five o'clock amplifying the unease. Hope's shoulders sagged under the day's weight, her mind a tumultuous sea of what-ifs, her resolve teetering on the precipice of a decision. The whole room seemed to hold its breath, awaiting the outcome that would dictate her next move, to quit if Sam leaves the company.

Suddenly, the door flung open with the force of the storm that raged within Sam. He entered, his presence a whirlwind of fury and determination, his eyes alight with a fiery intensity that commanded silence.

"Sam," Hope's voice faltered, a shaky attempt to pierce the thick air of tension. "How did it go with Phillips?"

Sam's gaze didn't waver from its target as he beelined for Damien, his stride purposeful and charged. Hope's words seemed to dissipate in the charged atmosphere, unheard.

Damien, taken aback by the intrusion, scrambled to regain his footing. "Sam, have you spoken to Phillips? What's the word?"

But Sam was not there to discuss Phillips. With a voice that cut sharply through the air, he demanded, "Weren't you supposed to pack and take your stuff today?"

Damien, momentarily flustered, rose from his seat. "I thought... Never mind. Just give me a minute." His eyes darted around, betraying his inner turmoil.

Damien wasn't satisfied. "So, how did it go with Phillips?" he pressed, an edge of challenge in his tone.

Damien's insistence met with Sam's evasive assurance. "You can relax, Damien. I haven't seen Phillips yet," Sam's voice carried a hint of finality, his words cloaked in an ominous undertone.

Suddenly, Sam's demeanor shifted as he produced a stack of documents from his briefcase. "You son of a bitch," he hissed, flinging the papers at Damien. "You have no shame."

The room froze as the papers fluttered down, each one a testament to Damien's betrayal. The evidence was undeniable, leaving Damien speechless in the wake of the revelation.

Sam, his voice thick with emotion, confronted him. "I found these in the boxes. Now I know why you wanted to hide them from me."

Damien, cornered and defeated, could only stammer, "Sam, I—"

"How much more did you want?" Sam interrupted, his voice rising in a crescendo of betrayal and hurt. "I would have trained you myself for my position. You only had to asked. You disgust me."

As Sam stood there, reeling from the storm of revelations, Damien's composure began to fracture, his voice taking on a raw, unfiltered edge that echoed years of suppressed bitterness. "You think this was about money, Sam?" he spat out, his words laced with a venom born of deep-seated envy. "It was never just about the money."

Damien paced the room, his movements erratic, as if fueled by the pent-up resentment that had simmered within him for years. "You, with your charmed life," he continued, his voice rising with every word. "Ever since college, it's always been Sam the star, Sam the golden boy. Business deals falling into your lap like ripe fruits, accolades and admiration at every turn. And there I was, always in your shadow, always the afterthought."

His eyes, now ablaze with a mixture of anger and pain, locked with Sam's. "You had everything, Sam. The career that skyrocketed while I got fired, the beautiful wife, the picture-perfect family. Did you ever stop to think how that felt for me? Toiling away, always steps behind, watching you effortlessly succeed in everything you touched?"

Damien's fists clenched at his sides as he paced, his voice a crescendo of anguish. "It gnawed at me, Sam. Every congratulatory pat on your back was a slap in my face. I was tired of being the one who always had to clap for you, tired of the patronizing nods.` You have no idea what it's like, living every day in the shadow of your friend's success, feeling like a constant failure in comparison."

He stopped pacing, standing still as the raw truth poured out of him. "That's why I did it. Not for the money, but to step out of your shadow, to prove that I'm not just the sidekick in your success story. I wanted to be seen, to be recognized for my worth, not just as Sam's friend, but as Damien in my own right."

Sam, visibly shaken, absorbed the words, the impact hitting him like a physical blow. The realization that Damien's friendship had been a facade, colored by envy and a desire to outshine him, left a bitter taste in his mouth. The bond they had built over the years, now tainted by the poison of jealousy, lay shattered at their feet.

Sam, shaken by the vehemence of Damien's words, stood frozen, a myriad of emotions flickering across his face. The hurt was palpable, a raw wound exposed to the sting of betrayal. "Then today is your luckiest day," Sam retorted, his voice a mix of sorrow and incredulity. "I've lost it all, haven't I? The job, the respect, the family…and the brother I thought I had in you."

Sam's voice, heavy with the burden of shattered trust, carried a final question that hung in the air, lingering long after it was spoken. "Did you get what you wanted, Damien? Did tearing down my life give you the satisfaction you craved?" Without waiting for an answer, he turned on his heel and stormed out of the office, leaving behind a door that echoed his departure with a resounding slam. Amidst the lingering echoes, he spotted Hope standing at her desk, a silent witness to the unraveling drama. Her finger still rested on the intercom button, a connection to the tumultuous scene that had unfolded moments ago.

As Sam's gaze met Hope's tear-filled eyes, she turned towards him, her astonishment etched across her face like a poignant canvas of sympathy and regret. "I'm so sorry, Sam. I never liked the son of a bitch," she confessed, her words a raw admission of the sentiments she had revealed for so long.

Damien calmly started packing up his stuff, resigned to the impending termination. He was almost done when a knock interrupted the uneasy silence. Without waiting for a response, Mr. Phillips opened the door and entered.

"Hey, Damien, got a minute?" Mr. Phillips began, and he proceeded to recount a bizarre conversation with Sam. Sam claimed to know the inner workings, stating that Emirates Genomic would sever ties if Sam remained, a blow that would cripple the company. In the interest of the company, Sam had chosen to resign.

"Is that all he said?" Damien questioned, his bafflement and astonishment evident.

Mr. Phillips continued, revealing that Sam had recommended Damien as his successor. The news left Damien uttering words in disbelief. Phillips assured him the job was his if he wanted it, emphasizing Sam's consistent loyalty to his friends. Damien, filled with appreciation, shook Mr. Phillips' hand.

A double knock on the door drew their attention, and Hope stood in the doorway announcing her departure for the day. In a sarcastic tone, she congratulated Damien on his promotion, claiming the door was open and she overheard the news.

Damien's response was curt, wanting her to leave immediately. "Thanks, Hope. See you tomorrow."

As she turned to exit, Hope hesitated, questioning Mr. Phillips about the source of the documents given to the sheiks. Mr. Phillips admitted Sam knew but wouldn't disclose.

"That's Sam Alright," said hope, seizing her moment, Hope dropped a bombshell. "You may find it interesting to know that it was Damien."

Mr. Phillips, shocked, turned to Damien for confirmation. Damien, mouth dry, remained silent with his head lowered. After a prolonged silence, Damien finally muttered, "It's complicated, sir."

Those words were enough for Mr. Phillips, a seasoned businessman, to connect the dots. "You son of a bitch!" he shouted.

"That's exactly what Sam called him, sir," Hope chimed in, leaving with a triumphant smile. The smile widened as she heard Phillips unleash his fury on Damien. "You're fucking fired. Get the fuck out of here." The door slammed shut, sealing Damien's fate in the wake of Hope's revelatory vendetta.

****

As the gears of time rolled back, the shadows of deceit and betrayal stretched long and sinister. In this shadowy realm, Damien, a master of malevolence, meticulously crafted a plot that would unravel Sam's life thread by thread. It all began with a seemingly benign gesture—a birthday gift, a sleek wireless keyboard, and mouse set that gleamed with the promise of efficiency and convenience.

Sam, unaware of the treacherous road ahead, welcomed the gift with open arms, his joy overshadowing the dark intent lurking within the seemingly innocent USB. Damien's malevolent gift was a modern-day Trojan horse, a devious scheme hidden beneath layers of technology.

As Sam integrated the new peripherals into his daily routine, every keystroke and click echoed in the cavernous depths of Damien's clandestine operations. Like a shadow, Damien lurked in the digital ether, manipulating and maneuvering through Sam's private world with a patience that was chilling in its precision.

The USB, a silent accomplice in this dark dance, became Damien's key to the vault of Sam's digital life. It was a gateway through which he siphoned passwords, communications, and intimate details, a feast of information laid bare for his taking.

The plot thickened as Damien delved deeper into the labyrinth of Sam's personal and professional secrets. His eyes, hungry for the damning evidence that would anchor his retribution, scoured through the stream of data. And then, like a predator striking at the heart of its prey, Damien found his golden opportunity in the sordid details of a bribe, a secret that would set the stage for Sam's downfall.

The dark dance of manipulation reached its climax when the deal was sealed, and funds seamlessly traversed from Emirates Genomics to Genesys. Anonymity cloaked Damien as he reached out to Emirates Genomics, a puppet master unveiling his masterstroke. With a devil's pact, he offered to expose the damning evidence in his possession, demanding only one retribution—Sam's termination.

The stage was set for a malevolent unveiling, a mystery of maleficent design spiraling towards its ominous resolution. Emotions tangled within the web of deceit, a sinister ballet where trust was shattered, and the puppet strings of vengeance were pulled with chilling precision.

Chapter 69

In the haunting aftermath of his departure from Genesys, Sam found himself navigating the desolation of a fractured existence. Behind the wheel, he aimlessly traversed the streets with no destination to anchor his weary soul. Each passing mile mirrored the unraveling threads of his life—his marriage, his father, his job, and now, the betrayal of his best friend. It was as if the cosmos itself had conspired against him, casting him adrift in a sea of relentless misfortune.

The weight of his losses bore down on Sam, a heavy burden that threatened to drown him in the abyss of despair. In this moment of profound solitude, he yearned for respite, a temporary escape from the relentless torrent of his shattered reality. The neon glow of a "Liquor" sign on a corner store flickered like a siren's call, reminiscent of the night before when the numbing embrace of tequila offered solace.

Entering the liquor store, Sam's purpose was crystal clear—a quest for an elixir that could hush the cacophony within, a momentary escape from the relentless pain that clung to him like an unyielding shadow. His eyes fixated on a particular bottle, a vessel of solace in the form of Don Julio Tequila.

Back in his car, the hum of the engine became a somber soundtrack to the uncertainty that tightly gripped him. Despite being lost in a city where he was anything but a stranger, Sam's eyes sought refuge in the Downtown skyline, as if yearning for a beacon of familiarity to pierce through the disarray of his emotions. In that poignant moment, an unspoken instinct guided him towards a place woven into the tapestry of his memories—the Marriott Hotel.

With no luggage in tow and a heart heavy with unspoken sorrows, Sam entered the hotel lobby. There, in a heartbreaking irony, he found himself requesting the honeymoon suite—a sanctuary of love and bliss that stood in stark contrast to the desolation that had become his reality.

Ascending to the twenty-second floor, we rediscover Sam in the very place where our tale commenced—the honeymoon suite, a sanctuary of love and promises now tainted by the shadows of his past. Here, amidst the echoes of a shared night with Nicole, a torrent of memories cascaded through Sam's mind as he unlatched the sliding door, confronting the precipice of his emotions.

Stepping onto the balcony, the city lights below sprawled out like a celestial canvas, each glimmer reminiscent of a star telling a story—yet this night unfolded a narrative steeped in melancholy. From this elevated perch, the urban landscape mirrored the starry night of that fateful evening, weaving a tale that echoed the pain and sorrow etched into the fabric of Sam's soul.

Uncorking the bottle of tequila, Sam welcomed the fiery cascade down his throat with a determined gulp, the sting of alcohol a harsh reminder of the pain he sought to drown. His coughing fit was a fleeting protest against the bitter reality, but he pushed through, pouring more into the void within.

Leaning over the balcony, the cityscape sprawled beneath him, but his gaze was drawn to the distant radio towers atop Mount Soledad, mere echoes of proximity to his abandoned home. The contrast of closeness and distance mirrored the tumult within him.

Returning to the room, he sought solace in the TV's flickering glow, channel surfing amidst the haze of intoxication. A casual drinker turned captive of the bottle, Sam succumbed to the numbing embrace, losing himself in the elusive dance of inebriation.

Back on the balcony, his perception blurred by alcohol's haze, he peered down at the street, unleashing words carried away by the indifferent wind. Yells escaped him, aimed at the oblivious couples below, a desperate attempt to share his unraveling tale.

"I was happy like you guys one day," he cried out, a lament for the innocence lost. "But I messed up. Don't you guys mess up like me." The chilling breeze, a sobering force, kissed his face, momentarily grounding him in the cold reality.

Putting the bottle aside, he stretched his arms into the wind, a momentary illusion of flight amid the chaos. "Why aren't you trying to destroy me?" he mused to the wind's gentle embrace. "The whole world has turned against me. Why haven't you? You probably need something from me before crossing me like that bastard Damien." His words, laden with a mix of despair and defiance, hung in the night air, absorbed by the indifferent city around him.

Bent over the balcony, Sam hung on the precipice of despair, pulling one leg over the edge and resting on the balcony wall. His voice, a fragile whisper, trembled through the night air, "I can't take it anymore."

Clutching the side wall for a moment's strength, he rose to stand straight on the perilous edge. "You win," he shouted at the sky, fingers slowly releasing their grip. A tender breeze brushed against his face, coaxing a melancholic smile. "You don't have to be nice to me," Sam murmured to the wind, head raised, eyes closed. "I won't give you a chance to hurt me."

With a measured slide towards the edge, his surrender seemed imminent. "See you all on the other side," Sam thought, loosening his grip. But in that fateful moment, the intrusive buzz of his phone sliced through the heavy silence, snapping his eyes open and his grip tight once more.

The blinking lights of the radio towers, like celestial messengers, whispered a silent plea—don't give up. Desperation filled him as he flipped open his phone, a fragile hope clinging to his soul, yearning to hear Nicole's voice for what might be the last time.

"Hello," Sam's voice trembled through the phone.

"Where are you, Sam?" Jacqueline's voice quivered with concern. She went on to share that Hope had reached out to Nicole, filling her in on the unfolding events at work. "Are you okay?" Jacqueline's worry echoed through the line, carrying a mother's concern.

"Am I okay?" Sam pondered, a heavy sigh laced with weariness escaping his lips. Jacqueline sensed the weight in his silence and gently urged him to share his whereabouts. She and Ariana, a lifeline in the darkness, were ready to come and get him.

In the quiet, a symphony of Sam's silent tears played, a heartbreaking melody. "Just talk to me," Jacqueline pleaded, a mother's desperation and love infused in her words. "It'll make you feel better. Please, Sam, would you do that for your mom?"

His grip tightened, Sam reluctantly stepped back from the ledge, sliding down to the floor. Confessions spilled forth—an unraveling of a life marked by loss, heartache, and betrayal.

Jacqueline responded, recognizing the return of the real Sam beneath the influence of alcohol. "You have to stay strong for all of us. So many people need you."

Sam bemoaned the mistakes that cost him Nicole, his job, and his sense of self. "Sometimes things happen for a reason," Jacqueline consoled, her voice gentle yet firm. "You've learned the real value of family, seen the truth about Damien. The pain won't fade easily, but you're stronger than you think."

Through the phone, Jacqueline heard Sam's heartache manifest as tears. "Sam," she whispered, her voice cracking. "My dear, everything is going to be okay. Let me come and get you. It's okay to cry; it's the beginning of your fight. Promise to stay strong, for everyone, including Nicole."

"I'm glad you called, Mom," Sam confessed, a sense of surrender mingling with gratitude. "Don't worry about me. I'll be alright. I've checked into a hotel. I'll see you tomorrow."

As the call with Jacqueline concluded, Sam found himself lingering in the hushed ambiance of the hotel room, the residual echoes of their conversation still reverberating in the air. A palpable silence enveloped him, punctuated only by the distant hum of the city beyond the window.

The weight of the second chance he'd been granted pressed upon him like a tangible force. Sam moved with deliberate slowness, as if each step carried the gravity of a life-altering revelation. He approached the bathroom, the remnants of the bottle in his hand, a visual testament to the emotional tempest that had gripped him just moments before.

With a solemn resolve, he poured the remaining contents down the sink, the amber liquid disappearing into the void, akin to the burdens he sought to release. The clinking sound of glass against porcelain resonated, marking a symbolic cleansing—a liberation from the self-imposed chains of despair.

Returning to the room, the bed beckoned like a sanctuary, and Sam succumbed to its embrace. He collapsed onto the mattress, his body a vessel for the torrent of memories that surged within. The room became a sanctuary for reflection, each breath laden with the weight of a haunted soul confronting the ghosts of his own existence.

In the dim light, the contours of his face betrayed the weariness etched into every line. Eyes closed, he navigated the labyrinth of his past, revisiting moments of joy and sorrow, love and loss. The bed, now a vessel for introspection, cradled him in its folds as he confronted the shadows that lingered in the corners of his consciousness.

The ghosts of his life danced in the room—a spectral ballet that played out the highs and lows, the victories and defeats. Sam lay there, a man at the crossroads, grappling with the complexities of his own narrative. The air seemed to thicken with the weight of introspection, and in that stillness, he sought solace, redemption, and the promise of a tomorrow unburdened by the ghosts that haunted his past.

Chapter 70

In the early morning hush, the shrill ring of Nicole's phone shattered the quietude. Blinking away the remnants of sleep, she glanced at the nightstand clock—6:17. The untimely call came from Sam, who preemptively apologized for the early intrusion. Without waiting for Nicole's response, he urgently expressed his desire to see the kids that day.

She informed Sam that she would be taking the kids to her parents before heading to work. Sam, in turn, declared his intention to be with them shortly and abruptly ended the call.

As Sam walked in later, Nicole, ever the elusive figure, tried to make a discreet exit before any awkward encounters. However, Sam had other plans. In a surprising turn, he declared his intention to whip up breakfast and invited Nicole to stay.

"Late for work," Nicole responded hastily, avoiding any lingering eye contact. It was a carefully crafted excuse, a veiled attempt to distance herself from the complexity of the situation. In truth, she wasn't running late; she had taken the day off, a deliberate choice to spend time with her parents and confide in them about the tumultuous events unfolding in her life.

As Nicole arrived at her parents' home, the familiar sight of her mother at the door brought a semblance of comfort. Her mother's eyes, always so perceptive, held a question that hung in the air, a silent inquiry into the absence of the children and the unrest that Nicole carried with her.

"Good morning," Nicole's voice, a soft echo of routine, met her mother's questioning gaze. The brief kiss they shared was a fleeting moment of comfort in the storm of her thoughts. "They're home with Sam," she explained, her words a simple brushstroke in the complex painting of her current life.

Inside, the house radiated a warmth that seemed foreign to Nicole's recent chill of isolation. As she exchanged morning kisses with her dad, a small gesture so deeply ingrained in their daily rituals, she felt a momentary lift in her spirits.

"Good morning," her dad greeted back, his hands presenting a plate of pancakes, an offering of love in the shape of breakfast. "You used to love my pancakes. See if you still like them."

A smile, tinged with nostalgia and the bittersweet taste of memories, spread across Nicole's face. "They're to die for, Dad." The words, spoken with a lightness she hadn't felt in a while, momentarily lifted the veil of her worries.

As they gathered around the breakfast table, the familiar cadence of family life filled the air. Laughter mingled with the clatter of dishes, each note a reminder of simpler times. Nicole's dad, drawn by the familiar theme of the "Gunsmoke" TV show, excused himself towards the television, declaring his allegiance to an unseen episode.

"That's my show," he announced, his voice a mix of determination and nostalgia. "I can't keep up talking with you girls, and I've never seen this episode."

Nicole, seizing the moment for a playful jest, teased, "Dad, you've seen every episode more than twenty times." Her laughter, light and genuine, echoed through the room, a temporary balm for the underlying tension that had brought her there.

As her mom returned with a fresh cup of coffee, the warmth of the gesture was not lost on Nicole. The gentle touch on her hand was more than just a mother's caress; it was an invitation to share, a bridge over the turbulent waters of her thoughts. "What's on your mind, my dear?" her mom asked, her voice a soft entreaty in the quiet morning.

"Is it that obvious?" Nicole responded, a half-hearted attempt at deflection.

Her mom's nod was gentle yet telling, her smile tinged with the wisdom of years spent deciphering her daughter's moods. The room, steeped in the comfort of familiar walls and shared memories, seemed to close around them, creating a space of understanding and intimacy.

Her mother's perceptive gaze held Nicole, a silent encouragement to peel back the layers of restraint. "When was the last time you took time off from work to come here?" she asked, her voice soft yet probing. The question, simple in its phrasing, was laden with the weight of unspoken concerns and the rarity of Nicole's visits away from the demands of her life.

Nicole felt the gentle probing of her mother's questions as an opening, a chance to voice the turmoil that had driven her to seek refuge in the safety of her childhood home.

Nicole hesitated, contemplating her parents' enduring marriage. "You and Dad have been married for so long, with lots of ups and downs. How do you—"

Her mother, perceptive and steering away from discussions about their own experiences, gently interrupted. "Everyone has their ups and downs, but I'm sure you're not here to talk about us. So tell me what's really on your mind."

Sitting upright, Nicole's gaze lingered on her father in the adjacent room. Summoning all her courage, she uttered, "I'm leaving Sam." The facade crumbled, tears streaming down her face.

Her mom's hand instinctively flew to her mouth and the words "oh my god" escaped her lips, expressing disbelief at the revelation. She sought the reason behind such a drastic decision.

Nicole explained, her voice laced with a mixture of hurt and anger, recounting Sam's reconnection with his childhood flame during their trip to Iran. "He betrayed me, Mom," she whispered, unwilling to let her father overhear the intimate details she wasn't yet ready to share with him.

In the aftermath of the revelation, her mom, still grappling with shock, attempted to offer perspective, suggesting that perhaps it was just a reunion with an old friend. Nicole, however, vehemently rejected the notion, emphasizing the breach of trust that initiated the entire ordeal.

"But there is a chance he's telling the truth," her mom countered, her tone gentle, a plea for reconsideration. "Are you ready to ruin your life, his, and the kids over what you're not certain about?"

The question hung in the air, a stark reminder of the precipice on which Nicole stood. It was a choice not just about her relationship with Sam but about the future of their family, a decision that bore the weight of all their lives entwined.

As Nicole poured out her heart, the image of Sam and his past love haunting her thoughts, she turned to her mother for wisdom. "I can't get over seeing them together. What would you do if Dad did that?" Her voice was a blend of desperation and need for maternal guidance, a hope that her mother's experiences could light the path ahead.

Her mother, contemplative and silent for a moment, watched her husband in the family room, the scenes of "Gunsmoke" playing like an old friend's tale. The way she observed him, with a smile that spoke volumes of their shared journey, suggested a deep, unspoken understanding of love and commitment.

"Do you believe Sam still loves you?" Her mother's voice cut through Nicole's turmoil, returning the conversation to the heart of the matter.

Nicole's affirmation was swift and sure, a testament to the bond she and Sam shared, marred but not destroyed. "I'm certain he does," she declared, her voice steady despite the storm within.

Her mother's response was gentle yet profound, a reflection on the nature of love and commitment. "The depth of your love for him, the purity and truth of it, that's the beauty of a relationship," she said, her voice soft and reflective. "Imagine the years ahead, the decisions made and the paths chosen. Ensure that your future self won't harbor regrets."

Nicole's mother's words were a tapestry of wisdom, weaving in the importance of mutual love, the joy of being cherished, and the irreplaceable glow of affection that endures through the years. It was an insight not just into a decision to be made but into a lifetime of love and the choices that shape it.

As Nicole absorbed her mother's words, her question about past doubts remained unspoken. Her mother's final wish was a simple yet profound hope for Nicole and Sam - to grow old together, with a love that reflects in their eyes every time they look at each other.

With a graceful movement, her mother stood, her actions speaking the love and dedication she held for her husband. As she placed a new cup of hot coffee next to him, the exchange of smiles between them was a testament to the enduring glow of love and mutual admiration - a subtle yet powerful affirmation of everything she had just imparted to Nicole. The scene was a living example of the love she described, a silent, beautiful answer to all of Nicole's unasked questions.

****

Pulling into the driveway, Nicole's first instinct was to scan for Sam's car, its absence marking the beginning of a new chapter of solitude and reflection. The quiet of the house welcomed her, a strange solace in the emptiness, yet crossing the threshold felt like stepping into a tangible aura of loss.

The home, once a lively hub of family activity, now echoed with a poignant silence. Each room, stripped of the immediate presence of her children and Sam, seemed to amplify her solitude, the walls reverberating with the ghostly laughter and chatter of happier times. A profound sense of longing settled within her, the knowledge of upcoming days without her children's vibrant energy turning the house into a shell of its former self.

Nicole's heart grew heavy as she absorbed the stillness, her eyes tracing the remnants of life scattered throughout the rooms—the toys left mid-adventure, the fading scent of recent meals. Each detail was a sharp reminder of the joy that once filled these spaces, now paused in a silent echo of the past.

Amidst the quiet, her gaze landed on a note from Sam, its presence a stark contrast to the emptiness around her. She unfolded it, the familiar handwriting a bittersweet tether to the world they shared. As she read, each word seemed to weigh heavily, laden with remorse and a plea for a new beginning.

Dear Nicole,
I'm be taking the kids out, hoping to bring a slice of normalcy back into their lives, even if just for a moment.

My heart aches as I write this, burdened with the regret of the pain I've caused you and our family. I am deeply ashamed of my actions, fully aware that the past cannot be undone. You've often blamed me for being trapped by the past, and I've taken your words to heart. It's time I anchor myself in the present, to foster a future we both dreamed of—a future I yearn to rebuild with you and our beautiful children by my side.

Mending the rift I've caused in your heart is a journey I know starts with a step you alone can decide to take—forgiveness. When I return with the kids later today, I'll be looking for a sign from you, a glimmer of hope that I can step across the threshold back into our lives, not just as a father but as the partner I failed to be.

I never intended to cause you pain,
Living without you is a thought I cannot bear,
My love for you remains undiminished, unwavering,
Sam

P.S. In the words of Prince, "How can u just leave me standing? Alone in a world so cold?" These lyrics echo my fear of a future without you, reminding me of the warmth your love brings into my life."

Nicole's gaze lingered on the final lines of the letter, where Sam's plea for forgiveness transitioned into a hopeful request for a signal from Nicole to come inside. His words hung in the air, a bridge between his remorseful departure and the uncertain future that awaited them. It was a clear message, leaving the next step in her hands, a silent acknowledgment that the path forward hinged on her response, her willingness to signal a readiness to embark on a journey of reconciliation or to continue navigating the waters of separation.

As Nicole absorbed the contents of the letter, Sam's words seemed to reverberate throughout the stillness of the house, each reading embedding them deeper into her heart. The quiet contemplation was abruptly pierced by the joyful chaos of her children's return. Their voices, vibrant with the day's excitement, filled the space with life once more.

"Hi, Mom! We had so much fun today!" they chimed, their energy infectious. Nicole welcomed them with open arms, her heart swelling with love as she listened to their stories, their laughter a soothing balm to her unsettled emotions.

It was Tara's question, however, that brought a sudden pause to the joyful reunion. "Dad's still in the car. Is there anything you want to tell him before he leaves?" Her innocent inquiry was a stark reminder of the message Sam awaited, the sign or signal that would dictate the next chapter of their lives.

Nicole's hesitation was palpable, the weight of decision pressing down on her. She considered her words carefully, her mind a battlefield of conflicting emotions and desires. Finally, she asked Tara to express her gratitude for the day with the children, a message polite yet noncommittal, avoiding the deeper conversation that loomed between her and Sam.

Tara, intuitive beyond her years, feigned a yawn and gently nudged her mother towards direct communication with Sam. "I'm tired, maybe you should tell him yourself." But Nicole, recognizing her daughter's subtle attempt to bridge the gap, instead turned to Cameron, entrusting him with the simple task of delivering her message. With this, Nicole steered clear of giving Sam any explicit sign of forgiveness or willingness to reconcile, her actions a silent testament to the turmoil that still lay unresolved within her.

As Tara animatedly recounted their day, Cameron darted back in, presenting Nicole with a framed picture. The framed picture in Cameron's hands was an unexpected bridge to the past, a tangible piece of a memory that seemed both distant and painfully close. Nicole accepted it, her fingers brushing over the glass as if to touch the joy encapsulated within.

Holding the framed picture, Nicole's gaze fixated on the joyful tableau of Sam and the children, their smiles immortalized against the backdrop of the majestic cruise liner. Her fingers hesitated over the glass, tracing the outlines of their faces, noting her conspicuous absence from the scene. It was a stark visual representation of her current turmoil, a family portrait with a missing piece.

"Dad said he proposed to you on that ship," Tara's voice, tinged with a mixture of curiosity and nostalgia, broke into her contemplation. "That's right," Nicole whispered, her voice laden with a sea of unspoken thoughts. As she held the picture, the weight of her absence in it pressed upon her, a symbolic prelude to a future she feared might unfold — a future where her place in their lives might mirror her absence in this captured moment.

The photograph, while highlighting the joy and unity of Sam and the children, inadvertently magnified the growing chasm between her and the family she cherished. It was a poignant reminder of the emotional distance that had crept into their lives, a distance that now seemed to parallel the physical space between her and the subjects of the photo.

As she continued to gaze at the image, Nicole grappled with the realization that just as she was absent from this picture, she might similarly find herself absent from future moments, her role as a central figure in their lives reduced to a peripheral one. The idea of an evolving family dynamic, one where she might no longer be at the forefront, was as unsettling as it was heartbreaking.

The laughter and banter of Tara and Cameron in the background were a bittersweet accompaniment to her thoughts. Nicole understood that the decisions made in the coming days would not only shape her relationship with Sam but also her presence in these irreplaceable family moments. The picture, a seemingly simple snapshot of a day out, now felt like a prophetic glimpse into a potential future — one where her place was uncertain, and her absence a silent void in the familial landscape.

Clutching the frame a little tighter, Nicole realized that the path she chose from here on out would influence not just her own journey but the tapestry of their family life. The notion of navigating a future, possibly at the periphery of this picture-perfect scene, was a motivation to tread thoughtfully, to make choices that considered not just the pain of the past but the promise of the days ahead. The photograph, with its joyful subjects and one notable absence, was a poignant crossroads, urging her to decide the role she would play in the unfolding chapters of their lives.

Chapter 71

After dropping the children off at home, Sam made a stop at Ariana's house. The fatigue from the day's events overcame him as he settled in to watch a movie, eventually succumbing to the allure of sleep. Jacqueline, ever considerate, gently roused him and guided him to the room that Ariana had thoughtfully prepared.

Expressing his gratitude, Sam patted Ariana on the back before making his way to the designated room. Fatigue weighed heavily on him, and as soon as his head touched the pillow, he surrendered to the embrace of slumber.

True to his early morning habit, Sam awoke with the dawn. With the luxury of time and nothing particular on his agenda, he found himself flipping through the pages of the Journal of Genetics. Amidst the scientific jargon, the images accompanying an article on Bloom Syndrome caught his attention, prompting him to delve into its contents.

The article illuminated the intricacies of Bloom Syndrome, highlighting its connection to an elevated risk of various forms of cancer. Like many genetic disorders, it was underscored that Bloom Syndrome is caused by a recessive mutant gene. In a moment of revelation, Sam absorbed the information that for the effects of the disease to manifest, both parents must pass the mutant gene to their offspring. Strikingly, parents who carry this gene could remain asymptomatic, as they possess one normal gene alongside the mutant one.

As Sam pondered the complexities, he internalized the genetic dance that dictates a child's inheritance—one set of genes from the mother, another from the father. In the case of carriers, where both parents harbor the mutant gene, there exists a one in four chance that their child will inherit both sets of the mutant gene, leading to the manifestation of Bloom Syndrome.

The quiet room, the dim light of dawn filtering through, became a contemplative space as Sam grappled with the implications of this genetic puzzle.

The morning unfolded as Sam emerged from his room, greeted by the inviting sight of a set breakfast table carefully arranged by his mother. Pleasantries were exchanged, with Jacqueline expressing hopes for a restful night's sleep.

Pouring himself a glass of tea, Sam settled at the table, his mind seemingly absorbed in a realm of contemplation. Jacqueline, ever perceptive, noted the unusual quietness in her son.

"You're unusually quiet this morning," she observed, a gentle curiosity in her tone.

Sam, breaking his silence, shared the current preoccupation of his mind—various genetic diseases. He lamented a wish that his professional focus had leaned more towards research, envisioning a path where he could have directly impacted lives instead of navigating the intricacies of genetic business like telling the sheiks which camel is genetically superior. A touch of regret lingered in his words.

Jacqueline, the perennial source of encouragement, responded with words that resonated deeply. She reminded Sam that it's never too late to follow a different path. With an inquisitive glint in her eyes, she posed a question that echoed with hope—whether it was possible to fix "bad genes."

Sam, caught between the advancements of science and the lingering limitations, explained that while progress was on the horizon, the science had not yet reached the point of transformative intervention. In the midst of contemplation, an idea sparked within him.

"Might there be a way to know about genetic issues beforehand?" Sam mused, his thoughts unfolding before him. A sudden surge of enthusiasm lit up his face as he considered the potential of this concept.

"That might just be the answer," he declared, rising from the table with newfound determination. "And I know where I should start." The room resonated with a renewed sense of purpose as Sam envisioned a future where his expertise in genetics could bridge the gap between science and proactive genetic health, stirring emotions of hope and possibility.

The journey to UCSD was a nostalgic one for Sam, each step echoing with memories of academic corridors and mentorship. Parking his car beside the imposing Genetics building, he ascended to the fifth floor, anticipation building with every floor the elevator conquered. Walking down the familiar hallway, Sam checked the names etched on office doors until he spotted the one that stirred a sense of reverence – Dr. Mills' name tag.

He knocked twice, the echo of his anticipation mingling with the faint response, "Come in."

Pushing open the door, Sam found Dr. Mills behind his desk, surrounded by stacks of paper, a testament to a lifetime dedicated to academia. Dr. Mills, recognizing the familiar face, took off his spectacles, and a warm smile lit up his features. "Sam, so good to see you," he greeted, slowly rising from his seat and approaching his former student.

Sam couldn't help but notice the toll time had taken on his old professor. The once sturdy figure now bore the weight of the years, reflected in the bowed back and the gentle etchings of wrinkles on his face. Dr. Mills, despite the visible signs of aging, emanated the same sweetness, care, and friendliness that had endeared him to generations of students. Approaching the ninth decade of his life, he remained an esteemed member of the biology department, a founding faculty member at UCSD.

Dr. Mills gestured toward a chair in front of his desk, and Sam took a seat, a flood of memories and emotions enveloping him. Hesitant yet compelled, Sam contemplated involving his mentor in the new idea that sparked within him. The memory of the day he had approached Dr. Mills with the concept of starting Genesys Company lingered vividly. Back then, Sam had wanted him as a startup partner, but Dr. Mills had gracefully declined, imparting wisdom that resonated even now. "This institution needs people like me to create people like you," he had gently explained, setting Sam on a path of growth and innovation.

Dr. Mills, with a careworn expression that mirrored that of a concerned family member, inquired about Nicole and the kids. Sam, with a mixture of gratitude and heaviness in his voice, laid bare the complexities of his family situation. However, determined to shift the narrative, he swiftly redirected the conversation toward his newfound idea, expressing his intent to make Dr. Mills another business proposition.

As Dr. Mills wiped his glasses with the corner of his T-shirt adorned with a vibrant DNA double helix, he settled back into his chair, his eyes fixed on Sam. The specter of impending retirement loomed, but his interest was fully engaged as Sam began to unravel the threads of his innovation.

"This is my last quarter at UCSD," Dr. Mills disclosed, acknowledging the imminent end to his academic journey. However, the prospect of Sam's idea rekindled the spark of curiosity in his eyes.

Sam, propelled by an infectious enthusiasm, shared the concept that had ignited in his mind that very morning. He acknowledged Dr. Mills's vast knowledge of genetic disorders, positioning him as a pivotal figure in this venture. Sam envisioned an automated machine capable of scrutinizing people's DNA for a multitude of known genetic mutations.

In animated tones, he painted a future where individuals worldwide could send in their DNA via a simple cheek swab to be analyzed at their center. The machines, he described, would meticulously examine genetic codes for anomalies, enabling individuals to discover if they carried any genetic disorders. Sam's eyes sparkled with the potential to revolutionize family planning, eradicating genetic disorders caused by recessive mutated genes like Tay-Sachs disease or Bloom Syndrome.

"And, of course," Sam emphasized with a knowing grin, "there's a lucrative side to it as well." The room buzzed with the excitement of innovation, a fusion of Sam's passion and Dr. Mills's wealth of knowledge, weaving the threads of a groundbreaking proposition.

Dr. Mills gently rubbed his temple, a sign of contemplation as he delved into the depths of Sam's innovative proposal. He acknowledged the potential, highlighting the condition that it would work only when the gene contributing to the syndrome and its location on the chromosome were already known—an unfortunate gap in current knowledge.

Sam, undeterred by the limitation, exuberantly declared, "But it's a start." He emphasized that their mission wouldn't be to uncover these genes or their locations; that's the work of other scientists. Instead, their machines' software would evolve with advancements in genetic research.

"Why do you keep saying 'we'?" Dr. Mills, not entirely convinced, questioned, revealing his uncertainty about joining this new venture.

Without a hint of hesitation, Sam responded, "No one has your passion, enthusiasm, or knowledge. And you're retiring. I know you too well; you're not going to just sit at home doing nothing."

Dr. Mills, contemplating the idea of retirement, shared that the school was nudging him toward it, and he was beginning to appreciate the prospect. Admitting his age and the need to relax, he seemed hesitant but intrigued.

Sam, with a knowing smile, interpreted his words, "I know that's your way of saying that you're in."

The conversation shifted to practicalities as Dr. Mills inquired about the business plan and the substantial upfront investment required. Sam revealed his plan to finance the project by selling his Genesys shares. The details unfolded as he envisioned Dr. Mills as the head scientist leading research and development, with Sam orchestrating the broader vision.

As Sam passionately laid out his plans, Dr. Mills, in a jesting tone, remarked, "Not bad for not having a plan. I wasn't sure if you will ever stop." He playfully acknowledged his inevitable boredom if confined to retirement, sealing the agreement with a commitment.
"Count me in, but you must first promise to work hard on your personal

life," he added, a silent hope echoing for Nicole's forgiveness in the undertones of his words.

Once Sam left the bustling campus behind, he found himself wandering through the streets, aimlessly navigating the urban landscape until his gaze settled on new office buildings available for lease along Noble Drive. Nestled a short distance from Freeway 805, the area had undergone rapid development, boasting fresh apartments, condominiums, and sleek office spaces. The abundance of vacancies hinted at the possibility of securing a reasonable rate for his budding enterprise.

Motivated by this potential, he dialed the leasing agent's number, leaving a message that echoed with the promise of a new beginning. As he exited the parking lot of the office building, his attention was drawn to a well-appointed apartment complex just across the street. The notion of establishing his own residence held a bitter taste for Sam, but the dwindling chances of Nicole's forgiveness and the weariness of his nomadic lifestyle nudged him toward this decision.

Before he knew it, Sam found himself inking leases for both the office and apartment, the ink on the contracts symbolizing the simultaneous unfolding of new ventures — an exciting and a poignant step towards reshaping his life.

****

"Is this really happening?" Jacqueline's voice trembled with uncertainty as she watched Sam meticulously pack his belongings, the weight of their impending separation reflected in the unspoken truth hovering between them—a divorce looming on the horizon. She couldn't hold back the stream of tears that welled up, silently expressing the ache of a family unraveling.

In an attempt to grasp at the fraying threads of what once was, she implored Sam to reconsider, questioning the necessity of Nicole and the children taking separate paths. Jacqueline's words carried the weight of a mother witnessing the fragmentation of her son's life, an emotional plea for unity over division.

"Do you think I want to live like this?" Sam paused, his weariness palpable as he settled on the bed, revealing a vulnerability that echoed through his words. "Like someone who doesn't belong anywhere?"

Sitting beside him, Jacqueline sought to console, assuring him that her intentions weren't to upset him, and fervently expressing her hope for the family's reconciliation through prayer.

Sam, burdened by the emptiness of his days, confessed to the void he faced upon waking each morning, a void only momentarily abated by the constant hum of activity. The desperation in his voice hinted at a fear of succumbing to the shadows of despair once again.

"What are you talking about?" Jacqueline's concern was immediate, probing the cryptic comment with worry etched on her face.

Sam sealed his suitcases, a tangible representation of his readiness to move forward. "I don't want to turn into a person who doesn't have a motive to live." With those heavy words, he left the house, leaving Jacqueline to grapple with the profound depths of her son's misery.

Sam compiled a list of individuals integral to his new venture, and with a determined spirit, he reached out to Hope, seeking their contact information.

As the conversation unfolded, Hope couldn't help but share the challenges at Sam's former workplace, emphasizing the void left by his absence. Mr. Phillips expressed regrets about Sam's departure, even in the face of potentially losing significant accounts.

In a moment that danced between seriousness and jest, Hope laid out her condition for involvement, playfully stating, "You got it Sam, but first, you must promise to hire me." Sam readily agreed, the anticipation of reuniting with his former associate adding to the excitement of his new endeavor.

With contagious enthusiasm, Sam delved into the intricate details of his plans and visions for the company. The conversation pivoted to the essence of their work: acquiring and analyzing genes. In this exchange, a metaphorical light bulb illuminated Sam's mind, birthing the name 'Genelyze' for his ambitious venture.

Eager to set the wheels in motion, Sam tasked Hope with assembling the key players in Dr. Mills' office for a presentation scheduled on Monday afternoon. Hope, buzzing with excitement, offered to take charge of the preparation, leaving Sam with the sense that every piece of the puzzle was seamlessly falling into place.

Sam's voice carried a warm note of gratitude as he addressed her in her native Portuguese, "Você é a melhor, Esperança." The use of her name in her mother tongue was a sign of deep respect and acknowledgment, a personal touch that underscored the significance of their collaboration. As their call concluded, the vision of Genelyze took on a sharper, more tangible form before him, filling him with a potent mix of anticipation and satisfaction. The air around him seemed charged with the promise of what was to come, marking the moment as the beginning of something truly groundbreaking.

Chapter 72

As the day wound down, Nicole settled into her desk, ready to wrap up the patients' prognosis notes before leaving. Her eyes drifted to the window, offering a brief respite from the demands of the day. The eighth floor of the Scripps Medical Center granted her a sweeping view of Balboa Park's lush greenery—a sanctuary that usually provided the solace needed to unwind after a hectic schedule.

Yet, in that moment of reflection, her own image stared back at her from the glass, revealing a void where happiness once thrived. The laughter that had been a constant companion during the days when Sam colored her life seemed like a distant memory. She reminisced about the times he would call her at work, his voice injecting joy into even the busiest hours. Opening her eyes, she noticed the soft smile that graced her face at the mere thought of him.

The familiar chime of "You've got mail" jolted her from this nostalgic reverie, and she returned to her desk. Clicking on the mailbox icon, she was met with a pleasant surprise—a missive from Sam with a simple yet powerful subject line: "Miss you." Hastily, she opened the email, eager to soak in the connection that transcended the physical distance between them.

My Dearest,

It's evident that you've chosen silence, and we both know this is a futile game, beneath the maturity we've always held in our relationship. I don't blame you for shutting me out; however, the weight of what we share lingers, and we can't continue down this path. One crucial matter demands our immediate attention—we must find a way for me to be a consistent part of the children's lives. I've deliberately kept my distance, not wanting to entangle them in the mess I've created.

I've made a grave mistake, one that's irreversible. Perhaps seeking the guidance of a family therapist could be a step forward, or if you have another suggestion, I'm open to it. I await the day when your forgiveness graces my life, but I understand the urgency of your final decision. It's not about moving on; it's about sparing our children and ourselves more pain as time unfolds.

I've rented an apartment not too far from our house, and I want you to hear it directly from me. The days of me wandering from one place to another had to end.

Reach out in any way you feel comfortable, so we may find a way forward. Consider all aspects in making your decision. Let's not compound mistakes; two wrongs don't make a right.

With Love, Sam

The realization hit Nicole like a wave, the words "Oh my god, he's moved on" echoing in her mind with the relentless rhythm of a beating drum. The finality of Sam's actions, the stark implications of his email, left her reeling as she drove home. The notion of a future diverging from the path they had once walked together, of Sam establishing a life possibly without her, was a thought more piercing than she had prepared for.

Consumed by a whirlwind of emotions, she instinctively reached for her phone to call Brenda, seeking solace in the comfort of her friend's voice. But as tears welled up, blurring her vision and choking her words, she ended the call and tossed the phone aside, unready to voice the chaos within.

Then, almost as if in response to her silent cry for help, Brenda's call illuminated the screen of her phone. Nicole stared at it, a lifeline within reach, yet she found herself immobilized, the tears flowing freely now, her heart aching with a mix of sorrow and fear. The phone's persistent vibration was a distant murmur compared to the storm of her thoughts, and eventually, it quieted down, surrendering to voicemail.

But Brenda, ever intuitive and concerned, didn't wait for a callback. Moments after Nicole arrived home, the doorbell rang, a prelude to Brenda's hurried entrance. Her face, a canvas of worry and care, mirrored the anxiety Nicole felt. Brenda's embrace was immediate and enveloping, a safe harbor in the tumult of Nicole's despair.

As Nicole leaned into her friend, the dam of her emotions broke. "He's moved on," she sobbed, the words spilling out amidst tears. Brenda, pulling back to look Nicole in the eyes, responded with her own mix of shock and protective indignation, "Really, already? Who's the slut?"

Nicole, through her tears, corrected the misunderstanding, "No, not that way. He got his own place." The clarification did little to ease the burden of her heart, as the reality of their situation sunk in deeper. The step Sam had taken was not one of infidelity but one of independence, a stride towards a new chapter that might not include her. The revelation, though devoid of betrayal, was no less painful, the future they had once envisioned together now fragmenting into two separate paths.

Brenda's perplexity was evident, her question a reflection of the mixed signals Nicole's actions and reactions had sent. "Isn't that what you wanted anyway?" she asked, her words sharp with confusion and concern. "You asked him to leave, which he did nicely. You even packed his stuff, and now you're upset that he's got a place to sleep."

Nicole could feel the logic in Brenda's words, but logic offered little solace to the turmoil swirling within her. "I thought that's what I wanted," she admitted, her voice a mixture of confusion and sorrow. "But now, I'm miserable. He used to depend on me for everything, and now it seems he doesn't need me at all. He's moved on."

Brenda, steadfast in her support, encouraged Nicole to take a step back, to assess the whirlwind of emotions from a distance. "Don't jump to conclusions," she urged. "Maybe you both still need each other more than you think." Her questions delved deeper, challenging Nicole to consider what she truly wanted, to confront the possibility of forgiveness and reconciliation.

"Have you even thought about what it would mean to forgive him?" Brenda asked, her voice gentle yet probing. It was an invitation for Nicole to explore the paths not taken, to consider the weight of her feelings against the gravity of her decisions.

The conversation was a dance around the delicate balance of heartache and hope, of pain and the potential for healing. As Nicole sat with Brenda's questions echoing in her mind, she realized that the decision to separate, while seemingly clear at the moment, had opened up a labyrinth of emotions and possibilities. In the quiet of her solitude, Nicole's heart waged a silent battle, a tumultuous struggle between love and hurt, trust and doubt. The shadows of Sam's past actions loomed large, casting an inescapable gloom over her thoughts. She was haunted by questions, each one a piercing jab at the fabric of her self-worth and their shared history.

Was she merely a placeholder, a transient presence compared to the profound connection Sam once shared with Roxana? Did thoughts of Roxana seep into their most intimate moments, a ghostly third in their union? The idea gnawed at her, a relentless whisper that refused to be silenced.

Nicole's jealousy, a slow-burning flame, had been sparked long before the current crisis. It was never about the fleeting relationships of Sam's past—the ones that had ended conclusively. It was Roxana, the one who got away, the one who, in Nicole's deepest fears, held a permanent lease in Sam's heart. This woman represented a chapter that Nicole feared was never truly closed in Sam's book of life.

The reunion between Sam and Roxana had been a visceral confirmation of her worst fears. It wasn't just a meeting; it was a rekindling, a physical manifestation of the emotional entanglement that Nicole had dreaded. The betrayal stung not just because of the act itself, but because it seemed to affirm that she had been living in the shadow of a love story that predated and perhaps, in her darkest thoughts, outranked her own.

In her agony, Nicole found herself at a crossroads. Part of her ached for the relief that forgiveness could bring, an end to the cycle of pain and recrimination that had ensnared them both. Yet another part, fierce and protective, resisted the pull of reconciliation. The specter of Sam's past was a barrier too daunting, a reminder of hurts too deep to simply erase.

As she navigated through the maelstrom of her emotions, Nicole realized that the path to forgiveness was not just about absolving Sam; it was about liberating herself from the chains of insecurity and resentment. But the shadows cast by the past were long and dark, and as much as she yearned for a way out of the pain, the way forward remained shrouded in doubt and fear.   Wrapped in Brenda's embrace, Nicole found a temporary haven from the storm of her emotions. Brenda's words were a balm, reminding her that the choice to reconcile with Sam lay in her hands alone, free from the shadows and whispers of doubt that had haunted her.

"Remember how he gave you those two stars on your first date?" Brenda coaxed a smile, drawing on the happier memories of their relationship. "He's always been that guy, the one to make grand gestures. That's the Sam who loves you."

Nicole's smile was faint, a brief flicker of warmth amidst the chill of her recent thoughts. "Yes, he did," she acknowledged, the memory a poignant reminder of the Sam she had fallen in love with. But that memory now battled with the image of him at Roxana's doorstep, a stark contrast that fueled her hesitation and pain.

Brenda, ever the supportive friend, recognized the conflict raging within Nicole. She didn't dismiss the hurt and betrayal that Nicole felt, but she saw the potential for redemption, for a second chance that could mend what had been broken. "People make mistakes, Nicole. Big, ugly mistakes. But that doesn't mean they can't come back from them. Maybe Sam deserves that chance too."

As she suggested responding to Sam's email and arranging for him to spend time with the children, Brenda's tone was gentle yet firm, steering Nicole towards a decision that considered not just the past, but the future of their family. "Start with something small," she advised, "like replying to his email or setting up a schedule for him with the kids. And hey, nothing helps thinking like a bit of fresh air and a double scoop of Ben and Jerry's New York Super Fudge Chunk. Works every time."

Nicole listened, the words and suggestions swirling in her mind alongside her own doubts and fears. Brenda's counsel was a guidepost in the fog, a nudge towards action amidst the paralysis of her pain. As she considered the next steps and prepared to leave, the idea of ice cream, of something so normal and comforting, was a stark reminder of the simplicity she longed to return to.

Chapter 73

Sam's days were marked by a persistent anticipation, a yearning for an email from Nicole that never arrived. Nights found him seeking solace in the familiar cadence of the David Letterman show, drifting into slumber with the elusive hope lingering in his subconscious. Dawn heralded a renewed urgency, the first order of business being the anxious scrutiny of his inbox. The void of Nicole's message left a palpable void.

A twist of fate altered the routine as he prepared to depart. A glaring notification revealed a missed call, Nicole's name stark against the screen. Disbelief hung heavy as he gingerly pressed each digit to redial, a surge of nerves coursing through him. The dial tone reverberated, building tension until, just before the final press, his phone stirred to life. Nicole's number illuminated the screen, a lifeline emerging from the digital abyss. The phone rang a second time, Sam inhaling deeply before mustering the courage to answer.

"Hello," Sam's voice was cautious, his greeting a tentative step into the unknown territory of their conversation. The simplicity of the word belied the whirlwind of emotions behind it, a mix of regret, hope, and fear.

"What did you want to talk about?" Nicole's voice was a sharp intrusion, her tone stripped of the warmth and intimacy that once defined their exchanges. The question, direct and cold, set the tone for the conversation, a clear indication of the barriers that now stood between them.

Sam's initial relief at the sound of her voice was quickly tempered by the reality of their situation. The connection they once shared felt fragile, the conversation a bridge over a chasm of hurt and misunderstanding.

Before he could articulate his thoughts, Nicole, in a tone that could cut through steel, questioned his desire to see the kids.

Sam's admission was heartfelt, a confession of the ache that had settled deep within him since their separation. "I do. I miss you all like crazy," he said, the longing in his voice unmistakable.

Nicole's retort was swift and biting, a reflection of the hurt and skepticism that had built up over time. "How can you miss home when you've got your own place now? Free to do whatever you want, whenever you want."

The frustration that had been simmering within Sam bubbled to the surface. "I got my place because you never made it clear where I stand. I'm too old to be crashing at friends' pads." His words, tinged with exasperation, highlighted the disarray and confusion that had driven his decisions.

As Nicole's voice rang through the phone, each word was heavy with the frustration and hurt that had been simmering beneath the surface. "My mistake that I wasn't clearer. Let me spell it out for you," she began, her tone sharp, a prelude to a declaration long held back. "You can nev—", but Sam, sensing the direction the conversation was taking, hastily cut in. "Wait," he pleaded, his voice urgent with the desire to steer away from the precipice they were inching towards.

"You didn't call to fight. I had no idea this would upset you so much. I'm still the same person," he insisted, his words a mixture of defense and plea. "I'll0 stay with Ariana if that's what it takes."

It was Nicole's turn to falter, her anger giving way to a more vulnerable expression of pain. "It felt like you moved on so easily after breaking my heart," she confessed, her voice quivering with the admission.

Sam, seizing the moment of softened defenses, shared his own desolation. "Where I am is very lonely, and being away from you and the kids is very hard." His words were a mirror to his soul, reflecting the depth of his loneliness and the earnest desire to mend what had been broken.

Nicole, perhaps touched by his candor, lightened the mood with a playful jibe. "As long as you keep feeling miserable, you can keep the apartment."

Sam's response was immediate and raw. "I feel like shit," he confessed, a stark acknowledgment of the magnitude of his regret. His words painted a picture of a man who recognized the true cost of his actions, mourning the loss of the most valuable thing in his life—Nicole's love.

Nicole's voice shifted, the intensity of the conversation transitioned into a more practical matter. "Besides making you feel bad, I called to see when you want to see the kids?" Her question was straightforward, a momentary step away from the rawness of their earlier exchange.

"Of course," Sam replied eagerly, the thought of seeing the kids infusing his voice with a rare brightness. "It's perfect. I'll go home shortly and have dinner ready by the time you get home." The suggestion was a hopeful attempt to intertwine their lives in the small, everyday ways they used to.

But Nicole cut him off, her tone calm yet unmistakable in its finality. "There is no 'we' anymore. I will probably stay with my parents. I'll stop by home to see the kids and pack a bag for the weekend." The decisiveness in her voice marked the emotional and physical distance that had solidified between them.

Sam's response was a mixture of understanding and sorrow. "I can't subject you to the anguish I'm experiencing. I understand the ache of yearning for home yet being unable to return." He proposed a compromise, suggesting a brief visit the next morning, an attempt to maintain some semblance of connection.

Nicole, however, remained steadfast. "It's not needed. It's too late for you to concern yourself with my feelings." The finality of her words closed any doors that might have been left ajar, signaling a firm step toward separation. The conversation ended with the unspoken weight of their emotions lingering, a testament to the depth of their shared history and the profound impact of their current estrangement. The silence that followed was a heavy curtain, marking the end of an era and the uncertain beginning of another.

****

As Nicole pulled into the driveway, Sam's car immediately caught her eye, the nanny's car conspicuously absent. Tara and Cameron, exuberant and full of joy, rushed towards her, their jubilant shouts echoing through the house, "Look, Mommy, Dad's come home!" They eagerly pulled her into the kitchen, where Sam was bustling about, preparing dinner.

"Hey," Sam greeted, taking a short step toward her. Nicole, her gaze shifting from the excited children to Sam, offered a cold acknowledgment, "Hey, food smells good."

Tara and Cameron, brimming with enthusiasm, proudly declared their assistance in preparing dinner, ecstatic to have it ready before Nicole's arrival. Nicole knelt down, enveloping Tara and Cameron in her arms, explaining that she couldn't stay for dinner but was sure it would be delicious.

Cameron's pout became apparent as he asked his mom why they couldn't have dinner as a family anymore. Feeling the weight of missing another family moment, Nicole concocted an excuse, mentioning she had to visit Aunt Brenda.

Tara pleaded, suggesting here mom see Brenda afterward, unless she would prefer having dinner with Brenda instead of them.

The gravity of the moment pressed on Nicole, and witnessing the excitement in her kids' eyes, she finally agreed to stay for dinner.

"Time to set the table," Sam seized the opportunity, urging the kids to help. Slowly approaching Nicole, he quietly inquired if her parents were expecting her for dinner. The silence from Nicole confirmed she hadn't even called them. With a joyous smile, Sam continued, "Look how happy they are."

As Nicole glanced at her children seated around the table, a wave of emotion swept over her. Taking a seat, she felt her heart melt at the sight of her family gathered in a semblance of togetherness. It dawned on her that this was the first time they were sharing a family dinner since she had taken the kids and left Iran. The air was thick with unspoken sentiments, each morsel of food carrying the weight of their collective journey.

The table, adorned with a simple spread prepared by Sam, bore witness to a reunion marred by the complexities of their fractured relationship. The familiar aroma of the dishes failed to mask the tension that lingered in the room. Although the children chattered and engaged in the innocent banter of siblings, the silence between Sam and Nicole spoke volumes.

Nicole's mind swirled with conflicting emotions. As she observed Sam moving about, serving dinner with a forced cheerfulness, she couldn't escape the memories of their shared past. The love they once had, the dreams they built together, and the painful fractures that led to her decision to leave—these thoughts circled her mind like a tempest.

On the other side of the table, Sam's efforts to create a semblance of normalcy masked the turmoil within. He grappled with the weight of his mistakes, contemplating the daunting task of winning back Nicole's love. The uncertainty of the future loomed large, and every gesture, every glance exchanged across the table, carried the weight of their unresolved feelings.

The clinking of utensils against plates filled the air, punctuating the silence. The children, unaware of the complexities that surrounded them, continued to enjoy their dinner, their laughter momentarily lifting the heavy atmosphere. As the evening unfolded, the shared meal became a bittersweet tableau—a tableau of a family, once whole, now navigating the jagged contours of a fractured love.

As dinner drew to a close, a subtle shift in dynamics occurred. Sam, breaking the traditional roles, insisted, "We got this. Just relax and look pretty for us," taking charge of clearing the table. The playful banter continued as Cameron teased, "Yes, Mom, just relax and look pretty for us," playfully taking away Nicole's plate. Tara joined in, suggesting a change in responsibilities, "that the ladies should relax tonight and the men do the work for a change," eliciting laughter and warm smiles from Sam and Nicole. In a jesting English butler accent, Sam declared, "Anything for my ladies," bowing theatrically.

After casually placing everything in the sink, Sam and Cameron returned to the table, ready for some quality time. However, Nicole, despite the jovial atmosphere, abruptly rose, expressing gratitude for the lovely dinner but stating she must prepare to leave. A somber undertone settled over the room, even the kids registering a sense of sorrow on their dad's face. Sam, attempting to mask his feelings, redirected his attention to the kitchen chores.

Tara, sensing the emotional undercurrent, offered to help, gently tugging on Sam's arm. However, Sam, putting on a brave front, assured the kids that he was almost done and encouraged them to start playing their favorite PS2 games. "I'll join you soon," he promised, his attempt to maintain a semblance of normalcy in the midst of shifting emotions.

As Sam paused from his kitchen chores, a contemplative expression settled on his face. The weight of unspoken emotions hung in the air as he slowly approached the bedroom door. With a hesitant breath, he summoned the courage to knock, the sound echoing through the room.

The door cracked open, revealing Nicole, a silent enigma withholding her words. Every gesture and silence seemed to be a calculated act to torment him. Sam, acknowledging the tension, expressed his gratitude for her decision to stay, emphasizing the significance it held for the kids. Nicole, her demeanor unyielding, offered a cold nod, stating that her choice was solely for the children. As she mentioned being busy with packing and wanting to leave early, Sam seized the moment, proposing to engage in a conversation while she prepared.

As Nicole reluctantly swayed the door open, she ushered Sam into the sanctuary of her private corner. The room bore witness to the silent struggle between them. Sam, stepping into the space laden with tension, inquired about Nicole's call to her parents.

Nicole, preoccupied with packing, responded, her words carrying an undercurrent of frustration, mentioning she would call them on the way. Sam, sensing the weight of the unspoken, acknowledged the difficulty of making such calls and pressed further, asking if she had already informed them about what happened in Iran. Nicole, with a slightly raised voice, affirmed that she had, adding an inquiry, "What's your point anyway?"

Sam, deciding to cut through the tension, asked for a moment to express an idea without being interrupted. Nicole, although resistant, halted her activities and sat on the bed, her gaze averted.

Sam paused mid-stride, the weight of the moment settling on his shoulders as he collected his scattered thoughts. "You've made it clear that only one of us can stay in the house. This is going to be a challenging time, but let's strive to make it as bearable as possible, for us and for the kids. I already got as place, and I believe it would be best if we shared it. You can stay there during my time with Tara and Cameron. I'm sure you'd find more comfort there than anywhere else."

With a deliberate motion, Sam reached into his pocket, his fingers wrapping around a small, cool metal object. He withdrew a Tiffany heart locket key-ring, its silver surface catching the light with a soft gleam. Gently, he opened the heart to reveal Tara and Cameron's smiling faces, immortalized on either side. "Here's the key," he offered, extending it towards her. "Please, take it—for them."

Nicole hesitated, her voice tinged with resignation. "They're going to be hurt, regardless. It's inevitable." She slowly reached out, her fingers brushing against Sam's as she accepted the keychain. "This might be a solution for now, but what about when the paperwork is finalized...?"

Sam's expression faltered, a mix of confusion and dismay flickering across his features. "Finalized? Are you already pursuing a divorce? Don't you think our marriage, our children, our entire life together warrants a chance at redemption?"

The silence that followed was a chasm, a void filled with the unsaid, the fears, and the lingering love that neither could fully dismiss. As he moved towards the door, his offer to Nicole was a testament to his desperation and resignation. "You can have anything you want. Just show me where to sign." His words were an olive branch, an acknowledgment of her pain and his role in it, a willing surrender to whatever path she chose.

Nicole's "Wait" was a cry from the heart, a last-ditch effort to communicate the turmoil within her. Tears welled up in her eyes, her heart echoing the anguish of her decision. She clarified that nothing had been filed yet. As she clarified her stance, her voice was a whisper of uncertainty, the idea of sharing his place a tentative step towards an uncertain future.

Sam turned back, the box for the keychain in his hand, a final gesture in the dance of their parting. He handed it to her, the address inside a silent symbol of a shared space that would now separate them. As he left the room, the echoes of their shared past, the laughter, the love, and the pain, seemed to hover in the air, a haunting reminder of what they had and what was slipping away. Their bedroom, once a sanctuary of their love, now bore witness to the fractures and fissures of a marriage coming undone. The keychain, the tears, and the heavy silence were the poignant epitomes of their current reality — a reality where love was overshadowed by loss.

In the cold solitude of the bathroom, the harsh fluorescent light cast unforgiving shadows across Sam's face as he stared at his reflection. His eyes, normally a source of warmth and laughter, were now dull with regret and frustration. The man looking back at him was a stranger, a physical embodiment of all his failures and shortcomings.

As he turned the tap, the water cascading down his face seemed to merge with his tears, each droplet a sad testament to the pain and remorse that swirled within him. The water, which should have been cleansing, felt heavy, each drop laden with the weight of his mistakes, the echoes of his choices reverberating in the hollow space of the bathroom.

Unable to bear the sight of his own reflection any longer, Sam's voice broke through the silence, a raw, painful acknowledgment of his reality. "You messed up," he told himself, the words a bitter mantra of self-reproach. The sound bounced off the tiles, surrounding him, enveloping him in a cocoon of despair.

In a desperate attempt to escape his own accusing gaze, he grabbed a towel, pressing it hard against his face as if to wipe away not just the water but the guilt and the pain. Behind the fabric, with his eyes tightly shut, he sought refuge from the relentless storm of his own making.

As the water continued to run, its sound a steady reminder of the world moving on, Sam remained frozen, caught in the grip of his own sorrow. The fogged-up mirror no longer held his image, but in its obscurity, it reflected the chaos of his inner world — blurred, indistinct, and overwhelming.

The bathroom had witnessed many moments of his life, but none as piercing as this. It stood as a silent observer to his breakdown, the walls holding the weight of his unspoken agony, the air thick with the residue of his shattered self. As Sam finally turned off the tap, the silence that followed was a stark reminder of the solitary path he now walked, a path lined with the repercussions of his actions and the daunting task of seeking redemption.

****

In the realm of Sam's apartment Nicole held the key locket in her hands, the familiar weight of it seemed to resonate with the depth of her emotions. She delicately turned it, revealing the cherished images of Tara and Cameron, their smiles a poignant echo of happier times. The locket, a small yet profound token, stirred a whisper of gratitude within her, a silent appreciation for Sam's uncanny ability to choose gifts that reached the deepest corners of her heart.

With a breath of anticipation, she turned the key in the lock, the click of the mechanism a prelude to the unknown. As the door swung open, a soft exclamation of wonder escaped her lips. The sight that greeted her was nothing short of magical, a transformation of the mundane into the extraordinary. The apartment, under Sam's thoughtful arrangement, had blossomed into a living dream, a testament to his understanding of her love for the sublime beauty of roses.

Each step she took was accompanied by a sense of awe as the fragrance of roses enveloped her. The large bouquet by the entrance was just the beginning, a fragrant invitation into a world crafted from love and regret, hope and yearning. The living room, with its soft pink roses, radiated a tranquil beauty, while the kitchen's lavender roses added a layer of aromatic charm.

Following the petal-strewn path, Nicole found herself drawn towards the bedroom, the heart of this enchanted realm. Here, the atmosphere was rich with the deep hues of burgundy roses, each one a silent witness to the intensity of Sam's feelings. The bed, adorned with long-stemmed red rosebuds, seemed to beckon her, while the solitary white rosebud on the pillow held a note, a silent scribe of Sam's deepest thoughts.

The framed pictures on the nightstand were a journey through time, each one a captured moment of joy, of family, of a shared life. The images of Tara and Cameron in their soccer attire brought a smile through her tears, a reminder of the vibrant energy and innocence of their children. The third frame, a snapshot of a youthful Nicole and Sam from decades past, was a window into a time of laughter and dreams, a vivid reminder of their journey together.

Seated amidst the floral tapestry, Nicole's touch lingered on the frames, her tears a silent testament to the tumult of emotions within her. Each image, each petal, each scent was a thread in the complex weave of their lives. The joy, the pain, the love, and the longing all converged in this moment, blurring the lines between then and now.

With trembling fingers, she reached for the note beneath the white rosebud, the anticipation of Sam's words adding a palpable tension to the air. As she unfolded the paper, her heart raced, each beat a drumroll to the revelation within. The note, a potential key to unlocking the next chapter, lay in her hands, the words a whisper of possibility in the silent symphony of their story.

My Dearest Nicole,

I find solace in your presence here. Amidst the chaos I've unintentionally woven into your days, you deserve a tranquil weekend, a respite from the stress that clings to you. Embrace this moment of liberation fully, relinquish the burdens, and let the winds of joy carry you away.

May your time be adorned with moments of pure delight, unmarred by worry or strife. Picture a future bathed in happiness for us all, and let that vision paint your weekend with the brightest colors imaginable.

Ever Yours,
Sam

Each word seemed to reach out from the page, a tender caress in the form of ink and paper. Tears welled in Nicole's eyes, not just from the pain of their past but from the poignant beauty of the hope that Sam offered. His words, "Ever Yours," resonated deeply, a reminder of the enduring bond that, despite everything, continued to link their hearts. With the note clutched gently in her hand, Nicole allowed herself a moment to envision the future that Sam painted, a future where happiness could once again be a tangible reality.

As the note rested on the nightstand, a silent witness to the turbulent emotions coursing through her, Nicole's touch on its edges was tender, almost reverent. She raised her eyes to the aged photograph, the youthful smiles of herself and Sam frozen in time, a poignant reminder of what once was. "How could you do this?" she murmured, the question less an accusation and more a pained query to the universe, or perhaps directly to the man in the photograph.

Her emotions were a whirlwind, swirling around her as she turned her gaze from the photograph to the five-thousand-piece puzzle displayed on the wall. It was a symbol of their partnership, of hours spent together in quiet concentration, fitting each piece into place. Now, it hung there as a testament to what they had built, each piece a reminder of their shared history, now encased in glass as if to preserve the memory of a more innocent time.

The flood of memories was overwhelming, and Nicole shook her head in a vain attempt to dispel the images and feelings that threatened to engulf her. She moved towards her bag, intent on leaving, only to be stopped by another carefully laid plan of Sam's — her favorite bottle of wine, a crystal glass, and a fruit basket arranged on the kitchen counter.

The sight of the wine, a token of their shared tastes and the many evenings they had spent sipping and talking into the night, was yet another emotional tug. The crystal glass sparkled under the lights, an invitation to indulge in the familiar ritual, while the fruit basket added a touch of care and thoughtfulness to the silent offering.

Nicole stood there, caught between the desire to flee from the pain and the undeniable pull of the life they had shared. Each item in the apartment, from the photograph to the puzzle to the wine, was a thread in the fabric of their shared existence, a fabric now frayed and torn but still holding the faintest outline of the beautiful tapestry it once was.

As she hovered in the kitchen, the room around her seemed to echo with the ghostly laughter and conversations of the past. The decision of whether to indulge in the wine, to allow herself a moment of reflection in the space Sam had created, weighed heavily on her. The night stretched out before her, a canvas yet to be painted with the decisions of the evening, each stroke a potential step towards healing or further heartache.

A soft knock interrupted her thoughts, prompting her to peer through the door's eyepiece. Two figures, one black and the other Asian, dressed in pristine white outfits, stood on the other side. With cautious curiosity, she opened the door. The black girl, Jessica, spoke before Nicole could utter a word. "Hello, Nicole, ready for your massage?" Jessica's words were a smooth melody of welcome, yet they left Nicole baffled. Her name on a stranger's lips was a puzzle yet to be solved.

Jessica, quickly backtracked, realizing her misstep. "Oops, forget anything I said, girl. I'm Jessica, and this is Natalie. We was supposed to give you this first." She handed Nicole a box of Godiva chocolates with a card delicately placed on top. In her perplexity, Nicole reached for the card.

Nicole unfolded the card with a growing sense of intrigue, revealing Sam's brief but heartfelt message: "Hi love, Please accept this gift of relaxation and melody. Sam."

The simplicity of his words carried an undercurrent of sincerity, and Nicole couldn't help but feel a mixture of emotions. A gift from Sam, the orchestrator of her life's recent upheaval, felt like an unexpected twist. The offerings on the kitchen counter, the puzzle on the wall, and the note on the nightstand, contemplating the complexity of the emotions entwined in this gesture. With a deep breath, she prepared herself for the uncharted journey of relaxation and melody Sam had curated for her. Nicole envisioned this as another considerate gift from Sam, and the prospect of some much-needed relaxation warmed her heart. Stepping back from the doorway, she graciously welcomed the duo into the space.

Nicole, enveloped in the fantasy Sam had meticulously crafted, followed Jessica's guidance to the bedroom. Jessica's voice gently reached her, promising to return after the preparations were complete. A white robe awaited her, promising a soft cocoon of comfort. As she undressed and embraced the silky robe, the air carried a soft tune, a prelude to the session awaiting her.

Stepping into the dimly lit room, Nicole found herself immersed in a dreamlike setting. The soft glow of scented candles danced around a massage table, and the soothing melodies from Natalie's harp enveloped the space. Jessica gently guided Nicole, her voice a soothing melody, "Please remove your robe and lay face down under the sheet." She turned around to give her some privacy.

Warm oil caressed Nicole's back, and the music transitioned seamlessly into the familiar strains of "Take Me with U" by Prince, a song woven into the fabric of her relationship with Sam. With her eyes closed, Nicole surrendered to the sensory experience, memories of that heavenly day flooding her consciousness.

Lost in the ambiance, Nicole softly remarked to Jessica about Sam likely sharing her favorite songs. "Yes, he did," Jessica answered in a hushed tone, in the midst of her skilled ministrations. In the next breath, she delved into her thoughts, expressing, "I can sense that Sam genuinely loves you. The flowers, this elaborate treatment—it's evident. Although, it feels like an apology in every gesture." Her words flowed effortlessly, a cascade of observations and insights, leaving no room for Nicole to interject or perhaps even desire a response.

Nicole, yearning for a moment of enjoyment and relaxation, couldn't resist engaging in the conversation. She playfully remarked to Jessica, "Are you a mind reader too? I know he still loves me but what makes you think he's done something wrong? Can't a girl get some flowers and a massage without it implying a hidden agenda?"

"Mind reader? Hardly," Jessica continued, her tone playful yet pointed. "But love, when a man goes beyond the usual to get you not just a bouquet but what seems like the entirety of Carlsbad's blossoms, it speaks volumes. And you, my dear, mentioning he 'still' loves you—well, that word 'still' carries the weight of untold stories. It's almost always a whisper of a third shadow in the story. So, who is she? Who's the one that stirred the pot?"

Nicole, attempting to keep things vague, simply stated, "It's complicated," hoping to brush off the probing questions.

Jessica's advice flowed with the raw honesty of personal experience, painting the complexities of love and betrayal with broad strokes. "It's always complicated, isn't it? Especially when you find yourself cast as the other woman," she said, her voice a blend of empathy and caution. "But here's my advice from someone who's walked through that storm—men like him, they wander for their momentary pleasures, but they always go back to the safety of their wives. Treasure the gifts, by all means, but guard your heart fiercely. I lingered too long in my own delusion; don't you make my mistake."

Nicole's response was tinged with a weary sadness. "It's not quite like that. I'm not the other woman; I'm the wife he betrayed. The thought of leaving crosses my mind because of our shared life crumbling under the weight of his actions."

Jessica's regret was palpable. "I'm sorry," she sighed, her previous assumptions dissolving into the air. "It's not for me to dictate a 'must' in your journey. Your heart, though broken, holds the map to what comes next."

Nicole's admission, "My heart shattered when I saw them together," laid bare the depth of her pain, a sentiment Jessica acknowledged with quiet understanding. "Healing takes time, and in that time, your heart's whisper will grow stronger, guiding you forward."

Natalie's fingers expertly weaved the melody into "Waiting for a Girl Like You" by Foreigner.

Nicole found herself immersed in a sea of thoughts, realizing that Sam was determined not to be easily forgotten. He knew her so intimately, orchestrating this elaborate plan within a mere few hours. "I mean how do you find a harpist on such a short notice?"

Jessica nodded, a remorseful smile playing on her lips. "Love, or the quest to reclaim it, often comes with a hefty price tag—emotionally and, evidently, financially. Sam's actions suggest a desperation to mend fences, to rewrite the ending to a story that veered off course."

In an attempt to escape the present, Nicole closed her eyes, seeking solace in memories of the past. However, an ominous vision of the future persistently intruded upon her thoughts, casting a shadow over her attempt to drown in nostalgia.

Jessica concluded the session by delicately wiping the fragrant oil from Nicole's body with a moist, warm towel, accompanied by the haunting melody of "When You're Gone" by the Cranberries, skillfully played by Natalie. As Nicole donned her robe, gratitude filled her as she expressed her sincere thanks to the duo.

As Nicole lay in her bed, the soft scent of the massage oils still lingering on her skin, she found herself caught in the delicate balance between two divergent paths. The rhythmic melody of the massage's lingering music played in her mind, echoing the conflicting emotions that danced within her.

On one hand, the past, filled with shared memories and the love that had once bound her and Sam together, tugged at her heartstrings. The framed pictures Sam had carefully chosen, the melody that interwove with the fabric of their relationship, all whispered of a history that refused to be easily forgotten. The roses, meticulously scattered like fragments of a once-perfect union, evoked a sense of yearning for what was.

On the other hand, the present was marred by the recent revelations, the hurtful truths that had left her heart shattered. The uncertainty of Sam's actions, the unanswered questions lingering in the air, painted a stark contrast to the idyllic scenes he had meticulously crafted. The weight of his transgressions bore heavily on her, a burden she struggled to reconcile with the love she still held.

Nicole grappled with the decision before her – to forgive or to let go. The conflicting emotions surged within her like a cyclone, pulling her in opposite directions. Could she find it in her heart to forgive Sam for the sake of the life they had built together? Or was the pain too deep, the breach irreparable?

Each choice carried its own weight, and the decision ahead was laden with the complexity of a love tested and a future uncertain. The night whispered softly, but the answers remained elusive, hidden in the recesses of her conflicted heart.

Chapter 74

Every day, like a ritual, Nicole would find herself standing by her office window, gazing out onto the bustling street below. The city's rhythm echoed around her, a stark contrast to the turmoil within. Amid the urban symphony, her eyes were drawn to the bold proclamation on the billboard across the street, a stark reminder of the tumultuous crossroads she found herself at.

"Get a divorce. Get a life," the words screamed at her, a concise command from a law firm eager to untangle the knots of fractured unions. Each week, the sign's declaration became a silent companion, a constant presence in the backdrop of her contemplation. The name and phone number glared at her, offering a lifeline to a future unknown.

The weeks passed, and Nicole's routine remained unchanged. She stood by the window, an unwitting spectator to the chaotic dance of the city. Her gaze lingered on the sign, a poignant symbol of the choices that loomed over her. The directive seemed straightforward, but her fingers, heavy with the weight of indecision, hesitated to dial the numbers.

The billboard became a silent witness to her internal struggle, an emblem of the emotional turbulence that accompanied the thought of unraveling a life once woven together. Each passing day etched the words deeper into her consciousness, a constant reminder of the crossroads she couldn't escape.

As the city outside continued its relentless march, Nicole's internal battle mirrored the urban chaos. The billboard stood as a sentinel to her hesitations, a visual echo of the complex emotions that surged within her. In the quiet moments by the window, amid the city's cacophony, the decision remained suspended, waiting for her fingers to find the strength to dial a number that could redefine her future.

As November's chill settled in, so did the frostiness of Sam's patience, nearing its end alongside the waning days of the month. Restless, he had pressed Nicole for a decision, a resolution to the limbo that held their lives in suspension. For a man accustomed to swift choices and decisive actions, the prolonged uncertainty tested the boundaries of his endurance. Nicole, on the surface, seemed poised to depart from Sam, but her hesitancy to act revealed a deeper, unspoken struggle.

After persistent appeals, Nicole relented, agreeing to unveil her decision immediately following the Thanksgiving weekend. The delay, perhaps fueled by a reluctance to confront the gravity of the choice or the shadow of Jacqueline's invitation, hung in the air. Jacqueline, undeterred by Nicole's initial hesitance, insisted she join them for Thanksgiving, brushing off any awkwardness that might arise. She divulged the imminent arrival of Farhad, his visa now approved, set to grace their Thanksgiving morning.

Nicole, feeling the tug of familial bonds and a hint of nostalgia, eventually accepted the invitation. Her words conveyed anticipation and a longing for connection, expressing the void that had grown in the absence of Jacqueline and Ariana. Yet, beneath the surface, unspoken tensions and unresolved complexities lingered, casting a shadow over the approaching Thanksgiving gathering—a day meant for gratitude, but for Nicole, laden with the weight of imminent decisions and the convergence of past and present. The approaching holiday was not just a marker on the calendar but a deadline for the future of her relationship with Sam.

As another mundane day wound down, Nicole found herself drawn to the panoramic cityscape beyond her office window. A familiar impulse stirred within her, urging her to break the silence with the familiar cadence of a phone call. The number on the billboard across the street had become an unspoken challenge, a numeric gauntlet she had hesitated to confront in the past.

Yet, as the calendar pages edged closer to Thanksgiving, a quiet resolve burgeoned within her. This time, as she extended her trembling fingers toward the phone, a newfound strength accompanied her actions. The toll-free number, previously an intimidating sequence of digits, seemed less formidable now, each press of the button echoing a step toward an uncertain but inevitable destination.

To her astonishment, when her gaze revisited the billboard, it no longer bore the stark declaration of a law office beckoning her toward divorce. Instead, a luminous announcement for The Wild Animal Park's Festival of Lights adorned the prominent space instead. A cascade of memories enveloped her consciousness, transporting her back to the joyous escapades of family outings to the vibrant event, where laughter and warmth abounded.

Tears welled in her eyes, not from the ghosts of lost possibilities, but from the spectral embrace of cherished moments. Was the universe orchestrating a subtle plea, imploring her to consider reconciliation rather than dissolution? The juxtaposition of the festival ad and her wavering thoughts formed a tableau of conflicting emotions.

Lost in the labyrinth of contemplation, Nicole's fingers moved autonomously, dialing the familiar numbers from muscle memory. Each digit marked a step, a decision, and soon, a voice emerged from the other end of the line, a threshold to an uncertain dialogue that could reshape the trajectory of her fractured relationship with Sam. The journey into the unknown had begun, guided by the whispers of nostalgia and the vanishing murmurings of hope.

Chapter 75

Thanksgiving morning painted the airport scene with a flurry of anticipation as everyone congregated to welcome Farhad to America. Ariana, wide-eyed and elated, kept a vigilant watch on the flight monitors. The collective excitement peaked when the word "LANDED" illuminated next to Farhad's flight number, triggering jubilant celebrations among the awaiting crowd. Sam, fueled by the festive air, seized the opportunity and sidled up to Nicole, curiosity etched on his face and asked if Ariana's imminent joy mirrored what he might experience upon hearing Nicole's decision. However, Nicole, wearing a furrowed brow, signaled that the airport wasn't the appropriate setting for such a conversation. Sam, feeling the weight of unspoken tension, let out a low growl of frustration, "is there ever a right time or place?" In a moment of exasperation, he walked away, leaving the unresolved emotions hanging in the air, much like the anticipation that lingered on this Thanksgiving morning.

Farhad's inaugural day in America unfolded like an odyssey of novelty and cultural contrasts. The freedom to sip beer without the looming specter of legal repercussions marked a departure from the restrictive norms of his native Iran, setting the stage for an array of unfamiliar experiences.

American football, a spectacle unlike the soccer that goes by the same name globally, introduced Farhad to a sport characterized by handball maneuvers, goalposts that resembled inverted soccer goals, and the captivating presence of spirited cheerleaders on the sidelines. The intricacies of the game, from the strategic handling of the ball to the pursuit of touchdowns, showcased a stark departure from the soccer-centric sporting culture he knew.

As the Dallas Cowboys clashed with the Miami Dolphins, the final score of 20-0 left Farhad marveling at the abundance of goals in American football, each point akin to a goal in the soccer matches he was accustomed to. The realization underscored the distinctive nature of this unfamiliar sport, weaving a tapestry of excitement and confusion for the Iranian newcomer.

Even the collective group pre-meal grace, a customary practice in American households, presented a departure from the traditions Farhad knew. In Iran, the ritual involved everyone reciting their thanks individually after the end of the meal.

Amidst the unfamiliarity, Farhad found himself on a journey of discovery, each experience contributing to the intricate mosaic of his first day in America. The day's encounters became more than mere novelties; they were glimpses into a culture distinct from his own, leaving him simultaneously enchanted and bewildered by the myriad differences that characterized his newfound American reality.

As the day's festivities waned and the laughter faded, Sam found himself helping to settle the kids into Nicole's car. The task was familiar yet heavy with unspoken words and lingering glances. As Nicole approached the driver's side, Sam couldn't contain the question that had been burning inside him. His voice, laced with a mix of hope and fear, broke the evening's calm. "Have you made up your mind?" he asked, his eyes searching hers for a hint of the decision that would shape their futures.

Nicole paused, the weight of the moment settling upon her shoulders. "I haven't decided yet," she admitted, her voice a low echo of the internal struggle that held her captive. Each word seemed to carry the burden of their shared past and the uncertain horizon of their future.

Sam, unable to mask his longing for a definitive answer, pressed on, his question a reflection of the desperation that gnawed at him. "Can you at least tell me which way you're leaning?" he pleaded, hoping for a glimpse into her thoughts, a clue to the decision that hung in the balance.

Nicole's response was tinged with frustration, a testament to the gravity of the choice before her. "This isn't a game, Sam. It's our lives we're talking about," she countered, her words a reminder of the profound impact of her pending decision. Her tone, a mix of weariness and resolve, underscored the seriousness with which she approached the crossroads they faced.

Sam, overwhelmed by the gravity of the situation, pleaded for a chance to be part of their lives again. The weight of Nicole's uncertainty hung in the air, and she began, "I'm uncertain about my final. . ."

As Nicole began to voice her indecision, Sam's impatience broke through the veneer of calm. "Then make up your mind," he insisted, the plea a sharp demand in the quiet night. His urgency was a raw expression of the turmoil that churned within him, a desire for clarity amidst the maelstrom of doubt.

Nicole's response was a blend of weariness and resolve. "What's the rush? Why are you doing this now? Don't ruin the day," she implored, her words a plea for a momentary reprieve from the relentless pressure of making a life-altering decision. Her request was not just for herself but for the delicate balance of their family life that hung in the balance.

But Sam, consumed by the need for closure, couldn't contain his demand. "I can't live like this anymore. I need an answer now," he declared, his voice a testament to the unbearable weight of living in limbo.

Nicole, her resolve crystallizing in the face of Sam's insistence, made a decisive move. Reaching for the manila envelope in the car, the car's interior light briefly illuminated her face, revealing the traces of tears and the undeniable strength that defined her. She drew out the stack of papers, each page a symbol of the end of their book of life. With deliberate movements, she signed where necessary, her signature a final stroke in the narrative of their marriage. Handing the envelope back to Sam, she delivered the verdict that would untangle their lives. "One more signature, and we're all done. I hope you can go on with your life now."

As she started the car, the finality of her actions settling around her like a heavy shroud, Nicole rolled down the window. Her last words to Sam were a poignant mix of regret and accusation. "Always remember that you made me do this on Thanksgiving Day. I still needed more time." The words were a lament, a reflection of the heartache that had led to this moment and the enduring pain that would follow.

With that, Nicole drove away, leaving Sam standing alone, the envelope in his hands a tangible representation of the end of their shared life. The documents within were more than just paper; they were the closing chapter of a love story that had once promised a lifetime.

As Sam stood there, the fading taillights of Nicole's car signaling her enduring departure, he found himself engulfed in the poignant aftermath of their exchange. The vanishing echoes of the engine's distant hum mirrored the widening gap between them, a tangible manifestation of the emotional chasm that had now taken residence in the spaces once shared.

The distance seemed to stretch infinitely, a silent testament to the profound shift that had just occurred. Sam, ordinarily decisive in his actions, now grappled with the realization that this breach was beyond immediate repair. It was forming a gulf, carved not only by the exchange of signed documents but also by the weight of countless unspoken words and the unresolved emotions that lingered in the air like a heavy fog.

The expanse of the chasm felt insurmountable, a metaphorical landscape of fractures and uncertainties. Sam's attempts to traverse it mentally were met with the harsh reality that certain distances could not be bridged with sheer willpower. The specter of their broken bond cast a pervasive shadow, dimming the memories of shared laughter, joy, and love.

In the aftermath of that decisive moment, Sam found himself standing on the precipice of an unknown future, the gravity of the situation settling heavily on his shoulders. The road ahead seemed shrouded in uncertainty, and the once-familiar landscape of their relationship had shifted into uncharted territory.

As the echoes of Nicole's departure dwindled, the weight of what had transpired bore down on Sam's heart. The emotional residue of their exchange clung to him like an indelible mark, leaving him to confront not only the present reality but also the potential irreversibility of the choices made on this Thanksgiving Day.

Chapter 76

For three days, the envelope lay untouched, an ominous presence in Sam's home, its unbroken seal a barrier between him and the finality of Nicole's decision. It was a heartbreak in paper form, its contents unknown yet deeply feared. Sam, in his reluctance to face the inevitable, had retreated into himself, his apartment now a sanctuary from the world and its painful realities.

Sleep became his only respite, a temporary escape from the constant tug of the envelope's presence. Yet, as night draped the world outside in its quiet darkness, a restless urge pulled Sam from his bed, compelling him to face what he had been avoiding. With each step towards his workspace, his heart grew heavier, the weight of the impending confrontation anchoring him in a deep sense of dread.

His workplace, usually a hub of activity and thought, now felt like a mausoleum of his former life, the dim light casting long shadows that seemed to whisper of better days. The Freeway 805 stretched out before him, unusually quiet, its stillness a stark contrast to the turmoil churning inside him. He felt adrift, disconnected from the world rushing by outside, a solitary figure grappling with the imminent collapse of everything he held dear.

As he stood by the window, the darkness outside seemed to seep in, filling the room with an oppressive sense of isolation. The freeway, typically a vein of life and movement, lay empty, a visual representation of the emptiness he felt. It was as if the world had paused, holding its breath as he braced himself to confront the reality sealed within the envelope.

With a deep, resigned breath, Sam sank into his chair, the darkness wrapping around him like a shroud. His mind wandered back through the years, retracing the path that had led him to this lonely precipice. Memories of laughter, love, and shared dreams flickered through his thoughts, each one a poignant reminder of what was about to be lost.

The night sky stretched out above Sam, an expanse of darkness punctuated by the twinkling of distant stars. Among them, the constellation Delphinus seemed to beckon to him, its celestial shape a comfort amidst the swirling turmoil of his thoughts. As he gazed upwards, two hours slipped by unnoticed, the stars guiding him on a journey through the past sixteen years of his life with Nicole.

Each star seemed to pulse with a memory, becoming luminous touchstones to moments of joy and sorrow, triumph and challenge. Sam found himself adrift in the sea of recollections, each constellation a chapter from the story of his life with Nicole.

He remembered their first kiss, a moment charged with the electricity of new beginnings. He could almost feel the nervous anticipation, the hesitant approach, and the eventual melding of two souls searching for connection. The stars twinkled in acknowledgment of the memory, a shared secret between him and the universe.

Then came the bittersweet farewell by Nicole's dormitory, a parting that held the promise of reunion. The stars seemed to dim slightly, echoing the melancholy of that moment, the aching desire to stay just a little longer.

The proposal, a moment of pure, unbridled emotion, shone brightly in his mind. He could see Nicole's tears, not of sorrow but of overwhelming joy, each one reflecting the commitment they were about to make. The stars above danced in celebration, casting their ethereal light on the memory.

But it was the memory of New Orleans that brought a gentle smile to his lips, the day when the heavens opened up and showered them with rain. It wasn't just water falling from the sky; it was as if the universe itself was pouring out its blessings upon them. He remembered Nicole's laughter, a sound that rang clear and true amidst the chaos as she held him under the monsoon.

"It's raining!" he had shouted, a statement of the obvious overwhelmed by the surreal joy of the moment.

"I know," she had replied, her laughter mingling with the sound of rain. Together, they had stood defiantly in the middle of Bourbon Street, the world around them scurrying for shelter. Their long loving kiss defied the elements, a testament to a love they believed was unassailable.

The night enveloped Sam in a quiet so profound it seemed to amplify the cascade of memories that flooded his mind. Each recollection was a vivid brushstroke painting the intricate tapestry of his life with Nicole. The memories came in waves, each one crashing over him with a force that left him breathless.

He was transported back to the hospital room, the sterile smell and the beeping monitors fading into the background as he focused on Nicole's strained face, her hand gripping his with a strength born of pain and anticipation. The birth of Tara was a moment of transcendental beauty, a point in time when life seemed to expand infinitely. The memory of cutting the umbilical cord was not just a physical act but a symbolic gesture of stepping into a new world of parenthood, a thread that bound them to a future filled with unknown joys and challenges.

Yet, the joy of Tara's birth was tinged with the stark terror of Cameron's arrival. The complications that arose were a cruel twist of fate, a sinister shadow that threatened to engulf their happiness. The hospital became a stage for a drama of life and death, each moment a precarious step in a dance with destiny. The relief that followed Cameron's safe arrival was a testament to their resilience, a shared triumph over the forces that sought to tear them apart.

In the solitude of the night, Sam's mind wandered through the laughter that once filled their home, the shared dreams and the simple pleasures that made up their daily lives. But intertwined with the joy were the strands of sorrow, the inevitable counterpart to the love they shared. Each memory, whether joyous or painful, was a chapter in the story of their lives together.

As the mental slideshow continued, the bittersweet image of Nicole passing the envelope to him emerged. In the theater of his mind, she dissolved away like the last star of his constellation, gracefully fading as if hiding behind the horizon. The poignant exchange, laden with unspoken words, left a lingering ache in his chest.

As Sam sat beneath the night sky, the stars continued their ancient dance, indifferent to the woes of one solitary man on Earth. Yet, in their silent vigil, they offered a sense of connection, a reminder that the universe was vast and his story was just one among countless others. The memories, both joyous and painful, were a testament to the life he had lived, the love he had shared, and the uncertainty of what lay ahead. As the night wore on, the constellation of Delphinus continued to shine, a celestial guide through the darkness of his reflections.

The envelope, a tangible relic of their co-authored memories, rested on his lap, as Sam's exhausted body finally surrendered to the relentless pull of sleep. His emotions, a tumultuous sea that had churned ceaselessly throughout the day, began to settle into a temporary calm. The envelope, once a harbinger of finality, now lay beside him, its presence a muted echo of the decisions that awaited him on the other side of slumber.

As he closed his eyes, the weight of the day's contemplations pressed down on him, yet in the vulnerability of rest, he found a fleeting escape. The room around him faded away, the envelope's stark reality softened by the gentle blur of drowsiness. It became a silent sentinel, watching over him as he ventured into the dreamscape, a place where the harsh edges of reality were smoothed into the fluid contours of imagination.

In his dreams, the memories of his life with Nicole played out like a series of vignettes, each one a poignant reminder of the love, laughter, pain, and sorrow that had colored their shared existence. The moments they had cherished, the challenges they had overcome, and the dreams they had nurtured all swirled together in a dance of shadow and light.

The early morning light filtered into the office, casting a hazy glow that seemed to blanket the usual buzz of the workplace. As Hope stepped through the quiet corridors, a sense of apprehension filled the air, the kind that foretold a story yet to unfold. Her routine morning walk was halted abruptly as she passed by Sam's office, the sight within arresting her steps.

There, in the semi-darkness, Sam lay surrendered to a fitful sleep, his body slumped in the chair, a stark silhouette of vulnerability. The office, usually a beacon of determination and energy, was now a still life of exhaustion and surrender. The sight of Sam, so unguarded and worn, struck a chord of empathy in Hope's heart.

Compelled by a mix of concern and compassion, she stepped into the room, her presence a quiet intrusion into the solitary world Sam had cocooned himself in. "Wake up, Sam," she whispered, her voice a gentle nudge against the heavy silence. Her hand reached out, rocking the chair slightly, the soft creaks a testament to the solitude of the night past.

Sam's awakening was a startled jolt back to reality, the sudden movement sending the envelope slipping from his lap to the floor. Disoriented, he looked around, his voice heavy with the remnants of sleep and burdened with the weight of unspoken thoughts. "What time is it?" he asked, a simple question loaded with the urgency of a man grappling with the fragments of a night spent in turmoil.

As Hope bent down to retrieve the envelope, her fingers traced the embossed logo, the insignia of a decision that held the finality of an end. Her words, filled with genuine sorrow, acknowledged the reality they all sensed but hoped wouldn't materialize. "Everyone knows them from their billboard ads. I'm so sorry that it had to come to this," she said, the envelope in her hand a symbol of the painful journey that lay ahead.

The revelation that Sam had yet to open the envelope lent a new layer of tension to the room. The unopened Pandora's box in his hands held the potential to alter the course of his life, the unknown contents a heavy weight on his already burdened shoulders. His admission, "I haven't looked inside yet, but she has signed them already," was a whisper of resignation, a reluctant acceptance of the inevitable change looming over him.

Hope, standing in the threshold between professional obligation and personal empathy, felt the enormity of Sam's plight. "I don't know what to say," she confessed, her voice soft, her words a subtle admission of the complexity of comforting someone standing on the precipice of such a profound personal upheaval. Her presence in the room was a balance of respect and concern, a witness to the intimate moment of vulnerability that Sam seldom displayed.

Her practical suggestion for him to freshen up was more than a mere directive; it was an unspoken gesture of care. "But I know a shower, a shave, and a change of clothing are in order right away." The advice, simple on the surface, was an attempt to offer Sam a momentary escape from the overwhelming reality, a chance to regroup and face the day with a renewed sense of self.

"You don't look so good," Hope added, the sympathetic half-smile accompanying her words an effort to lighten the heavy atmosphere. It was a gentle nudge, a reminder that despite the chaos that might lie within the sealed envelope, life, with its mundane necessities, continued.

Her suggestion for him to take the day off was an offering of respite, an acknowledgment that some battles were too personal, too raw to be faced amidst the demands of the professional world. "Just take the day off; we'll be fine here," she assured him, her words a beacon of solidarity and understanding.

Back in his apartment, Sam moved through the familiar motions of personal care: the hot water cascading over him, the scrape of the razor against his stubble, the exchange of worn clothes for something fresh. Yet, the mundane acts couldn't drown out the persistent pull of the unopened envelope on the table.

He stared at it, a vessel harboring the unknown, a Pandora's Box of emotions he was hesitant to unleash. The weight of its contents hung in the air, a palpable heaviness that seemed to resist his attempts to breach its secrets. In a surge of frustration, he flung the envelope across the room, a futile attempt to distance himself from the impending reality.

As the envelope soared through the air, Sam's fingers danced over his phone, dialing Nicole's number with a mix of trepidation and determination. The connection was established, and in the hushed twilight of an emotionally charged conversation, Sam's voice trembled over the line, carrying the weight of unspoken burdens. "Hi, how are the kids?" he ventured, the simplicity of the question barely masking the complexities beneath.

A somber "They just went to bed" echoed through the silent spaces, a subtle reminder of the altered dynamics between them.

As the conversation veered towards the unspoken, Sam broached the subject that lingered in the shadows. "I have the papers," he confessed, the words laden with a palpable hesitancy. "But just tell me what you want yourself."

Nicole's reply, though composed, bore the echoes of an emotional storm. "It's all in there. Were they not clear?" Her words hung in the air, a subtle challenge wrapped in layers of unexpressed pain.

"I haven't read them yet," Sam admitted, a revelation that felt like a confession of unread chapters in their shared story. "But you've had plenty of time," Nicole countered, her tone revealing a blend of impatience and an unspoken yearning for resolution.

In a moment of vulnerability, Sam exposed the raw truth. "You know that I won't object to anything you want." His willingness to acquiesce felt like a fragile bridge stretched across the chasm of their emotional distance.

"Sam, please don't make it any harder," Nicole pleaded, her voice bearing the fatigue of countless tears shed in the quiet hours of the night. "I'm tired of crying."

A pivotal moment unfolded as Sam, with a heavy heart, proposed a sacrifice. "Will the crying stop once I sign the papers?" His words carried the weight of an offer to sever the ties that bound them. "If you say yes and if you think you would feel better, I'll sign them and will bring them over right now. I won't even read them. Joint custody of the children is all I ask for."

Nicole, caught in the emotional tempest, acknowledged the impending storm. "I know the crying won't stop right away," she conceded, her voice a delicate admission of the emotional turbulence ahead. But Sam, interrupting her, laid bare his own wounds. "I'm at the lowest point of my life," he confessed. "We both need healing. Allow us to care for each other once again and heal together."

Nicole's response carried the weight of unspoken truths. "Listen to yourself. I give you the divorce papers, and you suggest we heal together. Just think about why we need healing in the first place." A catch in her throat betrayed the vulnerability beneath. "I tried, I tried very hard, but I couldn't forgive you." Nicole's confession was a whisper of defeat, a testament to the silent battles she had waged in the solitude of her thoughts. The inability to forgive, a barrier insurmountable, had led them to this precipice.

In the poignant shadows of an impending separation, Sam's words lingered like a haunting melody in the cold air. "It's strange that it had to happen this time of the year," he mused, the weight of nostalgia pulling at the edges of his voice. "I wish we could have one more Christmas together as a family."

The specter of traditions danced in the spaces between their words. "Actually, we always set the Christmas tree on the Thanksgiving Day weekend," Sam revealed, the echo of laughter and twinkling lights resonating through the bittersweet confession. "Tell the kids I'm sorry, and I'll try to make it up to them."

In a gentle counterpoint, Nicole, bearing the weight of her own emotions, offered a tender suggestion. "You should pick them up from school tomorrow and pick a tree together. They would love that."

Sam, momentarily buoyed by the prospect of shared moments, eagerly embraced the idea. "That would be perfect. I'll bring the signed papers," he promised, his words carrying the undertone of a vow to salvage fragments of normalcy amid the impending changes.

Yet, Nicole, cognizant of the fragility of their shared reality, urged caution. "Let's not ruin the day tomorrow. You could send them over later," she suggested, a plea for an undisturbed space where the innocence of childhood could still find refuge.

"Maybe after we come back from Mammoth Mountain," Sam interjected, his tone a wistful inquiry veiled in the mention of a cherished tradition—the annual ski trip during Christmas break.

The line hung heavy with unspoken sentiments as Nicole, perhaps unable to articulate the tumult of emotions, chose to sever the connection. "Have fun carrying the tree tomorrow," she uttered, the unspoken goodbye hanging in the air like the final note of a melancholic melody.

On the journey back home, the weight of anticipation hung heavy in the air for Nicole. The prospect of seeing Sam for the first time after serving him with the divorce papers was a surreal collision of the familiar and the unknown. As she navigated the winding roads, her mind painted vivid scenes of Sam and the kids, enveloped in the warmth of tradition, adorning the Christmas tree with both ornaments and cherished memories.

Arriving home, the melodic strains of Christmas music merged seamlessly with the euphoric laughter of children. The festive symphony welcomed Nicole as she stepped through the threshold, a bittersweet soundtrack to a once-shared life now undergoing a transformative shift. Making her way to the family room, she was met with the enchanting sight of a meticulously adorned Christmas tree, with Sam delicately placing the final piece—the star that crowned their shared memories.

Children, their faces illuminated with excitement, rushed toward their mother, eager to showcase their favorite ornaments. Sam descended the ladder, a tentative smile playing on his lips as he extended an invitation to Nicole. Would she do the honor of switching on the Christmas tree lights?

Acknowledging the beauty of the tree, Nicole approached Sam, a reciprocal story casting a silent shadow over the festive scene. As their hands brushed in the act of passing the switch, it marked their first contact in what felt like an eternity. In that fleeting touch, a subtle spark flickered in Sam's eyes—a glimpse of hope amid the emotional tumult. Nicole, however, offered only a serene smile, accepting the switch from Sam.

With a simple flick, the room transformed. The Christmas tree burst into a radiant display of lights, casting a soft glow that illuminated the space. In that luminous moment, a dim of hope permeated a house that had seemed barren of it, like a beacon cutting through the emotional shadows that had settled within the walls. The tree, now a symbol of resilience and livelihood, stood as a testament to the power of fleeting connections and the possibility of renewal in the face of inevitable change.

Brimming with holiday joy, Nicole summoned her children for a cozy huddle, the air around them crackling with the excitement of the upcoming holidays. Eyes sparkling with laughter, she asked Tara and Cameron about their Christmas wishes, a tradition that brought them all closer every year.

Tara, her voice bubbling with youthful enthusiasm, spoke of her longing for a pink ski jacket. Her vivid descriptions painted images of the snowy slopes of Mammoth Mountain, their usual Christmas retreat, where family warmth and chilly winds intermingled. The mention was a tender nod to the cherished memories they all held of skiing down those familiar trails. A glance exchanged between Nicole and Sam spoke volumes of their silent acknowledgment that he had something to do with her wish, Sam's subtle shrug a testament to the shifting sands beneath their family traditions.

Cameron, ever eager to forge his path, expressed his wish for a new set of skis, his own, free from the history of hand-me-downs. His bright eyes were filled with the dreams of swift descents and fresh snow, an individual stamp in the family's skiing legacy.

Nicole, with the wisdom and foresight of a mother's heart, gently steered the conversation. Her words were careful, laden with love and a hint of necessary redirection. "Let's think of something different this year, kids," she suggested, her voice calm yet firm, hinting at a departure from their annual pilgrimage to Mammoth. The news met with Tara's immediate and puzzled reaction, her young mind wrestling with the change in tradition.

In a bid to soften the blow and rekindle the excitement, Nicole hinted at a surprise destination, her tone playful yet evasive. "It's a secret for now," she said, a mysterious smile dancing on her lips. Yet, her eyes avoided Sam's, a silent admission that the plan was as much a mystery to her as it was to the children.

Sam, a quiet observer of the unfolding scene, noticed the unease beneath Nicole's facade. Her body language spoke of a journey she was planning without him, a future where the traditions they had created as a family would no longer include his presence.

In the midst of the festive chaos, Tara and Cameron's excitement bubbled over, their youthful energy filling the room as they eagerly pressed for details about their holiday destination. Sam, with a gentle smile, indulged their curiosity, subtly nudging Nicole to unveil the surprise. "Maybe Mom has something amazing planned," he hinted, his voice tinged with a bittersweet note that only Nicole could detect.

Nicole, caught in the wave of anticipation from the children and the knowing gaze from Sam, felt a moment of panic. Her eyes quickly scanned the room for a distraction, a source of inspiration. They settled on the "Bon Appétit" sign featuring the iconic Parisian skyline, a whimsical reminder of far-off places and dreams. Seizing the image as her impromptu escape, she announced with feigned enthusiasm, "We're going to Paris!"

The children's joy was immediate and infectious, their cheers filling the room with visions of the Eiffel Tower and French pastries dancing in their heads. Sam, amidst the celebration, felt a pang of sorrow tighten around his heart. He knew this trip was a fabrication, a placeholder for the truth that Nicole had yet to plan anything. More poignantly, he understood that even if the trip to Paris were real, his place in their family tableau was fading, soon to be a memory.

Sam's expression remained composed, a mask of supportive cheer for the sake of Tara and Cameron's delight. But behind his encouraging nods and smiles, a profound sadness lingered. He was keenly aware that their future family adventures would unfold without him, that his role in their lives was changing irrevocably.

As Nicole rode the wave of the children's excitement, promising adventures and sights to see, Sam quietly observed the scene, a silent sentinel of what was and what might never be. He clung to the joy in his children's eyes, allowing it to momentarily push away the reality of the divorce papers and the separate paths he and Nicole would soon walk

Amid the jubilation, Sam, aware of the strained dynamics, pulled his children close, expressing regret that work commitments would keep him from joining them. With a mix of disappointment and acceptance, the kids bid their father farewell, promising to bring back stories and memories. Sam, departing without a word to Nicole, carried an air of resignation.

Nicole, realizing the gravity of her actions, rushed after Sam, a desperate plea in her voice. She apologized and admitted her mistake, acknowledging the impossibility of them going together. Sam, frustrated and resigned, was about to close the car door, to leave Nicole grappling with her error.

In a last attempt to salvage the situation, Nicole vowed to make alternative plans closer to home. Sam, worn down but compassionate, as he had all the hopes of winning her back suggested they maintain the illusion for the kids and fully spoil them on the trip and break the news after the trip. Affirming she would have the signed divorce documents soon, with a heavy heart Sam departed. The air hung with the bittersweet scent of lost dreams and unspoken words, as both Nicole and Sam navigated the delicate dance of love slipping away.

Chapter 77

In the relentless hustle of life, Sam immersed himself in work, cloaking his solitude in long hours at the office. The only break came when compelled by the insistent beckoning of Hope or the gentle nudges from his mother. Returning to the echo-filled void of his apartment after work was a prospect he avoided like an unwelcome ghost.

Desperate for connection, Sam sought solace in the warmth of Ariana's home, where the comforting presence of Farhad and his mother provided a fleeting escape from the hollow silence that awaited him elsewhere. Alternatively, he sought refuge in the camaraderie of Luke, their moments together offering a temporary reprieve from the weight of his solitude.

In the midst of one such rendezvous, Sam found himself in the heart of Luke's surfboard manufacturing realm. Amid the scent of resin and the hum of machinery, Luke unraveled a revelation that resonated through Sam's emotional landscape. Brenda was embarking on the journey to France with Nicole too. Luke disclosed that Brenda had invited him to join this escapade, a gesture that Luke had to clear by Sam.

Caught in the crosscurrents of emotions, Luke hesitated, seeking Sam's tacit approval before committing. Sam, with a mix of nostalgia and a genuine desire for his friend's happiness, urged Luke to seize the opportunity without second thoughts. In a moment of candid reflection, Sam revealed his own yearning for such an adventure, silently lamenting the constraints that bound him.

In a moment fraught with unspoken weight, Luke sought reassurance from Sam once more. A solemn confirmation escaped Sam's lips, a silent plea shimmering behind his eyes as he implored

Luke to watch over them, safeguard their journey, and keep them cocooned within safety's embrace.

Luke, the playful surfer, couldn't mask his thoughts. "It really sucks seeing you guys split and at least if you and Roxana had sex, it wouldn't suck as much. But now it really sucks."

Epiphany dawned on Sam as he acknowledged the truth in Nicole's perspective. It extends beyond mere physicality; it delves into the painful realm of betrayal. Sam advised his friend, "I understand that you don't have absolute control over that thing in your pants, but hear me out." Sam's demeanor shifted, his voice carrying the weight of earnest sincerity, "never betray Brenda. If you truly believe she's the one, why hesitate? If there's one thing I've learned, it's to never let true passion pass you by. Seize the moment with Brenda, that free-spirited soul who's captured your heart. Embrace her vibrant essence, and together, create a life. Don't hesitate, don't look back. Live fully, fiercely, and without regret. Make every second count, all the way to the end. This is your moment, grasp it with both hands. Place that ring on her finger, and pledge that she'll be your sole love for the entirety of her life. Embrace her wholeheartedly and refuse to release that grasp. It's time to make the right choice."

In the quiet echoes of Sam's yearning, he found refuge in Luke, a desperate need to share a revelation that had long haunted him. "Roxana told me why she left. Something I never knew," Sam confessed, his voice tinged with the weight of untold secrets and unspoken pain. In response, Luke, not the best guardian of confidences, held space, waiting patiently for Sam to unravel the enigma.

Sam, aware that only a select few were privy to the secret Roxana had entrusted him with, hesitated. He questioned the trustworthiness of Luke's renowned "big mouth," a playful jab hinting at the gravity of what he was about to reveal. Yet, beneath the banter, Luke sensed the gravity of Sam's vulnerability, promising to keep the silence intact. It was a solemn pledge, enough for Sam to unleash the floodgates of his truth, unveiling the revelation that bound him in solitude—a son they shared.

Luke's voice softened as he delved into the narrative, each word reflecting a blend of empathy and personal pain. As he spoke of Saamaan and the irreplaceable role of a father, his story took on a deeply personal hue, revealing the contours of his own fatherless upbringing. "You see, Saamaan knows his father as Nader. And believe me, growing up with that certainty is a gift. You don't want to grow up shadowed by the mystery of your father's identity," he reflected, his voice tinged with a poignant yearning.

His story unfolded further, sketching the distant image of his own father, a man known to him only as a Pacific Southwest Airline pilot who spent only one fleeting weekend with his mother. "Roxana made a heart-wrenching choice, but she preserved that father-son bond for Saamaan. And that's commendable." Luke's words resonated with an understanding of the sacrifices made for the sake of a child's well-being. His own narrative was a testament to the longing and unanswered questions that shaped his youth.

With a wistful smile, Luke shared the whimsical yet heartbreaking ritual of his childhood. "Whenever I saw a PSA plane, I'd wave, hoping or just maybe imagining, my dad is waving back." The innocence of the gesture contrasted sharply with the pain of his unmet longing, painting a vivid picture of a boy yearning for a connection that was never there.

His advice to Sam was heartfelt and resolute. "The bond between a father and son is sacred. Don't let anything, not even your own pain or doubts, disrupt what Saamaan has. It's the best thing for him." Luke's voice held a conviction born of his own experiences, a plea for Sam to recognize the importance of a father's presence in a child's life.

As he concluded, there was a sense of solemnity in the air, a shared understanding of the deep emotional currents that ran beneath the surface of their conversation. Luke's story, interwoven with Sam's ongoing struggle, highlighted the complex tapestry of fatherhood, loss, and the enduring impact of the choices made in the name of love.

Chapter 78

Alone at is his apartment, bathed in the flickering glow of the TV, shadows danced across Sam's face, weaving an intricate tapestry that mirrored the somber depths of his memories. The amber liquid of tequila poured into a glass stirred echoes of regret as he revisited the pivotal moments that led him to this desolate juncture.

His mind retraced the painful steps: the moment Nicole confronted him about Roxana, a surge of shame engulfing him like an unrelenting tide. The memory of encountering Roxana in the jewelry store and the revelation of Saamaan's existence echoed through his consciousness. A yearning, a silent plea, emerged as he raised the tequila shot, wishing Roxana to be spared the harsh trials he himself is enduring.

In an impulsive gesture, tequila shot still in hand, Sam dialed Roxana's number, bridging the distance that mirrored the emotional chasm between them. The long-distance call materialized into Roxana's voice, a cautious "hello" that marked the resurrection of a connection he had thought forever severed. Sam, adopting the guise of a spy, playfully recited the code, "Is this the Aslani residence?"

"Saam?" Roxana's voice, a cocktail of surprise and recognition, crackled through the line, her incredulity breaking through the initial formality.

"Yeah, it's me," Sam admitted, shedding the playful facade for a moment of sincerity. "How have you been? How's Saamaan?"

Their conversation meandered through updates and mutual concerns until Roxana steered it toward the turbulent waters of Sam's marriage. "So, what's happening with you and Nicole?" she ventured, her tone a careful blend of curiosity and caution.

Sam sighed, the weight of his reality pressing down. "Well, it's... not so great. We're staring down the barrel of a divorce."

Roxana's response was soft yet firm, a mix of sympathy and stern advice. "Saam, whatever's going on, Nicole deserves the full truth before making her final decision."

He hesitated, the burden of secrets heavy on his shoulders. "Roxana, there are things I've kept from her, secrets of ours, as I promised I would."

"I know, Saam. But maybe it's time," Roxana encouraged, her concern palpable even across the miles. "You can and should tell her everything, Saam. It might not be too late to fix things."

"But what if it's beyond repair? What if I've already lost her?" Sam's voice was tinged with defeat.

Roxana's reply was a beacon in the dark, her conviction clear. "Saam, you sound defeated. You were never the one to back down. It's not in your nature. It's never too late for honesty, for vulnerability. Go to her, Saam. Spill your heart out, strip away the veils, and let the raw truth and honesty speak. Confess everything, lay everything bare. She must know it all to choose her path," she urged, her tone both gentle and insistent.

"You have my full support to unveil our secrets if it means mending what's broken between you and Nicole. Consider it my way of standing by you, of hoping for your happiness. I pray this brings healing," Roxana added, her words imbued with a mix of hope and solemnity.

Their exchange, a delicate dance of shared history and the possibility of redemption, continued until Roxana abruptly ended the call. Nader and Saamaan had returned, the tangible presence of family demanding her attention. As the connection severed, Sam found himself caught between the echoes of Roxana's encouragement and the formidable task that lay ahead. Discarding the tequila shot, he witnessed a faint glimmer of hope flickering in the shadows.

In the hushed tones of the next day, Sam's call to Nicole bore the weight of impending decisions. The gravity of the moment hung in the air as he somberly informed her about his intention to sign the divorce papers, promising to deliver them the following day. Yet, intertwined with this stark reality was a simple yet earnest request, a plea that held the potential to alter the course of their shared history.

As Nicole contemplated Sam's entreaty, her mind danced with possibilities. What could he possibly want? The answer, however, unfolded as a humble desire—a plea for a moment of her time. Sam longed for her to listen, to hear his side of the story, before the ink dried on their official separation. A request that, in its simplicity, carried the weight of unspoken emotions.

Nicole, in a moment of compassion, found his plea not only reasonable but achingly human. She agreed, setting the stage for a conversation that could reshape the contours of their fractured relationship. Unbeknownst to her, Sam, in his intimate understanding of her, had anticipated her acceptance.

With logistics falling into place, Sam revealed that he had arranged for the kids to be under the watchful eye of his mother and Arianna, a mere ten-minute drive away.

However, the timing posed a dilemma. Nicole pointed out that tomorrow is Christmas Eve and their imminent departure for Paris on Christmas Day. Sam, unwavering in his resolve, presented it as his sole request—a plea to untangle the threads of their shared history before they embarked on separate journeys. A subtle negotiation unfolded, with Sam proposing to pick up the kids in the morning and leaving them with Ariana, affording them a brief window for their crucial conversation. Nicole, swayed by the sincerity in his words, conceded to his timeline.

In an unexpected turn, Nicole extended her own plea—a request for Sam to stay for Christmas Eve, to share in the tradition of opening gifts on Christmas morning. Sam, the weight of impending separation momentarily lifted, found joy in her invitation. With a smile in his voice, he agreed, sealing a fragile pact for one last shared celebration. "Then," Sam offered, "I will give you a ride to the airport." The anticipation of their final moments together lingered, a poignant prelude to the inevitable parting of ways.

In the quiet serenity of the room, Sam's gaze lingered on the unassuming envelope resting on the coffee table. Its silent presence had become a familiar specter, a silent witness to the unfolding drama of his life. Yet, this time, the weight of decision hung heavy in the air, and

Sam felt the compelling need to relinquish control, to let Nicole decide the course of their destinies.

With a determined yet hesitant hand, Sam drew the large manila envelope closer. The papers, a harbinger of finality, awaited his acknowledgment. Unfazed by the words on the pages, Sam bypassed them, his eyes fixating on the last page, a solitary Post-it note acting as a guide. "Sign here," it beckoned, a stark directive reminiscent of a life-altering choice.

A palpable tension gripped the room as Sam, reminiscent of a condemned soul yearning for clemency, stole a glance at his phone. A breath held, a heartbeat suspended in the hope of a pardon. The screen remained unaltered—no calls, no messages, no pardon, from Nicole. The silence, a haunting reminder of the unspoken chasm between them, lingered, each passing second echoing the weight of uncertainty.

A hesitant pen met the paper, Sam's signature etching across the page like a plea for understanding. The final strokes were blurred, smudged by a tear that slipped from the corners of his eyes. It bore the weight of unspoken emotions, a silent testament to the depth of his heartache.

As the papers found their way back into the envelope, a sense of resignation settled over Sam. The documents, sealed and ready, became a harbinger of the fateful day looming on the horizon. The moment, heavy with the weight of unspoken farewells, bore witness to the silent surrender of a man who may have ran out of reasons to hope.

Chapter 79

The next day, Sam ventured to the house to reunite with the kids. After safely entrusting them to Ariana's care, he found himself standing before his own front door, a once-familiar threshold now fraught with uncertainty. Aware that his presence might not be welcomed, he hesitated, grappling with the notion of entering his own home uninvited.

Summoning a semblance of formality, Sam rang the bell, its chime announcing his arrival, even as he inserted the key to unlock the door. The heavy silence was broken by the creaking hinges as Nicole, almost coincidentally, appeared near the entrance. A fleeting moment of shared recognition lingered before she turned away, leaving Sam to navigate the awkward entry.

Inside, the air crackled with unspoken tension. Nicole, moving with deliberate indifference, headed for the kitchen. Undeterred, Sam followed, taking a seat at the table. In a small but poignant gesture, Nicole poured a cup of coffee for herself and a cup of tea for Sam. The clinking of cups echoed in the strained atmosphere, a silent acknowledgment of their fractured connection.

As Sam expressed gratitude for the unexpected gesture, a quiet note of appreciation punctuated the space between them—a fragile thread woven into the fabric of their complicated relationship, even in the midst of adversity.

As Sam lifted the tea to his lips, his gaze lingered on Nicole, whose smile seemed to shatter like fragile glass as she cast her eyes downward. The air between them held the weight of unspoken expectations, and Sam sensed her silent plea for him to delve into the heart of the matter.

With deliberate care, he placed the envelope on the table, a tangible embodiment of compliance with her request. The moment hung suspended, pregnant with anticipation, as Sam acknowledged her willingness to hear him out. Nicole, holding her coffee cup with an almost burdensome weight, sipped with a nod—a gesture that betrayed a mix of resignation and impatience, urging him to cut to the core.

Sam, feeling the gravity of the confession he was about to make, declared his intention to lay everything bare. He spoke of the wrongs he had committed, acknowledging the lack of malicious intent but grappling with the realization that his actions had set a chain of events in motion. The cup, now an inconsequential mass in Nicole's hands, seemed to carry the collective weight of their unified life journey.

As Sam delved into the narrative, he admitted, deep down, he always sensed that a profound and dramatic event must have unfolded, leading to Roxana's abrupt departure. Despite letting his curiosity fade into the background over time, the mere sight of her reignited the compelling urge to unearth the truth. The truth, he confessed, was initially sought to fill the void left by Roxana's sudden departure. He admitted to initiating the initial call and orchestrating a private meeting, driven by the hope of prying the truth from her. However, now that he had unraveled the truth, he confessed that he wished he had remained in the dark. The revelation weighed heavily on both of them, considering the profound impact it had on their lives. The admission was a fragile dance of regret, a glimpse into the internal turmoil that had marked his journey to revelation.

Nicole, her curiosity finally shattering the silence, delved into the conversation by inquiring about the secret. The notion that, within the enchanting confines of the garden, their dialogue had been restricted to mere words felt almost surreal. Sam reassured her, confirming his preparedness to unveil every detail, acknowledging that only the unadulterated truth held the key to liberation. Continuing, he reflected, "You saw me entering the garden, but even I was uncertain about my expectations as the gate closed behind me."

"I'd be deceiving you if I claimed it was all innocent," Sam confessed, casting a shadow over the conversation. The weight of his words hung in the air, a palpable tension that hinted at a revelation fraught with complexity.

As Sam continued, recounting how seemingly inconsequential exchanges had unraveled into a kiss, Nicole's grip on the coffee mug tightened to the point where it seemed as if the vessel might shatter, mirroring the fragility of their relationship. Yet, there was an underlying acknowledgment that this disclosure was merely the tip of the emotional iceberg.

Sam, sensing the gravity of the moment, unfolded the narrative further. The fleeting kiss, he explained, acted as a sudden awakening—a stark realization of the inherent impurity of their actions. In a shared moment of clarity, they both recognized that staining their lives with these unsanctioned actions would cast long, haunting shadows over the entirety of their existence. As they pulled away from each other, the weight of their mistakes hung heavy in the air. Sam, driven by a relentless pursuit of truth, pressed Roxana until her cries unraveled the hidden truth.

Nicole, her eyes widening, found herself on the precipice of revelation. Every sensory nerve alert, she braced herself for the unveiling of a truth that threatened to reshape the landscape of their connection. The emotional intensity in the room was palpable, as Sam prepared to expose the raw and unfiltered details that had remained buried beneath the surface.

"Nicole, I have a son with her," Sam confessed in a single breath. The revelation hung in the air, a heavy admission that would alter the course of their shared history. Nicole's jaw dropped in stunned disbelief, the shock almost causing her to lose grip on the coffee cup. Instinctively, she leaned back, creating a physical distance as if trying to shield herself from the weight of the revelation.

"You have a child with her," Nicole exclaimed, grappling with the magnitude of the revelation. Words eluded her momentarily, and the air crackled with the tension of the unexpected disclosure. Finally finding her voice, she declared that she had heard enough, signaling that it was time for him to leave.

"I will if you really want me to, but you promised to hear me out," pleaded Sam, a flicker of hope in his eyes. Nicole, torn between the desire to understand and the pain of the revelation, "you mean there is more," she remarked, her tone a mix of disbelief and anguish. Sam acknowledged the complexity of the situation, assuring her that understanding the full story was crucial. With a hesitant nod, Nicole allowed him to proceed, bracing herself for the storm of emotions that would accompany the unfolding truth.

In the hushed aftermath of Nicole's silence, Sam embarked on the journey of unraveling the complete narrative. Every word carried the weight of Roxana's unexpected pregnancy, the sacrifices made by Nader, and the heart-wrenching decision Roxana had to make—sacrificing her relationship with Sam for the sake of an unborn child, a clandestine truth known to only a select few. Nicole, initially consumed by rage and inner fire, found herself drawn into the narrative, the intensity of her emotions momentarily subdued.

As Sam's revelations concluded, a heavy silence enveloped the room, creating an unspoken space where each held their breath, waiting for the other to break the stillness. Nicole, inherently caring, finally spoke, her words laden with a complex mix of emotions. "I'm sorry. I don't know what to say, but it doesn't warrant a betrayal," she offered, her compassionate nature battling against the turmoil of emotions stirred by the revelation. The moment remained a tableau of unspoken emotions, a testament to the intricate web of feelings that had woven itself into the fabric of their lives—suspended by a fine thread, delicate yet bearing the weight of their shattered emotions.

"Betraying you was the last thing on my mind," Sam expressed, his words carrying the weight of regret and the earnest desire for redemption. In his explanation, he painted a picture of personal evolution—a journey toward becoming a better man, husband, and father. He pleaded for a chance, promising that if granted another opportunity, he would prove himself worthy of a second chapter.

Nicole, grappling with the whirlwind of emotions, needed time to process the revelations that had unfolded in rapid succession. Eventually, she suggested that Sam retrieve the kids, allowing her the solitude to prepare for their impending departure. As Sam rose to leave, he gently squeezed her hand, half expecting a rejection. To his surprise, her hand offered no resistance, prompting a tentative smile from him.

With a nod of obedience, Sam prepared to depart. However, before leaving, Nicole gestured toward the envelope on the table. "Why don't you hold on to this until we come back from France," she suggested. "I guess I can do that," Sam replied, accepting the envelope as he left to reunite with the kids. The room, now tinged with a mix of tension and hope, stood witness to a fragile moment in their complex journey of reconciliation.

As the day unfolded, Sam immersed himself in the comforting routine of home, creating precious moments with the kids, while Nicole tirelessly orchestrated the preparations for their upcoming journey. Night descended, casting its quiet spell over the household.

The pivotal moment arrived when Nicole, with a gentle command, directed the kids to ready themselves for bed. As she ascended the staircase, a pause ensued. In the dimly lit hallway, the hushed voices of Cameron and Tara reached her ears. The siblings, bound by a shared vulnerability, engaged in a quiet conversation that would inadvertently unravel the poignant wishes of their hearts.

"Tara," Cameron's soft voice echoed through the corridor, disrupting the tranquility of the evening. Tara, roused from a blissful reverie, responded with a question that held the weight of dreams interrupted. Cameron, whispering in the sacred intimacy of sibling confessions, inquired about Tara's bedtime wish. Tara, torn between the bonds of sibling camaraderie and the sanctity of her wish, declared with a mix of reluctance and love that revealing it to Cameron might shatter its potential to come true. Her words hung in the air like a delicate secret, charged with the power of unspoken hopes.

Undeterred, Cameron forged ahead, revealing his own heartfelt desire for Christmas. "I wished for Dad to come back home," he confessed, his words carrying the weight of a quiet desperation, a longing for a reunion that felt elusive in the vast expanse of their family's emotions.

A tender exchange unfolded as Tara, torn between the love for her brother and the sanctity of her own wish for Christmas night whispered. "That wish is mine, and it's what I wished for and you should wish for something else," her words a delicate plea echoing in the quiet sanctuary of their shared moments. Yet, he remained resolute, his heart's longing clear in the quiet sincerity of his words. "But that's all I want for Christmas," Cameron declared, his unwavering wish casting a bittersweet hue over the shared vulnerability of siblings bound by the intricacies of their family's story. Tears welled up in Nicole's eyes, a silent witness to the raw emotions unfolding in her children's exchange.

In a poignant tableau, Nicole entered Tara's room, where emotions lingered in the air like a delicate fragrance. She tucked Tara into bed, her heart heavy with the weight of unspoken wishes. Picking up Cameron, she carried him to his room, gently tucking him in with a motherly tenderness. As she hurriedly passed Sam, tears streaming down her face, he felt the searing impact of the pain he had caused his family.

In the wake of Nicole's departure, Sam stood in the hallway, haunted by the profound anguish he had inflicted. The walls echoed with the silent reverberations of wishes, both spoken and unspoken, weaving a tapestry of emotions that would shape their journey forward.

Chapter 80

Christmas day unfurled, ushering in the ritual of gift-opening. Handing the gifts to the children, joy illuminated their faces as they gleefully unwrapped each treasure. For a fleeting moment, a semblance of normalcy graced their lives.

Amidst the merriment, the final offering emerged from Sam to Nicole. A small box exchanged hands, and she, with a gracious smile, began the meticulous process of unveiling its contents. As Nicole unwrapped the carefully presented box from Sam, the delicate anticipation mingled with a wave of conflicting emotions. The sight of the matching bracelet and earrings, mirroring the necklace bestowed upon her during their anniversary, reflected Sam's thoughtful gesture. Each piece resonated with the shared history they had woven together—a tapestry of love, commitment, and the intricacies of their journey.

The elegance of the gift mirrored the genuine effort Sam had invested in choosing something meaningful. However, it served as a dual reminder—a symbol of their enduring love and a marker of the tumultuous day when Roxana, a figure from their past, resurfaced. The delicate dance between gratitude for Sam's thoughtfulness and the spectral echoes of that fateful day played out in Nicole's eyes.

In the intricate dance of emotions, she expressed gratitude for the gift, her voice carrying the undertones of a complex journey. Sam, sensing the delicate balance between joy and melancholy, hesitantly pulled her into a loose hug, a silent plea echoing in the embrace—a yearning to linger in the refuge of her arms, even if just for a moment longer.

At the airport, Sam bid farewell to everyone with heartfelt sentiments, entrusting Luke with the responsibility of safeguarding their loved ones. Turning to the kids, he urged them to be well-behaved and attentive to their mom's guidance. Finally, he found himself face to face with Nicole.

"Let's go, guys. Mom will catch up," Brenda artfully ushered the children away, creating a moment of private connection between Nicole and Sam. As they watched their children disappear into the bustling airport, Sam's eyes lingered with a wish that escaped his lips, carried away by the gentle breeze.

"Have a happy New Year," Sam expressed, a whispered hope hanging in the air, yearning for the promise of a brighter future. Nicole, in her quiet response, merely said, "I hope so," and gracefully walked away.

A sudden chill of despair gripped Sam as Nicole departed, leaving behind a void where hope once thrived. Her exit lacked the customary smile or wave, casting an ominous shadow on their connection. The invisible barrier between them, initially subtle, now morphed into an imposing wall that loomed taller and thicker with every step she took away.

In the throes of this emotional maelstrom, Sam found himself engulfed in an overwhelming sense of urgency. Without a formulated plan, a surge of raw emotion propelled him to defy the growing distance. In a spontaneous eruption of sentiment, he couldn't contain the yearning within him.

"Nicole!" Sam raced toward her. The sound of her name pierced through the air, a desperate plea that cut through the surrounding clamor. Surprised, she halted in her tracks. In this suspended moment, time seemed to elongate, allowing him to dissect every nuance of her movements frame by frame. As she turned, a cascade of hair danced in the air, framing her beautiful face like an ethereal halo. A flicker of hope ignited in Sam's eyes, a fleeting desire that she might reciprocate his impulsive dash, racing towards him to bridge the emotional chasm between them. In his daydream, he envisioned sweeping her off her feet, their reunion marked by a passionate kiss that defied the weight of their recent tribulations.

Perhaps, in this fantasy, the terminal would transform into a cinematic backdrop where applause would cascade from onlookers, celebrating their reconciliation as if scripted by the hand of fate. Alas, the harsh truth lingered – such grand gestures were confined to the realm of movies, where love stories unfold with cinematic perfection, not in the unpredictable, messy tapestry of real life.

His radiant smile wilted, mirroring the fading hues of a sunset, as Nicole stood steadfast before him. "What?" Her tone sliced through the charged air, a stark reminder of the distance between them.

Caught off guard, Sam found himself momentarily speechless. He lingered, feigning the need to catch his breath, as if time itself had conspired against him. The urgency in Nicole's demeanor was palpable as she tapped impatiently on her watch, a silent declaration that time was a luxury she couldn't afford to squander.

His attempt at formulating an excuse hung in the air. "Just wanted to say..." Sam began, the words dangling precariously on the precipice of truth and fabrication. He urged her to be cautious about the looming Y2K virus, weaving a tale of potential dangers in subway cars and elevators as the clock struck midnight on New Year's Eve.

"Is that it?" Nicole's skepticism reverberated in the question, her impatience bordering on exasperation.

In a moment of unguarded honesty, Sam revealed the core of his emotions. "I'll miss you." The words, laden with unspoken sentiments, lingered in the charged silence. Nicole, without a backward glance or a parting wave, shook her head in disbelief as she left, leaving Sam alone with the weight of his unexpressed emotions hanging in the air like the echoes of a fading melody.

Thirteen hours, marked by the passage of four movies and the shared consumption of three meals, became a distant memory as the captain's voice resonated through the cabin, announcing their impending landing at Charles De Gaulle airport. Stirring the kids awake, Nicole eagerly lifted the window shades, urging them to catch their first glimpse of Paris from above.

In the role of a surrogate father, Luke, attuned to the absence of their real dad, rose from the row in front. With an animated demeanor, he encouraged Tara and Cameron to spot the iconic Eiffel Tower as the plane descended. A flight attendant, interrupting the enchanting moment, hurriedly approached Luke, advising him to return to his seat and fasten his seatbelt.

"Oui, oui," Luke chuckled, settling back into his seat. Brenda, seizing the opportunity, pointed out the Eiffel Tower to Luke, his fingers gently brushing through her tousled hair. There was an unfamiliar intensity in his gaze, silently conveying the depth of his admiration for her morning allure. "Did I ever tell you how spellbound I was by your beauty from the very first day we met?"

"You might have, but feel free to say it again," Brenda playfully teased, her eyes twinkling with joy.

Luke, seizing the moment with a newfound sincerity, confessed that he couldn't fathom a life without her. He tightly held her hand, expressing his desire to spend the rest of his days with her. Brenda, amused by this sudden surge of romanticism, attributed it to the 'Paris effect.'

Unable to contain his emotions, Luke unbuckled his seatbelt and knelt in the cramped space between the seats. Ignoring the flight attendant's persistent reminders, he poured out his heart. "Whether I have one day or one hundred years left, I want to spend it all with you."

Nicole and the kids peeked through the spaces between the seats, their curiosity piqued. Luke, with a genuine smile lighting up his face, opened a ring box. "Brenda, will you marry me?" he asked, the question hanging in the air, surrounded by a hushed anticipation.

The gravity of the moment brought tears to Brenda's eyes, the silence pregnant with the weight of her response. Everyone in the vicinity held their breath, awaiting her answer. "Of course I will," she finally declared, sealing her response with a heartfelt kiss.

With practiced finesse, Luke resumed his seat, slipping the ring onto Brenda's finger. The collective sigh of relief and the subtle hum of congratulatory whispers filled the cabin, marking the beginning of a new chapter for Luke and Brenda amid the enchantment of Paris.

Brenda lifted her hand, the dazzling ring catching the light as she marveled at its beauty. Nicole, with a warm smile, extended her congratulations, playfully patting Luke on the shoulder. "You finally came to your senses," she teased, acknowledging the years it took for the couple to reach this milestone.

"Don't tease my fiancé," Brenda retorted, a playful glint in her eyes as she embraced Luke.

"Fiancé, I like my new title," Luke jested, proudly wearing the label as he gazed at his newly adorned fiancée.

Chapter 81

Brenda found herself captivated by the dazzling sight of her engagement ring, so much so that she missed most of the landmarks pointed out by the limo driver on their way to the hotel. The journey took them along the famous Avenue des Champs Elysees, where tempting restaurants and alluring shops adorned the street, and people gathered on the sidewalks, savoring the vibrant atmosphere.

Navigating through the Franklin D. Roosevelt roundabout, the limo turned into Avenue Montaigne, eventually coming to a stop at the prestigious Hotel Plaza Athenee. Nicole joined Brenda on the balcony of their room, where an awe-inspiring view unfolded before them. The Eiffel Tower, standing tall across the Seine, served as an iconic symbol of Paris and France, casting a spell of enchantment over the City of Light.

Known as the Iron Lady, this one-thousand-fifty-foot monument was originally constructed as the entrance arch for the 1889 World's Fair. It proudly held the title of the world's tallest structure until the completion of the Chrysler Building in 1930, gracing the skyline of New York City. The Eiffel Tower continues to be a global icon, drawing over seven million paid visitors annually and earning the distinction of being the most visited paid monument in the world.

In the following days, they immersed themselves in the vibrant tapestry of the city, exploring its iconic landmarks and indulging in the exquisite culinary delights it had to offer. Throughout this adventure, Sam maintained a daily connection with Luke and the kids, bridging the distance through heartfelt conversations over the phone. As the calendar pages turned, they found themselves on the brink of the final day of 1999, anticipating the momentous transition to a new year.

Chapter 82

On Friday December 31, under the soft winter sky, Nicole, her children, Brenda, and Luke emerged from Le Maurice Restaurant and strolled across Rue de Rivoli toward the serene expanse of the River Seine. The mild winter days had seen them traversing the city, exploring its myriad corners with every step. As fatigue set in, Cameron, expressing his weariness, voiced his desire to retreat to the hotel, yearning for the simplicity of relaxation and television. In a heartwarming gesture, Luke knelt down, inviting Cameron to hitch a ride on his back, a request the young boy cheerfully embraced as they continued their leisurely walk.

Nicole, sensing the need for rest, conveyed her intention to return to the hotel, ensuring the children would be revitalized for the grand New Year's Eve spectacle at the Eiffel Tower.

In a playful whisper, Luke turned to Brenda, injecting humor into the moment, "I wouldn't mind a nap after that lavish lunch, especially if you promise to be my delightful dessert."

"Oui, oui," Brenda responded with laughter, the lightness of their banter echoing through the enchanting streets of Paris.

As they made their way back to the hotel, Brenda gently reached for Nicole's hand, a silent gesture of support amid the unspoken struggles. "How are you holding up?" Brenda inquired, acknowledging the delicate nature of the topic. "I understand if you don't want to talk about it, but I wouldn't be much of a friend if I didn't ask."

Nicole mustered a faint, forced smile. "I know," she responded, leaving the conversation suspended in the air.

In a moment of raw candor, Brenda expressed her concern to Nicole, acknowledging Nicole's constant tears and questioning if divorce was truly what she wanted. "I never thought one signature could bring so much pain," Nicole admitted, revealing to Brenda for the first time that Sam had signed the paperwork and handed it to her before their departure. Brenda, ever supportive, asked a poignant question, "Do you regret it?" Her comforting hand rested on Nicole's back, a tender moment amid the fractures of life.

"I guess it's all done now," Nicole replied with a mix of resignation and acceptance. "Whether I regret it or not, it's all done."

Sensing the weight of the situation, Brenda offered solace, urging Nicole to set aside the thoughts, at least for the New Year. She encouraged her friend to make it the best New Year's Eve ever and insisted, "Let me see a smile now."

Nicole managed a feigned grin, prompting Brenda to playfully challenge her to do better. The two friends, embracing the power of distraction, shifted the conversation to happier topics, finding a temporary reprieve in the joyous moments until they reached the hotel.

Chapter 83

As the sun set for the last time in 1999, the night unfolded, draping Paris in a star-studded blanket. The Eiffel Tower mall began to swell with spectators, drawn to the anticipated fireworks that had been the buzz of the city for months. Nicole, seated in the comfort of her suite, sipped on a glass of red wine while gazing at the Tower illuminated with a warm orangeish glow.

In the quiet solitude of her suite, Nicole's gaze lingered on the mesmerizing glow of the Eiffel Tower. The vibrant lights, casting a warm and enchanting ambiance over the city, seemed to hold the promise of a new beginning. In the depth of that moment, a silent hope took root within her—a hope that the approaching New Year might usher in transformative changes, illuminating her life with newfound joy and possibilities.

Yet, intertwined with this optimistic yearning was the heavy weight of regret and self-awareness. The wish felt somewhat foolish, a poignant acknowledgment of the reality she had created. The decision to push Sam, the person she loved so deeply, out of her life echoed in her thoughts, casting a shadow over the anticipation of change. The clash between hope and regret painted a complex tapestry of emotions on her contemplative face.

As the lights of the Eiffel Tower continued to dance in the night, Nicole found herself caught in the duality of her desires—a desire for renewal and the painful acknowledgment of the choices that led to this moment. As Nicole's gaze shifted toward her children, their just-awakened faces held a mixture of innocence and anticipation. Their clothes, neatly laid out by Nicole in careful preparation, awaited them, a silent signal for the night's festivities to begin. She gently roused them, encouraging them to get ready for the evening that lay ahead.

In the melodic cadence of the night, Nicole sought solace in the connection with Brenda. "Nicole," Brenda's voice carried a note of excitement, "we'll be at your room in about an hour, around 11. I want you to look your best and get ready for an unforgettable night." The words held a subtle promise of shared laughter, camaraderie, and the warmth of friendship.

As Nicole prepared for the festivities, the prospect of the upcoming evening became a beacon of hope in the midst of uncertainty. Brenda's words lingered in the air, an assurance that, at least for tonight, joy would triumph over the complexities of life. The anticipation of the "best of times" held a unique allure, promising a respite from the weight of recent days and a chance to embrace the magic of the moment.

In the bewitching hour of eleven, Nicole adorned herself in a short, black, strapless dress that gracefully showcased her long, toned legs, elevated by the allure of high heels. The transformative ritual of preparation neared completion.

Her lips, adorned with dark burgundy lipstick, received the final, tender caress as she applied lip gloss. A glance into her jewelry box presented a myriad of options, yet her gaze gravitated persistently to a particular piece—the necklace bestowed upon her by Sam during their anniversary. With deliberation, she embraced the sentimental adornment around her neck, harmonizing it with the newly acquired Christmas set of earrings and bracelet.

Reflecting upon her reflection in the mirror, a genuine smile graced Nicole's lips. A gentle touch to the set of gifts from Sam evoked a cascade of emotions, infusing the moment with a profound sense of connection and history.

Amidst the enchanting backdrop of the Eiffel Tower's luminous display, Nicole and her children became immersed, losing all sense of time in the mesmerizing spectacle. Despite her own readiness for the evening, the serene moments shared with her children created an atmosphere of deep connection and belonging, prompting her to relinquish the habitual glance at the clock.

It was only after the passage of untracked time that a gentle knock on the door drew her attention. Upon opening the door, Nicole was greeted by Luke. With a playful smirk, she teasingly inquired, "Where is your beautiful fiancée?"

"Brenda wants to talk to you in private and asked me to take the kids to the lobby," Luke conveyed, a hint of nervousness lingered in his response hinting at a hidden agenda. Playfully, he deflected the situation with a familiar adage, "happy wife, happy life."

As Nicole ushered the children to accompany Uncle Luke to the lobby, she assured them of a swift reunion, leaving her alone with a curious blend of anticipation and uncertainty.

As Nicole made her way back to the balcony, eager to resume gazing at the brightly lit Tower, another knock echoed through the room. "It's about time," she murmured, anticipating Brenda's arrival. "What took you so long?" she playfully chided, swinging the door open. However, her words faded into silence as her eyes fell upon an unexpected sight—a delivery of immense beauty. Before her stood a large flower arrangement, a peacock tail of roses in vibrant hues, concealing the delivery person from her view.

Although the basket obstructed her line of sight, Nicole had a strong inkling about the sender. A card, perched at the front of the arrangement, confirmed her suspicions.

"When the day turns into the last day of all time"
"I can say I hope you're in these arms of mine"
"And when the night falls before that day I will cry"
"Cause without you all I can do is die"

The hauntingly poetic lines from Prince reassured her that Sam was the architect of this meticulously planned surprise, with Brenda and Luke acting as his secret agents. Reading the card again, Nicole asked the delivery person to place the basket on the table in her room, the fragrant blooms now bearing the weight of emotions that words struggled to convey.

As the delivery man turned to leave, Nicole couldn't stifle a sigh. Something about him seemed oddly familiar. To her surprise, the familiar silhouette emerged from the shadows. It wasn't just an ordinary delivery man; it was Sam, who was supposed to be miles away in California. Without hesitation, Sam dropped to one knee before her, his eyes reflecting a depth of emotion as profound as the words of Prince he had chosen.

"Those words... they're exactly how I feel about you," he confessed, voice laden with sincerity. "Cause without you, all I can do is die."

Stunned and shocked, Nicole found herself tongue-tied. She managed to force the words out, her voice a mix of disbelief and curiosity, "What are you doing here?" The air was charged with a complexity of emotions—surprise, uncertainty, and a flicker of something she couldn't quite place.

"Nicole, my love," Sam began, his voice carrying the weight of remorse and longing. He implored her to guide him on the path to rectifying his wrongs, expressing that he would willingly face any consequence to win back even a tiny corner of her heart. In an attempt to lighten the heavy atmosphere, he interjected, "By the way, you look stunning."

Nicole, her composure teetering on the edge, responded with a poignant declaration. She made it clear that he had shattered something precious, their trust, and she desired to move past him. The tears she held back threatened to stain her makeup as she posed a poignant question, "Why are you fighting this so much?"

"Because you are worth fighting for," Sam replied passionately. He unraveled a heartfelt confession, revealing the depth of his love. "You're the best thing that's ever happened to me. I love you not just for who you are but for who I become when I am with you. I love losing myself within you. I love every idiosyncrasy of yours, from your taste in boring subtitled foreign movies to the way you conquer long spaghetti strings in one go, getting sauce all over your pretty face. I adore the way your eyes narrow when you're mad and how your lips pout when you're upset. Please forgive me, and I promise not to make you pout anymore." The sincerity in his voice resonated with a raw vulnerability, laying bare the depth of his remorse and the fervor of his desire for redemption.

"Oh, Sam, you're torturing me," Nicole cried out, her emotions a turbulent sea. Summoning all her strength, she delivered the next words with a heavy heart. "Sam, I have let you go. I learned to live without you. Sorry, Sam. It's over."

Sam, keenly observant, pointed at the ring that lingered on her finger. "Is that why you're still wearing my ring?" A surge of fury propelled Nicole to remove the ring, flinging it at him with a force that mirrored her emotional turmoil. She declared with a sharp edge to her voice, "Here's your ring. If there's any shred of feeling left for me, then just leave." The air crackled with the intensity of their encounter, each word a poignant reminder of the love that once bound them and the pain that now threatened to sever all ties.

In this poignant moment, Sam found himself at the crossroads of desperation and acceptance. There's a limit to how much a man can unravel the tapestry of his wrongs, to how deeply he can crush his own pride in the pursuit of forgiveness. With the tattered remnants of his dignity, Sam turned away and walked toward the door.

In the quiet of that room, he retrieved the divorce papers from his side pocket and stooped to pick up the ring from the cold floor. His voice, tinged with regret and a thread of hope, trembled as he expressed, "I came here with the hope of tearing these papers together," gently placing the divorce papers beside the meticulously arranged flowers. With a wistful touch, he clarified that he left them there so she wouldn't have to witness this painful parting again when she returned home.

Sam carefully laid the ring atop the envelope, his eyes reflecting the weight of the gesture. "If I ever wanted to take this back, I would have never given it to you," he confessed with a mixture of resignation and sincerity. The door swung open, and he stepped out into the cool corridor, leaving behind the symbol of their union.

"Don't blame me for trying," Sam uttered with a poignant blend of sorrow and resignation, the words lingering in the room like a bittersweet melody. As the door closed behind him, it bore witness to the palpable barrier that emerged—a tangible separation marking the irrevocable finality of their encounter.

In the fading echoes of his footsteps, the room retained the hushed whispers of a love once vividly cherished. Each memory held fragments of shared laughter, stolen glances, and the tender moments that now seemed like distant constellations. The air itself seemed to carry the weight of their collective sighs, suspended between what once was and now lost.

The lingering resonance of Sam's parting words echoed through the silence, like a haunting refrain playing out the ebb and flow of emotions. The ache in his voice reverberated, leaving an indelible imprint on the room—a testament to the complexity of human connections and the inevitable heartaches that accompany the dissolution of love.

As the door closed with a soft thud, it sealed not just the physical space but also encapsulated the emotional chasm that had grown between them. The room, that could be a haven for shared dreams, now stood as a witness to the somber aftermath of a love that had weathered storms but ultimately succumbed to the relentless passage of time.

As the vibrant spectacle of the Eiffel Tower show unfolded, casting its radiant glow across the Parisian sky, Nicole found herself ensnared in the intricate dance of fireworks. The dazzling bursts of color mirrored the kaleidoscope of emotions raging within her. Yet, beneath the resplendent display, a profound heaviness settled over her, tethering her to the weight of the moment.

Her legs, once sturdy pillars that navigated the highs and lows of the past, now betrayed her. An overwhelming weakness coursed through them, compelling her to surrender to the solace of a nearby chair. The reverberations of each exploding firework seemed to echo the shattering of her own inner world, leaving her breathless in the wake of profound heartache.

In the quiet moments that followed, Nicole's tears, unbridled and raw, cascaded into her hands. The muffled sobs encapsulated the depth of her grief, a poignant soundtrack to the dissolution of a love once held dear. The celebratory atmosphere of New Year's Eve faded into insignificance as the reality of Sam's departure for good enveloped her.

Her trembling hands reached for the envelope and the ring, tangible relics of a love story that had unraveled. In that solemn moment, the paper and metal became more than mere objects; they were symbols of closure, encapsulating the painful acknowledgment that the chapter she had shared with Sam had reached its final page.

As the world outside continued to dazzle with the brilliance of fireworks, Nicole sat in the silent aftermath of Sam's departure, embracing the rawness of her emotions and the uncharted path that lay ahead. The Eiffel Tower, now a distant witness to her solitude, stood as a silent sentinel to the complexities of love and the profound ache of farewells.

The grandeur of the Eiffel Tower show reached a crescendo, unleashing a cascade of intense fireworks that painted the Parisian sky in vivid hues. From the lower tiers, explosions of light punctuated the night, sporadic bursts shooting out like fleeting memories etched against the Tower's silhouette.

In this spectacle of radiant chaos, Nicole found herself enveloped in a surreal ambiance. The scent of the flowers mingled with the choking aroma of gunpowder, creating a sensory landscape that mirrored the amalgamation of beauty and heartache.

With trembling hands, she delicately retrieved the papers from the envelope, unfolding the intricate dance of ink and emotion on the final page. Sam's smudged signature, a tangible echo of his presence, stared back at her. A solitary tear, heavy with the weight of unspoken farewells, fell onto the page, tracing a path alongside the ink. As the tear and the indigo stain merged, it was as if their shared history wept, bleeding onto the parchment.

In an overwhelming surge of emotion, she flung the divorce papers at the wall, their fluttering descent echoing the shattered fragments of her heart. The impact against the hard surface resonated with the finality of their separation, a silent reverberation through the room that mirrored the explosive display outside. With her face buried in her hands, Nicole surrendered to the grief, each sob an echo in the cavernous space of her solitude.

Sam lingered outside the closed door, an amalgamation of hope and uncertainty etched across his face. Laughter from jubilant hotel guests echoed in the hallway—revelers adorned in paper hats, blowing horns, their jollity a stark contrast to the quiet drama unfolding behind the closed door. "Heureuse nouvelle année," they joyfully exclaimed, extending New Year wishes without realizing the poignant tableau that stood adjacent to their celebration.

Sam managed a polite smile, the foreign words lost on him, as he watched them disappear down the corridor. The vibrant energy of the revelers seemed distant, incongruent with the gravity of the moment. Slowly, he began to tread towards the elevator, a silent observer in a whirlwind of festivities.

As the elevator doors parted, it revealed another couple lost in the throes of a New Year's kiss, adorned with paper hats and clutching horns. The shared exclamation of "Heureuse nouvelle année" echoed in the confined space, a chorus of celebration. Invited to join, Sam declined with a shake of his head, feigning an anticipation for someone yet to arrive.

The elevator doors closed, leaving him alone with an unobstructed view of the Eiffel Tower through a nearby window. The luminous display outside intensified, the fireworks casting an ethereal glow upon the iconic structure. The Tower, bathed in celestial light, seemed poised for an otherworldly ascent.

With the approaching countdown resonating in the air, Sam heard the familiar chime of the elevator opening once more. Sensing indifferent to the imminent transition into the New Year, he stepped inside and pressed the lobby button. As the door began to shut, a sudden interruption—the intrusion of a hand holding a flower—halted its closure. The door slid open to reveal Nicole, a delicate figure against the backdrop of celebratory chaos. The shared gaze between them encapsulated the unspoken emotions of a moment caught between the echoes of a fading year and the uncertain dawn of a new one.

As Nicole took a step backward, her voice trembled with a mix of pain and humor, "Didn't you say not to ride elevators on New Year's Eve?" Her words hung in the air, laden with the weight of their shared history. In response, Sam froze on the spot, the realization of his actions and the ensuing consequences immobilizing him. The elevator doors, oblivious to the emotional turmoil transpiring within, began to close again, a cruel reminder of the physical separation it threatened to impose.

A surge of desperation propelled Sam to action. As the elevator doors began to close, he defied the mechanical order, leaping out of the confined space to find himself standing before Nicole. The stark contrast between the bustling hallway and the intimate gravity of their encounter heightened the palpable tension between them.

The world outside exploded in a symphony of lights, the intense fireworks casting an ethereal glow over the Eiffel Tower—a spectacle that paled in comparison to the emotional intensity between them. As the countdown to the New Year approached its zenith, Nicole, her voice a fragile whisper, uttered words laced with vulnerability, "Sam Larabi, if you ever broke my heart again, I will kill you." The gravity of her declaration hung in the air, a testament to the tumultuous journey that had led them to this precipice.

In a heartbeat, Sam surrendered to the overwhelming surge of emotion, embracing Nicole and sealing their reunion with a fervent kiss. At that very moment, the clock struck midnight, and the night sky erupted into a dazzling display of fireworks. Nicole, caught in the whirlwind of emotions, delicately placed her ring into Sam's hand, a symbolic gesture of trust and commitment, as their lips remained entwined. With a tenderness that transcended words, Sam slipped the ring onto her finger, completing a circle of promises amidst the radiant backdrop of the New Year's spectacle.

"We missed the entire show," Nicole laughed between kisses. "What now?" Yet, in the warmth of their embrace, the vast distance and dark emptiness that once separated them dissipated, replaced by a newfound sense of completeness. Sam, overwhelmed with the depth of his emotions, found solace in the embrace of the woman he loved.

In that magical moment, Sam answered her question by quoting Prince, "Let's party like it's nineteen-ninety-nine." The words hung in the air, encapsulating the profound journey of love, loss, and redemption that had unfolded beneath the shower of fireworks—a celebration not just of the New Millennium, but of the resilient spirit of love that defied the challenges of life.

With a deep breath, Sam turned to Nicole, his eyes reflecting the colorful afterglow of the fireworks. "To new beginnings," he whispered, his voice heavy with emotion.

"To new beginnings," Nicole echoed, a tear of joy gliding down her cheek, sparkling like the fireworks that had just lit up the sky.

Made in the USA
Columbia, SC
22 February 2024

df0d846a-125a-47ee-92ed-b0c02c4d87f3R01